# Fall of the Florios

# Fall of the Florios

## A Novel

## Stefania Auci

Translated from the Italian by
Katherine Gregor and Howard Curtis

HarperVia

*An Imprint of* HarperCollins*Publishers*

Originally published as chapters 5 through 8 of the original Italian edition *L'inverno dei leoni* in Italy in 2021 by Nord.

FIRST HARPERVIA EDITION PUBLISHED IN 2024

Library of Congress Cataloging-in-Publication Data has been applied for.

ISBN 978-0-06-338915-1

24 25 26 27 28  LBC  5 4 3 2 1

To Eleonora and Federico,

for all the tenderness and affection.

I am very proud of you.

All around here the sky is bright and clear, seldom have I seen such a clear sky. Open your eyes, Captain, and say it yourself. Can you see a single cloud, however small, on the horizon?

—JOSEPH ROTH, *THE TALE OF THE 1002ND NIGHT*

# CONTENTS

# THE FLORIO FAMILY TREE

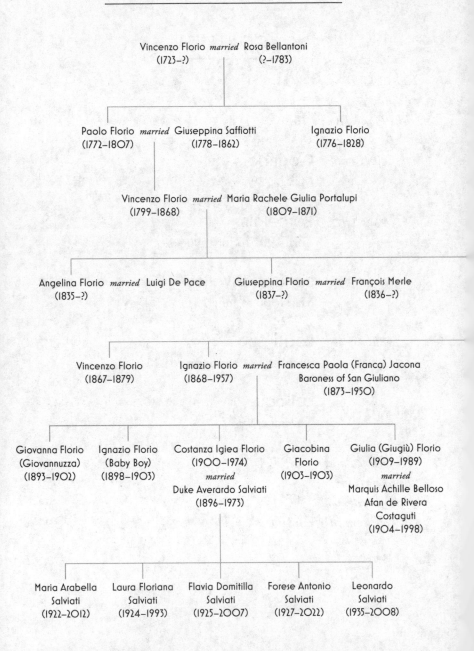

Vincenzo Florio *married* Rosa Bellantoni
(1723–?) (?–1783)

Paolo Florio *married* Giuseppina Saffiotti
(1772–1807) (1778–1862)

Ignazio Florio
(1776–1828)

Vincenzo Florio *married* Maria Rachele Giulia Portalupi
(1799–1868) (1809–1871)

Angelina Florio *married* Luigi De Pace
(1835–?)

Giuseppina Florio *married* François Merle
(1837–?) (1836–?)

Vincenzo Florio
(1867–1879)

Ignazio Florio *married* Francesca Paola (Franca) Jacona
(1868–1957) Baroness of San Giuliano
(1873–1950)

Giovanna Florio
(Giovannuzza)
(1893–1902)

Ignazio Florio
(Baby Boy)
(1898–1903)

Costanza Igiea Florio
(1900–1974)
*married*
Duke Averardo Salviati
(1896–1973)

Giacobina
Florio
(1903–1903)

Giulia (Giugiù) Florio
(1909–1989)
*married*
Marquis Achille Belloso
Afan de Rivera
Costaguti
(1904–1998)

Maria Arabella
Salviati
(1922–2012)

Laura Floriana
Salviati
(1924–1993)

Flavia Domitilla
Salviati
(1925–2007)

Forese Antonio
Salviati
(1927–2022)

Leonardo
Salviati
(1935–2008)

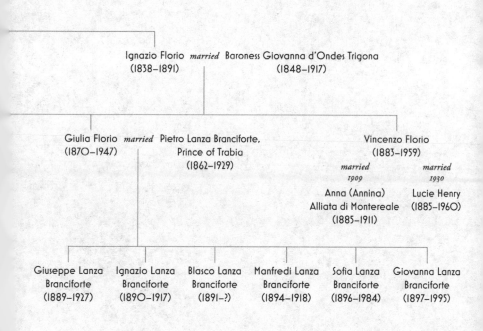

Ignazio Florio *married* Baroness Giovanna d'Ondes Trigona
(1838–1891) (1848–1917)

Giulia Florio *married* Pietro Lanza Branciforte,
(1870–1947) Prince of Trabia
(1862–1929)

Vincenzo Florio
(1883–1959)

*married*
*1909*

Anna (Annina)
Alliata di Montereale
(1885–1911)

*married*
*1930*

Lucie Henry
(1885–1960)

Giuseppe Lanza Branciforte (1889–1927)

Ignazio Lanza Branciforte (1890–1917)

Blasco Lanza Branciforte (1891–?)

Manfredi Lanza Branciforte (1894–1918)

Sofia Lanza Branciforte (1896–1984)

Giovanna Lanza Branciforte (1897–1995)

# PART ONE

# Cognac

March 1894 to March 1901

*Abballa quannu a fortuna sona.*
When fortune plays, dance.
—SICILIAN PROVERB

COGNAC IS A MATTER OF soil, wood, patience, and sea. Like whisky. Like marsala wine.

It is first mentioned as early as the seventeenth century, but since May 1, 1909, by government decree, the rest of the world has had to resign itself to producing ordinary "brandy," because cognac's one and only cradle is identifiable with the *département* of Charente, in South-West France. A chalky soil rich in marine sediment, covered in vine varieties like Ugni Blanc (a clone of the Trebbiano grape, planted in France after the devastation wrought by phylloxera in the late nineteenth century), Colombard, with its delicate yellow fruit, and Folle Blanche, with its compact clusters. In order to be considered cognac, at least 90 percent of the wine must come from one of these three grape varieties, either singly or in combination. The remaining 10 percent may be constituted by other grapes: Montils, Sémillon, Jurançon Blanc, Blanc Ramé, Select, or Sauvignon.

But that's not enough: there is a specific window for the harvest, usually from October to the first frosts. Then there are the barrels: the timber must be sourced from oaks in the Limousin and Tronçais forests. The staves mature in the open air, then are riveted just by iron hoops, so that neither nails nor glue may alter the flavor of the wine. Finally, they are toasted, in other words overheated on the inside, carefully and for a long time. Moreover, before the wine is poured into the barrels, it must be distilled, rigorously and at least twice, in the traditional Charentais alembic, first at 77 to 81°F, then at 158 to 162°F.

Only then is the wine left to rest, because all that is lovely and precious requires time, calm, patience. These ingredients may not be written down, but they are essential. You must wait, then wait some more, because nothing good can come into the world before its right time.

For cognac, that's at least two years but can be as much as fifty years or more. In these cellars, steeped in the smell of the Atlantic, in which the evaporation process is slow, blending the aroma of the alcohol with those of wood and sea air, the cognac assumes its characteristic flavors of vanilla, tobacco, cinnamon, and dried fruits, and turns amber, with a silky texture. Naturally, it decreases in volume by 3 to 5 percent year over year. The French recognize this as *la part des anges*, the angel's tithe. In the cellar, there's also a place called Paradis, named for the demijohns that hold cognac aged at least fifty years.

A girl, unfortunately.

*Ignazio's smile waned when the midwife gave him the news, and he accepted the compliments and good wishes with a mere nod. Then Diodata opened the door to Franca's bedroom, let him in, and placed in his arms a* cusuzza nica, *a tiny little thing, all red and bawling, wrapped in blankets to shield her from the November chill.*

*Franca was lying in bed, eyes closed and hands over her belly. The labor had been long and difficult.*

*She opened her eyes when she heard his approaching footsteps. "It's a girl. I'm sorry."*

*A wave of tenderness swept over Ignazio at these heartfelt words. He sat down beside her and kissed her forehead. "Our daughter Giovanna," he replied, handing her the baby. They were a family now, and no longer a couple struggling to find its equilibrium.*

Three months later, Giovannuzza has conquered his heart. Franca is still its queen, but the baby its princess.

The boy must come. It's just a matter of time. Casa Florio needs an heir. The doctor has said that Ignazio can soon resume spending time in his wife's bedroom, and that is one of the few recent pieces of good news.

January 1894 has been a difficult month. Few parties, barring those within the family, few opportunities for entertainment. They've been shut in at home, suitably guarded so that no one comes to bother *decent folk*.

Palermo is no longer safe.

Early in the new year, a state of siege was declared on the island. It was the result of riots incited by the Sicilian *Fasci*, the organization that drew farmhands and factory workers, men and women, all equally unhappy with the heavy taxes and the injustices they often had to bear. As unstoppable as contagion, the protests have spread from the city to the countryside and turned into actual insurrections. In Pietraperzia, Spaccaforno, Salemi, Campobello di Mazara, Mazara del Vallo, Misilmeri, Castelvetrano, Trapani, and Santa Ninfa, people have burned down the tollbooths and, brandishing weapons, assaulted public offices and jails, setting the prisoners free.

The island was in the grip of chaos, so much so that military intervention was required to restore order. The Piedmontese, as old people call them, came when ordered to by General Morra di Lavriano, granted full powers by the government, took out their rifles, and shot at everybody, women included. Nothing has been done against those who have tormented the farmers and factory workers, driving them to hunger and despair—far from it: every protest has had its share of dead and wounded, arrests and subsequent trials. Disappointment has added to disappointment, seeing that the current government is run by Francesco Crispi, a Sicilian and a former Garibaldi supporter, who took over from Giovanni Giolitti after the Banca Romana scandal.

There is a heavy calm at present, dictated by fear, maintained thanks to constant arrests and harsh sentencing. It is tempting to agree with Donna Ciccia, who grumbles that *that man* can't be trusted, that it feels like being back under Bourbon rule.

It is the evening and there is little light in the rooms or in the garden. A warm glow kindles the cognac in the glass Ignazio has just been holding. Its spicy, vaguely honeyed aroma fills the room.

A knock at the door. "Come in," he mutters, snatched away from his reading: a rundown of the *Britannia*, the Prince of Wales's cutter, being completed in a Glasgow shipyard and against which Ignazio's *Valkyrie* will compete next June in the Channel Race.

The door opens, revealing Franca's face. "Aren't you ready?"

"Not yet, my dear," he replies, putting his papers aside. "But how's Giovannuzza? Why was my *picciridda* crying so much this afternoon?"

"The nanny said she had a nasty colic. She spent a long time massaging her belly."

The thought of that soft, fragrant little body fills her with a tenderness she never imagined she could feel. In the beginning, after the pain of childbirth, she feared she would develop a kind of rejection of her daughter: the pain had been too much, the recovery too grueling. However, the baby conquered her with just a glance, instilling a warm, total love that eclipsed the rest of the world, shielding her from all unpleasantness.

Franca appoaches Ignazio. Since Giovannuzza's birth, her body has only become more voluptuous—if that were possible. Ignazio can't resist. He embraces her, kissing her neck. "You're a goddess," he whispers into her skin.

Franca laughs and lets him nuzzle her, even though it took Diodata nearly two hours to style her hair. Ignazio has been too tense lately, and she feels unable to provide the peace of mind he needs. But she wants to prevent him from seeking it in someone else's arms.

All sorts of things happened after that Banca Romana scandal, of course. For days stern-looking men poured in and out of the Olivuzza office, and Ignazio spent even more time on Piazza Marina than usual. Franca even heard that, after Credito Mobiliare closed its doors, Ignazio was obliged to pay five million lire, a figure she alternately perceived as both staggering and trifling. But what would she know about that? The dressmaker and the milliner first addressed their invoices to her mother and now directly to Ignazio . . . She did try to ask, but both Ignazio and Giovanna dismissed her with vague excuses and a general prescription "not to worry."

"Do we really have to go?" he asks, his face buried in Franca's hair. "Can't we go up to your bedroom?" He slips his hands under her robe, finds her corset, and caresses her breast.

She wriggles free, laughing, and pushes him away. "I never would have thought that I'd have to persuade my husband to go to the theater and a reception!" She closes her robe, flashing him a sidelong glance. "I'm going to finish getting ready . . . and so should you."

Ignazio smiles. "We'll talk about it on the way back," he says, releasing her only after kissing her wrist.

 ～

On the afternoon of March 4, 1894, the carriage of the Lanza di Trabias makes a stop outside the entrance to the Olivuzza. Pietro is the first to alight, followed by Giulia and a man with dark, wavy hair, a broad forehead, lively eyes, and a bushy mustache. The butler welcomes them before motioning them to the red marble staircase decorated with cascades of flowers. Franca is waiting at the top. She immediately stretches her arms to Giulia and Pietro, kisses them, and tells them to make themselves at home in the winter garden. Then she smiles at the other man. "Welcome, Maestro. You honor us with your presence." Lifting the hem of her skirt, she adds, "Please come with me. Our guests can't wait to meet you."

Giacomo Puccini follows Franca, ogling her curves as discreetly as he can. He is in Palermo for a performance of *Manon Lescaut*, which premiered last year in Turin, and the city has given him a magnificent welcome: applause while the curtains were still up, calls for him and the singers to come up on the stage, and a final ovation that made the entire Teatro Politeama quake. Franca and Ignazio met him last night at a dinner in his honor at Palazzo Butera and have invited him for tea, just to make his triumph complete.

Franca slows down, walks closer, and says, "Your *Manon* is a work that truly touches the soul, Maestro. I couldn't confess it to you last night, but it made me cry my eyes out."

Puccini appears confused, moved by her earnest compliment. He stops, takes Franca's hand, and kisses it. "Signora, your words mean more to me than last night's applause. I am honored and touched."

Franca hesitates, then says in one breath, "Why does great music make us suffer so?"

Puccini's large, dark eyes widen. He draws closer to Franca's ear and murmurs, "Because it takes up where words end. Just like beauty . . . I'm sure you know what I mean." He kisses her hand again.

Franca blushes, smiles, takes his arm, and carries on walking.

❦

"Ignazio!" The meaning behind Donna Giovanna's softly voiced call is unmistakable.

She also witnessed the scene: twice now Puccini bowed to kiss Franca's hand, and even whispered something in her ear. Familiarity—an intimacy?—that would surely cause Ignazio to lose his temper, as he waited for their guest by the door to the winter garden. She knows him only too well: he is jealous, possessive—never mind that he's unfaithful—because, just like a spoiled child, he can't bear to share his toys.

Franca and Puccini are now in front of Ignazio and he manages a smile. "Welcome, Maestro," he says, his voice a little too high-pitched. He then steps between his wife and the composer, ushering the latter to Giovanna, who, with Donna Ciccia, is entertaining a group of elderly women dressed in black.

Giovanna has prepared this afternoon's reception in every detail: she chose the flowers, table linen, silverware, china, the wide variety of tea blends in wooden boxes, and even the cakes. Everything is so perfect and elegant, it looks like a painting. *She still doesn't trust me*, Franca thinks, taking it all in.

She is roused from her thoughts by a giggle. It's the unmistakable voice of Tina Scalia Whitaker, the wife of Joseph Isaac Whitaker. Known to everyone simply as Pip, Joseph is the grandson of Ben Ingham, a crucial figure in Ignazio's grandfather Vincenzo's life. Possibly the most famous couple in Palermo, Pip and Tina could not be more different: he follows in the family tradition of producing and selling marsala wine, supplementing it with his true passions, archaeology and ornithology. Tina, on the other hand, the daughter of a general who supported Garibaldi, is a highly educated, intelligent woman who lives and breathes high society: no one is spared her barbs and sarcasm.

Franca turns to the women of the Whitaker family, who chat in a blend of English and Sicilian, and meets Tina's eye. The two women hold each other's gazes for a moment, and Franca catches in Tina's expression something between compassion and mockery. She knows Tina considers her beautiful and rather foolish, like an elegant doll on display, and nothing else. She purses her lips, thumbing her pearl-and-topaz necklace to summon courage, and greets Tina with a simple nod.

She is distracted by Ignazio's voice.

"The Teatro Politeama is very fine, but the acoustics aren't ideal," he is telling Puccini and the small crowd gathered around them. "I trust Teatro Massimo will soon be ready. I say this with a degree of pride, since even the roof over the building is made by my family's foundry."

"Then let me thank the patron of the arts who's creating a temple to opera in Palermo . . . and your foundry!" Puccini exclaims, amusing everyone.

In the ensuing silence, a stern-looking young woman steps forward. "Maestro . . . it's such a privilege to be able to speak to you . . . May I ask you a question?"

"Please do," Puccini replies with a smile.

"How—how do you write your music?"

"A musician's calling isn't like a proper job," he muses, "and it certainly has no breaks. Rather, it's like . . . a compulsion of the soul. Even now, standing with you, in my mind . . . in my soul, notes form and connect. It's a stream that finds no peace until it reaches the river. For example . . ." He goes to the piano little Vincenzo tortures twice a week during his music lessons.

The chatter ceases, cups are put down, even the waiters freeze.

In the unexpected silence, Franca approaches the piano and stares at Puccini, as though to encourage him.

His hands come to rest on the keyboard and a melody suddenly fills the room.

> *Che gelida manina, se la lasci riscaldar.*
> *Cercar che giova?*
> *Al buio non si trova.*
> *Ma per fortuna è una notte di luna,*
> *e qui la luna l'abbiamo vicina . . .*

Puccini plays and sings, and the air, fragrant with vanilla and tea, catches the notes, seemingly reluctant to let them vanish. Then he stops, his fingers hovering over the keys, his face flush with emotion.

As applause breaks out, he stands and bows to Franca. "I'm glad you've heard a fragment from my next opera. Remembering this moment will make it easier for me to complete it."

Franca blushes as Ignazio orders champagne to toast "Maestro Puccini's future triumph, hoping he will come back and have it performed in Palermo!" The men nod while the women sigh, thinking that this is indeed divine music.

But after drinking the toast, Puccini walks up to Franca again.

"You were splendid," she says, moved. "Thank you for this unhoped-for gift."

In response, Puccini takes both her hands and lifts them to his lips, to the hungry looks and insolent commentary of those present. *Isn't she allowing him to be too familiar? Does she think she's above the rules?*

"Thank you to your family for inviting me into your splendid home," he replies. "And thank you, Signora. You have an extraordinary light inside you, a precious light. I hope you may guard it forever."

Franca smiles, but her eyes momentarily mist over.

One person notices.

Her sister-in-law Giulia.

Palazzo Butera, the Lanza di Trabias' home, stands against the city walls, a stone's throw from Porta Felice. The winter garden looks out over a steely sea that mirrors the gray clouds of a day that's unusually dark for early May. The scent of dry leaves hovers in the air, of damp soil and budding flowers. Sitting in the willow-clad parlor, amid potted lemons and small banana trees, Franca and Giulia can speak freely while the children—Giulia's offspring and Vincenzo—play nearby, under the watchful eye of their governesses.

"So? Why did you want to see me?"

Franca grips the handle of the Sèvres china cup, imprinted with the Lanza di Trabia coat of arms. She wonders when Giulia became so curt, so different from the young woman who wrote her affectionate letters when Franca first joined the family. She doesn't want to judge her, though: she's been hardened by her tense relationship with her mother-in-law and the death of little Blasco. That was a tragedy whose magnitude she can only grasp now that she's a mother herself.

Somewhere from among the tress, Vincenzo shrieks and Giuseppe, Giulia's eldest, responds with a giggle. There's a patter of small feet, and the sound of a bouncing ball. It's odd to watch two boys, eleven and five, and know that they are uncle and nephew.

Giulia gives a faint smile, the first since Franca arrived, then looks at her, as though inviting her to speak.

"I want some advice," Franca says. "Honest advice, as though you were my true sister."

Giulia raises an eyebrow, then looks down at Franca's trembling fingers. She takes the cup away from her and places it on the coffee table, then leans back. "Why are you trembling?" She lowers her voice. "You're still scared of everything, aren't you? Scared of everyone judging you."

Franca blinks and nods, surprised, then casts her eyes down onto her bejeweled fingers.

"I was wondering when you'd finally realize that you can't carry on like this. You look like a soul in purgatory."

Franca clutches her skirt and her voice breaks. "Don't think I'm naive. Ignazio . . . I always assumed he was the one at the center of all the gossip, and I forced myself not to listen because, in the end, it's me he comes back to, it's me he's in love with. But people criticize me, too. I hear comments, little remarks whenever we go out . . . Last night, for instance, at the De Setas' house, he flirted in a truly vulgar manner with the lady of the house. I was mortified! At home, I feel like a guest, because I don't even need to talk: everybody turns to your mother. I feel even the servants find me odd. And your mother, even though she's a real saint, won't let me have a say in anything." Her outburst is like a dam bursting. A sob escapes her lips. "She always finds something to chide me for, and it's not just her but the whole city! Either I speak too little, or too much, how I dress . . . whatever I do it's wrong and I no longer know which way to turn."

Giulia shakes her head, while her face betrays emotions Franca has trouble interpreting, then raises an eyebrow. "You're too good, my dear Franca. Too good. You need to grow balls, or they'll tear you to shreds. And that also applies to my mother."

Franca's green eyes open wide. Giulia is using crass language that's almost archaic in its brutal sincerity. "Really?" she asks with a sob.

"Of course." Giulia stands up and walks to the windows. "You think I haven't noticed how you are?" She doesn't wait for her sister-in-law to follow her, and Franca has to rush after her.

"You are Donna Franca Florio now. Not my mother, who's a widow and thinks only of having Masses held in my father's name. You are Ignazio's wife, he's the head of the family, and you must commandeer what's yours, starting with respect." She seizes Franca's arms and speaks to her just inches from her face. "When I got married, my father told me that nobody should ever get the better of me. It was up to me to defend myself first and foremost, or my husband's family would stifle me. And it's what I'm telling you now." She stares at her intently. "I love my brother, but I know him: he's not always very bright; too many women prance around him. He's self-absorbed and doesn't realize you have troubles, that people criticize you partly because of him. I know him, he's not a bad soul, but he's so . . . so superficial. He couldn't begin to understand how you feel, *l'antisi puru ju chidde ca ti sparlano*—he doesn't even notice what's being said behind your back."

Lifting Franca's downcast face, which is pale from shame, Giulia ignores her tear-soaked eyelashes, grabs her by the shoulders, and shakes her.

"Look at me! It's up to you to protect yourself, because I know what the world says about us Florio women. That we spend too much money on dresses and jewels, that we depend on the family fortune, but that our heads are empty. And that we're too arrogant to stay in our place." Giulia clenches her hands into fists. "I don't care what they say. You shouldn't either; if you listen to them, you give them power. They're wretches who just prove they're envious by saying what they do. We have everything that they don't—that's why they malign us and will continue to do so."

Giulia is blunt. Fierce.

Franca has little idea of her sister-in-law's tribulations. She doesn't know that she, too, had to endure terrible humiliation, especially in the beginning, when her mother-in-law constantly threw Giulia's middle-class origins in her face before everyone. Then, for years, she never missed an opportunity to remind her that her marriage was little more than a contract. As for Pietro, he never stood up for his wife or supported her in any way.

Still, all those years taught Giulia not to give in, never to bow her head. They fueled in her a rage like the one her grandfather Vincenzo carried all his life, and while he had channeled it to dominate an entire city out to humiliate him, she channeled hers first as a shield, then as a weapon, to win the respect of the Lanza di Trabias. And now she truly is the lady of that house and family. She has achieved this partly by remembering her father's golden rule: there's nothing more precious than lucidity and self-control. Her father, Ignazio, also repeatedly told her, "Listen to your head, not your heart." She projects the image of a haughty, unapproachable woman, an image built for protection.

No, Franca has no way of fully knowing the price her sister-in-law had to pay to become what she is: a proud, determined, untouchable woman.

And that's precisely what Giulia wants to show Franca. That she has to earn her place among the Florios and in Palermo, because that's how it must be. There are no alternatives. And she can only achieve this by finding within her the required strength and detachment. She must let all that has hurt her wash over her, and erect fortified walls around her soul.

Franca looks into Giulia's face, nervously wipes her cheeks, and ponders.

To her mother-in-law, being a Florio means supporting her husband in every way, never giving him any reason to blame her or complain, shining at every social event, rising to any occasion. And when he makes mistakes, it is her duty to forgive him.

Giulia's depiction of reality, however, situates Ignazio in the background. There is only her, Franca, distinct from—free from?—her role as a wife. She must, first and foremost, be herself. She must be proud, rise above everything. Be untouchable. No criticism must ever hurt her, and if it does, her wound must heal instantaneously.

She loosens herself from Giulia's grip and takes a step back. This is all so far removed from what Giovanna has told her, from the way she was brought up: she has always been the obedient daughter, the respectful wife, and now . . . "But I—I've behaved well. I haven't protested, I haven't cried when he . . ." she murmurs in a voice steeped in grief. "Even when I found out that he was cheating on me, I—I've been a good wife, or at least I've tried to be."

"And that's where you've gone wrong: you've tried to please everybody. You shouldn't behave well: you should take what belongs to you by right and do so without fear of being judged. You're not a *picciridda* seeking her mother's approval anymore. Having a famous surname isn't enough. And giving your husband a son isn't enough to gain his respect either. Nor should you hope that my mother will step aside of her own volition. She'll do it once she sees that you measure up to the name you carry, and trust me, that won't happen easily or quickly. Remember, *chi po 'fari e 'un fa, campa scuntento*—he who can do something but doesn't do it ends up unhappy." Her voice softens, becomes a caress. "In Palermo, you don't get anything for nothing." She indicates the city beyond the *palazzo* walls, toward Cassaro. "In this city, everybody, from carters to princes, lives on bread and envy. Some would rather be killed than admit their mediocrity. Whenever you hear a criticism, remind yourself you're a Florio and they're not. If they say your jewels are garish, tell yourself that theirs are worth half the value of yours. If they pick on you for the way you dress, tell yourself that they don't have the figure, let alone the money, to wear your clothes. Remember that whenever you hear them talk behind your back. Keep it in mind and laugh, laugh at them for their mediocrity."

Franca listens.

Giulia's words open doors to unexplored rooms and give her a new outlook. It's like seeing herself in a mirror for the first time and discovering assets she never imagined she possessed, that reveal the infinite possibilities life can offer her.

Giulia watches her, understands, takes a step back, and smiles. She has seen true self-awareness light her face, something that will finally make her sister-in-law like her. "You mustn't be afraid. You were born to be a Florio." She pats her face. "You're not only beautiful; you also have intelligence, charm, and elegance. You have so much strength, the world won't be able to ignore it. Don't be afraid to be what you are. But remember: a child is always good, but a son is a blessing. You must get pregnant as soon as possible." Her voice drops, heavy with intimations. "With a son, it'll be easier. And you'll be freer."

Franca leaves Palazzo Butera with a spring in her step, followed by the governess and a still skipping Vincenzino, excited after playing. She looks ahead, indifferent to the sky that threatens to pour a spring shower down on her.

Yes. She has been silent, discreet, patient, compliant. But now she must learn.

Not to have doubts.

To claim what belongs to her.

To become Donna Franca Florio.

It's such a new thought, it makes her dizzy.

*To become myself.*

∽

A thunderclap in the distance.

Ignazio looks up from his papers and goes to the window. The sirocco winds of recent days are giving way to a gray sky bloated with sand that threatens La Cala and the black, glossy carriages heading to Foro Italico. Men in frock coats and women in their faille, taffeta, and muslin dresses crowd the final stretch of the Cassaro to show off and be seen. This is a new Palermo. In his childhood recollections, Palermo was elegant and discreet; now it has become brazen and irreverent. It used to peer through the shutters and make comments in private; now it stares you in the eye, ready to slander your clothes, your vehicle, and your social circle. Ignazio finds this insolence deeply irksome.

His gaze pauses on a washerwoman carrying a heap of laundry in a basket, dragging along a barefoot little boy. There are still hovels with very poor people at the margins of the *corso*, with haggard-looking women forever waiting for their men who work in factories or aboard ships. Palermo prefers not to see these people. He doesn't want to see them either, although his mother insists on him undertaking charity work. Yes, he knows it's important to the family name: the Florios actually have a soup kitchen, and Franca is a member of the Congregazione delle Dame del Giardinello, and is always generous, especially toward abandoned, unmarried young women . . . He is an entrepreneur: he provides jobs and bread to those employed by NGI and those who work at the Oretea and in the slipway—not to mention all his other businesses outside Palermo . . .

Lost in thought, Ignazio runs his fingers through his hair, then stops to avoid ruffling it. He looks at his reflection in the window: his waxed mustache, the carnation in his buttonhole, the perfect knot in his tie, clipped with a diamond pin. Impeccable.

But the papers on his desk, waiting to be signed, read, and acted on, ruin everything.

Sometimes, when he's alone in this office, he thinks he can hear sounds, as if the building is moaning in pain, or as if cracks are slowly opening behind the wood paneling. He knows it's absurd, but it makes him feel uneasy.

He steps away from the window and turns to admire the painting of the Marsala winery, which his father commissioned from Antonino Leto. There, before the building, the water is green and calm, the light warm and mellow.

He could do with that calm right now.

The Florios owe their fortune to the sea. It's a thought he has been wrangling with for weeks. He was asked to radically modernize his passenger steamers as a condition for the renewal of the conventions. He objected but said he would see to it, then put it off. And now he can no longer avoid that demand.

But where to find the money? The Credito Mobiliare issue— *Damn them!* he thinks—forced him to make a dent in the company's cash deposits. In order to save the Florio name, he honored the savings and checks of the bank's customers, covering them out of his personal pocket and shouldering all the losses. He also carried out the necessary procedure to get into Credito Mobiliare's deficit and recover the money, as well as the shares of personal capital he had invested, but it was hopeless. He saved the family's good name, true, but now he has practically no capital left, only a stack of useless credit instruments.

Papers, papers, papers. Nothing but papers.

There's no solution: he will have to ask the Banca Commerciale Italiana for credit, so that he can have the cash for these immediate expenses. He who has never stooped to ask for anything, be it money, trust, or credit.

And that's not all. There is something he deeply resents, even if he will never confess it to anyone. He is too proud to admit even to himself that he made an enormous error in judgment. Many people, starting with Domenico Gallotti and his brother-in-law, Pietro, advised him to be more cautious and not trust the reassurances of the bank's management.

And yet . . .

He thinks about his father, about what he would do in these circumstances. But Ignazio has to admit that his father would not have reached this stage. He would not have blindly trusted others, as Ignazio has done.

He almost feels relief that his father isn't here to witness his failure—relief, but equally a burning sense of bitterness, because he knows that, were he alive, he would shoot him an accusatory look and show him the door.

This is too much for Ignazio. He paces around the room, searching his memory for the person who drove him to make these decisions, encouraged these commitments—because it can't be his fault, oh no—and gives this error a first and last name.

Giovanni Laganà.

∽

Giovannuzza gurgles, mumbles, looks up, and giggles. Her mother, kneeling in front of her on the carpet, holds out her arms to her. The child takes a step, then another, held up by Mademoiselle Coudray, the nanny. This is a new experience for her, and she's giving it her all; you can tell by her look of concentration and her pressed lips.

"Come here, my dear heart, *cori meu*," Franca says encouragingly, clapping her hands.

As soon as she senses that the little girl is sure of her footing, the nanny lets go of her. Giovannuzza waddles to her mother, displaying tiny, pearl-like teeth.

Franca hugs her and showers her neck in kisses. "Well done, *picciridda!*"

"You shouldn't be on the floor. It's undignified."

Giovanna has suddenly appeared behind her, like a ghost.

Franca instinctively holds the child closer and glances up at her mother-in-law. "I'm in my daughter's room," she replies calmly. "We're playing, and no one's looking."

Giovanna lifts her chin at Mademoiselle Coudray, who blushes and makes to leave, but Franca stops her and places Giovannuzza in her arms. "*S'il vous plaît, emmenez-la dehors, qu'elle puisse respirer de l'air frais.*"

"You're indulging her," Giovanna mutters as soon as Mademoiselle Coudray and the child have left. "Girls need a firm hand. Even more so than boys."

With a hollow laugh, Franca stands up. "A firm hand? Your son has always done whatever he pleased and still behaves worse than a spoiled child!"

Giovanna tilts her head, taken aback by the outburst. "What do you mean?" she replies with irritation.

"Your son, my husband, is a spoiled child oblivious to the consequences of his actions. And don't pretend you don't know—everyone in Palermo is talking about it. Ever since that *chanteuse*"—she pulls a face—"arrived with her low-cut gowns, he's been going every night to the Alhambra, a *café chantant* in Foro Italico. He sits in the front row and waits for her after the show."

"Ah."

A single syllable.

Franca stares at her mother-in-law with rebellion in her eyes, but Giovanna does not avert her gaze. "I've already told you once, my girl, you must learn to look the other way."

"As a matter of fact, I have looked the other way. But that doesn't mean he has the right to act like this. Nor does it give you the right to criticize my daughter's upbringing."

Giovanna shudders. She is not used to being contradicted. "You should let yourself be guided by those with more experience than you, even as a mother—"

"By a mother who encourages her son's freedom to trample the bond of marriage? I'll never fail to show respect to him or this family: let that be clear. But I want my daughter to feel loved and to learn from the outset how important it is to defend her dignity. The honor of the family name comes later."

Giovanna is too stunned to reply immediately. She looks down at her wrinkled hands and caresses her husband's wedding band, held in place by her own. "Sometimes a name is the only thing that allows one to survive," she murmurs.

But Franca can't hear her: she has rushed out and left her here, alone in the middle of the room.

*That's how it is*, Giovanna thinks. The Florio name, which defines their social role, their importance, their power, was the anchor of their marriage, its *raison d'être*. And still is, even though when

Ignazio died a void opened before her, which she can only barely fill with prayers.

Her black dress catches the light from the window and traps it. The scent of the last flowers and the clip of the gardeners' shears cutting off dried branches come in through the window.

Giovanna looks at the door through which Franca left and thinks: *You still have a lot to learn, my girl.*

Franca leans against the doorjamb with her forehead, one hand on the key, the other over her heart, trying to soothe the tension. She takes deep breaths.

Diodata looks out from the wardrobe and gives a little bow. "Does the signora need me?"

"No, thank you. I have a headache and want to rest for a while. Don't let anyone in."

Diodata nods. "Would you like me to close the balcony doors?"

"Yes, please."

Alone at last, Franca kicks off her shoes and lies down on the bed, one arm over her eyes. The room is plunged in semi-darkness and the air smells of her perfumes. This is her refuge: whenever anyone—her mother-in-law, Ignazio, or Palermo—disturbs her peace of mind, she just needs to come into this room and look at the roses on the floor and the frescoes on the ceiling to recover.

She has never stopped thinking about what Giulia told her a few months earlier. That she must be strong and put herself first. But it's so exhausting to fight against those who judge her, criticize her, accuse her. How hard it is to be appreciated for who she is and not only for what she represents.

Franca is lulled into a light, comforting slumber that brushes these negative thoughts to the side.

This slumber, however, is broken by an annoying noise. Someone is knocking at the door.

Franca moans and turns over, putting a pillow over her head. "I said I didn't want to be disturbed!"

"It's me, darling, Ignazio. Let me in!" He knocks again, this time more insistently. "I have a surprise for you."

*A surprise.*

Bitterness sweeps over Franca, supplanting the serenity given her by sleep. Only a year ago, that word would have made her rush to him. But now she knows it's a sign, a tacit admission of guilt, the way Ignazio salves his conscience: with a gift for his wife, usually a valuable item, after betraying her and satisfying his mistress's whims.

Unsolicited compensation.

She gets off the bed, opens the door without deigning to look at him, sits down at her dressing table, and starts removing the pins from her hair in order to brush it.

Ignazio smiles in the mirror and strokes her neck, whispers a compliment, then places a leather jewelry box in her lap. "For my queen." He touches her cheek with the back of his hand. "Open it."

She sighs, takes the box, and turns it over in her hand. "Who is it?"

"What—what do you—?"

"Is it that *chanteuse* who performs practically naked at the Alhambra?"

"*Mon Dieu*, Franca, what are you saying?" Ignazio is astounded. "Can't I give my wife a present just like that, without a reason? Why these insinuations? It's not like you!"

She finally opens the box, which reveals a ring with a sapphire cabochon and a halo of diamonds. Then she turns to look at Ignazio. "A present 'without a reason'?" she says coldly. "The bigger your blunder, the bigger your gift, and that's the truth. Everybody knows you've cheated on me. Again." She fights back her tears. She won't cry. She mustn't. "Those rakes at the club told their wives, and they . . . they told me!"

Ignazio steps back, surprise and disappointment in his eyes. "And you believe—"

"Don't waste time denying it. I know everything in intimate detail: the evenings you spend with her, your toasts with the other club members to celebrate your conquest, and even that you've boasted about how . . . how willing she was. I've been spared nothing." She clutches the box and raises her voice. "And do you know what I replied to those vipers after they told me everything? That *their* husbands clearly knew everything because they were with *mine!*"

Ignazio is dumbfounded. He turns his back to her. "Bloody bastards . . ." he mumbles, then he faces her again, smiles, and tries to embrace her, but she wriggles free and pushes him away. "My darling, those women are making a fuss over nothing . . . Yes, I did attend the odd show and . . . and this woman has given me attention and smiles. But that's all." He scoffs. "Some men are even more envious than women and invent—"

"Envy?" Franca tosses her head back and laughs bitterly. "Of course they envy you! You sleep with the most beautiful women, shower them with money . . . I'd say envy is all they wear in your company!"

"Now, don't be vulgar."

"Oh, *I'm* vulgar, am I?" She jumps to her feet and hurls the ring at him. It bounces off the floor. "Damn it, I don't want it! I'm your wife, not some woman you can buy! Now get out! Go to that whore who's waiting for you with her legs spread open!"

Ignazio takes another step back and picks up the ring. Then he eyes Franca, who is ravaged by anger. "That's too much! You trust women's gossip more than your own husband," he mutters in a tone that's meant to be contemptuous. "I'll come back when you're more reasonable."

Franca is left motionless, her arms down by her sides, eyes closed.

She hears the door open, then slam shut.

Her flushed cheeks are now moist with tears. She weeps and feels the load, the anguish in her chest, swell and breathe, as though it were alive.

But it's not because she has been betrayed that she's crying. It's because she will forgive him. Yes, she will, and not because Giovanna told her always to do so.

She will forgive him because she loves him, truly loves him. And she hopes with her entire being that this love may change him and make him understand that he will never find another woman who loves him as she does. Every betrayal, though, is a fracture in her soul, into which creep disillusion and bitterness. So Franca cries harder and prays, desperately prays that these cracks do not shatter her.

Then she wipes her face with an irritated gesture, turns to the mirror, and looks at her reflection. She should not have let anger get the upper hand: now she's upset and her eyes are red. A splendid woman, but one whose face is distorted with anguish.

*What now?* she wonders. *What will it cost me to keep going this time?*

ᕲ

Hasty, determined footsteps herald Giovanni Laganà's arrival to Ignazio's office at NGI's headquarters on Piazza Marina.

He walks in confidently without even greeting Ignazio, who is standing by the window. On the contrary, he practically slams the door before sitting down opposite the desk, not waiting to be invited.

"You've informed me that you no longer require my services," he starts without preamble. "So be it. You're entitled. But you can't tell me this by letter, like I'm the lowliest peasant at the foundry. I don't deserve it, not after all I've done for you and your family." This hostility only scratches the surface of his barely contained rage. "I want to know why. What has led you to this decision? You must say it to my face."

Ignazio slowly goes to the desk, sits down, and regards him haughtily. "You may be furious, but I am aggrieved. You're asking me why. Because you betrayed my trust and that of my family. You hungered for more power and more money, and since I couldn't give it to you, you went to others and put my company and me in a bad light. You did it when you convinced me to trust Credito Mobiliare . . . I remember clearly how you insisted the bank was trustworthy, and look what it cost me! Do you deny it?" He doesn't give Laganà time to respond. "And now . . . Do you want to see the papers I received from Genoa? Letters written in your own hand!" He indicates a beige portfolio, by itself on the desk.

Laganà snatches it angrily and leafs through its contents.

"Did you think I'd never discover that you tried to stall the improvements to the ships so that the government wouldn't renew our conventions?" Ignazio points a finger at him. "You're not only a hypocrite and a liar but also a braggart. I'm the one who decides what to modernize, together with the board of directors. You took me for a fool and thought you could cheat me. Who do you think you are?"

Laganà doesn't seem to be listening. He drops the papers on the desk, shakes his head, and studies his hands: strong fingers, his skin spotted with age. Ignazio says nothing, waiting for his words to register. *He knows he's been found out*, he thinks. *He's going to say he's innocent and ask to explain . . .*

Instead, he is almost startled when Laganà looks up at him.

There is just one emotion on his face: contempt.

"Your problem, Don Ignazio, is that you believe everything you're told. I don't know if you're naive or a total imbecile. In any case, you're entirely incompetent."

Stunned, Ignazio sits motionless.

Outside, the wheels of carts and carriages squeak on the basalt, their sound filling the silence in the room. "You've been a disloyal administrator, you betrayed the trust of Casa Florio, and now . . . now you're insulting *me*?"

Laganà's lips form a straight, hard line under his gray-flecked mustache. "You, yes. I worked diligently for your father; I always advised him as best I could. My loyalty to Casa Florio has been un-impeachable, and now you accuse me of selling out our routes in order to give our competitors an advantage . . . On what grounds? Hearsay? Gossip?" He grabs the papers, crumples them, and tosses them aside.

"You negotiated with our rivals!"

Laganà laughs. A dark, bilious guffaw. "Now I understand. *Siti 'un fissa*—you're a fool!" He stares in disbelief. "You're weak, Don Ignazio. Casa Florio has no money in the till, and *senza dinari 'un si canta missa*—no money, no Mass. Do you realize you lack sufficient funds to get your fleet back into shape? And instead of thanking me for negotiating a stay of execution with your competitors and preventing them from pouncing and making mincemeat out of you, you're pointing the finger at me, who has always served you well—who defended you!"

*It's a threat*, Ignazio thinks, clutching the armrests of the chair that belonged to his father. *It's a threat and this scoundrel wants to scare me . . . to humiliate me.*

He grows more convinced that Laganà is a liar and a manipulator.

He tries to appear magnanimous. He wants to be, has to be. "And I thank you for your work. My father, too, would thank you if he were here, but, like me, he wouldn't have tolerated even the shadow of a doubt concerning your loyalty to Casa Florio." He joins his hands together. "For the sake of the past, I still respect you. I'm offering you the chance to leave without scandal and with an adequate settlement. It's up to you. Don't force me to fire and publicly disavow you."

Laganà returns a pitying look. "All you have of your father is his name. Soon, even that will carry no more influence. And the fault will be yours alone. Mind how you act and whom you heed: this is my last piece of advice to you. You're unable to see or realize the damage you're causing NGI. From now on everything that happens to Casa Florio will be the result of your decisions." He rises and brushes the brim of his hat. "You'll receive my resignation letter tomorrow without fail. It is I who doesn't want to work for you anymore. To be shown the door like this after so many years . . . No, I don't deserve it." He leans forward, and for a moment, Ignazio is almost afraid he is going to attack. "Only, you'll have to pay me, and a great deal, because my work and my loyalty come at a price."

Ignazio says nothing. Creaks seem to come from the walls, as though the wood paneling is contracting. Or maybe it's the sound of a Palermo that doesn't care.

Laganà reaches the door, stops, and turns. "This doesn't end here, *Signor* Florio," he says. "Because everything in life comes at a price, even ingratitude. Everything you've earned has been thanks to me, and sooner or later you'll have to give back."

The door slams behind him with a thud.

*Everything in life comes at a price. So obvious,* Ignazio tells himself, annoyed. Did Laganà think he'd get away with it? That he, Ignazio, was in some way inferior to his father? *What a joke!*

In the carriage on his way home, Ignazio thinks about what happened, barely aware that the sun has set and the temperature has plummeted. October has brought with it short days, as though its gusts of wind were intent on stealing the light.

By the time the gates of the Olivuzza open and the carriage draws up beside the large olive tree, his thoughts have altered. He wants laughter, champagne, music, and lighthearted chatter. It's been too arduous a day to spend the evening at home or in a small haunt. He will ask Franca what invitations she has received and will choose the most eccentric.

He finds his wife in Giovannuzza's room, standing opposite Mademoiselle Coudray and the little girl, who is clutching a silver spoon. Franca greets him and smiles. "Look at how clever our *picciridda* is," she says proudly. "She's learning to eat by herself."

Ignazio goes to the high chair. Giovannuzza lights up and reaches out with her arms, splashing semolina around. "Papapaa," she mumbles.

"Eat," he says, laughing and indicating her bowl.

The little girl drops the spoon on the floor and claps her hands. Momentarily, his worries subside. Laganà, figures that don't add up . . . nothing seems important anymore. But only for a moment. While Mademoiselle Coudray wipes Giovannuzza's mouth, Ignazio mutters to Franca, "I'd like to go out tonight. I need to clear my head."

She curls a lock of hair around her fingers. "I'd rather stay at home, Ignazio. Diodata told me there have been more protests and a carriage was attacked with stones. I'm worried."

"No, that's just servants' gossip. Go on, get ready."

Franca shakes her head. "Please, let's stay at home. Just for tonight. We're always out, and I'd like to spend a couple of hours with just you and our daughter."

"Home? Like paupers who can't afford to attend a party or accept an invitation?" Ignazio shakes his head and goes to the door. "I can't believe that you, of all people, are saying this to me!"

Franca follows him down the corridor and takes him by the arm. "I don't understand . . . Just for one night . . . I thought you'd be pleased to—"

"I want to go out! I can't bear being shut in here all the time!"

Franca lets go of him and lowers her head.

"You're welcome to act the governess, since it gives you so much fun." He walks past her with an angry step. "I'm going to Romualdo's and then to the club . . . or wherever else I feel like. Don't wait up."

"You're a sight for sore eyes! You haven't been around for a week. I'm invited to a card party—will you come along?"

Romualdo Trigona's house on Piazza della Rivoluzione doesn't have an ounce of the Olivuzza's modernity, but Ignazio loves to breathe in the scent of freedom radiated by the rooms of a bachelor. Romualdo is getting dressed in front of his bedroom mirror with his usual nonchalance. Around him, the bed, the mahogany chest, and the chairs are strewn haphazardly with jackets and ties.

"You own more clothes than a woman!" Ignazio exclaims.

"That's coming from the man who, every time he goes to his London tailor, orders enough jackets and suits to clothe an army," Romualdo replies. He holds a red moiré silk tie to his damask waistcoat and seeks Ignazio's opinion with a look.

Ignazio sniggers. "That makes you look like a couch, *curò*," he jests, gesturing to pick another tie. "The smooth satin one's better."

*Curò*—dear heart. Romualdo smiles at the comical but affectionate endearment Ignazio and Romualdo use with each other, follows his advice, and ties the plastron on while glancing sideways at him.

"What's wrong, Ignazio? You look glum . . ."

Ignazio shrugs his shoulders. "Trouble at NGI. And I got upset with Franca."

"What? Did she discover a peccadillo? Or have people been talking to her?"

"No, not this time. But she behaved in a way that annoyed me."

Romualdo inquires no further. Quarrels between those two are old news. "Why do you think I'm not married? To avoid rows and doors slammed in my face."

"Don't you have an understanding—"

"—with Giulia Tasca di Cutò's father? Yes, I do. But she's still too much of a *picciridda* for my taste, and I want to have some fun."

Ignazio leans back in the armchair. "Tell me about it. Franca grows hysterical whenever she hears about certain episodes. But this evening, when I wanted to go out with her, she got it into her head that we had to stay home and stare at each other, just us and the *picciridda*. Imagine that! A man works all day and then has to stay home like some pauper—a *puveriddu*!"

Romualdo shrugs as he combs his hair. "She's a woman," he states blankly, admiring his perfectly straight part, glossy with brilliantine. "And after a while, women want to stay home and be mothers."

"Fine, that's proper, but Franca can't keep me on a leash." He sighs. "I mean, she has to understand that a man has needs . . . That's been true since the dawn of time. It's not as if by indulging myself or having a mistress I love my wife any less. Franca is one thing, other women something else. Besides, I've seen to it that she wants for nothing."

"Women have gotten it into their heads that men are accountable to them . . ." Romualdo mutters, waving his hand as though to say: *Madness.*

Ignazio shakes his head. "It's not that: she's scared I won't want her anymore, and it gets on my nerves, because that's not how she'll stop me from doing certain things. I need other women. I want to enjoy myself, I want to be charmed by them and take what they offer me. Especially if they're really popular and desirable. I won't accept rejection. Is that a sin? Well then, I have a lifetime to confess and repent."

"And women do say yes to you . . . and in particular to your *picciuli*—your pocketbook." Romualdo lights a cigarette and blows the smoke out, laughing beneath his well-trimmed mustache. "Anyway, all this talk of women has made me feel like taking a stroll. Forget the card game—let's go to Casa delle Rose. I hear they have some new girls."

Red velvet, alcoves, lace robes that part to reveal smooth, firm bodies. Ignazio suddenly imagines all this and can practically smell the face powder and perfumes. Casa delle Rose is a refined place, a far cry from the brothels around Piazza Marina or in the neighborhood of the Oretea Foundry. There, a man can leave his burden of tiredness and worries at the door and find some peace, and—why not?—even some mirth.

"You're right, *curò*. Let's go," he says, jumping to his feet.

Romualdo stubs out his cigarette, retrieves his frock coat from the closet, and laughs to himself. It really doesn't take much to improve Ignazio's mood.

It's after midnight by the time Ignazio returns to the Olivuzza, the worse for several glasses of champagne, swaying slightly, clearly intoxicated. The evening was very enjoyable and the young woman he spent it with a real flower, a true Neapolitan beauty with jet-black eyes and a mouth that—

"You shouldn't come home at this time of night."

Giovanna is waiting for him at the top of the red staircase in her robe.

"It's late, *Maman*," Ignazio says with a sigh, suddenly irritated. "Whatever it is we need to discuss, can't we do it tomorrow? I have a headache."

She comes down a few steps and stops in front of him. "You stink of wine and whores like a libertine." Giovanna is quivering with indignation and anger. This is not how she raised her son. She doesn't recognize him. Her husband—God rest his soul— always showed respect to her and for the name he carried, and now her son appears to be doing everything in his power to dishonor them.

"I won't allow you to speak to me like that, even though you're my mother."

Ignazio raises his hand in an attempt to force her aside, but Giovanna seems made of marble. She puts a hand on his chest and nails him with a fierce glare. "You're acting recklessly. I heard what you did at NGI: throwing Laganà out like that was a dangerous thing to do. Now he's furious, and I don't blame him, because some things require skill. What now? Whom will you call on to replace him?"

"That's none of your business!" Ignazio nearly shouts. "What— now, on top of everything else, you want to tell me how to act at work? Would you like to wear a pair of pants and go to the office instead of me? Go ahead. You'd be doing me a favor!"

Giovanna stands motionless. Some things need to be said, and if she isn't the one to say them, no one will. For an instant, she almost blames her husband for leaving her to manage such an immature son on her own. "You're doing it all wrong, Ignazio. You should stay with your wife, she's a flower, but you yell at her and bolt. You had the *picciridda* months ago, so you should think about having a son instead of going around carousing like a . . ." She puts a hand over her mouth to restrain an insult. "You have a beautiful, faithful wife waiting for you; appreciate what you have instead of wasting time and money on other women."

Ignazio blushes, now totally sober. "Are you trying to butt into our bedroom, too, now?"

Giovanna's voice is like the slash of a razor. "I'm not interested in what you do. All I'm truly interested in is this family and its future." She steps aside, turning her back on him, and walks up the red marble stairs. "We don't count, you and I," she says. "All that matters is the Florio name, and you must measure up to it. Now go wash."

She leaves Ignazio standing there motionless on the stairs, staring blankly, suddenly nauseated. He retches, claps a hand over his mouth, and barely makes it out the front door before vomiting.

Then, resting his forehead against the wall, his vision blurred by the nausea, sweating and trembling, he looks down at his father's gold ring on his finger. Franca returned it to him during their honeymoon, saying that, as the head of the family, it was only right that he should wear it.

His father . . . He was certainly a true head of the family. Sober, cautious, and discreet. He defended the Florios' honor at all costs. He never humiliated his wife or dismissed an employee without a fair hearing.

But he, Ignazio? Who is he?

⌒

The ballroom is brightly lit. The crystal Murano chandeliers stain with gold the moldings around the doors, the mirrors above the French consoles, and the ivory damask curtains; against the walls, couches and ottomans await the guests, who are expected shortly.

Of the two ballrooms at the Olivuzza, Franca has elected this one, partly because it is in the older part of the house and is larger and more richly decorated. The first ball of Palermo's 1895 season will not be her and Ignazio's first, but it may be the most important because it will serve as the benchmark for all those to succeed it.

Franca's footsteps barely echo on the polished herringbone parquet, drowned out by the small orchestra tuning up: they will begin with a waltz, and she and Ignazio will open the dance. Servants in livery stand upright by the French doors leading to the garden, like a royal guard. Franca looks up at the light-colored ceiling, framed by gilded plaster cornices, and remembers how small she felt the first time she walked into this lavish room, and how thrilling it was to see torches illuminating the garden beyond the large glass doors.

She goes out onto the terrace. Long tables with refreshments have been arranged under the wrought-iron gazebo, covered with a white tarp. There are already Baccarat and Bohemian crystal carafes filled with lemonade and fruit juice laid out, as well as champagne and white wine in silver buckets so large you could bathe a baby in them. Large, gleaming trays mirror finely decorated glass coupes.

Franca nods to herself, then heads for the buffet hall, which was painted with frescoes by Antonino Leto when her father-in-law still lived. Here she finds Nino talking with the regular sommelier. The waiters have nearly finished setting bottles of Casa Florio's best marsala wine, as well as cognac, port, and brandy, on the tables.

Across the room, a waitress is laying out silver cutlery beside the Limoges dishes and cups. When she sees the mistress of the house, she blushes and gives a quick bow. "I'm done, Signora," she mutters apologetically before practically scurrying away.

Franca swallows a sigh of annoyance as she watches the young woman head downstairs. The servant women *must* stay in the kitchen during balls, partly because they have a lot to do, since, unlike other aristocratic households, the Florios don't just have a *monsù* with a handful of assistants but an entire battalion of cooks, who also take care of the baking. For this evening, Franca ordered fruit tartlets, *mille-feuilles* with chantilly, savarin and cream cakes, as well as Bavarian and sponge cakes. There is also *gelo di mellone*—the traditional Sicilian jellied watermelon pudding—various sorbets, and chalices brimming with candied fruit.

Furthermore, on the large table stand antique Neapolitan silver coffeepots with ebony and ivory handles, which she picked out from the large number of sets kept in the big cabinets and dressers at the Olivuzza. She strokes the linen of the blindingly white Flanders tablecloth, which has a satin runner with long tassels that brush against the floor, and smiles to herself, pleased, before motioning to Nino. "I gave instructions for the baskets of party favors to be decorated with lilies from the hothouse. Have you seen to it?"

The butler nods. "It's been done, Donna Franca. We've put the flowers in the ice room to keep them fresh, and at the right time we'll add them to the gifts for your guests."

"Good. As soon as the room is half filled, start serving the champagne. I want the guests to enjoy themselves and dance right away."

She says goodbye to the man, then walks through a series of rooms to the crimson salon, where, in agreement with Ignazio, she has had various gaming tables set up and arranged for an abundant supply of Tuscan cigars. A waiter is placing bottles of brandy and Florio cognac into a drinks cabinet, inlaid with tortoiseshell, ivory, and mother-of-pearl. Above hangs an Antonino Leto painting of boats with unfurled sails.

Next door, the drawing room reserved for the ladies is ready. Chinese and Japanese porcelain vases filled with flowers from the garden adorn the shelves, and lamps, covered with printed oriental silks, gently illuminate the beautiful paintings, including works by Francesco de Mura, Mattia Preti, and Francesco Solimena, that Franca has especially curated for this room.

Here, in the half-light, Franca finds Giovanna sitting on a couch, a black figure against the pink velvet. Her mother-in-law looks her up and down and smiles. "You've done everything so well," she says and holds out her hand.

Surprised, Franca takes it and sits down beside her.

"I feel as if I've stepped back in time, to when my Ignazio was alive, with all the rooms decorated and salons full of people dancing." Giovanna gives an uncertain smile. "My aunt, the princess of Sant'Elia, used to say that no parties could compete with ours." The memory of past joy softens her expression. She pulls her hand away. "Now go and welcome your guests."

Strolling across the last salon, Franca pauses in front of a mirror and brushes a lock of hair from her cheek. She is wearing a low-cut peach gown, hemmed by ivory lace, designed for her by Worth. In her bejeweled hand is a fan with mother-of-pearl inserts, while her beloved pearls encircle her neck.

Yes, everything is ready.

The Tasca di Cutòs are among the first to arrive: Giulia, now a dear friend of Franca's, with Alessandro, the young heir, and her younger sister Maria. The Tasca di Cutò family are regulars at the Olivuzza, one of the few Giovanna receives with pleasure, in memory of her friendship with Giulia's mother, Princess Giovanna Nicoletta Filangeri, who died a few months before Ignazio.

Franca greets everybody, then takes Giulia's arm. "Where's Romualdo, my dear?"

She responds with a vague gesture. "My future husband stayed behind with Ignazio to welcome my brother-in-law Giulio and his wife, Bice." She makes an irked grimace. "You know what it's like: when my sister arrives, they all fall at her feet."

Franca doesn't comment, but there's a flash of understanding in her eyes: Ignazio isn't immune to the charms of Beatrice Tasca di Cutò, wife of Giulio Tomasi, Duke of Palma and future Prince of Lampedusa, either. After all, from what they say, Bice is very skilled at "using her favors."

But Giulia is naturally pragmatic so doesn't pander to these thoughts. "I'd like to ask your advice about the dress for the civil ceremony . . . Would you accompany me to the dressmaker's tomorrow? You're the only one whose taste I trust."

Franca nods and gives her hand a squeeze.

"But right now I want to relay my father's regards to Donna Giovanna. Do you know where she is?"

"In the ladies' drawing room. Go on. We'll talk later."

She watches her vanish through the quilted velvet doors, then greets the other guests: first her sister-in-law, Giulia, and her husband, Pietro, then another dear friend, Stefanina Spadafora, who looks her up and down before letting out an exclamation of wonder at her elegant dress.

Franca smiles again. This smile, the dress, and the jewels are now her shield against fears, gossip, and envy—which resound stronger than ever this evening. This is the first ball of Palermo's season, and it must be unforgettable.

～

Romualdo Trigona sits down next to his friend. "What's wrong, *curò*? Aren't you having fun?"

Ignazio shrugs his shoulders. "*Camurrie*, you know. Troubles."

"Look over there . . . The ladies are all together. I believe they're crucifying us." Romualdo sniggers without waiting for an answer. Then he snags a coupe of champagne on the fly and savors it with his eyes closed. When he reopens them, he sees Pietro Lanza di Trabia watching him, amused.

"Perfect temperature! How many deliveries of ice did you have carted from the Madonie Mountains, Ignazio?"

But his friend hasn't even heard him. He looks lost in thought, his brow deeply furrowed.

Pietro laughs, soon joined by Romualdo. "Come on, Ignazio,

don't tell me you don't like Perrier-Jouët anymore! Oh, but perhaps I understand. You're sad because your wife's here and you can't ogle women."

Ignazio finally stirs. "No, it's not that." He hesitates. "I can't get that business of Laganà and his son out of my head."

Turning serious, Pietro shifts slightly to survey the room inconspicuously. There are couples dancing to the lively beat of a mazurka, the clicking of their heels on the parquet so loud that it almost overcomes the music. "Not here. Let's go outside."

They step out onto the large balcony overlooking the garden, not far from the tables where cakes and ice creams are being served. The grounds of the Olivuzza are a dark sea dotted with small torches to mark the paths. Here and there, strolling couples can be glimpsed, trailed by chaperones.

"He's nominated his son Augusto to run for Parliament's lower house and is trying to secure a seat in the Senate for himself," Ignazio explains once he is sure they are far from prying ears. "He's scheming to enter politics, says he's entitled to more because of how he served Casa Florio and the country." There is a blend of bitterness and irritation in his voice. "And then he has the gall to come and demand the compensation money I owe him."

Pietro looks first at him then at Romualdo. "Wait, that's something I'm not aware of. What's this about the Senate?"

Romualdo searches his jacket for his cigar case and matchbook. "It's the consequence for the mess your brother-in-law made when he fired Laganà, or rather when he rudely ousted him from NGI. Now the man is seeking revenge." He wipes his mouth with his hand. "Ignazio made a mess—that's what happened." He takes a puff and looks at the sky. "A real mess."

"*E iddu ora voli i picciuli e va faciennu scruscio*—now he wants the money, and he goes around gossiping," Ignazio says angrily to Pietro.

Romualdo looks at his empty glass and gestures to a waiter in the doorway of the balcony to bring him another.

Pietro puckers his lips in a disappointed grimace. Romualdo has been drinking a little too much of late, and it shows.

"I contacted various members of Parliament, who replied with a barrage of letters urging me to act 'with caution.' Do you realize he's trying to tell me what to do? I promised him compensation and he'll get it, but he'll have to sweat for it first. Besides, I don't even have that kind of money in the bank right now."

"Who told you he's proposing his son?" Romualdo asks, ignoring what Ignazio has just said. "I mean . . . there's a rumor going round, but I took it for speculation."

Ignazio puts his hands in his pockets and studies the perfect line of his English shoes. "Unfortunately not. Abele Damiani confirmed it: Laganà went to see him, bad-mouthed me, and asked him to speak to Crispi so that *he* may personally handle the procedure to anoint him senator. Damiani was embarrassed about telling me all that."

Romualdo shakes a hand. "I can't picture Damiani being embarrassed, but—"

"Oh, stop interrupting me all the time!"

Pietro and Romualdo are startled. Ignazio never loses his temper. He smooths his mustache, then rubs his hands together.

Pietro recognizes signs of self-consciousness. "Laganà is a shark, Ignazio. You should have known." The reprimand is justified.

"This business about his entering Parliament is shameful," Ignazio hisses. "*Iddu surci di cunnutto è*—he's a sewer rat. He mustn't become a senator."

Romualdo downs all his champagne in a gulp. "What about his son?"

"Augusto Laganà? He's supported by Crispi himself."

Pietro glances around, takes two chairs, and offers one to Romualdo. "It's not in your interest to go against Crispi, Ignazio. He's still Crispi."

"He was our lawyer, for crying out loud, so he should show some gratitude, but instead . . ." Ignazio tosses his head back and is momentarily lulled by the sounds of the party, voices and laughter billowing out through the open French doors. A world that belongs to him by right. He lifts a hand to block the light from the room, the night sky above him, beyond the volutes of the gazebo. "But he's almost eighty years old now and his downward spiral started quite a while ago. Hitching a cart to a dying horse is the best way to go nowhere fast. No, we need new energy, someone who wants to get ahead."

Pietro looks puzzled. "What do you mean?"

"He supports Laganà? Well, I'll support Rosario Garibaldi Bosco."

"The Socialist?" Pietro says, eyes open wide. "The one Crispi actually put in prison over the *Fasci* uprising?"

"Yes, him. Socialists have many sympathizers among the workers and sailors under my employment. We just need them to stir things a little and put pressure on those higher up. I've thought of everything. *Ca 'ti pari chi sugnu scimunito*—do I seem like an idiot to you?"

Pietro still watches him, unconvinced. "You risk being labeled a Socialist, like that hothead Alessandro Tasca di Cutò."

Romualdo throws up his hands without comment.

"Me? Not at all. This isn't about political ideology but what's in the best interests of Casa Florio. Crispi and his friends are trying to impose certain rules on me, but it's an antiquated plan of action and their politics have been superseded by fact. Money and titles no longer are enough to have sway in Parliament. If my family's strength lies in its factories and the people who work in them, then I must look for support among those who are interested that these companies continue to operate and prosper." Ignazio has spoken deliberately and softly, to make sure the others understand he is not joking.

"In other words, the workers." Romualdo raises his glass to him.

Ignazio nods. "If politics is a market, then I can afford to choose whom to support."

⌒

It's shortly after midnight. The elderly women gather in the salon reserved for them, to rest and chat in peace. On the other hand, in the crimson salon countless men play cards, wreathed in a thick cloud of smoke. Even so, the ballroom is teeming and, despite the open windows, sweltering.

Franca stands guard by the door to the buffet room with Emma di Villarosa and Giulia Tasca di Cutò, watching the dancers. She knows it—she can sense it: if there have been malicious remarks, they haven't caught on. Everything has been absolutely perfect: before her eyes, Palermo has eaten, danced, gossiped, and enjoyed itself.

"A truly wonderful party, Franca. Congratulations."

Franca turns to see Tina Whitaker, matronly and stern, with her husband, Pip. He has roamed all alone around the salons, admiring the collection of Capodimonte statuettes, and lingering for a good five minutes in front of a large group of porcelain figures by Filippo Tagliolini, with Hercules as the slave of Queen Omphale; as for Tina, she has, as always, been the center of attention, dishing out her repertoire of witticisms and barbs.

"Thank you, Tina," Franca replies, astounded that Palermo's bluntest woman has nothing else to say about her ball. "I hope you've had something from the cake buffet?"

"Yes. Your *monsù* has outdone himself. The jasmine ice cream is a delight. But now it's time for my husband and me to retire."

"Really? But it's still so early, not even one yet," Franca protests, although she knows Tina's habits.

Tina taps on her wrist while Pip stares uneasily down at his shoes. "You, Franca, are a woman made for socializing, but I think it inappropriate to overstay one's welcome."

Franca opens her hands in a gesture of resignation. "Very well. At least allow me to gift you a memento of this evening." She flashes Nino, who's behind her, a discreet signal and he briefly disappears before returning with a willow basket decorated with white lilies. Curious, a few guests approach.

"For you," Franca says, handing Tina a small jewelry box and Pip an oblong trinket wrapped in marbled paper. "For the ladies, we thought we'd have a charm made by the Fecarotta jewelers: a pomegranate in honor of the approaching fall," she explains as Tina closely inspects the knickknack. "And for the men a silver cigar holder." She leans toward Pip and says softly, "I'm sure you'll appreciate it."

Joseph Whitaker blushes.

Tina rolls her eyes, placing the charm back in its case, and slips it into her satin purse. "Once again, the Florios' hospitality proves to be unrivaled, my dear Franca." As she shakes hands, she glances at the couples dancing yet another mazurka and mutters, "Don't these people have families to go home to?" Then she leaves, holding Pip's arm.

Franca's sigh is echoed by Emma and Giulia, who remarks, "She can't help it. That woman must always spew a little poison."

Ignazio comes in from the terrace, sees Franca, and waves at her. She sees him, too, smiles and walks toward him.

One more waltz with him will seal a perfect evening.

༝༨

"Has he arrived?"

"Anytime now . . . When he comes, we must give him a hero's welcome!"

"The man's been in every jail on the mainland, and now he's a member of Parliament—all thanks to the Florios!"

"At long last, even the masters have realized they have to talk to us workers."

"Here's the steamer! It's here!"

"Hurrah for Rosario Garibaldi Bosco! Hurrah for the Florios!"

It's three o'clock in the morning, and yet it looks like noon in the harbor of Palermo. The pier and docks are crammed with workers from the Castellammare and Tribunali districts, awaiting their member of Parliament: Rosario Garibaldi Bosco, who was sentenced over two years ago, in February 1894, for leading the uprising of the Sicilian *Fasci*, of which he is also a founding member. He is not a worker but an accountant, his hands are not smeared with engine oil, nor are his lungs covered in soot, and yet he has fought for social justice since adolescence. In high school, he read propaganda leaflets out loud to illiterate workers, then, as a journalist, he wrote long articles in which he imagined a Sicily where the workers were free from the oppression of masters supported by the complicity of a repressive government.

Despite being in prison, he was a candidate for the left-wing Chamber and won at least three rounds, including one against Augusto Laganà, Giovanni's son. And when, in March 1896, an amnesty was issued to him and his companions, he was finally able to return to Palermo.

The steamship *Elettrico*, part of the NGI line, maneuvers slowly toward the pier. A few minutes later, Rosario Garibaldi Bosco appears at the top of the steps, greeted with cheers, cries of jubilation, and fervent waves of *Fasci* and Socialist Party flags.

The strain of his long imprisonment is evident: he is only thirty, but looks much older, as though he's suddenly aged, skinny and moving slowly. He gets off, greets his companions, then gives a long hug to his father, who is unable to hold back his tears.

As he heads home, surrounded by a stream of people, a carriage sets off, follows him, and stops in an adjacent street. Another half hour goes by before the crowd disperses and the shutters close on the balcony where Garibaldi Bosco has stepped out several times to thank everyone for their welcome.

Only then do Ignazio and another man, his face partly concealed by a hat, get out of the carriage, open the small front entrance, and climb the stone stairs. When Ignazio knocks on the door, the celebratory chatter inside the apartment suddenly falls silent.

Rosario himself opens the door. "You, here?" he exclaims, astounded.

He is in his shirtsleeves, and there are biscuit crumbs on his mustache. A little girl clings to his legs. She looks scared.

He picks her up. "Calm down, *nica mia*," he says with a smile. "They're not police officers." He kisses her, then puts her back down on the ground. "Go to *Mamma*, go," he says with a tap on her back. "Tell her I'm talking to . . . to some friends." He turns to the two men. "I'm sorry. I wasn't expecting you so soon. Come in."

He leads the way to a room behind a glass door and lights an oil lamp while the two men sit on a couch. Slightly uneasy, Ignazio speaks first. "We didn't want to draw attention to ourselves," he says apologetically. "You realize, of course, that it wouldn't benefit either of us if people found out we've met. Right, Erasmo?"

The Genoese Erasmo Piaggio took over Giovanni Laganà's position as director general of NGI some time ago: he's a stern, determined, capable, and unscrupulous man. He puts his hat down on his lap, smooths the tips of his mustache, and nods. Then he looks at Rosario expectantly.

Rosario rubs his hands on his thighs, searching for the right words. "I don't know how to express my gratitude. I heard you lobbied for the amnesty, supported my family, and allowed my companions to run an election campaign at the Oretea and the slipway. It's absurd that my companions and I should have been arrested. The military court didn't realize that if we'd wanted to, we could have unleashed a protest throughout the island."

"Or perhaps it did realize that," Piaggio remarks calmly.

Rosario nods, then lowers his head. "That's right. There are too many wrongs in this country, things crying out for justice, but the government seems deaf and blind to them." He pauses. "In any case, you know very well that the Socialist Party now has many sympathizers."

"Of course I do," Ignazio replies. "Alessandro Tasca di Cutò has been arrested for the same political views." Last September, he had to endure endless complaints from Romualdo, who had been questioned by the police for a long time about his brother-in-law's "subversive acquaintances." "As you can imagine, I don't share many of your views. But I do consider myself an intelligent person, and I believe that workers and farmers should command more importance. In other words, that their voices should be heard by our politicians in Rome."

Rosario stiffens. "If workers are taken care of, then they become more cooperative, and so a company can prosper. Is that what you mean?"

"Yes, exactly." Ignazio smiles. "You obtained our help for a series of reasons, not least to prevent the rise of a dishonest man, the son of someone who tried to harm Palermo and its seafaring in every way he could."

"Laganà's son. Augusto. He stood against me in the same district."

"That's right. His defeat was in my interests, of course, but also in the interests of the workers, because it involved preventing Sicily being excluded from the share of government agreements and commissions for repairs, which keep both the Oretea and the slipway alive."

Piaggio sits up and looks at Rosario. "What we're asking you, Signor Bosco," he says calmly but firmly, "is to be our voice with the workers. So that they understand fully the advantage they will gain by . . . by cooperating with us."

Rosario doesn't reply immediately. He sits down in an armchair and his gaze travels from Piaggio to Ignazio. "It's true that I'm indebted to you," he finally says. "And yes, in the case of Laganà, your interests tallied with mine. But don't think that my companions and I are ready to give up on our sacrosanct rights in exchange for the master's charity."

"Nobody's asking you to—" Piaggio begins.

"Let's be clear," Ignazio cuts in. "We used to be able to rely on Crispi, but he's old now, and after the Adua disaster, he has even more enemies. And I wouldn't be so sure of the new prime minister either: it's true that Rudinì is from Palermo, but he's a conservative at heart. No, Sicily needs new men who can listen to both politicians and workers and act accordingly. That's the future."

"Crispi has always first and foremost served the interests of those who voted for him and gotten others to vote for him." Rosario has dropped his voice, but there is no hesitation in his words.

"Indeed." Ignazio opens his arms. "He owes a great deal to my family, just as we owe him. But that's in the past. He can't begin to imagine how and why the world is changing. You do, on the other hand, and have the interests of our land at heart. Together, we can stop Sicily from being cast aside in the country's economy. Are you willing to help us?"

"My dear Giovanni, do you know what they say in my city? *Si voi pruvari li peni di lu 'nfernu, lu 'nvernu a Missina e l'estati 'n Palermu*—if you want a taste of hell, winter in Messina and summer in Palermo. But I'm sure you'll like it in Palermo, despite the sirocco wind." Marchese Antonio Starabba di Rudinì stroked his beard with a smile, then added, "And you'll do an excellent job."

Count Giovanni Codronchi Argeli returned the prime minister's smile. But his affable smile concealed the awareness that the highfalutin position—royal civil commissioner extraordinaire for Sicily—was in reality a very delicate task filled with hidden dangers.

Indeed, the island was a time bomb. Too much unrest, starting with the *Fasci*; widespread corruption and organized crime. Rudinì knew only too well that he needed to review the budgets, reorganize duties and taxes, examine the different departments of the administration, and replace corrupt civil servants. But in order to achieve all this, he needed to resort to a politician who was immune to influence and pressure, with no personal interests to defend and a free rein.

In other words, a non-Sicilian.

The serious, cautious, pensive Giovanni Codronchi Argeli—mayor of his birthplace, Imola, for over eight years—was the ideal candidate. Moreover, he would be useful in further undermining Crispi's influence, at the same time restricting the spread of Socialist ideas. Basically, strengthening the position of the Right on the island.

This was an ambitious design that required important allies, of prominent figures.

Like Ignazio Florio.

Ignazio is in fact invited to a meeting with the commissioner slated for early June 1896. Ignazio has been anticipating this moment since he first spoke with Rosario Garibaldi Bosco. Keeping the workers' demands under control as much as possible was only the first step; now the government has to be persuaded that the only way to prevent protests and uprisings—if not worse—is to create jobs, and a lot of them at that. He's been talking a lot to Piaggio, but in the end, the best solution seems to be to begin construction of a shipyard adjoining the careening basin, to extend the present slipway. A plan that failed three years ago because of hindering on the city's part.

Codronchi has made him wait. Two whole months. But now Ignazio is here, facing him, in his private office in the Royal Palace. He studies this stout man with his chubby cheeks and bushy gray mustache, with all the confidence of someone who knows Palermo and its residents like the back of his hand and not only through hearsay.

The city's sounds bleed through the open windows: peddlers crying, children chasing one another, a melody from a barrel organ. The two men have had coffee and exchanged pleasantries, but now the secretary removes the cups and leaves them alone, shutting the door behind him.

Giovanni Codronchi wipes the sweat from his wide forehead—Rudinì was right about summer in Palermo. "So. Personally, I'm in favor of your project, Don Ignazio. Building and repairing steamers would guarantee long-term commissions, and they, in turn, would ensure social calm."

Sitting cross-legged, hands on his lap, Ignazio nods. "I'm glad you agree." He leans in. "Palermo needs certainty: the crisis is making people nasty and encouraging them to follow certain bad actors who spin yarns about fabulous wages for all. The workers in my foundry—"

"—the Oretea."

"That's right. They're protesting because their wages haven't changed for years, but in particular because there have been many redundancies. But believe me, it was unavoidable: I'm a businessman. I must take care of the health of my business. We can't support them all." He frowns and gives a theatrical sigh. "They think that here in Sicily you can earn the same money as up north, as though we had the same roads and the same commissions. But the truth is that money doesn't circulate here; if it weren't for us Florios, and a handful of others, the island would already be abandoned: everybody would have gone to America or somewhere else. On the other hand, the government must understand that it's dangerous to have so much unemployment because there are hotheads who will use any excuse to their advantage."

"Yes, of course." Codronchi leans on the armrest of his chair and drums his fingers on the portfolio in front of him. "In my opinion, this project would weaken the radical elements. It's something close to the government's heart, in particular to our prime minister, who's from Palermo, like you. I'll personally see that it's supported, only . . ." He sits up in his chair and interlaces his fingers in front of his face. "You know better than I that Italian ship-building isn't in a good state at present. Livorno and Genoa are having difficulties, and commissions for new ships often end up abroad, in England . . ."

"Work engenders work, Commissioner, you know that. NGI has long been asked to modernize its steamers. If we had access to a shipyard, we could do so without having to travel to Genoa or even Southampton or the Clyde and dock ships there indefinitely. Besides, let's speak frankly: it's undeniable that the Genoese are working against Palermo, doing their best to hinder us. But if we managed to build ships here, we would provide jobs for new work-ers and receive commissions both for the careening basin and the foundry. That's why we need government funds: Casa Florio can provide much but not all. We can equip the shipyard, but we need tax breaks and to appropriate the public property bordering the tobacco factory."

Codronchi nods and rubs his lips. "You do know that those close to Crispi won't support your plan, don't you? And that you'll also encounter obstacles within the government?"

Ignazio leans back and crosses his hands on his belly. "Crispi's had his time, Commissioner. He's no longer the man my father respected." He lowers his voice. "Our concerns are very distant, if not incompatible, now. At present, we have other needs. If we could give jobs to workers, carpenters, and bricklayers, we would pull the rug from under the feet of the Socialists and anarchists, who would no longer be able to fuel discontent to unleash unrest. We must make room for new, forward-thinking forces that have Sicily's economic development at heart and see a future where in-stitutions and businesses can work together."

A seasoned politician, able to read between the lines, Codronchi nods. "You're an industrialist and financier capable of putting ingenuity and resources at the service of the public. Moreover, you're looking attentively to the future."

Ignazio's mouth forms the slow, self-assured smile of a man of the world. "Finance and politics must work in harmony. And it's up to people like you and me to make sure that happens."

~

"Heavens, what a mess!" Giulia exclaims, giving her sister-in-law a hug.

Franca has been waiting for her at the foot of the staircase overlooking the garden. They're surrounded by a retinue of gardeners and servants busy cleaning up after the visit of Wilhelm II, German Emperor and King of Prussia, Empress Augusta Victoria, and their children, Wilhelm and Eitel Friedrich: the royal family came to take tea with the Florios the day before.

"Yes, it's been a busy week, what with preparing the Olivuzza, deciding the menu, observing protocol . . . But thankfully everything went well. The kaiser especially enjoyed the almond cakes and the empress much admired the parrots in the aviary and the tall yuccas, while Vincenzino talked to young Wilhelm for a long time—after all, they're the same age . . ." She smiles. "He made quite a few grammatical mistakes, but his German pronunciation was perfect."

"And now you're clearly very tired," Giulia remarks, blunt as ever.

"Yes, a little," Franca admits, "but what I really need is to talk to someone who . . ." She looks down and lifts her foot. "Well . . . someone who isn't going to tell all Palermo that there's still dust on my shoes because I haven't had time to change . . ."

Giulia laughs. "So you sent for me. Come on; let's take a stroll through the garden. That way I'll also have dust on my shoes!"

She takes her arm and they head outside. The sun is setting, and it won't be long before darkness descends over the park.

"So . . . it sounds like everything went wonderfully well at the Whitakers, too, yesterday," Giulia exclaims cheerfully. "Tina sent me a note and told me everything."

"Yes, she wrote me, too. And she made sure to point out that the kaiser very much enjoyed her singing," Franca replies, toying with the string of pearls around her neck.

Giulia notices and squeezes her arm. "Are they new?" Franca lowers her head and nods. "Has Ignazio been foolish again?" she asks softly. "Is that why you got me to come here?"

"No . . . I mean yes. He gave me these pearls and you know what that means." Her pause is filled with bitterness. "They say pearls bring tears. I never wanted to believe it, because to me they're some of the most beautiful things in the world. And yet, invariably, they have brought me to tears. I don't even know who the . . . the lucky one is this time . . ." She sighs and straightens up. "I definitely know how some things work in a marriage now. Even Romualdo has a mistress, although he only recently got married."

Giulia shrugs her shoulders. "Unfortunately, Romualdo and my brother are cut from the same cloth." She stops and looks Franca in the eye. "You've achieved remarkable self-control; you've learned how to swallow such things. But I know you can't help thinking about it."

Giulia hugs her, wishing she could confront her brother and make him act with more discretion, tell him outright that he's tormenting Franca, but she knows it would be pointless. So she releases herself from the hug and changes the subject abruptly.

"Now that even the kaiser's praised her voice, we're going to have to hear yet again how Wagner went into ecstasies when he heard Tina sing *Lohengrin*! Still, we should be sympathetic: Mother

Nature has been generous to her in terms of voice and wit, though certainly not beauty . . ."

Franca's lips wrinkle in a wicked smile. "Fortunately, her daughters are more attractive than her and have no artistic pretensions."

They giggle and, for a while, walk in the silence of the garden, broken only by the voice of Vincenzino playing with his velocipede under the watch of Donna Ciccia and Giovanna. Giulia goes over to greet her mother and brother.

Suddenly, Franca glimpses a man among the trees, just past the hedges. He looks like a peasant, with his brown jacket and worn-out boots. He looks at her, greets her by raising his hand to his hat, then vanishes.

She frowns and stops. "Is it really necessary to have these people around?" she asks Giovanna, who is now next to her.

Giovanna looks at the man in the trees, little more now than a shape in the shadows, purses her lips, and nods. "You're right," she murmurs. "I'll tell Saro to speak with him so that they're more discreet . . . But it's always best to have them nearby, because you never know what might happen." She looks at her son. "Don't move," she commands as she strides back to the villa.

The boy waits for his mother to be far enough away, then runs down the paths to the aviary.

"Vincenzo, come back here!" Giulia shouts.

He waves and disappears beyond a rosebush. Giulia opens her arms in exasperation. "My mother will be furious now. Vincenzo is too spoiled and doesn't obey anyone. He told me the other day that he wants to shoot the parrots and that—"

Franca isn't listening. The man has walked away, but she still feels his presence. She can feel his eyes watching her through the trees, sensing him. "That man worries and frightens me."

"I can understand," Giulia murmurs. "I don't like having

these . . . these oafs around either, but it can't be helped. Whether it's here, in the country, in Trabia or in Bagheria, there's always someone watching our backs. Pietro's terrified of abductions."

"I see his point, but . . ." Franca looks around, reluctant to speak too loudly. "You know, not long ago, Audrey, Joss's sister—Joss is Pip Whitaker's older brother—was kidnapped, and he had to pay, pay a lot, to get her back. It's so sad!"

Giulia nods. "Yes, I heard. Poor darling. Apparently, she had nightmares for days on end. They told me it happened at the Favorita; it seems there were four of them and they beat up the groom who was escorting her. I don't know what I'd do if something like that happened to my children."

"You'd pay, like Joss. They asked for a hundred thousand lire, and he paid it without a word of protest. The prefect tried to intervene, but the Whitakers wouldn't talk. They had a good fright and chose not to make a fuss."

The cry of the eagle, followed by Vincenzino's voice, sounds from the aviary. Giulia's face darkens. "Oh God! If they ever took my brother, Mother would die."

Franca hugs her. "It's not going to happen," she says, but her voice doesn't instill as much confidence as she'd wish.

She remembers how, a while back, she chided Francesco Noto, the head gardener, for badly pruning a rosebush she had brought from England. Ignazio waited for her to come back into the house, then took her aside, embraced her, and whispered, "Please, *mon aimée*, always treat that man with respect, and his brother Pietro, the doorkeeper, too. They're . . . friends who help us keep the peace."

Since then, Franca has noticed that nobody addresses those two without first making a gesture of deference. Nobody. But she hasn't pressed the issue any further: although she's been wrapped in cotton wool, she knows how certain things work.

Suddenly, she spots Saro, Ignazio's valet, rushing to the stables. He's nervous and almost forgets to greet her.

Seconds later, Giovanna steps out of the villa and gives her a nod.

Franca nods back, takes Giulia's arm, and calls Vincenzino, telling him to come back to the house with them.

She keeps her back to the garden. She doesn't want to see.

$\backsim$

August 10, 1897, is bright and warm. Palermo slumbers, its eyes still half shut, the light of dawn bullying its way through the shutters and doors left ajar.

A servant woman crosses the sequence of salons, parlors, and rooms on the ground floor of the Olivuzza; she's shaking, and practically stumbles as she turns to look at Giovanna, who's falling behind her, hands clenched over her stomach, back stiff, and face stony. As she passes the mirrors, they briefly reflect the image of the young fighter who came into this house thirty years ago, instead of a tired and unhappy old woman.

The servant woman practically rushes into the buffet room and indicates one of the dressers, its doors wide open. "Careful," she mutters in consternation. "Look!"

Empty. The dresser is empty.

The silver trays, the pitchers, and the teapots have vanished. The large embossed-silver basin she bought in Naples when her Vincenzino was still alive is no longer there. The flowers it contained are strewn under the mahogany tables, trampled by feet that have left muddy prints.

"What else is missing?" Giovanna asks in a frail voice.

The servant puts a hand over her mouth and points at the next room. "Two of those French somethings, the ones you use for holding fruit . . ." She hesitates, embarrassed and frightened. God forbid Donna Giovanna might think *she's* in any way involved.

"The two *épergnes*?" Giovanna's voice is shrill. She looks to the ceiling, as though she could see the images of what happened last night on it. She takes a deep breath, trying to calm her anger. "Where's Nino?" she asks in a steadier tone.

As though summoned by her words, the butler appears at the dining room door. Giovanna blindly trusts this man who worked for ages in Favignana, in their house near the *tonnara*, and has been at the Olivuzza for the past four years. She has never needed his calm and his all-seeing eye more than she does now.

"I'm here, Donna Giovanna. It seems that the French alabaster vases and your son's golden snuff boxes are also missing." He clears his throat. "And that's not all. They've also taken Signorina Giovannuzza's toys. There are footprints all the way down the corridor."

Giovanna feels a tightening in her chest.

The child.

Their bedroom, their privacy, has been violated. A burglary in Casa Florio.

*Contempt.* An insult to their power. Thieves in her home. Thieves taking her things, the things she has collected, chosen, looked after. Not just objects but memories, like those two antique alabaster vases she and her beloved Ignazio bought in Paris from a dealer on Place des Vosges.

*How dare they?* Giovanna looks around and an unpleasant sensation runs through her, one that goes beyond fear. Beyond contempt.

Nausea.

She looks at the muddy footprints—*filthy feet*, she thinks with disdain—at the finger smears on the polished mahogany, at the trampled flowers. It's as if these marks defile her own body and clothes.

"Clean everything up," she orders the servant woman. "All of it!" she adds more loudly, not bothering to conceal her rage. "And you, Nino, make a detailed inventory of all that's missing. Get the servant women to help you. I need to know what these wretches have stolen."

She turns on her heels and marches out of the room and down the steps to the garden. The fresh air brings her no relief. On the contrary. She discovers more muddy footprints on the steps, a sign that the burglars must have entered and left here.

She should call Ignazio, but he's still asleep. He recently returned from a cruise on the Aegean, aboard his new yacht the *Aegusa*, the ancient name for Favignana. A well-deserved vacation: a year ago, the creation of the Anglo-Sicilian Sulfur Company, which involved both British and French entrepreneurs, succeeded thanks to Ignazio's intervention and is now yielding a good profit. Then, more recently, Nathaniel Rothschild came to Palermo on his yacht, *Veglia*, and there followed an uninterrupted series of receptions, visits, tours of the city, and work meetings. When the illustrious guest finally departed, Ignazio suggested this cruise to the whole family, but she didn't feel like leaving Palermo, telling herself that the children should enjoy themselves without an elderly woman weighing them down. So she stayed here, with only Donna Ciccia and her embroidery for company.

Never before has she been afraid of staying at the Olivuzza on her own. Never in all these years.

She walks into the green salon and pauses in the middle of this room where she has spent so many peaceful moments. She wanders amid the furniture, strokes her husband's photographs, picks up a few items, as if to reassure herself that they are still here, then looks at her hands. The skin is flecked by age spots, her fingers dry and contracted. She looks up: on a table stand her workbasket, the missal, the ivory crucifix, the candles in their silver holders, and the vermeil matchbox. In the corner display cabinet, there are a few porcelain statuettes. On the small table next to the couch, she spots the crystal vase with fresh flowers and the photographs of her Vincenzino and Ignazio in their silver frames. Everything looks intact.

It is a world in which she has never felt the slightest unease. The Florio name has always been powerful and feared, always enough to defend her.

But now everything has been trampled, just like the flowers upstairs.

That is what truly frightens her most.

⌒

After waking Ignazio, Giovanna goes into her daughter-in-law's bedroom. Franca abruptly lifts her head. Diodata has informed her what happened, and she is unable to conceal her fear. After helping her mistress into her robe, Diodata leaves, muttering insults at "those undignified rogues with no God or family."

There is a sea of jewels on the bed. Franca has emptied the gold mesh bag where she keeps them to account for anything missing. Many are gifts from Ignazio: bracelets, rings, gold and platinum necklaces with diamonds, sapphires, emeralds, and many, many pearls gleaming in the morning light. Giovannuzza, who has long black hair and green eyes, is sitting on the bed, still in her nightdress, playing, slipping on rings that are too large for her fingers and slide off into the sheets.

"They haven't touched anything of mine," Franca says, hugging her daughter. "They've only taken the tin toys from—from her room," she adds, unable to utter the child's name. "Good God! What if she'd ended up like Audrey Whitaker . . ."

Giovanna lets her eyes wander over the floor decorated with rose petals. She never liked this room but has always thought it perfect for Franca. "But she didn't," she replies flatly.

She looks straight at her, her eyes more eloquent than words.

Franca lets go of her daughter. "Ignazio won't call the police, will he?"

Giovanna shakes her head. "*Chisti 'un sunnu cose di sbirri*—this is not police business."

The police can't be trusted: they're all foreigners and know nothing of Palermo. They barge into your home, speaking in that singsong accent of theirs, pose irrelevant questions, and frame victims as culprits. Some things can be dealt with quickly and without unnecessary escalation. "He's already talking with Noto. We pay him, and handsomely at that." Her voice is hoarse, like stone against stone. The anger she feels is there, seething beneath her words, barely concealed by the stern tone. "We give him money, even got him a job, and what does he do?"

"How is that possible?" Ignazio shouts furiously, banging his fist on the desk. The inkwell clinks, the pens roll. Then he drops his voice and his anger turns into a lash. "We pay you—you and your brother—to watch, and not exactly pennies . . . and now I discover that my home has been burglarized?"

Hair slicked back, his face angular, Francesco Noto torments the brim of his hat. He looks more uneasy than contrite, possibly even annoyed: he isn't used to being treated like this. "Don

Ignazio, it pains me to hear you speak this way. I'd never have thought that—"

"But it was precisely your duty to prevent these dogs from despoiling my home, taking my things and my mother's. They even broke into my *picciridda*'s room! What will they do next time? Kidnap her or my brother? If you don't feel capable of fixing this, just say so. The world is full of people I could use instead of you."

The look in the man's deep-set eyes becomes a glare. A wary expression appears beneath his bushy eyebrows. "You'd better watch what you say, Don Ignazio. We have always shown you respect."

Ignazio does not appear to have picked up on Noto's intimations, or else deliberately ignores them. "Respect is given to those who give it to you. You know better than I that it's measured in actions, Don Ciccio. Where were you both?"

The man hesitates before replying. It isn't an embarrassed silence but rather the silence of someone deciding what to say and how. "Somebody has offended you because of our shortcomings, and for that I apologize. My brother and I will make sure everything you've lost is returned to you, to the last pin. A gentleman like yourself can't have burglars upsetting your wife and your mother, who's a saint." He raises his eyes only slightly but nails Ignazio with his look. "We will make sure nobody bothers you or your family again."

To Ignazio, these words douse the fire, ringing of promise. His breathing, shallow from anger, relaxes. "I truly hope so, Signor Noto."

*Signor Noto* and not *Don Ciccio*. An unequivocal sign.

Francesco Noto squints slightly. "Consider it done. Don't worry."

A cough, then another.

"I don't like it." Giovanna sighs, fingering her beads. She usually recites the rosary with Donna Ciccia, but she's on her own today because her friend is bedridden. For some time now she has suffered pains, severe at times, in her legs.

Sitting on a bench, Giovannuzza is playing with Fanny, her favorite china doll—a present from Aunt Giulia—in the gentle light of a mild October day. She's thin and pale, and is often pestered by an irritating cough. The long days spent by the sea in Favignana at first, then the tour across the Aegean, have not helped her. Giovanna is worried.

She would like to mention it to Franca again and ask her to do something. Perhaps, she thinks, Giovannuzza should repeat the treatment with cluster pine essence tablets, which they had ordered straight from Paris, and seemed to bring some relief. Of course, they had to jump through all sorts of hoops to get Giovannuzza to swallow them: she had rebelled, kept her mouth firmly closed, and had once even vomited over the nanny's skirt.

But Franca has gone out to the dressmaker's with Giulia Trigona, and she heard her say that afterward they would be having lunch at Palazzo Butera with Giulia's daughter. She's going to have to wait until the afternoon to speak with her. And then she'll have to endure being dismissed as an overly anxious old woman.

*Maybe I'd better take Giovannuzza back indoors*, she thinks, but doesn't have the heart to do so. It's a gentle, fragrant day, the scent of the yucca flowers mingling with the jasmine that still blooms along the outside wall of the Olivuzza. *And the sunshine is good for both of them*, she thinks, stroking the child's face.

Giovannuzza coughs a few more times but pauses only briefly

before returning to dressing Fanny with the miniature clothes her mother gave her, clothes identical to her own.

Not far from them, Vincenzino is trying to climb onto his new velocipede, helped by a manservant. When he finally succeeds, he laughs happily.

Sometimes Giovanna sees in him *the other* Vincenzino, the first-born who for the past eighteen years has been asleep next to his father and grandfather in the chapel of the Santa Maria di Gesù Cemetery.

She misses him. She misses all her departed. During this period when the light takes on the color of honey and the air is filled with garden smells, she thinks she can almost hear their voices carried on the wind: her mother, who died over twenty-five years ago, stiffened by illness; her son, whose voice did not have time to deepen as boys' voices do when they become adults; Ignazio, with his calm, self-assured voice.

It's his voice she misses most of all. She misses his warmth, his hands, his gestures. At times, she can still feel his eyes on her and hear his laughter. She has kept his clothes in an attic at the Olivuzza and occasionally goes there, opens the trunks, strokes the fabrics, smells them, and searches for a trace or a sign of him. The memory of him, though, like the fabrics, has faded.

Six years have passed since he died. Years of grieving during which Giovanna has felt her heart wither and turn into a piece of parchment in her rib cage. Love stopped hurting her only after it was transformed into a memory, belonging only to her.

*It's unfair*, she thinks, taking a handkerchief from her sleeve. *He should be here with me, with all of us.*

If he were still living, Ignazio would now be fifty-nine: a perfect age to still rule Casa Florio, but also to at least partly shed some responsibilities and enjoy some peace and quiet with her. Ignazziddu would have had the chance to gain experience at his side, to learn, to . . . grow up. She sighs. Her son is twenty-nine, but in many ways he's as impulsive and immature as a boy.

There's a pitter-patter of small feet. Giovanna looks up. There stands Giovannuzza, her granddaughter, eyes as green as her mother's, only gentler and more innocent.

"What are you doing, *Oma*?" she asks.

Behind her, the German nanny is picking up the toys. It was Franca who wanted her; Giovanna would have preferred an English nanny.

"I'm praying," she replies, lifting the rosary beads.

"Why?"

"Sometimes to pray is to remember. It's the only way to keep near those you loved the most, those no longer here."

Giovannuzza looks at her inquisitively. She doesn't understand but with an ordinary child's intuition senses that her grandmother is sad, very sad. She takes her hand. "But I'm here, so you don't have to remember me. *Kommst du?*"

She nods. "I'm coming, sweetheart." Then she frees her hand from her granddaughter's and says, "You go ahead and call Vincenzino."

The little girl runs off, holding Fanny tight to her chest, loudly calling the uncle who is only ten years her senior.

Giovanna looks up at the house. Following Ignazio's death, the Olivuzza seemed huge to her, as though his absence had rendered its vast rooms pointless. Only with time has she learned to live within them, or at least not to be crushed by them. Her eyes run across the façade and linger on the window of her husband's bedroom.

She glimpses it in the blink of an eye. *A shadow.*

She instinctively crosses herself, then looks away and starts off walking, head down. Alone.

As usual, her ghosts follow.

⌒

Concern for her granddaughter keeps Giovanna awake days later. She wanders through the rooms of the Olivuzza in her robe and shawl, cradling her unfailing rosary beads, eyes filled with sadness. She now sleeps little, as old people do, and her rest is fitful, tormented by worries and memories.

From the kitchens, she hears the clinking of dishes and the chatter of maids preparing to clean the rooms. Despite her protests—"That city's air won't be good for her, not to mention the dampness . . ."—Franca has insisted on taking Giovannuzza to Venice with her. Ignazio is in Rome on business, with Vincenzo. He said it has something to do with taxes.

Giovanna slowly heads to the kitchens: she's expecting a group of noblewomen for tea today. She wants to enlist them in various charitable ventures, her embroidery school in particular, and has decided to ask *Monsù* to make Belgian wafers with gooseberry jam, possibly with English-style focaccias and bread rolls with butter and orange marmalade.

But something suddenly catches her eyes and forces her to stop. She retraces her steps, looks around, and blinks.

The alabaster vases she and her husband bought in Paris, and which were stolen early in August, are there in front of her, on the shelf where she placed them twenty years ago.

Giovanna hesitates, confused, frightened even. Then she goes closer and touches them.

There is no doubt about it. They are real. They're *her* vases.

She's suddenly overwhelmed by a kind of frenzy. She runs across the checkered floor, the parquet of the ballroom, to the buffet room. She opens dressers, cabinets, and cupboards, throwing doors and drawers open. She touches the silverware in disbelief: it's shiny and very clean. She takes a coffeepot, turns it upside down, and, her lips quivering, seeks the mark of Antonio Alvino, the Neapolitan silversmith. Here it is, unmistakable. She closes the dresser again slowly, nodding to herself.

The last room is Giovannuzza's. On the floor, in the basket, are the child's tin toys.

Everything that was stolen is back in its place.

*Francesco Noto has demanded respect.*

Giovanna picks up the bell to call Nino but puts it back down immediately. *It's pointless*, she thinks. *None of the servants will say anything. They'll only be relieved that it's all been sorted out.*

The excitement has been violent; she needs some fresh air. But she only takes a few steps down the garden alley before she sees a man standing under a palm tree. It's the head gardener, and he's obviously waiting for her.

Francesco Noto removes his hat and gives a little bow. "Donna Giovanna, *assabbinirìca* . . ."

She nods. "I must thank you for myself and on behalf of my family, Don Francesco," she says, going to him. The hem of her black robe brushes against the man's dusty shoes.

"I'm glad." He doesn't look into her face; his eyes seem to be drifting around the garden, where his brother Pietro, the doorkeeper, must be. "It was two men from the village, two coachmen. They ask you to forgive them for their slight."

"Who? Their names."

"Vincenzo Lo Porto and Giuseppe Caruso. We've removed them from the Olivuzza."

Giovanna nods again. That is sufficient for her.

What she doesn't know is *how* the issue was sorted. She has no idea that Lo Porto's and Caruso's families are desperately looking for them, because although they have been dismissed from the Olivuzza, they haven't gone to America or Tunisia, as some people said.

Everybody in the district knows it. You can't go against the Noto brothers, embarrass them in front of the Florios, and think you'll get away with it.

Of course, the Notos, too, did some foolish things, not least asking Pip's older brother, Joss Whitaker, for a gift, and then not sharing it with Lo Porto and Caruso, their friends.

And that's no way to treat friends.

Some say that the two coachmen slighted the Florios to even things out with the Notos. Others, that they wanted to undermine the Notos. There are so many rumors . . .

Except that the Notos couldn't tolerate that kind of slight. No, Giovanna doesn't know about these things, nor does she want to.

She does find out by the end of November, as she's about to climb into the carriage that will take her to the convent of the Sisters of Charity for the Thirteen-Day Novena in honor of Saint Lucy. Accompanied by an increasingly stooped and slow Donna Ciccia, a valet is helping her into the carriage when two women approach her, wrapped in dark shawls that shield them from the tramontana.

"Donna Giovanna!" the younger woman cries. "Signora, you must hear us out!" Her hair is gathered in a severe bun and she is wearing humble but clean clothes. The skin over her cheekbones is taut and she has large, hungry eyes, dark with grief. "You owe it to us," she says, clinging to the carriage door.

Taken by surprise, Giovanna takes a step back. "*Chi vuliti di mia? Cu 'site?* Who are you? What do you want from me?" she asks curtly.

"We're the wives of Giuseppe Caruso and Vincenzo Lo Porto," the other woman replies. She looks the same age as Giovanna but is actually much younger: sorrow and shame have suddenly aged her. She's wearing a dress that may not even be hers, hanging loose and short. "Look at us, Donna Giovanna. Look at us: we're women and mothers just like you. We have children but no one to support us."

Giovanna becomes stone-faced. "You come to ask me for money because you have to raise your hungry children? It's your husbands you should be angry with, it's them you should ask. They should have considered this before breaking into my house to steal! Instead, they've fled like cowards."

Vincenzo Lo Porto's wife comes closer. "My husband hasn't gone anywhere," she hisses, her eyes red from crying. "I've nowhere to light a candle or lay a flower. Thanks to you, I've been left without a husband."

Giovanna freezes. She feels Donna Ciccia stiffen behind her, hears her labored breathing.

She looks at Giuseppe Caruso's wife, who's holding her hands tight over her belly. The woman nods. "Even my father-in-law knows: he's asked for justice; he said he'd go all the way to Rome if they didn't tell him what happened to his son. And they left a murdered dog outside our front door." She takes Giovanna's wrist and squeezes it. "Now do you understand?" she whispers in despair.

"There were others who wanted to take a lot more than a handful of silverware from you, you know?" Lo Porto's wife's face is now a hand's breadth away from hers. "That they wanted to kidnap your son or your granddaughter? It's already happened to other people, you know . . ."

This is too much for Giovanna. She takes a step back and wriggles free, practically shoving her away. "Let go of me," she commands. At that moment, the coachman grabs the woman by the arms and pulls her back. Giovanna takes advantage of this to get into the carriage, although the other woman tries to yank her out. Donna Ciccia slaps the woman's hand.

"Let's go," Giovanna orders, breathless, her heart beating fast. She puts a hand on her chest. "Go, let's go!" she says again, more loudly, while the two women scream, kick and punch the door.

At last, the carriage takes off and their cries are drowned out by the sound of the wheels on the cobblestones and Donna Ciccia's labored breathing.

Giovanna can barely speak and clasps her black-gloved hands.

"Did you know this?" Donna Ciccia asks.

Giovanna swallows air and seeks comfort in a hasty *Hail Mary* but fails. A lump of guilt and nausea tightens her stomach. "No."

"You saw, didn't you? Their clothes."

She nods just once, her eyes focusing on the window without seeing.

Black. The two women were in mourning. Like widows.

And they officially become widows a few weeks later, when their husbands' bodies are discovered in a pothole in a storehouse just outside the city.

They were murdered a few days after the burglary. They never left Palermo.

This business reaches the ears of a police commissioner who transfers to Palermo from the north a year later. An inflexible man accustomed to annihilating his enemies, the way he did years earlier when he arrested two hundred members of Fratellanza di Favara, a criminal organization responsible for a long string of murders.

His mission, as entrusted by the government, is to put an end to the Mafia, the criminal organization everybody is talking about and that seems to evade all laws. In addition, he will have to plunge his hands into the mud puddle where political power and crime overlap before the whole system is compromised. A system where the criminals are at the service of senators, aristocrats, and prominent figures "who protect and defend them so that they, in turn, can be protected and defended by them," as the commissioner writes in his extensive report. Discovering that the Florios were burglarized, he tries to question Giovanna but to no avail. He tries to speak to the Whitakers and shed light on Audrey's kidnapping and extortion but receives only silence in return.

He comes to understand many things, this man with a square jaw and a blond beard, named Ermanno Sangiorgi. For instance, he begins to understand the organization: the system of families, the heads of the districts, the *picciotti*, and the oath of loyalty . . . A structure that will remain practically unchanged nearly a hundred years later in the statements of Tommaso Buscetta, the Boss of Two Worlds. These statements were given first before Giovanni Falcone during a secret interrogation that would last six months, then at the first true Mafia trial, which will drag on for six years, from 1986 to 1992. A structure responsible for the attacks that would claim the lives of Falcone and Paolo Borsellino, respectively four and six months after the end of the trial.

Yes, Ermanno Sangiorgi will understand many things about the Mafia—but succeed in proving very few.

⌒

March 1898 is unsure of itself and takes hesitant steps, like a toddler. Even on sunny days, a chilly wind shakes the garden of the Olivuzza, ruffling the tops of the trees.

Through the window of the small parlor adjacent to her bedroom, Franca watches the shadows forming under the palm trees and listens to the rustling leaves. It reminds her of the sea lapping the hull of the *Aegusa* and the cruise Ignazio organized in the Eastern Mediterranean last summer. She recalls the rugged beauty of the Aegean Islands; the clear waters of the Turkish coast; the charm of Constantinople, as insidious as poison; the narrow streets in Corfu she and Giulia traversed laughing, while Giovannuzza trotted behind them with the nanny; that wind that smelled of oregano and rosemary . . .

She sighs, her heart heavy with nostalgia. She would like to see the Aegean sunsets again, have another glass of Nykteri—called "night wine" because the grapes are picked before dawn—and feel Ignazio's arms enfold her, embracing her and nobody else but her.

Only, he can't, not while she's in this state.

She pats her belly. Not long to go before she gives birth.

*Matri sant'Anna, let it be a boy* has been her prayer ever since she discovered she was pregnant. *A boy for Casa Florio, for me. For Ignazio, who finally might stop looking elsewhere for what I can give him.*

Because that's how it is. Ignazio is still collecting women—as long as they're young and beautiful, and never mind if they're aristocrats or of ill repute. It's a miracle he hasn't caught any diseases: he's clearly cautious in that respect.

Besides, why should he be discreet when, among their Palermo acquaintances, there's not a couple one could call faithful? With a blend of anger and sorrow, Franca remembers what Giulia, Romualdo Trigona's wife, told her a few weeks ago. That her husband now has a steady mistress and that she's made up her mind: she will no longer just sit and watch. She doesn't care what people think: she wants to be free to live her life, to love and be happy.

And yet people *still* find a way to hurt Franca.

The last time was only a couple of days ago. Luckily, Maruzza came . . .

For some time now, she's had a companion, Countess Maruzza Bardesono, a middle-aged woman with sharp features and a stern expression. Raised in a wealthy family, she was left alone and with no means of support when her brother died. Someone told Franca she was looking for work, and Franca arranged to meet her, more out of a sense of duty than need. But she was struck by her ladylike manners, her education, and the aura of self-confidence she gave off, and immediately offered her the position. Franca has never regretted it.

That day, Maruzza came into Franca's bedroom to return her copy of *L'Amuleto*, the latest novel by Neera, a female author they both love. She found Franca in tears, her head resting on her dressing table, and clutching a sheet of paper. The floor was strewn with hairbrushes, combs, perfume bottles, and skin creams hurled in a fit of anger.

"What's the matter, Donna Franca? Are you unwell?" Maruzza asked, putting the book down on the bed.

Still sobbing, Franca handed her the sheet of paper.

Maruzza's face turned scarlet as she read the letter. "Filthy people!" she exclaimed. "Anonymous letters are the tools of cowards . . . and to send them to a pregnant woman on top of everything else! Shame on them!"

"I don't know who these women are that he frequents, and I don't want to know," Franca said. "I've always accepted it because I know that he loves me and will come back to me." She stood up and looked into Maruzza's eyes. "But lately I've been increasingly wondering whether I would do better to leave. Just my daughter and me on our own."

Maruzza took her by the arms. "Donna Franca, I've gotten to know you a little. May I speak frankly?"

She nodded.

"You have everything a woman can wish for. Health, beauty, an angel of a daughter, affectionate and intelligent. And . . . all this." She made a sweeping gesture to indicate the bedroom. "You're about to become a mother again, remember?"

"But . . ."

"We're all of us alone, Donna Franca, men and women. Money, titles, and social standing don't matter. We're all of us looking for something we don't have, something we lack. Except that a man is given the weapons to fight his battles. A woman, on the other hand, has to earn these, and if she obtains them, it's usually at a high price. You're lucky because you have many weapons at your disposal and have even learned to use them. Many women don't have any at all. They're *useless things*, like the one who wrote this letter . . ."

Franca frowned and looked down at the letter, as though trying to find something to confirm what Maruzza had just said.

"Yes, of course, it's a woman," Maruzza continued. "You see, some women don't even search for weapons, because in order to find them they'd have to change too many things, starting with the way they think. They'd have to stop deluding themselves—just as Neera says . . ." She picked up the book, leafed through it, and found the page she wanted. "'Not having the energy to seek out that which would be truly to their advantage, they latch on to the nearest, most comfortable lesson,'" she read. "They're afraid to live, so they turn into little women who're frightened of everything, only finding strength by judging others. But their bitterness turns to bile and stifles them, so they have to expel it somehow, even if it means writing letters like this one. They're unhappy people, Donna Franca. Yes, they envy you your money, your clothes, and your jewels. But trust me, they attack you above all because they see the kind of woman you are. You have courage. You know of your husband's exploits, but you continue with your head held high, you don't hide, you don't stoop to the same level, you don't allow anyone to compromise your dignity. You're always conscious of the name you carry."

Franca sat back down. "Are you saying I should feel sorry for the woman who wrote this letter?"

"Yes. Then there are the other women . . ."

"The . . . the other women?"

"The debauchees your husband showers with jewels. Of course, they only have a few weapons . . . but know how to use them only too well!" Maruzza laughed joylessly. "Think about it: they're also pitiful. They see themselves as important but fail to realize that men use them just for fun. Mistresses who last only a few weeks, who end up jilted without the slightest regret, cast aside like old dolls."

Franca could not conceal her surprise at these words, so unpleasant and yet so true. Her mind drew a parallel between Maruzza and her sister-in-law, Giulia. Two very different women who had, however, told her the same thing: that she was a plant with solid roots and shouldn't be afraid to blossom and reach out for the sky with her branches. She was destined to grow and become stronger and stronger.

And yet . . .

"But why does it still hurt so much even after all this time?" she asked herself more than Maruzza.

The woman sighed, then replied with an embittered smile, "Love is an ungrateful beast, Donna Franca. It bites the hand that feeds it and licks the one that strikes it. To love forever, to love truly, means to have no memory."

A stabbing pain in her back, so sharp it shakes her whole body.

Franca practically leaps out of the armchair in the parlor and catches her breath. *Could it be a contraction?* she wonders. She reaches out for the bell to summon a maid, who immediately appears at the door.

"Yes, Donna Franca?"

"Call Countess Bardesono, please. Tell her to come right away."

Another pang. Since the conversation about the anonymous letter a month earlier, her bond with Maruzza has grown stronger, more intimate. Franca instinctively gave her name, not her mother-in-law's.

Quick footsteps echo on the landing. The door opens. Franca lifts her head and catches Maruzza's gentle gaze. But she doubles over immediately afterward, restraining a moan; she turns pale and struggles to breathe.

Maruzza puts a hand on her forehead, then pulls it away. "Have the pains started? Would you like me to call the doctor? Or your mother?"

*Your mother*, not *Donna Giovanna*. Yes, Maruzza knows her well.

"The midwife and the doctor . . . and yes, my mother. She can stay here for a couple of d—"

Another pang in the belly. Franca wraps her fingers around Maruzza's wrist.

"They're too close together," she mutters, panic in her eyes. "They just started out of the blue . . ."

Maruzza waves her hand. "The second child always comes quicker than the first. Would you like me to call your husband?"

Ignazio. Franca wants him at her side. Knowing that he's waiting at home would lend her strength, of course. But where is he? At the NGI office or out and about? He left without saying a word, just planting a hasty kiss goodbye on the tips of her lips, before she saw him run off, impeccably dressed as usual, with the customary carnation in his buttonhole.

"Ask Saro where he is," she murmurs.

With one hand gripping Maruzza's arm, the other supporting her lower back, Franca stands up and takes a couple of steps. The bed has been made, the clothes hung back in the closet. A mellow light filters through the window, and everything is immersed in calmness and expectation. There are some white flowers standing on the chest of drawers and their perfume nauseates her.

"Take them out," she tells Maruzza. Another pang radiates through her lower belly. There is no doubt: her second child is about to be born.

Focusing, breath after breath. Blood pumping through her veins as waves of pain wash over her, receding only to strike again more fiercely. Her body rebels and opens. Her mind goes blank because it cannot bear these contractions, the feeling that her belly is about to be torn in two.

Then calm arrives with the final contraction. It's a kind of dull resignation. *Yes, I'm about to die*, Franca accepts, bathed in sweat, blood, and amniotic fluid, and almost wishes it would be so, because she's exhausted and can't tolerate the distress any longer. She shakes her head and lets out a sob.

"I can't," she murmurs to her mother, who's holding her hand. "I can't do it."

Also perspiring, Costanza squeezes her hand and wipes her daughter's forehead. "Of course you can," she says. "You did it with Giovanna! And it was very hard with her, remember?"

Opposite her, bent between her legs, the midwife emits something between a giggle and a huff. "Signorina Giovanna wasn't well positioned. I had to turn her! But this one is the right way round, only he's quite big. Push, and may Saint Anne help us."

Franca does not reply. She feels the pressure of another contraction, hunches forward, and suppresses her impulse to vomit. She has to free herself now and allow her child to be born. She pushes.

"Stop . . . That's enough . . ." The midwife puts a hand on her belly, straightens, and pats Franca's hand. "He's about to come out. When I tell you to, push, then stop. Now!"

Franca screams. She feels something sliding out of her, as though a vital organ is being removed from her. She outstretches her hand, but she's exhausted; she has no strength to ask, to know. She collapses back on the pillows, eyes closed.

It's over. Whatever it was, it's over.

A long moment elapses.

Then, a wail.

She opens her eyes and sees her mother. She's happy, laughing and crying at the same time, hands over her mouth, nodding. "*Masculu è!* A boy!"

He's still attached to her, bloodstained, covered in the white amniotic sac. But the baby's a boy, healthy, alive, with large eyes and a mouth pursed in a crying fit that speaks of all the pain of his first breath.

It's a boy. It's the heir.

⌒

"*Masculu è!*" The shout echoes throughout the house. Giovanna has broken the news to Ignazio, who's been waiting in the first-floor parlor with Romualdo Trigona, Giulia, and his brother-in-law, Pietro.

It's been years, perhaps not since childhood, since he last saw the radiant smile his mother flashes as she tells him, "It's a boy, my son! At last!"

Ignazio immediately orders champagne and for all the servants to have a glass, too, then drinks a toast with his friends and relatives, hugs them, and lifts his arms to the sky. The nanny brings Giovannuzza to her father to celebrate, and he picks her up, twirls her in the air, and plants a kiss on her forehead, before kissing his sister, Giulia.

He's happy. After five years, finally, an heir! Financial problems? The sailing crisis and the money that's never enough? It's all so remote. The demands of the foundry workers? They don't matter. There's a new Ignazio—because that's what he'll be named—now. Like his father, he'll carry on the family name and history.

Another glass of champagne, then he calls Saro.

The man stops by the door and bows. "Hearty congratulations, Don Ignazio."

Ignazio goes up to him, beaming, takes him by the shoulders, and looks into his eyes. "I need a few bottles of marsala wine. But not just any bottles—my grandfather's ones, stored at the far end of the cellar. Send someone to fetch them and bring them upstairs, quickly."

Saro stares, astounded, and walks away. Ignazio looks around, then lifts the silver bowl in the middle of the table before tipping it over to empty it of an arrangement of dried flowers. Tapping it like a drum, he strides across the house to the red salon that connects his and Franca's apartments. Romualdo follows him up the stairs with a laugh. Pietro, though, looks puzzled, and before he can climb the first step, he is stopped by Giovanna and Giulia, who carries Giovannuzza in her arms.

"What's my brother doing?" Giulia asks, confused.

Pietro shrugs. "How should I know? He told Saro to bring up some marsala wine."

Giovanna shakes her head, rolling her eyes to the ceiling. "God knows what he has in mind . . ."

Giulia leaves Giovannuzza to the care of the governess, grabs her skirt, and rushes up the stairs, followed by her mother. *All we need is for him to distress Franca with one of his "bright" ideas*, she thinks. She knows what it is to give birth, just as she knows that men can't begin to imagine it. The two women march down the corridor, then stop amid the plants in the winter garden. All of a sudden, they hear heavy breathing and the clink of glass.

It's Saro, loaded down with dusty bottles.

Giovanna is outraged. "What are you doing?"

"Don Ignazio told me . . ." Saro begins, stopping to catch his breath.

Ignazio's voice booms nearby. "Saro! Saro, where are you?" He looks out of Franca's room, eyes sparkling with excitement, gestures for him to come in, then steps back inside.

This singular procession sets off again and reaches Franca, who is sitting up in bed, pale and exhausted, but smiling. Her mother is holding the baby in her arms, waiting for the wet nurse to finish preparing his swaddling clothes.

Ignazio puts down the bowl on the dressing table, then takes the bottles of marsala wine and pours them in. The room fills with the sharp scent of alcohol, adding to the salty odor of sweat and a subtler, metallic note of blood.

Once he has finished, Ignazio turns to his mother-in-law and holds out his arms. Costanza doesn't know what to do and looks to her daughter, but Franca is laughing. She nods because she knows what her husband wants to do and is happy. Giulia, too, realizes and seizes her brother's hand. "Wait!" she shouts, laughing. She picks up the pitcher of water for the baby's bath and pours it into the bowl before everyone's astonished eyes. "You must dilute the marsala or he could get hurt! He's only just been born!"

Naked in his father's arms, the baby opens his eyes. Ignazio pauses for a second and gazes at this creature with its wrinkled face and red skin. It's his son. His and his adored Franca's.

Holding the baby over his forearm, he lowers him over the bowl, scooping up some of the liquid in his cupped hand, and wets his head. Then he immerses him completely.

There are cries of outrage behind him.

"What are you doing? Christening him?" Giovanna shouts, such a baptism blasphemous to her.

Giulia has a hand over her mouth, torn between laughter and indignation. Behind her aunt, Giovannuzza watches the scene, eyes wide open.

But Ignazio doesn't see or listen to anyone. He searches for Franca with his eyes. She laughs and claps her hands. Her face has a gentleness he will carry within him all his life.

Life, yes. The one he has always pursued, and that seemed to have escaped him for so long.

He has been haunted by death since his grandfather died on almost the same day as he was born. Then by his brother Vincenzo's death. And finally by his father's. He has tried to forget this grief with Franca, and not just with her.

With many, too many, women. And with the whims and follies his huge wealth allowed.

Only now does he know he can find some peace. Because there's life cradled in his arms. There's a future—for him and Casa Florio.

The baby opens his eyes wide and bursts into uncontrollable bawling, but Ignazio moistens his lips with a finger covered in liquor. "You must remember this taste, even before the taste of milk."

He rests him on his chest, heedless of the fact that he, too, is going to stink of liquor. "This is what made us what we are: the Florios."

⌒

"Don Ignazio . . . the factory workers are here." Saro has come into the office and is peering into the square through the curtains. Sitting at his desk, Ignazio exchanges a puzzled glance with Erasmo Piaggio, who occupies the chair opposite him, then rises and takes a peek over his valet's shoulder, followed by the NGI director. Indeed, there are ten or so workers waiting outside the entrance, talking with Pietro Noto, the doorkeeper.

"What are they doing here?" Ignazio grumbles.

"Perhaps they want an explanation for the delay in the works," Piaggio suggests.

Ignazio sits back down at his desk. "It's hard to explain to them that since Codronchi left his post last July, everything has become very complicated. We can only hope that this new company we've decided to set up," he says, tapping his index finger on the papers in front of him, "will restart things . . ." He suddenly gets up. "I really hope they haven't come here to ask for another raise! Would they have the gall, after what happened in January? We should speak to Garibaldi Bosco again: he's the only one who can get them to pipe down. These constant protests are such a bore . . ."

"They've come to pay their respects for the baby's birth." Giovanna is in the doorway. She has appeared without a sound and now regards her son with an air of reproach. "I told the doorkeeper to let them in." Then she turns to Saro. "Bring some more chairs here, then lay the desk with biscuits and wine. They're our workers and we must receive them with courtesy," she adds, preempting her son's objection, since his eyes have already widened. "That's what your father would have done." As she walks away, she thinks with some bitterness that her Ignazio would have gone to the Oretea Foundry in person to announce the birth of his heir, just as he did when Vincenzino was born.

Shortly afterward, the workers' heavy footsteps echo in the Olivuzza corridors, leaving dust on the rugs and staining the parquet. Dressed in their Sunday clothes, the men look around, intimidated by the enormous paintings, the elaborate flower arrangements, the gold and the stuccos, and, above all, by the house's seemingly endless labyrinth. They were not expecting to come in; the doorkeeper had said he would pass on their message to Don Ignazio and that they could return home. Then Donna Giovanna, *u' principale*'s widow— *recamatierna*, peace be with him, he was a great gentleman—had appeared and simply said, "You are welcome. Come in," and had headed to the office, once her husband's, now Ignazio's.

They walk past the green salon and glimpse Donna Ciccia, sitting in an armchair, slumbering with her mouth open. Some laugh, but only for an instant: immediately afterward they see Ignazio's portrait in a silver frame. They stop and cross themselves.

Giovanna watches them and feels her eyes well up. A worker of an advanced age, with a large gray mustache, steals a look at her. "He was a true father to us all," he conveys. "The Lord took him away too soon."

She nods hastily, then turns her back on them and continues walking to the office. Ignazio is by the door, with Piaggio. On the desk, cleared of papers and folders, stand bottles of wine and trays with biscuits. Beside them lie linen napkins embroidered with Ignazio's and Franca's initials.

The workers line up against the wall, and the worker with the gray mustache approaches Ignazio. "Your Excellency, I've— we've—come to . . . to . . ."

". . . congratulate you," finishes a young man at the end of the room. His eyes are intelligent, and he's the best dressed among them.

"Congratulations—yes. The birth of the *picciriddu* is a blessing not just for you but the whole Casa Florio, and we're very glad you decided to name him after your father, *u' principale*, peace be with him."

"Amen," Giovanna whispers from the end of the room.

"Thank you. It's very kind of you to come all this way," Ignazio mumbles, sticking his thumbs into the pockets of his waistcoat. "Can I offer you some refreshments? I imagine you came on foot."

"On foot and with an escort."

It's the young man again, and the sarcasm in his voice hasn't escaped anyone. Piaggio raises his eyebrows, goes to the window, and sees, in a corner of the piazza, a group of carabinieri. Then, as the men shuffle to the desk to take a glass of wine and a biscuit, he turns to the young man. "And you are . . . ?"

"Nicola Amodeo. Lathe turner at the Oretea."

"Well, Signor Amodeo, I should say the escort is a necessary precaution, considering the protests outside the NGI offices last January." It has taken Piaggio a fraction of a second to realize that this fellow is no ordinary factory worker. He holds his head high and answered confidently. *He's a union man, or worse.* "They were difficult decisions for us, too, you know? Making people redundant is never pleasant, but until work on the shipyard begins, the foundry cannot afford to employ more people than is absolutely necessary."

Ignazio approaches the two men, nodding.

"You don't realize how unfortunate January was for Palermo's poor." Amodeo shakes his head. "Firing the apprentices was a hard blow. They only asked for a raise because everything has gone up in price, starting with bread. Instead of hearing them out you threw them out and reported them to the police. And now nobody will hire them because they've been smeared as anarchists."

"Come now, you exaggerate!" Piaggio exclaims. "They were only apprentices, ungrateful hotheads who'd set up a picket line for no reason. Besides, you said it yourself: everything is getting more expensive everywhere. Taxes, for one!" He gestures at the waiter, who draws near balancing a tray with glasses of marsala wine. "In my shoes, you would have done the same. Punishing a few reminds everyone else who's boss."

Amodeo refuses the wine. "You fired them without giving them a chance to explain," he replies curtly.

"What were we supposed to do after the protests—hire them back?" Ignazio says. "Some thugs are like rats in a granary: they eat everything in a second."

Amodeo lowers his head. "Don Ignazio, you don't understand that there's hunger here, severe hunger, and hunger is dangerous. The January protest wasn't just made up of us from the foundry and the slipway but carpenters, bricklayers, stonecutters, too . . . There were folk from the Tribunali district and Monte di Pietà, Castellammare—even from Zisa and Acqua dei Corsari. Palermo needs jobs."

"Do you think I don't know?" Ignazio raises his voice, his lips curled in an exasperated grimace. "For as long as we had Codronchi, the shipyard project was moving forward . . . The ground was soon to be broken. I even went to Rome to push, beg, and plot . . . Now everything's come to a standstill at the ministry, you can't mention money, and no one wants to back us. Not to mention the fact that there are protests all over Italy and the government has other things on its plate. It doesn't depend on us!"

The young worker shakes his head again, with a disheartened smile. "It also depends on you, Don Ignazio."

"I—"

Giovanna interrupts him, a hand on his arm, making him turn. "Here's Franca with the *picciriddu*. Come."

Ignazio looks up. His wife has appeared in the doorway, supported by Maruzza. Behind them, the nanny is holding the lace bundle in which the baby is wrapped.

The workers welcome them with a round of applause, muttering blessings—"May the Lord always watch over you and protect you"—and congratulations to the mother and the child.

*My Franca is still pale*, Ignazio thinks. It's only been a few days since the birth and she's struggling to recover. A wave of tenderness melts his chest. He will organize a summer trip for her and the whole family, maybe on their train, so they don't have to tire themselves and can enjoy all the comforts of private carriages. Yes, they'll go back to Paris and perhaps Germany, too, he tells himself, the thought claiming his first smile of the day.

The main thing is to get away from Palermo and all this misery.

Ignazio is pacing up and down the room nervously, trying to vent his ill humor.

The second-floor dining room in the Olivuzza has never been his favorite; the mahogany furniture is too large and too dark, the silver chandeliers too heavy and antiquated. And he has always hated the two antique coral and brass peacocks that form a wheel over the mantel, just as he's hated the giant fireguard. But a year has passed since the birth of Ignazio—whom everyone calls Baby

87

Boy—so it's time for him and Franca to take up being the beating heart of Palermo's social life again. Even if that means welcoming with full honors certain characters he particularly dislikes, as he's doing this evening.

He stops by the table. "Montebello-style eggs?" he says with a huff, looking at the menu. "For an after-theater supper?"

Franca comes in, draped in a black lace dress and an ivory silk shawl. She isn't wearing a necklace, only two bangles and the Cartier pearl earrings Ignazio gave her during their honeymoon. Once again, she has recovered her pre-pregnancy figure. The costliest creams—from Charles Fay's Veloutine to Pinaud and Meyer's cold cream—the cold baths to tone her skin, and regular massages have helped, but she's now thinking of going to Paris to undergo a treatment that should make her face like glazed porcelain. She's been told it's a very painful process and that, at twenty-six, she doesn't need it *yet*.

"If you must know, my dear," she says in a velvety voice, "D'Annunzio adores eggs. But as you can see, there is also lobster in tartare sauce, asparagus in a frothy dressing, and, to crown it all, a *trionfo di gola*." She turns away and sighs. "What a charming, peculiar man . . . We spoke at length during the interval between acts three and four, you know."

"Oh, so he came to you as soon as the booing started . . ."

"What do you mean? It was a triumph! Eight curtain calls in the first act alone . . . It was those stupid students in the gallery making a racket. Apparently, they even smashed the panes in the theater's double doors. Besides, Gabriele's works are always daring and provoke debate. And this wonderful *Gioconda* is no exception. Partly thanks to Eleonora Duse and Zacconi, who are—"

"You call him by his first name," Ignazio interrupts coldly. "He's a lothario who's unafraid to flirt."

Franca focuses on the bodice of her dress and blows away an invisible speck of lint. "Takes one to know one, right?" She gestures at the servant and hands him her shawl, asking him to return it to Diodata.

Ignazio stares. "It's too revealing without the shawl."

Franca shoots him a glance that's a blend of frostiness and disbelief. "I believe this may be the first time you've said that to a woman. Or do you also say it to your . . . your lady friends?"

"What's that got to do with anything? Everybody knows that D'Annunzio is very *sensitive* to beautiful women. You're a beautiful woman and he wants to add you to his conquests. And don't bother denying it! I saw it in the way he was looking at you this evening, by the manner he was speaking to you—"

"I guess you can spot certain male hunting characteristics."

Ignazio scowls. "Don't joke, Franca."

She waves her hand with annoyance. "He's asked me for a 'lucky charm' for his new play and I promised I'd give him one. I was thinking of a grain of coral . . . Besides, if you'd really been paying attention, you would have seen that we were talking with Jules Claretie."

"But he's the manager of the Comédie-Française, and I'll bet he's half a pederast, like so many theater people. I'm not joking, Franca: keep away from D'Annunzio." Ignazio grabs her by the wrist.

She frees herself. "I know all about you. I know how much you spend on your mistresses, where you go, and even which perfume they use because I can smell it on you. The gossip about you is so predictable I no longer listen to it. And now you act the jealous husband all because I spoke to a man in front of an entire theater? How ridiculous!"

"I've no intention of being seen as a cuckold by the whole of Palermo."

Franca throws her head back with a loud laugh. "Good! How does it feel to be on the other side, for once? To see others long for something you have but have no regard for?" She strokes her neck and slides her fingers into her neckline, determined to provoke him. "What do you suppose other men think when they see you fool around with their wives?"

Ignazio turns scarlet. "How dare you . . ."

"I'm your wife and I do dare. But enough now. Or do you want to make yourself ridiculous in front of everybody?"

They are interrupted by a discreet but peremptory cough. Master Nino is by the door. "Count and Countess Trigona and Monsieur Claretie have arrived. Shall I let them in?"

Franca lifts the hem of her skirt. "I'll go welcome them," she says, and after flashing Ignazio one last frosty look, she bustles past him and out of the room, with a spring in her step.

❧

"Your wife looks splendid tonight, *curò*," Romualdo whispers, jutting his chin in the direction of Franca, who is engaged in a lively conversation with Giulia and Monsieur Claretie. "Everyone's noticed, including our poet. He's watched her more than the show."

Giuseppe Monroy laughs into his thin mustache. "You shouldn't say that to our Ignazziddu. Can't you see he's already on edge?"

"Noodles, that's all you two are," Ignazio hisses.

"But apparently Eleonora Duse knows how to rein him in." Giuseppe seizes a bottle of champagne and pours himself a drink in front of the astonished waiter. "She's quite a woman, that one. Look at those eyes: they're oozing flames! And what poise, what a bosom!"

Meanwhile, footsteps echo in the corridor, and there's the sound of male voices and a deep, throaty woman's laugh. Franca and Giulia exchange glances and go to the door. Gabriele d'Annunzio is the first to make an entrance in his very own style, arms open and palms facing upward. He goes straight to Franca, takes her hands, and lifts them first to his lips, then to his heart. "Donna Franca, this house is a worthy frame for your splendor."

"Thank you, Maestro," she replies with a smile. "May I present Countess Giulia Trigona, a dear friend of mine?"

Dressed in a fiery-red dress, Giulia makes a comical curtsy.

D'Annunzio smiles and bows in return. "*Enchanté, Madame.* Palermo must indeed be very happy that the beauty of her daughters rivals that of the nereid Actaea. You are as graceful as a light breeze, as the southern breath of the Mediterranean."

"Come now, stop flattering us," Franca exclaims. "Or else our husbands, jealous as they are, will feel honor bound to challenge you to a duel."

"They wouldn't be the first!" D'Annunzio replies in a booming voice. "I've heard the rumble of death on other occasions . . ."

By the entrance to the dining hall, wrapped in a pale gray cloak embroidered with glass beads that range in color from white to silver, a woman observes the scene with a smile that's a blend of irony and bitterness. She walks up to Franca. "He can't help it. He always has to show off to a beautiful woman." She proffers her hand. "I am Eleonora Duse. It's a pleasure to meet you, Donna Franca."

Franca briefly hesitates. Close up, without stage makeup, her long hair down to her shoulders, Eleonora Duse is not simply attractive or sensual. She is magnetic. She is the embodiment of elegance in her gestures as well as maintaining a figure of such perfect beauty that she seems unreal. "The honor is mine," Franca finally replies. "It was a privilege to see your performance this evening. You gave a voice to Silvia's inner torment, and you were able to convey something even more difficult: her physical suffering. With a simple blink of your eyelashes—"

"Only a sensitive woman knows how tightly love and suffering are bound together," Eleanora replies.

Franca smiles and invites her to sit down. A man suddenly appears in the doorway, breathless, with soft but determined features and lively eyes.

"Ah, here's my sculptor!" D'Annunzio exclaims.

Ermete Zacconi, who plays sculptor Lucio Settala, Silvia's husband, in *Gioconda*, gives Franca a bow and shakes her hand. "It's an honor, Donna Franca. Forgive me for being late, but I always need a moment's quiet after the show . . ."

"I can imagine, Signor Zacconi. Your character is so intense that . . . it made me shed more than one tear."

"Not from horror, I hope!" D'Annunzio has rushed to her and is squeezing her hand with a falsely modest look in his eyes.

"From pure and true emotion, I can assure you, Maestro."

He kisses her hand and smiles. Ignazio tries to meet Franca's eyes to communicate a silent reproach, but she turns her back on him and motions to all the guests to take their seats at the table.

∽

As soon as Franca and Ignazio are seated at their respective ends of the table, with D'Annunzio to Franca's right and Eleanora Dusa to Ignazio's left, the waiters serve dishes covered with silver domes. The fragrance of eggs and freshly baked bread spreads through the room.

"Montebello-style eggs? You spoil me too much!" D'Annunzio exclaims, sampling a mouthful without taking his eyes off Franca.

Ignazio seethes. Giuseppe exchanges glances with Romualdo, who sniggers.

During the pause between the lobster and the asparagus, D'Annunzio interlaces his fingers under his chin and looks at her. "You have a swan's neck, Signora. The earrings you're wearing make it look shorter and distract from your wondrous beauty." He waves at the Cartier drops. "Take them off."

"Really?"

"Yes."

Franca obediently removes one and looks at her reflection in the surface of the silver carafe in front of her. He draws closer, practically brushing against her cheek. "You see? You should wear only necklaces and *corsages* that show off your throat."

Franca nods, removes the other earring, and again looks at herself.

"You're right," she says, admiring her reflection.

Exasperated at the other end of the table, all Ignazio can think of is when he will be alone with his wife. He definitely can't bear all this familiarity. Moreover, he's convinced that Franca is taking advantage of D'Annunzio's attentions to take her revenge on him. *I'll show her! Does she think she's the only one allowed to make a scene?*

He pulls himself together only when he catches Romualdo looking at him, clearly trying to let him know that his ill humor is now obvious to everyone present. He orders a white Pinot to be served and gets to his feet. "I'd like to propose a toast to our guests," he announces. "But especially to Signora Duse, whose talent outshines even her charm."

The actress gives him a grateful smile, then looks at the hostess. "It's as important for a woman to see her intelligence recognized as it is to receive a compliment on her beauty. Don't you think, Donna Franca?"

Franca nods. "Men often think our sensitivity is a limitation rather than an asset, and that it places us beneath them. We see and understand everything, often choosing to keep silent, but they don't appear to notice."

Giulia Trigona bows her head and stares at the embroidery of the linen tablecloth. "Or, worse, they think that their status as husbands and fathers puts them above boundaries," she says, "and that allows them to humiliate and insult their wives in front of everyone."

Romualdo Trigona turns pale and bows his head over his plate.

"My muse cannot be stifled by the thick fog of everyday life." D'Annunzio looks at Eleonora Duse and raises his glass to her. "That is why I have rejected countless daily miseries and elected to live beyond them, free from the nets and ties that a mediocre society like ours tightens around the individual. For me, freedom is sacrosanct, and applies to both men and women."

Eleonora shakes her head and puts her fork down. "That also means evading any obligation that comes with a relationship. In other words, not taking moral accountability for one's own choices."

"On the contrary: to honor individual freedom as our only goddess means taking *all* the responsibilities that derive from this choice." D'Annunzio indicates the manager of the Comédie-Française. "Monsieur Claretie will no doubt confirm that in France, thanks to divorce, the vow of marriage no longer means eternal suffering . . . A sign, precisely, of admirable freedom of thought."

Claretie nods, then dabs his lips. "Far be it from me to diminish the sanctity of marriage," he says calmly. "However, I do think that artists should avoid relationships. Art demands freedom, partly because it often generates internal changes that can hurt others."

"Paradoxically, the theater, with its masks, uncovers the hypocrisy of human relations," Zacconi says, joining in. "You can allow yourself to say everything and its opposite through the words of a poet."

"Come now, let's not exaggerate!" Ignazio says in slightly too shrill a voice, his eyes fixed on Franca. "Marriage is the foundation of a virtuous society. It defines the roles, helps us raise children, and marks the boundary between what's licit and illicit. Denying its importance is pure madness."

Franca raises her eyebrows. "Really?" She puts her glass of wine down and strokes its base. "I think it's our behavior that speaks for us—our actions, not words or statements. It's a question of dignity, of self-respect and decency, because form and substance often coincide. You, Signor Zacconi, define it as 'hypocrisy,' but I prefer to think of it as a genuine respect for others, starting with one's own family and the name we carry."

Eleonora Duse studies her, then a smile slowly appears on her lips. She raises her glass. "How can I disagree with you, Donna Franca?"

Franca will remember this evening and these words many years later, in the darkness of a movie theater, watching a frail, intense elderly woman play the part of a mother reunited with the son she once abandoned, now an adult. She will search her face in vain for the Eleonora Duse she knew and admired. And she won't be able to stop herself from wondering if in the end, her spirit, like her body, and like the title of the movie, turned to ashes.

Because not even the most combative, intelligent women can escape such a fate. Franca has learned that lesson.

A mild winter welcomes the new century to Palermo. The city a reporter from *Corriere della Sera* has described as "Italy's most beautiful" is celebrating it by finally showing off its sophisticated soul to everyone. Villas and houses with pretty wrought-iron gratings and well-manicured gardens emerge in the area occupied by the 1891 National Exhibition; silent streets unfurl from Via della Libertà, the city's broad new road that echoes a Parisian boulevard. It is indeed Paris that Palermo seeks to emulate: you can tell by the stores with their stained-glass windows, the jewelers who display brooches and rings inspired by Cartier, the milliners appropriating patterns from *La Mode Illustrée* and *La Mode Parisienne*, and, of course, by the ever growing *cafés chantants*, filled with lights and mirrors, wide zinc counters, and tables with velvet chairs. Next door is the historic Gulì cake shop, the Cavalier Bruno confectionery, and the Caffè di Sicilia, where men discuss politics and business. Tearooms exclusively catering to women open shop: here, surrounded by walls decorated with floral paintings and oriental- or Arabian-style furnishing, ladies can drink tea or enjoy water ices and sorbets without fear of being hassled by dandies. The Teatro Massimo—completed at last—is closed, but its reputation as the third largest theater in Europe after the Paris Opéra and Vienna's Staatsoper remains intact, and Palermo's residents can still satisfy their desire for socializing at the seaside resorts of Acquasanta, Sammuzzo, and Arenella.

Exactly halfway between Palermo and the Arenella, where Villa dei Quattro Pizzi—now seldom used by the Florios—stands, there is the Domville family villa, a neo-Gothic house Ignazio has bought and completely transformed. Renaming it Villa Igiea, he intends to turn it into the most *à la page* sanatorium in Europe. An airy building with wide-open spaces, filled with light, and equipped with two hundred rooms overlooking the garden and, therefore, the sea. Behind the complex is Monte Pellegrino, from which wafts a scent of earth mixed with rue and oregano. The contrast of colors and fragrances is as unusual as it is energizing.

"And this is the terrace: three thousand square meters . . . almost thirty-two thousand three hundred square feet," Ignazio says in English. "It's winter, and yet here, in the open air, the temperature is very pleasant and the air invigorating, very useful for treating bronchial and lung disease."

He watches his guests' reactions to the splendid terrace and the magnificent Gulf of Palermo bathed in the January sun. The men nod, commenting in low voices, but seem reluctant to commit. And yet he is proud of this place and has spent a considerable sum on bringing to Sicily these eleven British physicians, so that they can attend the villa's opening. How can they not be excited by its potential?

"You may have noticed the linoleum floors. The entire building is fireproof and heated with tiled stoves and fireplaces—"

"If you will allow me, Don Ignazio, I'd like to add that the disinfection and laundry facilities, as well as the laboratories, are situated at a certain distance from the complex, to avoid disturbing the stay of our guests and ensure more hygiene."

The man who interrupted is skinny, with jet-black eyes and a large gray mustache. He is Vincenzo Cervello, professor of medicine and pharmacology at the University of Palermo, and about to be appointed health director of Villa Igiea, where he will have the opportunity to test his innovative treatment method for pulmonary disease: keeping patients in a room filled with paraldehyde, or formaldehyde, chloral, and iodoform vapor. A treatment as innovative as it is controversial: the group of British doctors has listened to his explanations with clear reservations and repeatedly tried asking him embarrassing questions. But Cervello has always ardently defended the efficacy of his treatment.

"—a stay which, as you see, we've crafted with attention to every detail in order to ensure comfort and discretion," Ignazio says, completing his sentence. "And now, gentlemen, I'll leave you for a couple of hours. Should you wish to visit the city, there are carriages at your disposal. May I remind you that there's a gala dinner this evening and that it will be my pleasure to have you as my guests."

The odd smile finally appears among the men's faces. A few look around, peering between the hedges and the trees in the garden. There is a moment of hesitation. "And your wife . . . She will be there, won't she?" the youngest of the group asks shyly.

Ignazio smiles through clenched teeth. "But of course. My wife can't wait to meet you, gentlemen."

There is a contented murmur in the group as they walk away.

With a sigh, Ignazio leans on the balustrade overlooking the sea. "Thank God it's over," he whispers to Professor Cervello. "Are you sure they didn't get as far as the second-floor rooms?"

"I'm absolutely certain. And they only saw the main area in the kitchen. Moreover, they visited just one laboratory and one of the therapy rooms."

Ignazio nods. The work is far from complete; it will be weeks before the sanatorium can receive guests. There have been the usual delays owing to lazy workmen, materials failing to arrive, and a bureaucracy slow to issue permits. In addition, there are the maintenance costs, already considerable, as one of the guests noted during a tête-à-tête with Ignazio over a brandy a few evenings ago.

Ignazio smiled diplomatically and avoided replying.

Never mind. Everything must appear perfect to these luminaries, and Villa Igiea ready to open. That way they will recommend this elegant place, kissed by sun and sea, fitted out with the most modern equipment, to their wealthy patients. And once they're here, Professor Cervello's effective treatment will do the rest.

Just as the two men go back into the building, a servant, barely older than a boy, appears at the end of the corridor and runs straight to Ignazio, who chides him sharply. "Slowly, damn it! There must be peace and quiet here!"

"*Mi scusasse*, excuse me, Don Ignazio. But there's a telegram and—"

Ignazio snatches it from his hand and dismisses him. The boy walks away practically on tiptoe.

Ignazio reads quickly, then squeezes Professor Cervello's arm. "Thank you, God! He's not coming! Minister Baccelli can't attend the opening of Villa Igiea! We have to postpone!"

Professor Cervello smiles in disbelief, his hand over his mouth. "We have time to complete the work and open in the spring . . ."

They shake hands.

"What a stroke of luck! I'll announce it at the gala dinner tonight. Oh, and I'll look devastated, I'll apologize profusely . . ."

"I gather few will be paying attention anyway," Cervello remarks, emboldened by the news. "I do believe the Englishmen's primary objective is to meet your wife."

Ignazio crumples the telegram and puts it in his pocket. "They can look at my Franca all they like. There's something they'll notice right away."

"What?" Cervello asks, intrigued.

Ignazio smiles. "My wife is pregnant again."

⌒

"My dear Ettore!" Franca exclaims.

A cigarillo firmly wedged between his lips, Ettore De Maria Bergler is busy stirring various shades of green in a bowl. At the sound of Franca's voice, he immediately raises his head and turns with a smile. The recollection of a spring many years ago, of a charcoal portrait from a time when she was still a young ingenue, certain that Ignazio did not even notice other women, flashes between them. He holds out a paint-soiled hand and kisses her knuckles. "Donna Franca, what a pleasure to see you! Have you come to see how we're getting on with the work?"

She nods and crosses her hands over her belly.

Her third child is due a couple of months from now: after her adored Giovannuzza and Baby Boy, another son would fill her with joy. This hall will have to be ready by then, since it is where the guests for the baby's christening will be entertained.

"Well, we've already done a great deal. Michele Cortegiani and Luigi Di Giovanni are almost ahead of me."

Franca looks up at two men sitting on scaffolding, putting the final touches to a wreath of roses. "Hello, Signor Cortegiani! Hello, Signor Di Giovanni!"

"My respects, Donna Franca," they reply in unison.

Nymphs draped in diaphanous clothes are dancing above her. "Magnificent," she murmurs, turning in a circle to see the frescoes coming to life. "There's something . . . something magical about these creatures."

"I'm convinced that art is magic and that it should be experienced without prejudice—don't you agree?"

She sighs and nods. A friend to writers and painters, she knows only too well how important it is for every work of art to be shrouded in mystery. By now, though, she has learned to spot the artists' minor and major obsessions, their pettiness, and, above all, their fears, since she finds these even in the letters Puccini and D'Annunzio write her. "That's right. You artists are creatures both powerful and frail."

The painter raises his eyebrows, takes a handkerchief from his pocket, and dabs a trickle of sweat from his face. "The problem nowadays is that there's no humility. Some people think they're entitled to make harsh criticism after seeing just one painting or hearing just one opera." He hands the bowl to an assistant and tells him to continue mixing the color, then wipes his hands with a cloth. "Come, let's go into the garden," he says with a smile. "It's a mild April and I don't want you to strain yourself any more than you should."

They walk along the corridor and down the winding staircase to the large terrace overlooking the sea, where wrought-iron furniture has been arranged. Franca sits down with a sigh of relief, feeling all her pregnancy-related tiredness.

De Maria Bergler does not appear to notice. "You look so . . . so radiant," he exclaims. "Oh, how I'd like to paint you right now, in this spring light!"

"You're always too kind," Franca replies, although she knows the painter is right: in recent months, Ignazio has started loving her passionately again, and the rumors about his "distractions" seem to have dwindled. Her rediscovered serenity is obvious. She has almost stopped thinking about the other women: they may hold

Ignazio's attention, but she is the mother of his children. They have the crumbs, she the banquet. Above all, she is proud of herself: her outward image has never been marred, not even for a moment.

"So—how are you?"

"The little devil is champing at the bit," Franca murmurs, patting her belly. The baby responds with a light kick in her side.

"We'll have completed the work in time for the birth. Can you smell primer, oil, glue, and especially wood? It's from the furniture designed by your dear friend Ernesto Basile; the porters have just delivered it from the Vittorio Ducrot factory and it's still in packaging. If you like, I can show it to you later. You'll see; in the end it'll feel like being in a garden during spring."

"Or in a dream place outside time," Franca replies, smiling. Because that is what she has in mind. An exclusive hotel reserved for international aristocracy, facing what Goethe described as *des schönsten aller Vorgebirge der Welt*, "the most beautiful promontory in the world." A refuge for regenerating body and mind.

It was her idea.

When Ignazio realized that Villa Igiea would never become the luxury sanatorium he had pictured—too much red tape, money, and, above all, too many doubts about the efficacy of Professor Cervello's course of treatment—he withdrew into an angry silence, emerging only to hurl invectives at ill fortune, claiming he was cursed for living on such a backward island.

Franca let him vent. Then, one evening, she recalled nostalgically their trip to Saint Moritz, Nice, and Cannes and, with a sigh, added how lovely it would be to have, here in Palermo, a luxury hotel like the ones they usually frequented . . .

Ignazio stared at her, then cried, "But of course! How true, my dear Franca! To hell with the sanatorium! *Our* Villa Igiea can become the finest luxury hotel in Europe!" He took her hands and kissed her.

They spent entire afternoons with their good friend Ernesto Basile, discussing their picture of the place: from the furniture in the bedrooms and salons to the lawn tennis courts (Ignazio was an enthusiastic player); from the scenic garden, with its bridges and staircases, to the telegraph station; from the possibility of making a few boats, and even one of their yachts, available to their guests, to the excellent cuisine, which—Franca would not budge on this— had to be run by a French chef and team, just as the maître d' and sommelier would be French, too. Thanks to the mild Sicilian climate, the hotel would always be open, even in winter. Ignazio told them how one of the British doctors had said, "Here in Sicily, January is like a warm June in England!" before going to bathe in the sea, followed by his colleagues.

She and Ignazio laughed so much together, complicit as never before. Franca made suggestions and explained; he listened. She felt—and still feels—like a part of this project. Besides, she loves this place far from the city, its fragrance of flowers and algae, and the way the sunlight bounces off the sea and along the city's coastline, bathing it in gold and bronze. She loves it so much, she has decided to reserve an entire floor of Villa Igiea for herself, Ignazio, and their children.

She runs her fingers down her gold and Sciacca coral necklace. "I'd like to move here as soon as possible, you know? The Olivuzza is like a seaport . . . there's always chaos, what with all the servants and guests going back and forth. I need peace and quiet now more than ever."

"Of course! Besides, what better place than one named after the goddess of health?"

Franca laughs. "Ah, if only you knew . . . At the beginning, when

my husband was still thinking of making this complex into a sanatorium, he tortured himself for weeks, unsure whether Igiea was
spelled with an *i* or without. In the end, dear D'Annunzio told
him that the goddess's name was actually Igiea." Her face softens.
"If it's a girl, that's what my husband wants to call her. But I so
wish it's a boy."

"Fate will decide. The important thing is that he or she is
healthy. And how is Donna Giovanna?"

"She's well, thank you. She's decided to stay at the Olivuzza,"
she adds even though the painter did not ask. But Franca is so
relieved that her mother-in-law decided to stay at the villa with her
youngest son, she cannot conceal it; it shows in her voice as well
as on her face. Ever since she arrived at the Olivuzza, now seven
years ago, Giovanna's lifestyle has remained the same, punctuated
by prayer, embroidery, melancholy, and regret. The veil of grief and
sadness over her apartment is now a shadow no amount of light
can dispel.

No, it's far better to breathe the sunlight, the life, and the
warmth of this place.

"A few days ago," the painter says, "I heard your husband talking to Ernesto about the possibility of building a little house in the
grounds of the Olivuzza for your brother-in-law."

"Yes. He's been mentioning this project for a while. I'm not
sure I fully agree, because it would mean turning the garden upside down and knocking down the little temple, but there you go.
Where his brother is concerned, he won't listen to either me or his
mother. Vincenzo is seventeen now and has asked him for *more
room and more freedom*." She stresses the last words.

The painter represses a jab behind his diplomatic smile. In
actual fact, the youngest Florio is already taking all the room
and freedom he wants: on the one hand, with his passion for

automobiles—he boasts about knowing every bolt and strap—on the other hand, with his collection of female conquests, not unlike that of his brother. *How two reprobates like them came out of a virtuous couple like Ignazio and Giovanna Florio is a mystery*, De Maria Bergler thinks, but takes care not to voice aloud.

He stands up. "I'm very sorry, Donna Franca, I must get back to work. But may I tell you something first? My contribution aside, I'm sure Villa Igiea will be an extraordinary place, and everyone will envy us for it. I don't think it would have been the same with a sanatorium. It was a good thing your husband changed his mind."

"Only people lacking imagination refuse to change their minds. And fools," Franca replies with a smile. "And yes, I agree with you. Maybe my optimism comes from my joy at this new pregnancy, but I'm also convinced that Villa Igiea will show the world the extraordinary beauty of Palermo."

On this April Sunday, the sun is already bright, chasing after the shadows of the trees on Piazza Marina, while the southwest wind raises clouds of dust on the *balate* of the Cassaro. Ignazio had to go to Villa Igiea first thing in the morning to talk to the foreman about the finish on the railings overlooking the sea. Afterward, he would have gladly lingered and taken a stroll in the garden, only he had an important appointment.

He is now in the NGI building, rereading a letter.

It is the draft of the missive he sent almost a year ago to the *Giornale di Sicilia*: a long, detailed list of everything necessary to lift the island from its perennial difficulties. "Project Sicily" was what he called it, and it proposed converting extensive farmland to intensive, building oil production plants, relaunching the mining of sulfur, experimentally growing sorghum and beet, replanting vines corroded by phylloxera, campaigning farmers to adopt modernized farming techniques, and facilitating legislation. That was the plan of action for the Sicilian Agriculture Consortium he had longed for, gathering around him eighteen thousand people—aristocrats, intellectuals, and politicians—all united by the belief that the time had come to act to revamp the island's economy.

But the government proved more generous with its words than its purse. The project lost momentum. From the ashes of disappointment, though, a new idea was born, which immediately aroused Ignazio's enthusiasm: to set up a newspaper.

He has thought about it carefully. The interests of Casa Florio would gain high visibility in the columns of a paper. Besides, a newspaper could become an indispensable tool for influencing public opinion. For example, it could criticize the decisions of a government making everybody unhappy by imposing taxes but providing no assistance. Once politicians realize that ordinary people are no longer following them, but are actually hostile to them, they can only change their line of action.

Last, but not least, a newspaper is the way to show everyone what the future holds. A newspaper will give a voice to discontent and hope.

To *his* concerns.

These are no longer his father's times, when a man could alter the destiny of an entire city by himself. Besides, his father had Crispi watching his back. Crispi has faded, so has Rudinì, and now Luigi Pelloux is head of the government, knows nothing about Sicily, and thinks he can solve everything with carabinieri and their rifles. Ignazio makes a gesture of annoyance. A few days ago, on April 8, Pelloux actually suspended support to shipbuilding, plunging the completion of the Palermo construction site into a serious crisis. *You can't talk to these northern politicians anymore,* he thinks angrily. *There are things they just don't understand, and then you have to call in an army and face them and give them a fright. You must involve the people.*

He looks around. The building is silent. No squeaking, no creaking today. Even the cracks seem to have vanished.

There is a knock at the door. An imposing figure of a man appears.

"Come in, my dear Rudinì, come in!"

Carlo Starabba di Rudinì, the former prime minister's eldest son, is a large, elegantly dressed man with thick, dark whiskers.

"Are you ready?" Ignazio asks.

"Above all, I'm honored. Being the owner of a new paper is no mean feat. The director is waiting for us at the office, isn't he?"

"Yes, Morello must already be there," Ignazio replies with a nod, focusing his attention on a pilot's book hanging on the wall, showing the Calabrian coast and the Strait of Messina. "You know, he's from Bagnara Calabra, like my great-grandfather. Strange coincidence."

"I thought he was from Rome. Didn't he used to write for *La Tribuna*?"

"Yes. Right—time to go."

It is cool, dark, and comforting inside the vehicle. Toying with his diamond cuff links—two large stones that light up his wrists— Ignazio holds back a sigh and crosses his fingers to conceal his tension.

"And how is your father?"

"He's well, thank you. Still mad at Pelloux," Rudinì replies with a shrug.

"I can understand that—he has every reason to be," Ignazio

says. "You know I've always supported him with conviction and been his loyal ally. And I understand why he's opposed to the current government, which is obsessed with a normalization that certainly isn't helping Sicily and the south as a whole. As if Sicily was identical to Piedmont or Tuscany! We survived the Bourbons, and yet we can't shake off the shackles and the wicked taxes imposed on us by the Rome government . . . while enterprises in the north have free rein, of course!"

Carlo di Rudinì pulls a bitter grimace. "When my father was in the government, he always made sure he protected the interests of Southern Italy, and Sicily in particular. We're still a very young nation, and we come from different administrations. We were all unified too hastily. Italy, my dear Don Ignazio, was born divided. Those who made Italy forty years ago didn't realize how different the south and the north were, and now we're paying the consequences."

Ignazio nods. "That's right: after the unification, Sicily and Sicilians were cast aside like an old shoe. No plans, no innovations; only accusations of leeching money, having no skills, and being . . . peasants." He practically spits out the word. "It's one of the reasons I founded the Agriculture Consortium, because I was confident we could achieve something concrete and modern. While elsewhere landowners are a political force people listen to and help, here they're considered on a par with idiots."

Rudinì gives him a skeptical sideways glance. Casa Florio has received many subsidies and has never been short of political support, starting with the naval concessions. But Ignazziddu Florio has neither his grandfather's authority nor his father's temperament. He has goodwill and brilliant ideas, certainly, but he's fickle: a flag that waves with the wind. And when it comes to production, he definitely hasn't distinguished himself for his innovation: he should be spending more—and more wisely—on his companies, whereas they are in fact limping along, like the Oretea, unable to keep up with the businesses in Northern Italy. Even so, Rudinì gives him credit for his awareness of social issues and knows he's a rich, powerful man with an extensive network. That's why he has gotten involved in the creation of the newspaper.

As though reading his mind, Ignazio leans forward and squeezes his arm. "I'm sure that with this venture we'll stir things up. This newspaper will operate under the banner of free information! I'll exploit my international contacts for news from all over the world and many prominent people will write for us: Colajanni, Capuana . . . even the great D'Annunzio assures me he'll work with us. The *Giornale di Sicilia* has done a lot, but now it's time someone truly defended the interests of Sicilians. Everybody agrees on this point: even Filippo Lo Vetere, a Socialist and not some aristocrat perched on his throne. Fighting between landowners and farmers is pointless, he says. No one will help us; we have to help ourselves."

Ignazio wants to add that he has even thought about how to attract a readership by offering prizes, like vases or dinner sets from his ceramics factory, but he has no time. The vehicle has reached Via dei Cintorinai, location of the newspaper's headquarters. Its first issue is to be published today, and it will go a long way, a very long way. For many generations, it will narrate the bitter life of Palermo with sincerity and courage; some of the most important figures in Sicilian and Italian journalism will learn their trade at its desks. And, before it finally closes down, some of its journalists will die at the hands of the Mafia.

*L'Ora,* Sicily's new daily political gazette.

᠙

Costanza Igiea Florio is born on June 4, 1900. She is called simply Igiea and welcomed by her family as a promise of happiness for the new century.

Only, this time the Casa Florio workers do not partake in the festivities. None of them shows up at the Olivuzza to celebrate the birth. There's nothing to celebrate when there's no work.

Between June and November, in fact, the subsidies for building new ships are cut, and this measure causes damage to the shipyards in the north—except that they already have orders—and brings the ones in the south to their knees. The Palermo yard, still incomplete, is the first to suffer. NGI has to suspend work, and Ignazio is forced to lay off hundreds of workers.

In circumstances overshadowed by the assassination of King Umberto I, it seems pointless to turn to Rome, which issues only empty reassurances, indicating its fear of a possible uprising and issuing a call to keep an eye on potential instigators and, if necessary, have them immediately arrested. In Palermo, even charity is denied: the prefect requests a subsidy for struggling families, but the government refuses; the prefect ends up withdrawing the application, afraid to set a dangerous precedent.

There is a rise in the number of unemployed families—almost two thousand at the start of 1900.

The city taxes go up, too, in a clumsy attempt to bring the budget, now in chronic deficit, into line.

And a single sentence, whispered by all—the Oretea workers, the clerks, the artisans, the porters, the sailors in the shipyard—rides the long, endless wave of hunger, despair, and uncertainty. An unforgiving accusation.

*Ignazio Florio is a liar.*

He said the shipyard would bring well-being to the city. He claimed that the economy would be given a new impetus. He promised bread and work for everyone.

Instead, Palermo is now inactive and can only watch from afar that colossal, unfinished shipyard that's slowly becoming obsolete before it was ever operational.

And it's Ignazio Florio's fault.

⌒

The dawn of February 27, 1901, is full of shivering, of shawls thrown over shoulders, mountains dusted with snow, and a lead-gray sky. It is only really cold in Sicily during the month of February.

This chill comes to the Olivuzza, cuts through the walls and the windows wedged with woolen rags to stop the drafts, dampens the heat of the warmers, and reaches Ignazio under the blankets.

Strangely, he is already awake. As a matter of fact, he has hardly slept. He is thirty but feels twice as old this morning.

Shivering, he gets out of bed, puts on his robe, goes into his study, asks for coffee and a cognac, and gives orders that he not be disturbed.

He looks at the stack of papers on his desk, not wanting to even touch them. And yet here they are, demanding to be reckoned with. Debts to banks, above all to the Banca Commerciale Italiana, which loaned him cash after that mess with Credito Mobiliare. He got into debt back then, so had to offer a portion of his NGI shares as collateral.

And now he has discovered that the orders for military ships he was counting on after the government cancelled the funds to build civilian steamers have been given to the shipyards in Naples and

Genoa. Palermo and the Florios have been excluded. Nothing for them, not even crumbs.

Which means those shares are worth little, very little now, and the banks want other collateral, other guarantees.

He rings the bell. "Call Morello at the paper right away," he tells the servant who appears at the door. Then he sits back down at his desk, feeling as though the ground has vanished from beneath his feet, and that he has nothing to hold on to, to keep from falling.

He suddenly hears a vague sound, like a subdued moan.

Here they are, the creaks that herald collapse.

Ignazio bangs a fist on his desk. If only he had delved deeper into the soundness of Credito Mobiliare years ago, before investing capital in it. If only he had listened to those who were advising him to stay away from it during the Banca Romana scandal. If only he hadn't covered the savers' losses out of his own pocket . . .

Instead, Casa Florio has been paying the consequences of those choices for eight years.

There has been very little help from Rome and, he now realizes, there will be increasingly less. Politics has become a constant gamble, with alliances that are both precarious and unstable; the government is forever changing leaders—Luigi Pelloux was succeeded by the elderly Giuseppe Saracco, and, from a few days ago, by Giuseppe Zanardelli, another politician from the north—and it's impossible to form a continuous, *productive* relationship with a minister or an undersecretary, because they do nothing but grab whatever they can and protect their own interests and the interests of those who have done them favors.

Northern industrialists are the ones with all the political power now. They have the factories and the shipyards as well as the forward-looking steel industries. They are able to load their products onto trains and get them anywhere quickly, not giving a damn about transportation by ship.

For a moment, the air presses against his stomach, as though iron dust has landed in the bottom of his lungs. He abruptly expels it with a hoarse sound, part stifled cry, part sob.

*How did we get to this point? How did I get here?* he wonders, staring at a painting of his *Valkyrie*, commissioned shortly before he sold the yacht. It brings back happy memories: he recalls the days when he had time on his hands and a mind free to devote himself to regattas, tournaments, games of lawn tennis. He has little of that left now: there are the parties, of course, and . . . those small distractions he grants himself every now and then.

He has always loved life, sport, adventure. Instead, he is nailed to a desk—just like his father—and has to find a way out of this impasse, and nobody, nobody seems willing to help him. Not even Alessandro Tasca di Cutò, who has become an influential Socialist, wants to listen to him. The last time they spoke, he told Ignazio that his shipyard's fate had been sealed by his delusions of grandeur, and the workers would be the ones to pay for his irresponsible actions. On his way out, he warned him: "People are scared of losing everything, Ignazio. And fear gives rise to chaos. Remember that." Then he left without saying goodbye.

*People?*

I'm *the one who's scared of losing everything.*

Because now there's a risk that the Palermo shipyard will never be completed.

And that *he* will go bankrupt.

"No," he utters softly, slapping his hands on the desk. "It can't be."

He must react. But how? Who can he turn to for help?

*How dare they do this to me? To the Florios?*

࿐

On February 28, 1901, the editorial in *L'Ora*, written by Rastignac—aka Vincenzo Morello—has a harsh title: "Forgotten."

So Sicily has been forgotten! . . . Palermo has been awarded special treatment; but only to exclude it from all the benefits enjoyed now or in the future by the other regions . . . In the laws and regulations, it is always Sicily that is forgotten, even though the crisis here is more serious than in other places, even though work has long been suspended in Palermo's factories.

This adds fuel to the fire, stoking the fears of a city that has been denied everything: its glorious past, the possibility of counting for something in a now-united Italy, a future of hope and progress.

And so Palermo raises its head. It does so with a wrath aroused by fear, yes, but above all by a violated dignity.

The concrete result is the first proper citywide strike, not just a protest by the workers at the Oretea Foundry or the shipyard site. Naturally, the strikes start with the trade unions in the Molo district, where the shipyard site is located, but laborers, coachmen, tailors, fishermen, barbers, gardeners, fruit sellers, bricklayers, bakers, and carpenters also take part. Because everyone knows that if the Florios don't resume construction, everything will collapse, and it's not as if the government cares about there being no more bread or work in Palermo; they just mind their own business, as they always have.

The Cassaro is filling with people: women and children head the procession, marching with the workers. They file past the NGI building to the Royal Palace, a torrent that swells at every street, every crossroads, until it becomes an overflowing river. The carabinieri are patrolling the streets, going after the leaders of the protest; the police are raiding the homes of workers who belong to the union.

But the residents of Palermo do not comply, they shout and react, and spitting turns to punching, to kicking the bars, and the strike turns into a guerilla struggle, with law-enforcement agents hunting down the protesters and the latter attacking barracks and stores; they sow devastation, they loot, because that's how it goes, because hunger is hunger and fear is fear.

*Semu fangu d'in tierra*, the *Palermitani* think: we are mud from the earth, people worth nothing, who must be whipped into submission, jailed like criminals, shot at. So the clash worsens and the violence increases: a bayonet attack by the Bersaglieri is met with stones, billboards are stacked and set fire to, while daggers, sabers, and pistols are produced. The unions that started the protests now fear they can no longer control the people's fury.

In fact, after one last message from Zanardelli, filled with vague reassurances and improbable promises, they take fright, yield, and announce the end of the strike.

But nothing has changed.

On March 3, 1901, stressed and worn out, Ignazio is looking through the window of the offices of *L'Ora*. He has felt the city quiver for two days, as though about to explode. He has sensed the mounting tension on the streets, his unease fueled by his own despair. He has witnessed clashes, cursed Socialists as well as Roman politicians and their official telegrams: one from Crispi—as useless and rhetorical as its sender—and those from Giovanni

Giolitti, minister of the interior, and Zanardelli, who actually sent him a personal telegram, asking him to use his influence to calm the waters.

*So now he speaks to me*, Ignazio thought. *Now that he's scared.*

Morello makes the final corrections to his editorial, then walks to the window. "They're already arresting dozens of people," he says. "If Rome insists on not understanding what truly happened here and continues to suppress, they're criminals. Giolitti and Zanardelli will have the dead on their conscience." He searches for his cigar case in the pocket of his jacket.

Ignazio lights his cigar for him, declines his offer of one, and bites his lip.

"Oh, and then a—a friend of mine gave me a telegram two Palermo members of Parliament, Pietro Bonanno and Vittorio Emanuele Orlando, sent Zanardelli: they accuse you of instigating the strike because you're in financial straits and want to use it as blackmail. And they say I'm your accomplice." Morello shakes his head. "I've seen a lot, Don Ignazio, ever since the times of *La Tribuna*, and I've spoken a lot, and never been afraid." He breathes out smoke and walks away from the window, back to the leather chair by his desk. "I've been accused of many things: of being a lackey to power and of being anti-establishment," he says with a touch of amusement. "Rubbish. The idea of being the instigator of a strike fills me with pride, not shame or fear, as those two would wish."

"In spite of Bonanno and Orlando's slanders, Palermo's members of Parliament have sided with the strike and against the exclusion of the commissions: Baron Chiaramonte Bordonaro, the Prince of Camporeale, and, naturally, my brother-in-law, Pietro. The rich and the poor together. Never before has the city been so united." Ignazio slowly walks to the other chair and slumps down opposite Morello. He can smell the warm aroma of his cigar.

"Prefect De Seta also tried to intervene in favor of the strikers' requests . . ."

"And the police commissioner decided to oppose him. The government going against itself: that's where we're at . . . and they go accusing me of speculating with public money and having 'delusions of grandeur,' as Tasca di Cutò says." He makes a gesture of annoyance and starts tapping the floor with his foot. There's a burst of angry shouting from the street, but it's immediately quenched. "Even if that were true, the problem isn't me and my losses: it's the workers we're having to let go because we no longer have a reason to keep them if there's no work. And that makes me furious: people look at the Florios as if we were the root of all evil, after all we've done, all *I've* done for this city . . . and I'm sure those bastards at the *Giornale di Sicilia* will pick up these absurdities and even broadcast them!"

"They're doing their jobs, Don Ignazio, just as I'm doing mine." Morello's raised eyebrow speaks volumes. "But you must take advantage of the moment. You have a respected family name and the support of most of Palermo's politicians. Not all, of course, since the Socialists and those two are a case apart, but it doesn't really matter. Lobby—do it now. They'll have to give in a little in Rome if they want to avoid a civil war breaking out soon. Then people will trust you again, the scandalmongers will be forced to eat their words, and the workers will see that *u' principale* knows how to command respect."

Ignazio nods, but a fear is taking root inside him and rising to his stomach. He no longer knows how much power his name holds in Rome: once upon a time, the papers would never have entertained certain criticisms, let alone printed them.

*All you have of your father is his name. Soon, even that will carry no more influence. And the fault will be yours alone*, Laganà prophesied a few years ago.

Ignazio swallows air; even though he can't admit it to himself, that day has come.

ᔐ

"This one?"

"Well, the green velvet matches your eyes, *Checchina*, but the dress doesn't . . . seem appropriate." Francesca has become a charming, relaxed woman. Having gotten over Amerigo's death, she remarried a couple of years ago and now divides her time between Palermo, Florence, and Paris with her husband, Maximilien Grimaud, Count d'Orsay.

"Wait . . ." says Stefanina Spadafora, who has recently married Giulio Cesare Pajno but put her honeymoon preparations on hold to help Franca with this difficult decision. She draws on the ebony cigarette holder held tightly between her fingers and lets out a puff of smoke. "No, Francesca's correct: not quite right yet."

"You're about to pose for one of Italy's—if not Europe's—most famous painters, *ma chère*. You can't look like a Catholic schoolgirl." Giulia Trigona is lying at the foot of the bed, leaning her head on her hand, vaguely bored. Her skirt is riding up her ankles, revealing her long, toned legs.

In a robe and slip, Franca holds the dress away from her, indicates the neckline, and gives her friends an eloquent look, but Stefanina waves her hand as if to say no, no point in insisting, it won't do. She gets up and walks across the room, treading on the rose-petaled tiles, to investigate the perfumes. She opens a bottle. "A true symphony of spices! What is it?"

Franca nods without turning. It's called La Marescialla and was created by the Pharmaceutical Workshop of Santa Maria Novella. A present from her mother, she explains as she paces the room, absorbed in thought, looking at the cherubs on the ceiling.

"What about the pomegranate-red dress?" Francesca says, slipping off her shoes and sitting down in the armchair left vacant by Stefanina. "You can get away with it. You've an enviable body even after three pregnancies."

"No, that would be too obvious," Franca replies. "I need something . . ." She taps her lips with her fingertips. She goes to the large closet to the left of the bed, opens it, and studies it, hands on her hips. She needs something that will astound. Something that reminds everyone that she is "the One and Only," as D'Annunzio called her, and that no woman can compete with her, not even that Lina Cavalieri her husband decided to bring to Palermo despite everything, even despite the strikes and protests that have turned the whole city upside down.

Yes, of course Ignazio is worried. As a matter of fact, he's in Rome right now, talking to ministers and Sicilian politicians in order to sort out the shipyard business, which is still dragging on. But when he returns—and here Franca feels a pang of resentment— he'll go straight to the Teatro Massimo to watch the rehearsals for *La Bohème* rather than to his family or his Oretea workers.

He even had the audacity to justify himself before leaving: "I'm the impresario, so I need to make sure everything's in order."

*Fool.*

Franca drums her fingers on the closet door. Does he really think she knows nothing? She did tell him once: "I always know everything, Ignazio." By now he should have realized that the more aggressively you hide certain things, the more likely they are to come to light, especially when a peacock like him does them.

All she needs is a sign—a new English suit, a sudden late-evening commitment, special care of his mustache—to know there's a new conquest on the horizon, a new affair to maintain.

As for people—still whispering, snickering, and hinting—Franca now knows that gossip is an ever-hungry animal, and if it doesn't find new carrion to pick at, it chews over whatever there is. And so she provides them with a humorous response and watches them as they tear her to pieces, or else shows off a new piece of jewelry, knowing full well they'll try to find out what *the other one* is like.

That's right: here, too, Ignazio is as brazen as he is predictable. After the umpteenth adventure, he will appear before her with a gift—a sapphire ring, a platinum bracelet, a diamond necklace—in lieu of reparation. And it will often be similar to the one he has given his current sweetheart.

The jewels always come: sometimes during the betrayal, sometimes once the affair is over. She has learned to measure the importance Ignazio bestows on the women with whom he cheats on her from the value of the items he gives her. But she knows that his remorse has the consistency of ash.

It's different with Lina Cavalieri, though.

Lina, the dressmaker's daughter, the violet seller, the folder of newspapers, who first conquered Rome and Naples, then the Folies Bergère in Paris and the London Empire. She has a silvery voice, yes, but above all she's very beautiful, with a face like a Madonna, a pair of very dark eyes, and a sinner's body that moves with brazen sensuality. Men go crazy for her: Franca has heard that eight carts were once needed to remove the flowers that had been thrown to her on the stage. And she knows how to use their fanaticism: that innocent appearance—she always performs without makeup or jewels—conceals a soul of iron. Last year, Lina decided to become an opera singer: she debuted in Lisbon with *I Pagliacci* and it was such a critical failure that anybody else would have stepped away quietly, crushed by shame. Anybody else but her. She bravely continued to perform, and now—after filling theaters in Warsaw and Naples—she's coming to Palermo, admired, awaited, desired.

It's the first time that Ignazio has paraded his mistress before the entire city, pitting her directly against Franca. He flirted with doing this a couple of years ago, after bedding Agustina Carolina del Carmen Otero Iglesias, known to everyone as simply "la Belle Otero." Another singer and dancer of obscure origins, a woman who could use her body with ease and had a healthy dose of cynicism. Ignazio didn't shy away from boasting about that conquest—and of her generous favors—with his friends at the club, stooping to vulgar details that reached Franca's ears, making her shudder with disdain.

But that was his typical male ego.

This is an insult.

Years ago, Franca would have suffered, breaking down in tears, torturing herself with humiliation. But now she has changed and has learned to turn sorrow into anger. She's discovered the explosive power of resentment, the strength produced by the awareness of one's self-worth. She no longer stews in embarrassment, no longer asks herself if she's gone wrong somewhere. She's learned to think for herself and to protect herself from the pain he inflicts on her. It's an odd feeling, this feeling she has for Ignazio, a blend of jealousy and affection, of humiliation and regret. Regret for what they were and for what has been thrown away.

*No, Ignazio's no fool. He's just selfish and unable to truly love.*

It's this final straw, though, that has made her put aside any lingering reservations and agree to pose for Giovanni Boldini, the most acclaimed, most talked-about portrait painter of the day. He is their guest: Ignazio has invited him to the Olivuzza because he wants Boldini to paint her portrait, like those he's already done of various high-society noblewomen across Europe. And, with his typical arrogance, Ignazio has requested the artist display Franca's portrait in Venice, at the exhibition he's holding next summer.

Franca shakes her head, pondering Ignazio's inability to weigh the consequences, to go beyond the immediate surface of things: all he has thought about is the social prestige and the envy this charming wife of his will generate. He hasn't realized that Boldini has a way of painting that seems to bare the soul, and that he paints women as creatures of flesh and desire. His women have just made love, relishing the pleasure derived from it.

She has no wish to appear so naked and exposed, but at the same time, she's tempted to let herself go and reveal what she could be. Sensual. Full of passion.

She's tempted to show the world, and her husband, who she truly is.

She picks a cream-colored dress, considers it for a moment, then puts it back.

Someone knocks at the door. It's Giovannuzza, followed by her governess and a couple of pugs, who aren't so much running as rolling behind her.

"Has the painter arrived, *Maman*? Can I see, too?" asks the little girl, staring at the clothes. Fascinated, she reaches out with her small hand and touches the fabrics. "Beautiful . . ." she murmurs.

Franca doesn't answer, looking now at a dress hanging in the most remote part of the closet, a dress she hasn't yet worn because Ignazio thinks it's too daring.

Jealous. Him. It would be funny if it weren't so infuriating.

"*Maman?*" the child insists in a pleading tone.

The governess is trying to send out the dogs, which have started licking the guests' shoes, making them shriek in protest.

"No, my love. This is not for children." Smiling with satisfaction, Franca turns and gives her a caress. "I'll have a portrait commissioned of you, too, when you're older. But now *geh und spiel im anderen Zimmer, su.*"

Giovannuzza huffs and sulks. "But *they're* allowed . . ." she says, indicating the women.

"*They're* grown-ups, Giovannuzza. And please show respect to adults."

Head down and tight-lipped, the child marches out. She doesn't say goodbye to anyone, not even Francesca, who always spoils her.

"She could have stayed . . ." Francesca says.

"No." Franca moves about the room slowly, picks up a cigarette in a holder from an ashtray and takes a drag. A habit she picked up on her last trip to France. She finds smoking very relaxing.

Her friends watch her and wait.

Giulia Trigona detects something the others can't see. As someone who, like Franca, suffers the excesses of an unfaithful and, it's rumored, violent husband, she says, "What's on your mind, Franca?"

Without replying, she slips off her robe, down to her bloomers and camisole, and looks in the mirror. Then she heads to the closet and takes out the dress she picked earlier, with Diodata's help.

A murmur of astonishment runs through her friends. The black carved-silk velvet dress, draped so that it accentuates her waist, makes her look even taller and more regal. It comes with a bib specially designed to highlight her long neck and make the dress more modest by covering the low neckline.

Franca takes the bib, looks at it, and throws it on the bed.

*No.*

She doesn't want it to be a respectable society lady's pose.

She wants to be looked at.

She studies herself in the mirror and shakes her head, and her loose, black hair shifts on her shoulders. There's still something missing.

She pushes her dress halfway down, freeing her chest from the fabric, then removes the camisole. Her breasts—white and full—are those of a girl, not a woman with three children. Stefanina leans forward and bursts out laughing. "Like that?" she asks, wide-eyed, while Francesca puts her hands to her mouth and mutters, "*Mon Dieu!*"

Giulia snickers. "Ignazio will have a shock when he returns to Palermo," she says, implying that he will deserve it.

Franca ignores their reactions, pulls up the bodice, and asks Diodata to secure the row of buttons.

She's almost breathless, but it's what she wants. This is her way to fight Ignazio's blind stupidity. And the envy of the *Palermitani*.

This isn't a dress; it's a suit of armor.

Still on the bed, Giulia watches with a vague smile. "Of course, if you want your husband to suffer a moment's embarrassment, that's the perfect dress. But you know what people will say, don't you?"

While Diodata starts styling her hair, Franca shrugs. "He asked Boldini to do a portrait of me. He'll have to accept my choice of attire," she replies, applying a touch of red to her lips. She indicates the flap on the bedside table. "Could you fetch me my jewelry bag, please?"

Giulia obeys, places the heavy bag among the silk dresses and sheets, and opens it.

Pure envy flashes across the faces of the three friends. None of them boasts such a collection of rings, necklaces, and bracelets of comparable weight or elegance.

Franca half closes her eyes, mentally separating Ignazio's gifts—the jewels that have the names of women—from her own. Those she chose carefully, almost lovingly, because—after her children—there's nothing dearer to her. These jewels are a mark of what Franca Florio is to the eyes of the world: beautiful, wealthy, and powerful.

She stands up and rummages among boxes and velvet pouches. Here they are, her pearls. She lets them slide between her fingers, caressing them. Then she links the necklaces together and, finally, adds the one with the twin pearls, as large as cherries. She puts it on, and the pearls cascade down her black dress like a waterfall of light.

Franca takes one final look in the mirror and tries to slow her breathing.

"Let's go."

Short, stout, his voice graceless, Giovanni Boldini has chosen a small, secluded drawing room with pale-colored walls and an oblique light to illuminate the amber skin of the lady of the house. A luminosity full of green and spring, warm like the air flowing in through the half-closed shutter of that turbulent March. Around them, dark damask armchairs; on the floor, a huge Persian rug. Franca's friends follow her, chatting and deciding where to sit, while she informs the servant woman that she is not to be disturbed. The door closes. The painter, who has already prepared the base on the canvas, studies her for a few seconds, his hands joined on his chest.

"I swear you're a vision, Donna Franca." He has a hint of a French accent—he has been living in Paris for thirty years.

She smiles, but only with her eyes. "I didn't consult you about the dress. Are you happy with it?"

She opens her arms to be admired, but the painter stops her. "Almost . . ." He takes her by the wrist, as though to lead her in a dance. "We need a little more light." He steps back, hands on his hips. Franca tries to imagine how he sees her; then she senses it and that makes her feel uneasy.

Stefanina approaches. "Another necklace?"

Boldini nods, practically skipping. "Yes, something to highlight her neckline . . . a brooch or a pendant."

Franca puts her hand on her friend's shoulder. "Remember the gold bangles I bought in Istanbul? Grab those, please. And the orchid-shaped diamond and platinum brooch, the one Ignazio gave me on our first wedding anniversary."

Stefanina vanishes behind the door, while the other women seat themselves in the armchairs. Boldini is thinking, conducting Franca around the room, searching for the best light. He lifts the pearls to her face, drops them again, wraps them around her, then lets them go, all the while muttering in a blend of Ferrarese and French. She herself is so slim and beautiful, it's almost comical to see this small man next to her.

"Mmm . . . it's really hard to find the right angle for you. You're so . . ." He makes a gesture that could be vulgar, but he manages to spin it as appreciative. Stefanina returns with the jewels and Franca puts them on. No, the bangles aren't suitable: the sleeve of the dress covers them. The brooch is better and gives even more light to the velvet drapery patterns.

Boldini goes to the large canvas. The portrait will be true to life and Franca will appear as tall as she stands now. He slides his glasses to the tip of his nose and starts to sketch the outline of her figure, but stops, mid-stroke, when he reaches the line of her shoulders. He looks at Francesca. "Excuse me, Signora . . . Could you lend Donna Franca your shawl?"

"My . . . Oh, yes, of course, here it is."

Laughing, Francesca hands her shawl to Franca, who doesn't know what to do with it, prompting a giggle.

Concentrating, Boldini asks her to position it around her body, so that the white fabric may light up her bare shoulders. Her black hair glistens in the spring light as she plays with the shawl, draping it around herself.

Then she turns her head to catch a remark from Giulia. That's when the painter stops her. "Like this! Stay still like this!" he commands, his eyes wide. He climbs onto a platform he uses when he paints, and sketches long, intense strokes, trying to capture the light.

Franca obeys. Taken by surprise, engrossed, her lips half open, her hip thrust forward in a sensual motion that ripples from her arm, like a wave.

She doesn't know that at this moment a painting is being created that will turn her into a legend.

# PART TWO

# Porcelain

### April 1901 to July 1904

*Li malanni trasino du sfilazzu di la porta.*
Bad luck comes in through the cracks in the door.
—SICILIAN PROVERB

I T STANDS JUST OVER TEN centimeters tall, white, decorated with floral patterns. This is the vase Marco Polo brought back from China in 1295, now safely kept in Saint Mark's Basilica in Venice. First and foremost, it is a concrete symbol of an obsession that began in the East as far back as the Neolithic period, an obsession destined to spread throughout the world: porcelain. For many centuries, this delicate but sturdy ceramic—sometimes so thin that, in the words of Abū Zayd al-Sīrāfī in 851, you can see "the glimmer of water" through it—remains a mystery to the West. For instance, according to Marco Polo, those who made cups and dishes "collect[ed] a type of soil from a sort of mine, gather[ed] it into large mounds, and [left] it there, in the wind, rain, and sun, without touching it, for thirty or forty years." In 1557, the scholar Giulio Cesare Scaligero claimed that "those who manufacture [porcelain] use eggshells and finely ground, pulverized shells soaked in water [ . . . ] It forms the vases that are buried underground [and are not] dug up for a hundred years." During that same period, in Florence, under the patronage of Francesco I de' Medici, "soft porcelain" is first produced. Instead of being derived from kaolin and feldspar, this emulation is 15 to 25 percent white clay and quartz: objects thus produced resemble porcelain but are much more fragile (as a matter of fact, only fifty-nine examples survive) and with various imperfections. In any case, shortly afterward, first the Portuguese, then the Dutch, start importing "true" porcelain to Europe, which immediately becomes an object of desire so expensive that it is considered "white gold."

Another in search of the secret formula is Count Ehrenfried Walther von Tschirnhaus, who, at the start of the eighteenth century, investigates the melting point for a number of substances, including kaolin. He gets nowhere, so King Augustus II forces the alchemist Johann Friedrich Böttger to assist him. Their experiments find success in 1708: now the West can also produce "its" porcelain. Von Tschirnhaus dies shortly afterward, but the king moves Böttger's laboratory to Albrechtsburg Castle, near Meissen, and by 1710, the factory is already in full swing. Thanks to sculptor and chief molder Johann Joachim Kändler, it reaches its artistic peak (one of Elizabeth II's wedding gifts is a Meissen porcelain set).

The secret of porcelain is no longer as well guarded and leaking it can be very profitable. So, within the space of a few years, we see the establishment of factories in Höchst (characterized by Johann Peter Melchior's figurines), Vienna (with baroque-style designs), Sèvres (where the "Pompadour rose" is perfected in honor of Louis XV's mistress, also patroness of the plant), and around Limoges (favored by the discovery of nearby kaolin deposits). This stretches across many countries, including Denmark, whose products are noted for their signature use of cobalt blue, and of course England, where Josiah Spode refines bone china by adding animal-bone powder to the mixture, yielding an incredibly light and translucent porcelain.

In Italy, in 1735, Marchese Carlo Ginori opens a plant in Doccia (specializing in tableware and household goods, owned by the family until 1896). In 1743, King Charles III of Spain and his wife set up the Royal Factory of Capodimonte: thanks to the discovery of kaolin deposits in Calabria, its output will outshine Germany and France in artistry and refinement. In fact, Capodimonte mainly produces small sculpture sets that show off the molders' skill and the uniquely milky tone of its porcelain.

The French Revolution and subsequent upheavals mark the end of this first glorious period of porcelain in Europe. With the disappearance of the royal courts that supported these factories—and not just financially—the law of profit takes over, prioritizing usage over art. It seems like a sad conclusion to a beautiful story, but it is not. The very fact that porcelain has become a household material may actually make its true mystery even more fascinating: a mystery Edmund de Waal comments on in his *The White Road*, pointing out that although porcelain is white and hard, "you can see the sunlight shine through . . . It is alchemy."

This evening, Palermo is a courtesan in search of lovers: a sensual, envious woman who squints to conceal her venom, a woman who wants to see and be seen. That is why she shows herself off, sparing no expense: S-shaped dresses or dresses with softer silhouettes, to be worn without a bodice, as the new French fashion demands; feather fans, lace gloves, mother-of-pearl binoculars, glowing jewelry, smiles, blown kisses, compliments.

And the Teatro Massimo is—literally—her stage, where everything happens in full view, albeit under the veil of elegant hypocrisy.

But of all the performances played out among the orchestra seats and in the boxes—the furtive gestures of lovers, mothers parading their eligible daughters, mutterings about the latest scandal, stern glances reminding others of unpaid debts—there is one, on this 15th of April, 1901, that has yet to begin and that everyone awaits with impatience. A show that could have the makings of a drama. Or else a *pochade*.

*This is going to be quite a spectacle*, architect Ernesto Basile thinks, a pince-nez perched on his aquiline nose. He is sitting in the orchestra section next to his wife and, as always before a performance, is mesmerized by the formal grace of the auditorium he designed. And while surveying the stage, he glimpses—only for a second—Ignazio around a corner of the curtain. He peers up at the Florios' box. It's still empty.

Ignazio Florio's mistress is about to make her Palermo debut in *La Bohème*—as Mimì, naturally. And Franca Florio never misses a premiere.

The lights dim. With a rustle of fabrics, the audience proceeds to seat itself. The musicians flip open their scores, and the first violin plays an A for the orchestra to tune to.

There is a murmur. Vincenzo has appeared in the Florios' box. He is now eighteen, with a sensual, mischievous face and a laid-back attitude that drives women crazy. He is seldom seen at the theater, much preferring sporting activities. His 12-horsepower FIAT is parked outside the Massimo—a vehicle in which he darts around the city, raising clouds of dust and protests from passersby.

While Vincenzo glances around inquisitively, Giovanna arrives, dressed in black silk, tight-lipped, her brow slightly furrowed. Vincenzo kisses her on the cheek and helps her to the seat in front of his before sitting down himself.

The murmur in the orchestra section grows more intense. Some spectators pretend to speak to their neighbors while stealing glances at the box; others just stare unashamedly.

The large curtain—on which Giuseppe Sciuti chose to depict Roger II's coronation procession—ripples slightly, as though breathing.

Franca appears practically out of thin air, clothed in a splendid coral dress. She stands still for a few seconds, her eyes taking in the orchestra section, accepting the glances, indifferent to these expressions of curiosity. Then she smiles at Vincenzo, who is offering her a chair, and sits down beside her mother-in-law. Her face is calm, composed, almost expressionless. Her eyes are fixed on the stage, in anticipation. Tonight's *La Bohème* might well have been staged for her alone.

Palermo falls silent.

Even the conductor, who has reached the podium in the meantime, seems to be waiting for a sign from her. From the back of the orchestra seats, someone claps, and timid applause spreads throughout the house. The conductor bows. The curtain opens.

From his corner behind the curtain, Ignazio catches sight of her.

Anger and anxiety course through him. Yes, he was hoping that Franca would find an excuse not to attend this evening, but instead, she is here. It's an act of defiance, of that he's certain.

Actually, it's revenge.

They had a fierce row when he arrived from Rome. All because of that third-rate painter and his portrait, so vulgar it makes Franca look like a dancer at a *café chantant*. That damned Boldini saw in his wife what only *he* had the right to see, starting with her long legs. And he had even gone so far as to put them on the canvas, for the eyes of those gossipmongers Stefanina Pajno, Francesca Grimaud d'Orsay, and Giulia Trigona. But the last straw had been when Franca, perfectly calm, told him that the portrait was a "*tableau fascinant.*" *Shame on her!*

Ignazio slaps the wall and starts pacing up and down, dodging technicians and a wardrobe assistant carrying an armful of costumes.

"What's the matter, Ignazio?" Lina Cavalieri asks, coming up to him and putting a hand on his arm. "You should be here to calm *me* down, but instead . . ."

He takes a deep breath. "No, no, you'll be wonderful. You'll bewitch them all just as you did me."

This woman has not merely stoked his desire but set his soul alight. From the first moment he laid eyes on her, he wanted her in his bed, and he succeeded. Never mind that her hobbies are so costly and that she forces him to follow her around Italy. She's worth every penny.

"Oh, yes, I know," Lina replies, throwing her costume shawl over her shoulders. She unfastens one button on her blouse, revealing a patch of milky skin, and stares at Ignazio with a blend of innocence and sensuality. Then she slips her fingers through his and lets him kiss her hand. Finally, she raises her head and looks at the boxes. "Is your wife here?"

Ignazio nods. "She never misses an opening night."

"I assume she knows . . ."

He hesitates before saying, "She's a woman who knows how to behave in public." His delivery is carefree, successfully masking his anger.

"I hope so," Lina says, anxiety clouding her dark eyes.

Ignazio strokes her face. "Whatever happens, just remember: you're in one of Europe's most beautiful theaters, full of people who wish only to hear you sing."

Lina would like to reply that they are mainly here to see *her* and that her singing skills are secondary, but there's no time: the stage manager signals her to approach. Ignazio pushes her away gently and watches her solemnly walk onto the stage. Lina looks more like a disgraced noblewoman than a shy, naive seamstress. But she has such a powerful presence that she even upstages a tenor like

Alessandro Bonci, loved by audiences for his virtuosity. Lina sings with sensual abandon, and with a physicality that makes up for her thin voice. She moves elegantly, smiles at Rodolfo as though he were the only man in the world, and even blushes.

> *Altro di me non saprei narrare.*
> *Sono la sua vicina*
> *Che la vien fuori d'ora a importunare . . .*

The hisses start at the end of Mimì's aria.

One, two, ten, a hundred.

The orchestra freezes. A shudder runs through the front seats; audience members exchange looks of disbelief. Some leap to their feet to applaud, but shouts and insults rain down from the gallery, joined by protests from the boxes. Amid all the screaming, shoving, and calling, the ushers struggle to calm the audience, even threatening to eject the unruliest. But to no avail.

In the general confusion, Lina turns to Ignazio, frowning, her hand tight in Bonci's: the tenor is petrified and lost.

Ignazio attempts some gestures of reassurance, but a single thought cuts through the noise. Once again, Palermo is refusing to side with him. No artist has ever had such a hostile reception. How is it possible that this city fails to understand the honor it has received? All the theaters and courts in Europe are fighting over Lina Cavalieri; she's pursued by impresarios, honored by princes and tycoons. But just look at the *Palermitani*—what are they doing?

They're hissing her.

He can smell hostility in the air now. It has the dry odor of pyrite, and just like gunpowder, it has caught fire, engendering chaos. And to think that he's done everything to make sure that

Lina would receive the right amount of applause. He contributed a tidy sum of money to the theater ushers, paid for a large claque . . .

But it seems he's not the only one to have had that idea.

It's a surprising thought.

He takes a step forward, his eyes searching for his family's box. While Vincenzo covers a sneer with his hand and his mother casts her eyes down in embarrassment, Franca stares at the stage with an unfathomable expression, the hint of a smile on her lips.

Ignazio follows the line of her gaze, like a thread. At the other end, Lina stares back.

He realizes with a shudder that he's witnessing a territorial fight between lionesses, a silent war between two fierce creatures who are testing each other, indifferent to their surroundings.

*Franca.*

She's behind this avalanche of hissing. Not directly, of course—she didn't have to be. *She has so many friends and admirers willing to please her, they probably needed just one word to unleash hell.*

*And to show everybody who is really in charge.*

As the orchestra finally resumes playing, Ignazio stands motionless. The first scene will soon be over and he'll have to comfort Lina, though that won't be hard: tears and accusations are not her style. She's a brave woman who has gotten ahead by dealing as many blows as she receives. This courage, this pride, is another thing Ignazio admires.

But he hasn't realized until this evening how far his own wife has come. As an honored, faithful mother of a family, of course, but that's not the point.

The point is that, in their marriage, he is the weak link.

And always will be.

The large hall in the High Court of Bologna is heaving, cloaked in a haze of cigarette smoke that makes everyone present open their eyes wide. Holding his hat and stick, Ignazio walks in and looks around. Before him stand the long benches occupied by reporters and lawyers; above the high-backed chairs of the judges there is the public. Many recognize him: he can tell from the murmur traveling across the courtroom and the inquisitive looks directed at him.

"This way, Signor Florio." A clerk of the court motions to him, and Ignazio steps toward him hesitantly, forcing himself to keep his eyes on the judges and not the cage where, wedged between two policemen on a wooden bench, Raffaele Palizzolo sits. Still, the two men's gazes meet for a moment and Ignazio is startled: Palizzolo's face is very gaunt and he's lost so much weight that his suit, although a well-tailored one, hangs loose on him. But his back is straight and his expression calm. He nods slightly at Ignazio and even gives him a faint smile.

Eight years have passed since the murder of Emanuele Notarbartolo: eight years during which the law has strived not to lose itself in a network of false leads, silences, and red herrings. A confused trial bordering on farce took place in Milan two years ago: the accused were two railroad workers who, since they rode the train where Notarbartolo was murdered, must have been accomplices. During that trial, however, Leopoldo, the victim's son, took the stand and, showing great courage, drew the grim portrait of a Palermo bound by ties of patronage, where people do not shy from anything—even killing—in order to maintain their privileges, and he named Palizzolo as the mastermind behind his father's murder.

In the ensuing commotion, the Chamber granted permission to proceed, and on December 8, 1899, the chief of police had Palizzolo arrested. A few days later, the Milan trial was suspended, only to resume in Bologna two months ago, on September 9, 1901.

Ignazio sits in the witness stand, crosses his legs, and rests his hands on his lap. He feels an unease he's struggling to shake off. Until now, he's managed to keep his embarrassment in check, but here in this courtroom it's not easy. He's never wanted to have anything to do with the law and, above all, can't accept that his name—as well as those of many figures from respectable Palermo society—should be dragged into this business. He's so nervous that he even quarreled with Lina yesterday for offering to come with him to Bologna, although she would have steered clear of the courtroom.

Giovanni Battista Frigotto, the presiding judge, begins the questioning. "Are you Signor Ignazio Florio, son of the late Ignazio?"

He nods.

"And your profession is . . ."

Ignazio clears his throat. "I'm an industrialist."

Frigotto raises an eyebrow. "Do you not also own a store?"

"An old family business, yes. I run a winery producing marsala, I own Navigazione Generale Italiana, and—"

"We haven't summoned you all the way from Palermo to hear about your wealth," Frigotto interjects. He regards Ignazio as though he were a jumped-up peasant, ignorant of courtroom etiquette.

"It was you who asked about my work," Ignazio replies irritably, "and in any case it's a matter of public record."

"Maybe where you come from, Signor Florio. But we're in Bologna now and hardly anyone should be expected to know the details of who you are and what you do for a living."

There is rumbling in the public gallery, even some mocking laughter. In the crowd, Ignazio spots a journalist from Catania whom he knows by sight: he's chatting to a colleague, a sarcastic smile on his lips. But when he realizes that Ignazio is looking at him, he abruptly drops his head and starts scribbling in his notebook.

"So, Signor Florio . . . You've been called here as a witness for the defense. Do you know the accused, Raffaele Palizzolo?"

He nods.

"Speak up, Signore."

He coughs. "Yes." He turns to look at Palizzolo, who gives him a gentle smile, as though apologizing for the inconvenience. But his eyes carry a warning only a fellow Sicilian could glean, and Ignazio feels a shudder run up his spine. Ignazio turns back to Frigotto, who has assumed a stern look, perhaps to intimidate him.

"Signor Florio, have you ever heard of the Mafia?"

Ignazio practically jumps. "No."

"I repeat: have you ever heard of a crime association called the Mafia?"

"And I repeat I haven't."

Frigotto pulls a face. "Strange. In the public security dispatches from Palermo, we read that you, like so many others, hire . . . certain individuals to ensure the safety of your property. And that said individuals are members of a criminal association to which the accused also allegedly belongs. In other words, the Mafia."

Ignazio shuffles on his chair. "They are workers I hire from the district I live in. Very honest people, men of honor. As for member of Parliament Palizzolo—"

"*Signor* Palizzolo," Frigotto corrects.

"—he's a very important person in Palermo, always willing to help those who turn to him in times of need."

"Must I remind you that you're under oath, Signor Florio?"

Ignazio crosses his arms. "I'm perfectly aware of that. My family has known Raffaele Palizzolo for a long time, he's even related to my wife, and—"

"—and you manipulated him so that he would obtain favors for you in Parliament. Come now, don't take offense; it's a well-known fact that you Sicilians are always helping one another, caring little whether you turn to honest men or shady characters."

A murmur rises in the courtroom. This time, the southern reporters protest these conjectures. Even Giuseppe Marchesano, one of the lawyers of the prosecution, voices his loud indignation.

Encouraged, Ignazio leans forward. "The thing is, Your Honor, a 'storekeeper' like me must think about the future of his business and knows that a loud voice is required to be heard by the institutions. Member of Parliament Palizzolo has always had Sicily's interests at heart—"

"—and those of the Florios!" a voice from the public shouts. Ignazio turns abruptly and recognizes the journalist: he's from Palermo and writes for *La Battaglia*, the Socialist newspaper owned by Alessandro Tasca di Cutò.

Marchesano gets to his feet. "Signor Florio, we called you here in order to clarify a specific instance. Is it true that Raffaele Palizzolo offered to sell you a property called Villa Gentile for you to use to build homes for your factory workers?"

Ignazio frowns. "Yes, but I declined."

"Why?"

"Oh, I can't remember."

"If Palizzolo had asked to borrow a large sum of money from you, would you have lent it to him?"

"If I could spare it, yes, of course. As I've already said, he's someone I know, and so does my family—"

"Do you think Palizzolo is capable of committing murder or of orchestrating one?"

Ignazio stares, eyes wide open. "No, absolutely not!" he practically shouts. "Besides, it was only after that strange trial in Milan that his name came up, and—"

"Thank you," Marchesano says, interrupting. "I have no more questions, Your Honor."

"You may go, Signor Florio," Frigotto says without even looking at him.

Ignazio is so annoyed, he barely notices the thick fog outside the courthouse. He strides across the square, raising and lowering his stick. *How dare the judge treat me like that? Besides, what does he know about certain things? You have to live in Sicily to understand. You have to eat salt and dust, swallow if you don't want to be chewed up, become a dog if you don't want to be gnawed on like a bone . . .* He suddenly stops and takes a deep breath of cold air. This fog, which hides the city from him, turning buildings, passersby, and carriages into ghosts, draws a despondent sigh from him. *No, you northerners know nothing. You think you're holy and forget that one can only reach heaven by knowing sin. And in Sicily, the one sin no one escapes is that of knowing and being unable to speak.*

"Donna Franca . . ." The maid stands in the doorway, motionless, a hand on the jamb. "Sorry to disturb you, but your daughter is unwell. She has a fever."

Franca is sitting at the dressing table in her bedroom in Villa

Igiea. She looks up from the gold mesh bag into which she is replacing the jewels she wore last night at the Lanza di Mazzarinos' dinner. She prefers to do it herself, not trusting the maids or even Diodata.

The room is cluttered with suitcases and trunks, and the lady's maid is packing day and evening clothes, robes, and shoes. Tomorrow, Franca, her mother, and the children are traveling to Bavaria, having spent the month of July in Tunis. Earlier, in May, they were in Favignana to watch the *mattanza* with the Trigonas and the Duke and Duchess of Palma, Giulio and Bice, the duke's brother, Ciccio Lampedusa, Carlo di Rudinì, Francesca Grimaud d'Orsay, and other relatives and friends, including the D'Ondes cousins and Ettore De Maria Bergler. They were very pleasant days, marked by strolls around the island and boat trips, but also by long, lazy chats and informal dinners.

At least until Empress Eugenia, Napoleon III's widow, arrived. Polite and melancholy, the elderly woman conquered everybody's affection and observed the *mattanza* with great interest, even letting out the odd cry of surprise. Naturally, Franca attended to every detail of her stay and threw a sumptuous dinner, for which she received extensive praise. The empress congratulated her in particular: just a few weeks earlier, Franca had been appointed lady-in-waiting at the court of Queen Elena.

Not being of noble birth, however, Ignazio had not been appointed a gentleman of the king, and that had significantly rankled him. An irritation that only piled onto his recent disappointment with the outcome of the Palizzolo trial—which ended with a heavy, thirty-year jail sentence—and the inconvenience of having to delay his departure for Favignana because he had to attend the solemn ceremonies for the anniversary of Francesco Crispi's death a year earlier, on August 11, 1901. And so, in the blazing sun, Ignazio had joined a procession of Chamber and Senate representatives, and, upon reaching Capuchin cemetery, was forced to endure not only a never-ending commemorative speech but also the display of Crispi's recently embalmed corpse.

*You became a mummy and a mummy you'll stay*, Ignazio thought, giving him a final glance and wiping the sweat off himself.

So he arrived in Favignana in a foul mood and let off steam by hovering around Bice in front of both her husband and Franca. And Bice certainly didn't dismiss him.

As usual, Franca looked the other way. Being recognized as a lady-in-waiting had renewed her pride, as well as satisfied her sense of revenge. She was no longer just the beautiful wife and mother of the heir to one of Europe's wealthiest families: she now had every right to host monarchs in her home and enjoy their esteem. One fling more or less—what did it matter?

The empress also wished to say goodbye to the children before leaving. Franca smiles with tenderness at the memory of Giovannuzza's and Baby Boy's drowsy faces, and of Bice's little Giuseppe Tomasi, dressed to the nines at seven in the morning to be presented to the royal guest before she boarded her yacht. Igiea, however, was left sleeping in her cradle.

She rouses herself. "Who's unwell? Igiea or Giovannuzza?" she asks with a hint of annoyance. If one of her daughters is ill, they will have to postpone their departure for at least a couple of days, and she really wants to escape the heat of Palermo. And Ignazio, whose presence has been insufferable of late. She needs fresh air, people, and mirth.

"Signorina Giovannuzza." The maid stands waiting, her fingers interlaced, and appears nervous.

"I'm coming."

Franca crosses the rooms in her robe, the silk weaving around her ankles, her footsteps muffled by the rugs. She enters Giovannuzza's room and finds the little girl in bed, cheeks flushed with fever, eyes puffy and half shut. It isn't the first time it's struck Franca that she looks older than eight, perhaps because of that melancholy air she's always had, or maybe because she's tall and slender, like her mother.

"*Maman . . .*" Giovannuzza mutters hoarsely, stretching out her hand.

"How are you feeling, my love?"

"Mmm . . . My head really hurts and . . . *ich habe Durst . . .*" Franca looks for the bottle of water on the bedside table.

The governess rushes to a table in the middle of the room, pours a glass of water, and hands it to Franca before returning to the foot of the bed.

Franca helps Giovannuzza prop herself on the pillows. The child takes a sip, but then violently coughs the liquid up onto the bedsheets.

"It hurts everywhere, *Mamma*," she whispers and bursts into plaintive tears.

Franca mops her face with a handkerchief and strokes it. She's hot. Too hot.

Something shudders inside her. Giovannuzza has always been a source of concern, but this doesn't seem like one of her usual mild fevers.

"Call the doctor," she tells the governess. "Not ours; he'd take too long. The hotel one." She kisses the child and holds her tight. "I'm here," she whispers, rocking her. "*Hab keine Angst, mein Schatz . . .* Don't be scared, my love . . ."

The doctor, who arrives shortly afterward, is a thin, serious-looking man with a face marked by years and experience. Franca, who has changed her clothes, watches the examination with growing anxiety. The doctor smiles at Giovannuzza and treats her very gently: you can tell from his expression that he is tense.

They exit the room and stand behind the door. Maruzza arrives.

"Well?" Franca asks, tormenting her handkerchief.

"I'm afraid it's typhoid fever," the doctor replies. "Her eyes are puffy, she has a high fever, her reflexes are slow . . . All symptoms of infection."

Franca puts her hands to her mouth and stares at the closed door. "What . . . how could she have contracted it?"

He opens his arms wide. "She could have drunk infected water or eaten something contaminated. Who knows? No use wondering how she got it now. If anything, make sure to isolate her from others and keep her clean. Tell the servants to boil the laundry they use for her."

Franca keeps staring at the doctor, bewildered. "I'll see to that," Maruzza says, squeezing Franca's arm.

"Meanwhile, I can do a bit of bloodletting to ease her headache, and I'll administer twenty-five drops of iodine in a glass of milk, since apparently it's . . ."

Franca isn't listening. Despite the heat, she feels as though a layer of ice has settled over her. "My baby . . ." she murmurs. "My Giovannuzza . . ." She touches the door, as though her caress could reach her daughter.

The doctor bows his head. "You might as well know right away, Donna Franca: it's going to be a difficult illness to tackle. My advice is to take the girl somewhere less sultry, where she can breathe more easily, away from the humidity of the sea."

Franca pulls herself together and clears her throat. "She can't travel, can she?"

The doctor shakes his head.

"But what if we took her to our Villa ai Colli, outside Palermo?"

"Yes, that would be better." He squeezes her hand and smiles. "Let me know."

Giovannuzza is transferred from Villa Igiea to Villa ai Colli by automobile. Vincenzo drives, joking with his niece in an attempt to make her laugh. This dark-eyed little girl has a special place in his heart, and she has always returned her uncle's kind-hearted affection. But now, nestled in a bundle of blankets and sheets, Giovannuzza can only manage a few faint smiles. For most of the journey, she is lethargic, breathing with difficulty, and every now and again moans and hugs her beloved Fanny, her porcelain doll, dressed all in pink. She falls asleep halfway through the journey. Franca tucks her in and removes the doll.

*What's wrong? What's happened to you, my little one?* she thinks, feeling her heart twist in a vise of anxiety.

The vehicle stops in a cloud of dust outside the entrance to the villa.

"You'll be better off here," Vincenzo tells Giovannuzza, picking her up in his arms to carry her into the house. "As soon as you're well, I'll take you out for a spin. We'll drive so fast your hat'll fly off, and we'll go as far as Cape Gallo, to see the fishermen come back from the sea."

"Thank you, Uncle," she says, reaching out to pull his thin mustache, a game they've played since she first managed to climb onto his lap. Then she turns, and her eyes search for her mother.

Franca comes to her. "What is it, my love?"

"Fanny . . ."

Franca turns to Maruzza, who is holding another blanket and a basket of toys from which the doll protrudes. She hands it to Giovannuzza, who hugs it. "Fanny's also cold, so cold . . ." she murmurs.

The maids waiting outside the villa hear her and, without waiting for Franca's order, run to warm the child's bed.

⌒

That evening, when Ignazio opens the door to the room prepared for Giovannuzza, he is taken aback by the balsamic aromas that fill the air, intended to help the girl breathe more easily. The child's face is like a red blotch on the pillow, while Franca's is like marble.

He goes to his daughter and kisses her, and she opens her eyes slightly. "Oh, Daddy," she says. "I feel awful . . ."

"I know, dear heart," he replies, resting a hand on her cheek and immediately withdrawing it because her skin is so hot. He looks up at Franca. She's sitting on the other side of the bed, her anxious eyes fixed on him. It's the first time in ages that she's asked him to help close the wounds gaping in her heart. It's obvious that she wishes she could take her daughter's place so as not to see her suffer so much.

Ignazio, too, is terrified by the question he reads in her eyes. They stare at each other for a moment, then he motions to Franca to follow him out of the room.

No sooner has he closed the door than she bursts into tears. "She's very ill, Ignazio, and I don't know what to do. God help us . . ."

Without replying, Ignazio holds her tight and strokes her hair, something he hasn't done in a long time, a once loving gesture that is now only comforting, but at least it momentarily succeeds in soothing their anxiety. Franca welcomes him with a sigh and relaxes against his chest.

"I'm scared," she says in a breath.

*I'm scared, too*, he thinks, unable to speak, because that smell brings back the memory of the room where his brother Vincenzo died, and the one where his father passed away. The knot in his stomach silences him: the acrid stench of a body trying to shield itself from disease, imprisoned in a stillness too similar to death.

He can't bear the thought that his daughter could die, that she might share his brother's fate. So when, the next day, Giovannuzza slips into a deep, at times delirious, slumber, Ignazio reaches for the only weapons he has: power and money.

He sends for Augusto Murri, lecturer in clinical medicine at the University of Bologna. He is a medical genius, the author of fundamental treatises on fevers and brain damage, renowned both in Italy and abroad. Everyone—friends, acquaintances, and doctors—says he is the best. The only one who could save her.

As the whole family gathers at Villa ai Colli, Ignazio calls him to Palermo. He arranges a special train to Naples for him, from there a steamer to Sicily, and, finally, an automobile to the villa.

Meanwhile, outside the gates, Palermo holds its breath. A little girl, an innocent soul, is ill. Disagreements, envy, and gossip are put aside; servants arrive to ask for news on behalf of their masters, bringing notes with wishes for a speedy recovery or indicating that rosaries are being said for Giovannuzza. But the news is always worse. The child is unconscious for prolonged periods, isn't eating, and hardly recognizes anyone besides her mother and the grandmother whose name she bears.

By the time Dr. Murri arrives, Giovannuzza has been unconscious for several hours. Franca is at her bedside, pale, overwhelmed, her black locks hanging around her face, eyes puffy from crying, and a dirty handkerchief in her hands. She has repeatedly tried to wake her daughter, to give her a sip of milk or moisten her parched lips with cold water, but the little girl, *her* little girl, is no longer responsive.

Augusto Murri is a sixty-year-old who walks with a slight stoop and gives off an air of quiet confidence. His hair is receding at the temples, and he has a bushy handlebar mustache. He signals to Franca to leave the room, but she just straightens up on the chair and keeps staring at him. Ignazio joins her.

They will not move from here.

Murri auscultates the child's chest, checks her reflexes, and tries to stir her. He feels a lump in his throat, seeing the expression on the faces of these parents about whom even he has read in the society columns. But the trips, the jewels, the splendid parties are meaningless now. Now they are just a father and a mother brought together by all-encompassing fear.

When the maids come to straighten the bed, the elderly physician motions the couple to follow him outside. In the corridor, the two grandmothers, Giovanna and Costanza, stand with Maruzza, hands clutching the crowns of their rosaries.

He clears his throat and speaks slowly, looking down. "I'm sorry. I don't think it's typhoid fever." He makes a long, heavy pause. "It's meningitis."

"No!" Franca topples, and before Ignazio can reach her, Costanza rushes to put her arm around her waist to keep her from collapsing. Maruzza hastens over, too. The women cling to one another, heads together, unable to speak. Silent tears run down Franca's face, her eyes blank, her face ashen.

The word is like a rock that sinks to the bottom of her consciousness. *Meningitis, meningitis, meningitis . . .* She starts trembling, and her mother holds her tighter, bursting into tears.

Ignazio is motionless, feeling caught in a vortex that sucks in all the air, the people, the objects, even the light. "But then . . ." he says but is unable to continue. He glances out of the window that overlooks the garden and for a moment he thinks he can see his father strolling about with Vincenzo in the orange grove he loved so much.

The doctor's voice stirs him out of his reverie. "We'll administer the required treatment. There's still time for intervention, and we'll do our best to give her help and relief. But just as no two things are identical, no two patients are alike either, so little Giovanna must be attended to very carefully, minute by minute. I have to be frank, however: the chances of recovery are very low. Even if she does recover, her speech or movements could be severely impaired." He looks at Franca, who seems about to faint. "You must be very strong, Signora. You have difficult days ahead."

Franca's hand reaches out for Ignazio's.

She needs to feel near her daughter's father. In spite of all that has happened in recent years, she wants the certainty that they can still be united. That they can traverse another stretch of road together. That love hasn't been completely extinguished. That they will face this grief side by side. That he won't leave her on her own in the darkest hours. That the void opening before them won't swallow them whole.

A thread of hope remains, and she clings to it. To that slender thread. Will the illness have consequences? No matter—they'll tackle them together. She'll stay with Giovannuzza and help her become the woman she has always imagined.

She can't and won't understand that there's a fine line between illusion and hope, and that when love overlaps with despair it can conjure the most painful lie.

⟶

Shortly before dawn on August 14, 1902, Franca wakes up after dozing off next to Giovannuzza. In the garden of the villa, the birds are chirping, greeting the day and the still faint light that filters through the white curtains.

The room is cool, and a delicate scent of grass has chased away the smell of the fumigants.

The little girl is lying on her side, her back to them, very still, her black braids on the pillow. Franca leans over to look at her and touches her gently: she feels cooler and less flushed. The governess has fallen asleep on the chair, and the house is immersed in silence.

For a moment, Franca thinks that perhaps the treatment has been effective. That the fever has dropped and Giovannuzza is going to wake up. Who cares if she'll limp or speak in an odd way? They'll find the best doctors to treat her, they'll take her to France or England, they'll plan long stays in Favignana, where she'll be able to breathe sea air and heal, away from prying eyes. Just as long as she's alive. Alive.

She touches her cheek once again.

That's when she realizes that her little girl is not cool but cold. That she's not pale but ashen. That all the dreams, wishes, and aspirations she had for her are shattered. That Giovannuzza will never grow up, that Franca will never see her in a wedding dress or be at her side when she becomes a mother.

Fanny, her porcelain doll, has ended up at the bottom of the bed. Franca picks it up and places it in the child's arms. She caresses her again and murmurs an "I love you" that will have no response, because her child will never again throw her arms around her and say, "I love you, too, *Mamma!*"

Something cracks open in Franca's soul and grief gushes out, spreading, choking her.

Her daughter, Giovanna Florio, is dead.

That's when Franca starts screaming.

⌒

In the tormented days that follow Giovannuzza's burial, Ignazio attempts to help Franca in the only way he knows how: by trying to take her away from Palermo, by keeping her far from the places where the memory of their eldest child is rooted. But when he asks her where she wants to go—London? Paris? Bavaria? Possibly Egypt?—Franca stares at him blankly for a long time, then utters one word: "Favignana."

So they board the *Virginia*, the steam launch they use to get to the island, and find themselves alone in the large house outside the harbor, not far from the *tonnara*. Franca goes out early in the morning and returns home only in the late afternoon; she says she goes "walking," and by evening she's so tired that she retires without dining. Ignazio tries to occupy his days with letters from Palermo concerning the Oretea, but he's worried.

So, one morning he decides to follow her.

His wife's figure, even smaller in the black outfit, moves like a ghost along the paths leading to the mountain behind the *tonnara*. She walks, gesticulates, sometimes laughs. Every now and then she stops, looks at the sea, then turns back. Again and again.

It's only when Ignazio draws closer that he understands.

She's talking to Giovannuzza, telling her that her mother loves her, that her dolls are waiting for her, that next summer they'll all go bathing together, that she'll gift her an evening dress for her birthday. She calls her softly, the way she used to when the little girl played hide-and-seek with the children of their guests.

Franca wanted to come to Favignana because she was happy with Giovannuzza here.

It's a desperate, heart-wrenching way to be close to her.

Ignazio retraces his steps, a pang in his heart and tears stinging his eyes. Death hasn't just taken his daughter away, it's now sapping his wife's peace of mind and beauty, and he cannot allow that—no. Too many things have already been stolen from him, and he can't even bear to think about what would happen if Franca lost her mind. It's better, a thousand times better, to go home.

But, once in Palermo, Franca shuts herself in the child's room in the Olivuzza for hours on end. She has given instructions for no one to touch it; she doesn't even want Giovannuzza's clothes to be removed from the closet. It still smells of her, an aroma of talcum powder and violet, and her hairbrushes are still on the dressing table. When she closes her eyes, she can hear her walking about the room with her light footsteps. She sits on the bed, one hand on the pillow, the other clutching a porcelain doll. Not Fanny. Fanny is with her, in the coffin.

This is how her mother-in-law finds her one October afternoon. Giovanna has led the children in prayers for their sister "who's gone to heaven with the angels," then played with them for a while. Both Baby Boy, who's four and a half years old, and Igiea, who's two and a half, are really suffering in their mother's absence and are moody and restless.

Giovanna sits down quietly next to Franca. Both are dressed in black, one stiffly, unfamiliar grief gnawing her flesh, the other stooped from the weight of years. Franca lowers her eyes and holds the doll tighter. She doesn't want to hear that she must pull herself together, that she must be strong because she has two children who need her attention, that in any case she can have more babies. Too many people have told her that, starting with Giulia and Maruzza. All that achieved was to make her angrier.

Because you can't die at the age of eight. And you don't have a child to replace another.

Giovanna holds her silver and coral rosary in one hand and clasps a photograph to her chest with the other. She shows it to Franca. "I don't know if you've ever seen this picture of my Vincenzino. He was twelve." She holds out the photograph of a little boy with a shy, gentle expression, dressed as a musketeer. "He was a beautiful *picciriddu*. *Sangu meo*, he was so sweet natured. He was being groomed to head this family, and my husband, *recamatierna*, would make him study and was always encouraging him. But he was too frail, too frail." Her voice breaks.

Franca opens her eyes and turns to her.

Looking at Giovanna is like seeing her own reflection.

She listens to her in spite of herself. Her grief, she thinks, is one of a kind and belongs to her alone. She lays the doll down on the bed and asks, "How did you feel afterward?"

"As though my skin had been removed." Giovanna slides her hand over the bed and caresses the doll's face as though it's her granddaughter's. "The Lord should have taken me instead of her," she says. "I'm old and my life is over. But she—she was a flower."

Franca looks up. On that old woman's face, its gray skin and lined cheeks, she senses the bitterness of a life without love or tenderness, and a resignation perhaps even more painful than grief. And she realizes that she has never seen her mother-in-law truly smile except when she was with her grandchildren. Especially Giovannuzza.

"You'll always think about her. About everything she could have done but will never do, about the fact that you won't see her grow up and will never find out what she could have been. *T'addumannirai soccu fa*—you'll wonder what she's doing—and only afterward remember she's dead. You'll see clothes, toys . . . *cose che ci vulissi accattari*—things you want to buy her—and remember you can't. Those are the real wounds, and they never heal, they always stay open."

"Will it never end, then?" Franca says in a breath.

Giovanna responds in the same way. "Never. I also lost a husband and God only knows how much I loved him . . . But losing a child is beyond anything one can imagine." She raises her hand to her chest and clenches it in a fist. "*Comu si t'ascippassero u cori.*"

Like someone tearing your heart out. Yes, that's how you feel. For a moment, Franca relives the birth of her daughter, when she felt her slide out of her. Maybe that was already when she began to lose her.

Giovanna taps her on the shoulder and gets to her feet. She's expected for dinner, she says gently. She can refuse condolence visits, but she must feed herself for the sake of those who are left.

Franca nods: yes, she'll come down to eat. But once she's alone again, she slowly lets herself slide onto the bed and curl up. The lamp her mother-in-law left on illuminates her sharp profile. She puts a hand over her eyes, wishing she could no longer see, or hear, or deal with anything or anyone. She wishes she were as old as Giovanna, old and resigned, so that she could no longer feel anything besides the pains of a body unable to contest the passage of time. Instead, she's twenty-nine years old and the creature who gave her more love than anyone else in her life has been snatched away from her. And she must go on.

⌁

"Excuse me, Don Ignazio . . ." There's a servant waiting by the door of the green salon. "The Prince di Cutò is here. Shall I let him in?"

Ignazio abruptly looks up from the papers he has been perusing. He forgot about this engagement. He massages his tired face. "Yes, of course."

Alessandro Tasca di Cutò appears shortly afterward and stands in the doorway, waiting, fiddling with the brim of his hat, looking at Baby Boy, who's on the rug, playing with a tin train.

"Step in," Ignazio says, rising from the couch. "Thank you for coming."

Alessandro approaches. "I've come to express my condolences. I've already spoken to your mother-in-law and had hoped to see your wife—"

"Franca is still very distressed and isn't receiving anyone," Ignazio replies vacantly. He runs his fingers through his son's blond curls, and the child immediately raises his head and reaches out with his little arms. He's more restless than usual, doing everything to keep his father's attention, hating to part from him.

"I know," Alessandro quickly says. "My sister Giulia told me. That's why I put it off for so long, and for that I apologize."

Ignazio turns to the little table where he left some documents, slams shut a file labeled CAPRERA, and says, "Let's go into the garden—that way I can let the *picciriddu* run around. And I think you also enjoy . . . being outdoors."

Alessandro pulls a face without a reply. He's used to these digs by now. He spent five months in Ucciardone Prison, following a sentence for slandering the former mayor of Palermo, Emanuele Paternò, whom he had accused of mismanaging the city's administration. The sentence triggered many protests in solidarity with the man everyone now calls "the red prince" for his Socialist notions.

"Come on, Baby Boy, let's go outside." The child immediately grabs Ignazio's hand and drags him toward the French doors. Once they are in the garden, Baby Boy runs ahead, shouting that he wants to get on the velocipede Uncle Vincenzo has given him. With a nod, Ignazio signals a servant to keep an eye on his son.

The two men walk in silence for a while beneath a sky stained with gray clouds. Alessandro speaks first. "I'm glad to see that at least you're back at work."

"I try." Ignazio pulls his eyes away from the stone bench outside the aviary, where Giovannuzza would often sit with her mother. "Besides, there's much to do. And Casa Florio never stops."

"Of course. Business waits for no man, sadly. I see you're working on the new steamer, the *Caprera* . . . When are you thinking of launching?"

*The red prince is certainly far-seeing*, Ignazio thinks with annoyance, but he has no intention of revealing anything. And he certainly doesn't want to make public the tension between him and Erasmo Piaggio or the fact that he's losing trust in the Genoese administrator because of his many—too many?—interests up north . . . The heart of NGI is in Palermo and in Palermo it must stay. "Next year, I hope," he finally replies. "But first I have a few . . . issues to resolve."

"And how is the consortium for citrus production? I know you've secured some advantageous sales contracts."

"Not enough to cover the costs . . . But that's a secondary issue, at least for me. What I'm interested in is that the shipyard be finally completed: building the *Caprera* will be proof that we can compete with Tuscan and Ligurian yards on an equal footing. But it's so hard to persuade those who have no intention of listening to you . . . Rome *in primis*, obviously."

"Indeed, there's cautious optimism among the workers. After last year's redundancies—"

"Still harping on that?" Ignazio lashes. "Aren't you tired of talking about it? Or is it that you don't know how to spend your evenings at the Trade Union Center you Socialists wanted so much?"

Alessandro stiffens. "You know perfectly well that the Trade Union Center was wanted, as you put it, principally by Garibaldi Bosco. And he's certainly not hostile to either you or Casa Florio. On the contrary—"

"Right, whereas you're convinced that everything that doesn't work in Sicily is the fault of entrepreneurs like myself, who are full of wrong notions, and that all it takes is to call on ordinary people to unite for the situation to change. You've written about this over and over in *La Battaglia*."

"You can't bear that a newspaper proves *L'Ora* wrong at least once a week, can you? I've often wondered what you did to prompt Morello to go back to *La Tribuna* and make that Sardinian Medardo Riccio the paper's editor in chief . . ."

A metallic clang disrupts the peace of the garden. The parrots in the aviary start flitting about, and a small flock of doves rises from the palm trees. A black automobile appears in the avenue, raising a cloud of pebbles and dust, and stops in front of them.

Vincenzo, wearing a cloth cap and dust glasses, gets out and shakes Alessandro's hand. If he picks up on the tension between the guest and his brother, he doesn't let on. "I'm back from the station. Everything's ready for the departure, at last."

Ignazio frowns. "Where are you going?"

"The Côte d'Azur. I'm bored with Palermo. And after what happened to the *nica*, the Olivuzza is too gloomy."

Alessandro gives a faint smile halfway between irony and sadness. Not even a serious bereavement can hamper the fun-loving habits of the younger Florio.

Ignazio indicates something behind his brother. "And who's going to see to *that* work?" he asks irritably.

Smoothing his hair with his hand, Vincenzo turns and looks at the building being erected amid a chaos of wooden planks, stones, bricks, and lime pails. It looks more like a fairy-tale castle than a villa, with two winding staircases and cast-iron merlons on the balconies and the roofs, over which stands a turret. "Oh, yes, the *villino!*" he exclaims. "Basile has outdone himself, don't you think?" he says to Alessandro. "And I definitely didn't make it easy for him," he adds with a snicker. "I wanted something that would suggest a castle, with baroque but also Romanesque elements, typical of the south, but equally Nordic . . . Not to mention the inside: I asked him to make sure one could go upstairs straight from the garage, without going outdoors, and he did as I asked! He's basically managed to create something truly original, like I wanted." He looks at the little villa with pride. "But it's practically finished, and I don't think those men on the scaffolding need me."

"With what this kind of building costs," Alessandro mutters, "you could feed tens of *those men*'s families for a year."

"Probably. But in all honesty, I don't care two hoots about them," Vincenzo replies, smiling at Alessandro's outraged expression.

"Still acting like a *picciriddu*," Ignazio says with a sigh.

"That's what life is: pursuing a new pleasure once the old one bores you." Vincenzo looks at his brother again. "And I don't intend to miss out on a single one."

After Alessandro Tasca di Cutò has left, Ignazio goes home, mulling over his brother's final words. Yes, that daredevil's right. Perhaps it's a little insouciance that Franca needs. The odd smile and occasion for cheer. His thoughts turn to certainty by the time he reaches her apartments, finding them plunged in a semi-darkness similar to the stagnation in his mother's rooms. It's as though the walls are oozing sadness, exhaling illness.

Life in this house has become a burden.

The Côte d'Azur, the sun, sea, warmth, friends . . . He's sure Franca will resist at first. When she does, he'll write to the Rothschilds, who generally spend their winters on the Côte d'Azur, and ask them to coax her. It'll take him a while, but he'll manage it: they'll board their train, go to the hotel in Beaulieu-sur-Mer Franca likes so much, the Hôtel Métropole, and spend Christmas there.

He, too, needs to go back to living.

Rocked by the train, Franca has fallen asleep on the navy-blue banquette, her head resting on Ignazio's shoulder. For the past few days, she seems to be reaching out to him, as if she finds a little solace only through contact with her husband. In bed, she's unable to fall asleep except in his embrace. Ignazio is confused. He has always lacked the insight to interpret women's feelings. He understands their desires, their urges, picks up on their sensual messages, anticipates their bad moods, but not their need for affection. Not that. It's expressed in a language foreign to him.

Still, he senses that Giovannuzza's death—she was their firstborn, the one who made them a family—may open a chasm between them, and he can't bear the thought of that. It would be yet more evidence of weakness, of the umpteenth failure. Admittedly in private, not public, but he now desperately clings to the few certainties he has. And, for better or worse, Franca is a certainty, so he responds to her requests for affection. He becomes available, devotes time, attention, and tenderness to her. *D'Annunzio's right*, he thinks, *my wife is unique.* All this grief has affected neither her beauty nor her grace. And despite everything, he loves her. In his own way, but he does love her.

One evening, shortly after their arrival at the Hôtel Métropole, Ignazio catches himself looking at her in a way he hasn't for some time. Franca is sitting at the dressing table; she has sent Diodata away and is removing pins from her hair. The shawl-like collar of her robe barely covers her neck. Her face is serious, but her expression is calm and engrossed. They dined in their room, alone, and Franca even got through an entire bowl of fish soup, something she hadn't managed in a while. He goes to her, puts his hands on her shoulders, and caresses them as far as the arms, pulling the robe down to her elbows. Her skin puckers under his fingers. Franca's lips part, and she stops, hands clutching the comb.

Ignazio hesitates, then touches her neck with his lips.

He wants her as he hasn't in a long time.

Franca shudders. Is she frightened? Ignazio can't tell. It's as if he, a seasoned seducer, no longer knows how to treat the frail creature his wife has become. He lifts a hand and strokes her face, and she abandons herself to his caress, her eyes closed. She seems uncertain, as though afraid to let go. Then she turns, searching for his lips, letting him help her chase away the grief of death with love. And restore some life to her.

~~~

Since that night, Franca has looked more serene. They have gone on a couple of excursions with Vincenzo—although he always drives too fast in that beloved automobile of his—and they spent New Year's Eve with their children: Baby Boy wanted to dip his lips in the champagne, but then pulled a face that made everyone laugh; clinging to her mother, Igiea watched the fireworks, eyes agog, and after a couple of frightened shrieks, laughed and clapped her little hands.

Now they're on the grounds of the Métropole, a huge garden with palm and citrus trees that stretches almost as far as the sea. In the January sun, Franca is reading, reclining in a deck chair, her black lace-trimmed dress bunched around her legs; Baby Boy is chasing after pigeons; and Ignazio is walking around with a Verascope in his hand. It's a present from Vincenzo, who's been dabbling in photography for the past few months. Ignazio hopes it'll bring a smile to his wife's face.

Every so often, Franca raises her eyes from her book and looks at her husband, who keeps frowning, seemingly incapable of making up his mind when it comes to taking a picture. Baby Boy suddenly grabs him by the leg and starts yelling that he, too, wants a *toto*-camera. Since Giovannuzza died, he has been throwing lots of tantrums and is always on edge. Ignazio ignores him for a while, but when the child hurls himself on the ground and starts beating with his fists, he scolds him.

Rushing to him, even Franca is unable to calm him down. Impatiently, Ignazio calls over the nanny to take the child away before he disturbs the other guests. The young woman comes running, her golden plaits bouncing.

"*Occupez-vous de lui, s'il vous plaît. Peut-être qu'il a faim . . .*" Franca says.

The nanny shakes her head. "*Il vient de manger, Madame Florio. Mais il n'a pas beaucoup dormi . . .*" She bends down and picks up Baby Boy. "*Que se passe-t-il, mon ange? Allons faire une petite sieste, hein?*" She walks away with the child, who keeps screaming and trying to free himself.

Franca returns to her deck chair, followed by Ignazio, who sits down beside her, taking her hand. Her large green eyes aren't yet fully calm, but the despair seems to have abated.

*Maybe the chasm between us is closing*, Ignazio thinks. *Maybe there's hope for us yet.* He often repeats this to himself, while trying not to stare too long at the hotel's charming female guests.

Franca motions him to come closer. "We've received an invitation from the Rothschilds for this evening. Dinner and a card game, a small get-together for just a few close friends."

"Would you like to go, Franca darling? Do you feel up to it?"

"Only if you'd like to go, too."

He gives her a light kiss on the forehead and nods. After the first, blissful few years of marriage, Franca gradually stopped relying on him, at times even going against his wishes, as was the case with the Boldini portrait. He felt her drifting away from him and did nothing to stop her. On the contrary: he replaced her with women who were apparently more passionate, liberated . . . fresher. Like his brother, he always needed something new, strong emotions, to feel free of any ties. But now he realizes that, besides love, Franca has always given him something else: respect. A respect the world insists on denying him, or rather accords only to the name he carries or his wealth. No matter what he's done or said, Franca has always remained above any pettiness. Unlike others, and despite everything, she has trusted him and *still does*. Even though he's been so harsh, so . . . ungrateful toward her. Mulling over this, Ignazio goes to write the Rothschilds a note accepting their invitation.

He instinctively turns to look at her and finds in her eyes something of the love he feared he had lost forever.

⌒

This evening, Franca wears a plain black dress and a long string of pearls. As Diodata dresses her hair, she catches Ignazio's eyes in the mirror and sees in them an admiration that warms her heart.

Before leaving, they drop into the makeshift nursery. Igiea is sitting on the rug with a doll, obviously sleepy but unable to rest because Baby Boy keeps throwing tantrums. He throws toys on the floor, refuses to put on his nightgown, and yells that he wants to go to the beach. He wriggles out of the nanny's grip, hugging his mother's legs. Franca bends down to pat him, trying to placate him, but the child won't listen.

"Enough already, Ignazino!" his father says. The child bursts into tears.

Face flushed, the nanny picks him up and speaks to him gently, then murmurs to Franca, exasperated, "He didn't even want to eat, *alors* . . ."

Franca shakes her head. "Try reading him a story. That usually calms him down." She bends down to kiss Igiea. "We have to go. It's getting late."

Ignazio follows her out the door. He gives her his arm, and they walk in silence along the Métropole's luxurious corridors and down the stairs, before the admiring eyes of other guests. Ignazio stiffens, but Franca seems indifferent. When he takes her hand in the car, though, it feels cold, and he realizes she's been as nervous as him.

"Are you all right?" he asks.

She nods, intertwines her fingers with his, and squeezes.

The tenderness, that old sweetness that warms his heart, is still there, a tiny flame that persists. They are finding each other again. Stronger than before.

The evening passes calmly, amid chatter and gossip about the latest scandal: the Archduchess Louise of Austria, wife of the Crown Prince of Saxony, mother of six children and expecting a seventh, has run off with André Giron, her eldest son's tutor, causing deep dismay in all the courts of Europe. After dinner, Franca and the women play faro, while Ignazio follows the men to the *fumoir*. There, the topic of conversation is the duel that took place two weeks ago in Nice, in the garden of Count Rohozinski's villa: two French fencing masters had boasted that their school was the best, and two offended Italian masters had challenged them. Ignazio is bombarded with questions because everybody knows that Vincenzo lent the duelists and seconds the automobiles that allowed them to escape the police when they tried to stop the duel. But he knows nothing of the ins and outs of the matter and downplays it, claiming that the only duels he is interested in are those at sea.

It's almost midnight when a valet from the Métropole arrives. He stops at the door, panting, his hands shaking. He asks for the Florios and says they must return to the hotel immediately.

Ignazio appears. "What's this about?"

The valet shakes his head. "*Retournez à l'hôtel, je vous en prie,*

*Monsieur Florio. Vite, vite!"* he practically shouts. *"Vite, vite!"* he repeats, running away.

Meanwhile, Franca has joined Ignazio and looks at him, perplexed. "What . . . what happened?"

"I don't know."

While the guests and hosts gather around, worried, a car is called to take them back to the Métropole.

Neither of them speaks in the car. Various theories crowd Ignazio's mind. An automobile accident involving Vincenzo? A burglary or a fire at the Olivuzza? What if something's happened to his mother, who's now elderly and tired? It would be awful to think of her alone and far away . . . Has something happened to one of his companies? *No, it's the middle of the night.*

As they near the hotel, he feels his anxiety rising. He fiddles with his father's ring, clenches and unclenches his hand. Next to him, Franca is as white as a sheet, fidgeting in her seat, crushing her gloves.

When they get out of the car, the manager of the Métropole comes running toward them along the red carpet. He grabs Ignazio's hands and says something.

Even years from now, he will be unable to remember most of the words. Because some memories are so painful, they burrow deep in one's soul, concealed by a merciful curtain of darkness in those who have them.

An accident.

"What accident?" Ignazio asks, while Franca starts shaking.

"A dreadful accident, Monsieur Florio! There's a doctor, he came right away, we tried to bring him round, but—"

"Who?" Ignazio yells, and it's as if someone else is asking the question, because a black mist is falling over his eyes, and there's no more sound in his throat. Franca collapses next to him, but he doesn't have the strength to help her.

He's gasping for breath, and yet he manages to repeat, "Who?" as he brushes past the man.

He comes across Baby Boy's nanny and barely recognizes her. But he sees that she's screaming and crying.

He pushes her aside violently and she falls to the ground.

*Baby Boy.*

*Ignazino.*

He starts to run, past servants, up the stairs, his heart exploding between his ribs.

The long corridor, the red carpet, the flickering lights, the door wide open, a man and a police officer next to the bed. His son.

Motionless.

Ignazio sways.

He reaches the bed, comes crashing down on his knees, stretches out with his hand. The child's eyes are open and there's a trickle of saliva at the corner of his mouth. He's in his nightgown, his blond hair spread on the pillow.

Ignazio shakes him. "Baby Boy," he calls in a voice that sounds very far away. "Baby Boy . . . Ignazino . . ."

A hand comes to rest on his shoulder, but he doesn't even feel it. It's over. All over. Because it isn't just his son who's died. It's the future of Casa Florio.

The Florios return to Palermo with a white coffin. Baby Boy will sleep next to his sister, who died less than six months ago, sheltered by the cypresses of the Santa Maria di Gesù Cemetery. He takes with him a mystery nobody will ever solve. The medical report only says that his heart stopped. But that saliva on his lips . . .

Ignazio refused an autopsy. "At least spare him that indignity," he mumbled when the pathologist asked his permission. A fall? A lethal dose of sleeping draft the nanny gave him to have some peace and quiet or to go to a romantic rendezvous? These thoughts are barbed wire, cutting to the touch. So he casts them aside.

It's not as if it changes anything.

After all, his son is dead.

After all, he can't even help himself.

*A heart has stopped. No, two hearts: his and mine,* Ignazio thinks in his study, late at night, while reaching for one of the last remaining bottles of cognac. He's had to suspend the production of cognac as well as table wines. The excessive costs, together with a serious phylloxera infestation in the vineyards of western Sicily, have brought the Marsala winery to its knees. And not just his: the Whitakers have the same problem.

The cracks are widening. The creaking louder. He can hear it echoing in his head.

He pounds his fist on the papers covering his desk, then slumps onto them, his head resting on his arms, eyes shut, heart thumping in his temples.

He wants to cry but can't.

*Where's the sense in all this?* he wonders. Why insist on fighting when there's no one to carry on his battle? What's left if what he inherited from his father and grandfather is destined to end with him? What can his family cling to now? A son is a branch reaching to the sky. But if it snaps, no leaf can spring from it.

That's how Ignazio feels. Dried up. Snapped in two.

In the days following Baby Boy's death, in the still, silent house, Ignazio even thought that it would be better to give up. To end it all.

He's wrapped that anger around himself like a cloak. Suffering and remorse keep him from sleeping; for the first time, he's afraid he'll never be able to escape this house where the ghosts outnumber the living.

Emptiness, darkness, silence. Oblivion has become attractive, and certainly less cruel than what's here at the Olivuzza. He's almost drunk on this feeling, this possibility of vanishing without saying anything to anyone, of letting himself go. But then it occurs to him that everybody—even Franca, perhaps—would label him a coward, half a man, incapable of fighting for what little he has left. A weakling, unlike his father and grandfather.

So he's carried on living. Or rather, let himself live.

A few weeks pass by.

Empty, silent, pointless.

But then maybe someone in heaven sees Franca and Ignazio and takes pity.

Yes, that must be it. Because there's a miracle.

Franca discovers that she's pregnant. After the initial disbelief comes joy: great, unexpected, and, for these reasons, absolute. They hug, tears mixing with smiles, and hold their sole remaining child, little Igiea.

*Maybe we can still be a happy family*, Ignazio tells himself. *Maybe fate is giving us another chance.*

"A trip to Venice?"

"Actually, more like a lengthy stay."

"You're very weak, Donna Franca. I don't recommend any travel, especially in your state. You're only four months gone and—"

"I'll be careful. I'll stay in the hotel as much as I can and rest. My mother and Maruzza will always be with me. I promise I'll behave, Doctor. Please . . ."

The doctor shakes his head. But then his stern lips give way to an indulgent smile. "Very well, then. But do be careful . . ."

The stay in Venice was Ignazio's idea. As always, he's convinced that running away from the hurt helps erase the suffering. The truth is, he can no longer bear the oppressive atmosphere of the Olivuzza and wants an excuse to escape his obligations.

So Venice it is. The Hotel Danieli, a close-knit group of friends who will help Franca feel better and let him off the hook. They are joined by Stefanina Pajno, the Villarosa sisters and their husbands, Giulia Trigona, and the other Giulia, Ignazio's sister, as well as, naturally, Franca's mother, Costanza, and Maruzza.

These are quiet months. Franca takes short strolls with her female friends or her mother, indulges in gondola rides to admire Venice and its reflection in the water, and raptly takes in the alternating ocher plaster, white karst stone, and marble that trims the windows. Her hand sometimes seeks Ignazio's and she gives him a tired smile as their image is reflected in the dark water of the canals. In the evening, she retires to their suite to play cards; they are often visited by Vera and Maddalena Papadopoli, the twin daughters of Senator Niccolò, a wealthy banker of Greek origin who maintains an interest in coins.

Costanza immediately regards the two women with suspicion: too beautiful, high cheekbones, and haughtiness in their eyes, self-confident and relaxed. She knows because she has seen it before, even if she has always bit her tongue. She has never meddled in her daughter's marriage. But her son-in-law is quick to lose his head over women like them. *I don't like them*, she thinks whenever she sees them strut up the steps of the Danieli flaunting that regal air.

But Franca laughs at their gossip and enjoys their sparkling, witty conversation. Besides, they're always kind to her: they bring her bunches of flowers, fragrant *zaleti* to dunk in dessert wine, or baskets of *bussolai* freshly baked by their cook.

One bright late-September afternoon, Costanza is getting ready to go out, as she does whenever she can because forced rest causes severe pains in her back and legs, pains that have been exacerbated by the humidity in Venice. Franca is asleep, one hand on her belly, the other splayed out on the pillow. She tucks Franca in like she did when she was a child and tells Diodata to let her rest.

With a slight limp, Costanza heads for the bookshop at the end of the Procuratie Vecchie. Franca has ordered *Elias Portolu* by Grazia Deledda: everybody's gushing about the book, and she'd like to present it to Franca when she wakes.

She spots him at the entrance to the *merceria*, at the foot of the Torre dell'Orologio. He's sitting in a café in Piazza San Marco, and there's a woman opposite him, a woman so beautiful and elegant that she seems born for admiration: copper hair, ivory skin, penetrating eyes, full lips. Ignazio is admiring her, but that's not all. He leans toward her, tickles her ear, from which a coral and gold earring hangs, and kisses her hand. The woman laughs: a shrill laugh bursting with mirth and sensuality. Then she ruffles Ignazio's hair with her gloved hand, quickly pats his cheek, and casts down her eyes to conceal a smile.

Costanza freezes. People walk past her, bumping into her, but she's unable to move. She leans against a pillar, seeking comfort in the solidity of the stone. Upset, she holds back a retch.

Ignazio's audacity has crossed the line. His wife is here, just a few steps away, pregnant, after losing two children. And he's flirting. *In public.*

He looks up and sees her. He turns pale, drops his head, and lets go of the woman's hand.

That's when Costanza Jacona Notarbartolo di Villarosa, Baroness of San Giuliano, does something she has never done in her almost sixty years.

She locks eyes with Ignazio, swivels her head to the side, and spits on the ground.

It doesn't take Costanza long to discover that the woman's name is Anna Morosini, known to all as "the doge's wife," partly because since her husband moved to Paris, she's relocated to Palazzo Da Mula and had the Morosini coat of arms fixed on the staircase, the ducal hat above it. She is the uncontested queen of Venetian high society: her balls are unmissable events, her parties legendary, and the salon in her *palazzo* is the gathering place of politicians and intellectuals, from the kaiser to the ubiquitous D'Annunzio. Anna is in many ways similar to Franca, starting with her green eyes and statuesque body. She is even a lady-in-waiting. At the same time, she couldn't be more different: free, lively, cheerful, and brazen.

And Ignazio is very much attracted to her.

It matters not how it happens. Maybe a remark by the Papadopoli twins, or something heard during a walk, or an imprudent act from Ignazio: singing before the mirror while grooming his beard with special care one morning. The fact is that by mid-October, Franca discovers her husband's new fling.

On her way back from one of her strolls, Costanza finds her slumped in an armchair, in her robe, rubbing her hard, swollen belly.

"He won't even stop for his child . . ." Franca murmurs, struggling to hold back her tears. "He's just left, and do you know what he said to me? 'I'm off to a boat ride with some friends.' Friends! I shouted back that he should save his lies because I knew he was going to see the Morosini woman, and that he doesn't even have the decency to hide. He didn't reply. He ran away and slammed the door. That's all he ever does: run away."

Costanza hugs her daughter. "Be brave," she murmurs in her ear, gripping her tight. "He's a man and you're a woman. You know how it is, but you can choose how to react. Not for his sake but for the *picciriddu*'s. You know what he's like . . . Don't get worked up—it won't help. Leave him to it." She takes Franca's face between her hands and forces Franca to look at her. "Women are stronger, my love. Stronger than anything, because they know life and death and are unafraid to face them both."

But Franca feels so brittle she could shatter. She hugs her mother back but feels a hot clump of emotions, a blend of anger, pain, and disappointment. Once again, Ignazio has betrayed her trust and run away, abandoning her to her memories and the weight of their children's deaths. He's run away from this room, from her, from their marriage. And that's something Franca can't stomach, simply can't, not after all that's happened, not after his promises to stay by her side and help. She has always told herself that Ignazio loves her in his own way, but now it is no longer enough.

Forced to lie down on the bed because of pain in her lower belly and back, Franca gazes out the window at the church of Santa Maria della Salute and prays that it may be a boy. That he be born healthy. That Ignazio change his ways. That her life might stop sliding down this slippery slope, because she can no longer endure it, she no longer has the strength.

All she wants is a little love and a little peace of mind.

She sends her husband a message, swallowing her bitterness and humiliation as she writes it, addressing it to Palazzo Da Mula. She asks him to join her so that they may spend an afternoon together, because she doesn't want to be alone and her mother and Maruzza are no longer enough for her.

He is her husband and he has a responsibility toward her.

The servant returns and hands her back the envelope, unopened, his eyes downcast. "They said that . . . that Signor Florio has gone out . . . with the *contessa* on a boat ride."

Franca takes the envelope and dismisses the boy with a nod. Left alone, she throws it into the fire.

The afternoon draws to a close, approaching darkness. The golden October light warms Venice's walls and baked brick before it is swallowed by the mist rising from the canals. Franca paces her room, watched by her mother and Maruzza, who exchange worried glances. They try to distract her by talking about the controversy surrounding her portrait: Boldini exhibited it here at the Venice Biennale, but it didn't have the hoped-for reception; on the contrary, there was fierce criticism. Franca shrugs in response. She still likes that painting, she says. She doesn't add that what she likes in particular is the vision of her that the portrait has captured forever: a beautiful, sensual, self-confident woman. When was the last time she felt like that?

In the end, she dismisses both women. She assures them she will be fine. Yes, she's going to rest in bed. Only . . .

The ceiling in the Danieli suite—a blue sky with cupids looking down—irritates her. The light coming in through the windows transforms the cherubs into little demons that mock her naïveté and weakness.

This is what she has become, this is how she feels. Fragile. Only at night do some thoughts manifest themselves in all their clarity, only at night can she face them head-on and admit the many, too many, mistakes she has made in her life. Marriage to an unreliable man, a boy who has always refused to grow up, whom she has been unable to keep in check. Her febrile attention to high society—to jewels, gossip, trips—with which she has filled her days, distracting her from what's truly important. The time stolen from her children by parties and receptions because she thought she had all the time in the world. Instead, that time is over, those children gone. And her sense of guilt weighs heavy, like a stone.

She has always hoped that her love was strong enough to pierce Ignazio's heart, to occupy the whole of it. She believed that her children were left in safe hands, that, after all, they didn't need her all that much. On top of that, she has always had to carry out her social duties: that, above all, was what being Donna Franca Florio meant! But it's not enough to receive the absolution her soul needs. *How many lies must you tell yourself to unburden your heart?* she thinks, her remorse becoming a lump in her throat. *If not, you would end up crushed, unable to live.*

She hugs her belly and tears crowd her eyelids. "I won't make the same mistakes with you," she promises the child she feels stirring within her. "I'll always stay close to you," she whispers.

She falls asleep like that, curled up on the bed, waiting. She is woken by the click of a key turning in the lock and glances at the bedside clock: three in the morning.

Ignazio moves about the room carefully, leaving a trail of iris fragrance in his wake.

She turns on the light abruptly. "Did you have fun on the boat?" Franca squints, her eyes like blades. "I guess you did. Everybody says it's hard to get bored with Contessa Morosini."

Ignazio starts while fiddling with his cuff links. One of them falls to the floor and he bends down to pick it up, cursing the gossipmongers who won't keep quiet. He was hoping to postpone the inevitable clash till morning. He has already seen a beautiful emerald pendant in the window of Missiaglia . . .

"People talk, my *ammatula* Franca. I wanted to tell you today, but it would have been pointless, you were so upset . . . Yes, it's true, Contessa Morosini is very beautiful and knows everybody in Venice. You can't go anywhere without running into her. And today she volunteered her boat for a trip around the lagoon." He rolls up his sleeves, goes to her, and lightly pats her face. "I brought you here so you could find peace. Do you really think I'd be so insensitive as to do something like that?"

Franca turns away with a grimace. "Go and wash up, please. You stink of her perfume." She places a hand on his chest and pushes him away.

Ignazio can't stand feeling trapped. He grabs her by the wrist and forces her to look at him. "Calm down! Now that I think about it, why can't I go out? Should I only see men?"

Franca can't hold back her tears anymore. "You!" She strikes him on the chest again, violently. "You don't care about me," she shouts. "We've lost two children, I'm pregnant, and all you do is—"

He grabs her by the arms and shakes her. "What are you saying? I beg you, my love . . ."

"You never change, do you? You just can't! Always running away from everything. From responsibilities, from fear, even from me, because you're unable to bear too much grief, right? You're a coward!"

"How dare you?" Ignazio is furious. Because Franca is right. His wife's words have struck where it hurts most, in that gray area of his soul he hasn't the courage to face. A sense of guilt also strikes him now, because, damn it, it's all true.

"Yes, that's what you are: a coward," Franca repeats under her breath. It's a judgment that admits no objection.

He stands up violently and walks away. His stomach is ablaze, maybe from too much champagne, or maybe Franca's words have split him in two. He doesn't face this part of himself often. On the contrary, he keeps it well hidden, and if he happens to glimpse it, he always repeats the same refrain: that he's a man, that some urges are natural, that his wife has never wanted for anything, that in any case he's always careful . . . well, almost always. Besides, everyone does it, so why should he be any different? *Damn them! Why do they pick on me? Don't they know they could harm the baby? Mindless people!*

Franca sobs violently. "Do you know how I feel? Humiliated! Cast aside because I'm expecting your child!" she yells, gripping the sheets. She struggles off the bed and goes and confronts him, while he opens his hands wide, trying to calm her. "You have to drop that woman," she says, pointing a finger at him, eyes filled with rage. "Her and the others, if there are any more, and stop making a fool of yourself. I don't want to hear another word about her. You owe me that, Ignazio. You owe it to me and to your child."

Ignazio is suddenly afraid: he's never seen Franca so livid during a quarrel and is worried for her health. He takes her trembling hands. "I promise. But calm down, I beg you." He kisses her eyelids. "Come now, to bed." He kisses her knuckles and slowly hugs her. "You're tired, dear heart," he says. "The doctor told you that you must rest, that you mustn't get upset . . ."

He is answered only by sobs.

They go to bed, he half dressed, she in her robe, and fall asleep.

Franca will wake with a start the next morning, with severe pains in her belly. She recognizes them right away: contractions.

But it's soon, too soon.

Giacobina Florio is born on October 14, 1903, almost two months early.

It is a difficult delivery. The baby is thin and purple. She dies the same evening, after a few hours of agony.

ᴄ২

Silence.

Franca looks up and squints. The light is aggressive and the sheets too coarse.

For a moment, she wonders where she is, and why her chest feels compressed. Because she's alone—but only for an instant. It all comes back to her, and her breath catches in her throat.

The faint lapping of the waves in the harbor drifts in through the half-open window. The room—plain, almost monastic in comparison with the one at the Olivuzza or Villa Igiea—is in the Favignana house. Diodata, Maruzza, and a young housekeeper are moving about the quarters, careful not to disturb her, but always vigilant, as Ignazio ordered. "Stay close to her," he told Maruzza before leaving, having brought them to the island aboard the *Virginia*. "My wife is—is upset. Make sure she doesn't do anything foolish."

They spoke very softly, but she heard everything.

*It's not so far-fetched*, Franca thought with detachment. On the contrary. It would bring her relief. Peace.

She grabs her robe, slips it on, and shakes her head, causing her hair to cascade down her shoulders in large waves. On her dressing table, amid brushes and jewels, stands a bottle of laudanum-based anxiolytic. Its golden shadow stretches across the marble tabletop, colliding with that of a glass half filled with water. Not far from here is the ivory bottle containing the cocaine prescribed for weakness and depression.

Franca laughs bitterly.

As if a little powder and a few drops could subdue what's inside her.

Three children dead in just over a year.

She rummages through her things for a cigarette and the holder. She smokes slowly, her green eyes reflecting Favignana's turquoise sea. It's an unusually clear day for February.

Clear and cold. Only, she doesn't feel the external cold. Instead, the chill inside her seems to absorb everything. Her strength. The light. Hunger. Thirst.

Perhaps she's dead but doesn't know it yet. She can't cry anymore; she doesn't know how to. Her tears stop at the lashes, refusing to fall, as though turning to stone. *No, that's not it*, she tells herself, stubbing the cigarette out in an ashtray littered with butts. If she were dead, she wouldn't feel so much pain.

Or perhaps she is, and this is her hell.

She calls Diodata, drinks some coffee, but doesn't touch the cookies. She has lost a lot of weight in the past few weeks. There's almost no need to tighten her corset anymore. Ignazio writes her, sends her telegrams inquiring how she is . . . but can't stay close to her anymore. And perhaps she doesn't want him here either. With Baby Boy, her Ignazino, they have lost their joy and future. And even if you can live without joy, there's nothing you can do without a future. Hope died with Giacobina.

Something snapped.

She picks up her hat and shawl, both black. On her chest, she wears a medallion with portraits of her children.

Outside, the island is stirred by a gentle but cold breeze. Some of the islanders glance at her and a couple of women give her little curtsies. Franca doesn't look at anyone. She plods down the narrow street flanking the villa, going almost as far as the town hall, then turns to the sea. The same route every day, the same slow footsteps.

She walks on, and the hem of her dress gets dusty, taking on the golden white of the tuff. Near the *tonnara*, some men remove their hats and greet her. She acknowledges them and nods.

She can feel their looks of commiseration, their pity, but she doesn't care. She no longer feels anything, neither annoyance nor resentment. In her soul there's an expanse of lavalike blackness where there no longer exists any trace of life, nor a possibility of its being reborn.

Sounds and smells of labor drift from the *tonnara* as she walks around it: the thudding of hammers, the rustle of nets being mended, the pungent smoke from the burners with pitch for the keels that need caulking. There are still months to go before the *tonnara* are immersed, but men and tools are already getting ready for those May days, after the Feast of the Holy Crucifix. Since their marriage, she and Ignazio have almost never missed this strange celebration of death and life, where the fragrance of the sea mingles with the reek of tuna blood.

She turns the corner and finds herself at a small basin with a slip of rock rolling down to the harbor. There, the water is clean and soon runs deep. To the right is the dock for the ships, still locked up in the warehouses.

The water.

It's so blue, so clear.

*It must be very cold*, she thinks, trying to walk down among the rocks to touch it. But it's calm and the lapping against the rocks seems to soothe her a little.

How good it would be to stop feeling this grief. This pressure in her chest that never leaves her. If she could distance herself from life, be immune to anger, envy, jealousy, and anxiety. It would mean no longer feeling any joy, but who cares?

What is life without love? Without the joy of children? Without the warmth of a man?

Besides, how would she benefit from feeling? Life gives nothing for free: fate granted her beauty, wealth, and good luck, but that very luck turned against her. She experienced a great love and, in return, received only betrayals. She had wealth, but her most beautiful jewels, her children, were snatched from her. She inspired admiration and envy, but now only pity and regret.

*Happiness is a will-o'-the-wisp, a phantom, something with only the appearance of reality. And life is a trickster—that's the truth. It promises, lets you savor delights, then wrenches them away in the most painful way possible.*

She no longer believes in life.

She studies her bare hands, stripped of jewels except for her wedding band and engagement ring. At times, when she wants to torture herself, she remembers those white headstones, the silk lilies of the valley hanging from the sides of the tombs. She recalls the muslin in which they are wrapped. She remembers the details of their clothes, their stiff, cold little hands. They died and took everything with them.

She resumes looking at the sea. *It's not fair,* she thinks. If fate had to rage against her, why didn't it strike directly, instead of attacking her children? They were three innocents.

It's like feeling the weight of a curse, an ancient *magarìa*, an injustice that hasn't been put right and only now finds satisfaction. Only, Franca doesn't want to give it satisfaction. If life wants to rage against her, she will put an end to it. She will withdraw from the game.

She walks almost as far as the sea.

She can imagine very well what could happen. The very thought of it comforts and warms her bosom, bringing relief.

At first, the water would be so cold it would take her breath away. The salt would blind her and irritate her throat. She would try to surface, but by then her clothes, swollen with water, would drag her down. Her chest would hurt, of course, and she would be frightened, but then the chill would envelop her and take her to the bottom in an embrace like a mother carrying her child to bed, to sleep.

Yes, death can be a mother.

She has heard that, near the end, those about to drown feel a kind of strange well-being, a profound peace. Maybe her father felt it eight years ago, when he drowned in the waters outside Livorno. Not Giovannuzza, lulled to death by the fever. Not Ignazino, his little heart suddenly giving out. Not Giacobina, who didn't even have the chance to open her eyes. When she thinks of those three children, the first memory that comes to her is of pressing a little body tight against her, a body growing increasingly cold despite her attempts to share her warmth.

The cold. She has so much of it. It never goes away.

*Perhaps this truly is the only hope I have left*, she considers, while pushing farther on. She removes her hat and throws the shawl aside. She won't need them, she thinks. She even dismisses the notion that what she's about to do is a mortal sin, or that it will be a scandal.

Nothing matters to her anymore.

Even breathing is a chore. All she wants is to stop feeling so awful. To disappear.

"*Me figghiu muriu quannu avia tririci anni*—my son was thirteen when he died. He died with his father. They went fishing and never came back."

The voice reaches her after the sea has already lapped her boots.

She turns. Up above stands a woman dressed in black, huddled in a woolen shawl. She speaks without looking at her. She is small, like a little girl, and yet her voice sounds loud and clear.

"Your son?"

"He was my life, my only son. My husband left me with two daughters, and I thought of them. It's only them that stopped me." The woman walks with difficulty across the rocks. "The Lord giveth and the Lord taketh away."

A sob escapes Franca. She shakes her head, annoyed. How dare this stranger speak to her like this? Hers weren't a fisherman's children! She wants to snap that this woman can't possibly understand, that her entire life and her family are falling to pieces, but a lump in her throat prevents her from speaking.

The old woman now looks at her attentively. "This is our curse," she continues, her voice hoarse with age. "*E di ccà 'un putemu scappari*—and we can't escape it."

Franca feels naked. Feeling tears escape her eyes, she looks away. It's as if this stranger knows her intention and is confronting her with the reality: that you can't run away when you still have responsibilities.

"My little girl," Franca mutters. Igiea stayed back in Palermo with the governess and her mother-in-law. She pictures her in those now abundantly empty rooms. She covers her mouth with her hands but is unable to stifle her sobs and starts crying. She cries for a long time, until the collar of her dress is soaked, she cries all the grief inside her that hasn't yet found a way out. She cries for herself, for her children's lost love, for the burning grief of what was not and now can never be, for the marriage she once believed in, that grew empty from the inside. She cries because she feels like a name, an object, not a person.

She walks away from the sea, but never will she stop hearing its call.

⌒

When Franca returns to the Olivuzza, a few weeks later, Palermo watches her with a mixture of pity and suspicion. It scrutinizes her, trying to detect traces of grief in her face. The city wants to know and see.

And Franca lets the city feed on her. She shows herself, looking splendid, on the occasion of a new visit by the kaiser and his wife: wearing her legendary pearls, she shows them around her brother-in-law's new *villino*—now completed—and lets herself be photographed at the foot of the stairs of this masterpiece designed by Ernesto Basile. At Villa Igiea, she receives Prince Philipp of Saxe-Coburg and Gotha and throws him an unforgettable party, as she does for the Vanderbilts, who have come to Palermo on board the yacht. She attends the unveiling of Benedetto Civiletti's statue of Ignazio Florio, standing next to Giovanna, who doesn't hold back her tears, and surrounded by workers who have come especially from Marsala. She is there for the launch of the *Caprera*, the first steamer from the shipyard. She celebrates with the whole city the homecoming of Raffaele Palizzolo, acquitted at the Court of Appeal, due to insufficient evidence, on the charge of being the architect behind Emanuele Notarbartolo's murder. And on the occasion of the Feast of Saint Rosalia, she repurposes one of NGI's steamers as a true floating garden from which the guests can enjoy the fireworks.

Never a concession, never a word out of place, never a trace of the grief that has scorched her inside. But the smile has left her eyes, leaving in its stead a detached look.

As though nothing could ever touch her again. As though, truly, she were dead.

# PART THREE

# Lily of the Valley

May 1906 to June 1911

*Cu prima nun pensa, all'ultimu suspira.*
He who does not think, first sighs in the end.
—SICILIAN PROVERB

T HE LILY OF THE VALLEY is a delicate plant. Small, with very white bell-shaped flowers and a scent so unique as to give it its name: the Italian *mughetto* comes from the French *muguet*, which in turn derives from *muscade*: "smelling of musk." D'Annunzio clearly refers to this when, in his play *Iron*, he has Mortella say: "How fresh you are! You smell of rain, of shells, and of *mughetto*."

A plant born of pain, at least according to legend: either from the tears of Eve as she's expelled from the Garden of Eden or the tears of the Virgin Mary beneath the cross. But also from the tears shed by Freya, the Norse goddess of fertility and strength, when, as a prisoner in Asgard, she reminisces about spring in her homeland.

A plant that brings good luck, at least in France. On May 1, 1561, Charles IX is offered the flower's stem as a good luck gift and decides that every year thereafter, on that same day, he will distribute lily of the valley to the ladies of the court. The tradition is then lost, only to be revived on May 1, 1900, in Paris, when the great fashion houses organize a party and gift lilies of the valley to both their workers and their customers. Then, on April 24, 1941, when Marshal Pétain establishes the Festival of Work and Social Concord, he replaces the dog rose, symbol of International Workers' Day since 1891, with the lily of the valley. Even now, especially in the Paris region, lilies of the valley are given on the 1st of May. And Christian Dior adopts the flower as a symbol, even dedicating his spring and summer collection to it in 1954.

A plant linked to the idea of a pure, virginal love—the reason why it is used in brides' bouquets. Only recently has it been discovered that this tradition has a scientific basis: the scent of the lily of the valley actually derives from an aromatic aldehyde called bourgeonal, which not only doubles the motility of the sperm of mammals but also attracts them like a kind of magnet. In addition, it is the only scent in the world to which males are more sensitive than females.

A useful plant. As far back as the mid-sixteenth century, the Sienese scientist Pietro Andrea Mattioli, in his commentaries on the works of Dioscorides, asserts that the lily of the valley serves to fortify the heart, especially if one is suffering palpitations. At the end of the nineteenth century, the French doctor Germain Sée confirms its health benefits for the heart and also emphasizes its effectiveness as a diuretic.

An untrustworthy plant. Ingested accidentally, it can trigger states of confusion, an irregular heartbeat, and strong abdominal pains that may last for several days.

A plant as soft and as delicate as it is dangerous. Just like love.

The outline of the Madonie distinguishes itself against the clear light of dawn. The sun is climbing the peaks, erasing the darkness and coloring them with light, while from the sea a cool wind blows, bringing with it the smell of sea salt and grass.

But this aroma cannot overcome other scents, stronger scents, scents that are foreign to these lands halfway between the sea and the countryside.

Engine oil. Fuel. Exhaust fumes.

The wind carries a jumble of words, encouragements, oaths shouted in English, French, German. Or in Italian, with a strong northern accent. Over everything, though, hovers the cacophony of engines rumbling, sputtering, roaring.

Mechanics. Drivers. Automobiles.

It is only five in the morning, but the plain of Campofelice, at the foot of the Madonie, is already crowded with people. Thirty special trains have arrived from Palermo, Catania, and Messina. Some people have even camped out all night just to be here. Now the waiting crowd pushes against the fence, which will shield it from neither the clouds of dust nor the stones thrown up by the automobiles racing by at almost 50 kilometers an hour.

Over to one side, along a stretch of tarred road, are the telegraph office and the wooden stands for the sponsors and the press. Opposite, there is another stand, adorned with garlands and pennants, reserved for the most important guests. The excitement is tangible here, too, even among those with little interest in the race: women mainly wanting to see and be seen; men looking askance at these dangerous, clattering machines. But they all know they can't afford to miss an event that's being talked about everywhere, in Italy and abroad.

An event. Because that is what this race is, and has always been, in Vincenzo Florio's mind. A valuable opportunity for visibility, assertion, modernization. For himself, for his family, for the whole of Sicily. Given that the future is late in arriving on his island, he has decided to bring it here himself. It's not the first time a Florio has had this aim. The grandfather whose name he shares did something very similar.

That's why he has struggled, heedless of all obstacles. He has ordered fields to be flattened and paths and mule tracks to be cleared at his own expense, even spreading tar along the circuit to prevent the dust from reducing the drivers' visibility; he has not only paid the shepherds to keep their sheep away from the road but also contracted certain "gentlemen" to stop damage being caused to the cars and the teams. He has ensured that carabinieri will be present, police officers posted along the route, as well as a company of Bersaglieri on bicycles to serve as couriers; he has brought in timekeepers from the Automobile Club of Milan; he has engaged a cameraman to film the departure and arrival; he has set up a tote kiosk for the betting; he has arranged for a luxurious steamer, the *Umberto I*, to take drivers and mechanics to Genoa straight after the race, so that they can get to Milan, where the Gold Cup, another important competition, will be held. And now he is ready to celebrate his triumph with medals, cups, and trophies created by the great silversmith Lalique, who has also designed the winner's prize for this Targa Florio.

That's why he has involved the whole family. Even Franca has let herself be persuaded to be driven along part of the circuit in a car with other ladies to appreciate the harsh beauty of the Madonie. But above all, Vincenzo has called upon her expertise in organizing social events, which is how he overcame her diffidence. Parties, dinners, buffets, excursions: everything has been arranged by Franca with her usual flair. The one who has been more difficult to involve is Ignazio, who's basically lazy and thinks of nothing but women. But, given that he always wants to shine, to be the best in everything, Vincenzo put pressure on him and managed to secure the money necessary for this undertaking, although with a lot of grumbling and complaining. And he has even succeeded—though he didn't have to make too much effort, because she loves him—to drag little Igiea into this *tourbillon*: she's even told him she wants to be a driver when she grows up.

Vincenzo is a manipulator. He knows it, and the members of his family know it, too, but they accept this side of his character with an indulgent smile.

So it's with a smug air that Vincenzo, in sporty clothes and English shoes, now walks among the drivers and the mechanics. He's become a handsome man: the features of his face are fine, his mustache underlines his well-drawn nose, and his mouth, often curled in a smile, is soft, almost feminine. As the light increases, he observes the cars gradually acquiring shape and consistency. They are different from the cars that are now quite common even in Palermo. Where those resemble carriages, with seats like couches and a steering wheel like the helm of a ship, these are narrow and streamlined. Even when they're idling, they give him the thrill of speed.

He waves at Vincenzo Lancia, who's already at the wheel of his FIAT, then walks up to a man in overalls, with a thick mustache and a chef's hat on his head, who's arguing animatedly in French with a mechanic and pointing at the pedals.

Vincenzo smiles. "*Avez-vous encore des problèmes, Monsieur Bablot?*"

Paul Bablot wipes a hand dirty with oil and grease on his overalls, then holds it out to Vincenzo, who shakes it.

"Well . . . the journey wasn't exactly a walk. The damp has made the engine flood and we're having to fine-tune it yet again. This race of yours is quite a challenge, Monsieur Florio. The course is . . . unusual, to say the least."

"It's how Count Di Isnello and I wanted it. We were inspired by the Gordon Bennett Cup. We wanted a course that brought out the best of both the cars and the drivers. And it had to be a circuit, so spectators could watch more than one lap. People here have never seen so many cars together in one place. I'm sure there are a few peasants who've never seen cars at all. It'll be an experience you'll never forget. And anyway, at least you managed to get here. Just think of those who couldn't even start."

There is a hint of annoyance in Vincenzo's smile. He glances over at a group of men in sporting clothes who are examining the cars with a critical eye. Some are talking loudly in French, making no attempt to hide their anger. *And how could it be otherwise?* he thinks. An NGI strike in Genoa blocked their cars, which didn't arrive in time for the regulation tests and checks. So, instead of participants in the race, they now find themselves mere spectators.

"We invested so much in this race," Vincenzo continues, visibly irritated, "and we've ended up hostage to a few unskilled *porteurs*. In Italy, unfortunately, there's no respect for anything. This is an event that could rejuvenate Sicily and bring it into the modern world, but they don't give a damn!"

Bablot shrugs as he gets into his car. "I understand your disappointment, but as far as I'm concerned, the fewer competitors there are, the better. Although, to be honest, I'm not worried: my Berliet is extraordinary!"

He signals to the mechanic to take his hands off the cylinders and tries to start the engine, which responds with a rumble.

Vincenzo nods and turns to look at another car, a 35-horsepower Hotchkiss with the number 2 on the radiator. On board, bent over the pedals, is a woman whose black hair is gathered in a bun. All at once, in a fluid motion, the woman gets out of the car to check the radiator, wiping her hands on her apron, which she wears over a garment that comes down to her calves. Only at a second glance does Vincenzo realize she's wearing a pair of very wide pants.

Everyone in racing circles knows and respects Madame Motan Le Blon, and they are used to always seeing her with her husband, Hubert: an unusual couple, united by an overwhelming passion for cars.

But here, of course, a woman mechanic attracts attention.

And in fact, as Vincenzo approaches her, he overhears a comment: "Look, a woman working like a man!" followed by an ironic laugh.

Vincenzo turns with a frown, but it's impossible to tell who uttered these words. When he then returns his gaze to Madame Le Blon, he sees that she's smiling.

"I hear them, even though I don't understand them," she says with a shrug. "Some looks don't need explanation: they're wondering why a woman is fiddling with a carburetor instead of staying at home, looking after her children." She takes off her apron, lays it down, then wraps her scarf, tying it under her chin. "If chatter bothered me, I would have stopped ages ago. But racing with my husband is one of the things that makes me happiest, and nothing and no one is going to dissuade me from doing it. In fact, let me tell you something . . ." She lowers her voice and comes closer. She gives off a vague smell of sweat, oil, and lavender soap. "I can drive as well as he can, better in fact. I already drove a steam Serpollet in Nice. A wonderful experience."

"My wife isn't afraid of speed." Hubert Le Blon comes up behind her, placing a hand on her back before kissing her cheek tenderly. "Her control of the car is really remarkable. She could make a few drivers of my acquaintance eat her dust."

Vincenzo bids the man farewell and kisses Madame Le Blon's hand, thinking that he wouldn't at all mind competing with this woman.

"Signor Florio, we're almost there!"

These words have been said by a young man with bushy eyebrows and mustache and two penetrating dark eyes. Once, jokingly, Vincenzo asked Alessandro Cagno if his nanny nursed him with motor oil instead of milk. He's twenty-three, the same age as Vincenzo, and has been racing for five years, having learned the ropes as a mechanic in Luigi Storero's workshop in Turin and then at Giovanni Angeli's FIAT, for which he also drives. He participated as a mechanic in the 1903 Paris–Madrid race, known as the "race of death," called off in Bordeaux after an excessive number of accidents, including one that resulted in the death of Marcel Renault. Between 1904 and 1905 Cagno distinguished himself in the Gordon Bennett Cup. Most recently, he won the prestigious uphill race on Mont Ventoux.

"Signor Cagno, good morning! Is it true that in Turin they've written a song about you?"

Cagno seems embarrassed. "Actually it's also about Felice Nazzaro and Lancia."

"And about your Itala, I think?"

"I'm the one who'll make the Itala sing today," Cagno replies, putting his cap on his head. "You'll see how well it warbles."

Vincenzo bursts out laughing and waves his hand. Then he turns toward the stands, looking for his brother and Franca, who are staying with the Lanza di Trabias and the Trigonas at the Grand Hotel delle Terme at Termini Imerese, a building with elegant lines designed by Giuseppe Damiani Almeyda and chosen to house the drivers and Palermo high society. Not seeing them, he shakes his head. They haven't arrived yet. He'd like to say hello to Ignazio at least, to share a moment with him.

Then all at once a pink patch appears, darting between the cars, appearing and disappearing in the swarm of drivers and mechanics. Surprised, he follows it with his eyes. Only when the patch stops next to Monsieur Bablot's Berliet does he recognize it.

"Annina!" he cries.

Anna Alliata di Montereale—Annina, as everyone calls her—is the younger sister of one of Franca's closest friends, Maria Concetta Vannucci, Princess of Petrulla. Annina is a few years younger than him, and they've known each other forever.

She turns, recognizes him, and comes over, her hat in her hand. Her eyes are bright with enthusiasm, her cheeks red.

"Annina, what on earth are you doing here? You're going to get yourself dirty!"

"Who cares? It's so nice to be in the middle of these automobiles, so amusing! You know something? I'd like to buy one!" She looks down at the lace hem of her dress, which is spattered with mud, and her boots, which now are marred by more than one oil stain. She shakes her head. "But *Maman* says such things are not for women. What nonsense!"

Vincenzo isn't sure how to reply. Annina and he have often spoken, during balls and dinners, but always on formal occasions. He always thought her a lively and intelligent young woman, but the passion lighting her face right now is a new discovery. "Your mother's a prudent woman," he says awkwardly. "Since she became a widow, she's had to take care of the whole family."

"No, it's not that. The fact is, she has such . . . antiquated ideas." Annina's eyes cloud over with annoyance. "She ought to understand that going for a little ride in a coach and four is a thing of the past. That the future is already here."

"It isn't easy to go from one era to another," Vincenzo remarks, his thoughts turning to his own mother. She has remained at the Olivuzza, maintaining that she had to attend Donna Ciccia, who can hardly move these days, but he knows she would never have come in a million years anyway.

At that moment, some of the people involved with the organization appear in the crowd. Perhaps they're looking for him. He turns his back on them. *Not now*, he thinks.

"You know, right at the start, when I used to race along the avenues of the Olivuzza, my mother would say that I ruined the garden and made the birds in her aviary die of broken hearts. But she's an old woman, you have to understand. On the other hand, Ignazio certainly isn't old, and he's called me irresponsible more than once. But that's because he's a born coward. Just imagine, he doesn't even want to ride a horse, because he's afraid of the speed."

Annina laughs and gives him a sidelong glance. "But . . . you *are* a little bit irresponsible, aren't you?"

He smiles. "A little," he replies with unusual candor. What he doesn't tell her is that speed is something that makes the blood sing in his veins, something that makes him feel alive, sends shivers down his spine. And that her laugh has the same effect on him.

"Don Vincenzo!" One of the mechanics is striding toward him. "We were looking for you, Signore."

Vincenzo nods and says he'll join them immediately. Then he turns back to Annina. "Go up to the stand. Your mother must be getting worried."

"All right. But you must promise me you'll take me for a ride in one of your cars."

He smiles. "Yes, I promise. Soon."

Annina turns, takes a step away, then turns again and places a gloved hand on Vincenzo's hand. Her voice is a whisper that ought to be drowned out by the roar of the engines but instead echoes clearly. "Today has assured me that it's pointless to wait for dreams to come true. One has to take the first step. One has to dream on a grand scale. Thank you for demonstrating that it's possible to realize one's desires."

Ignazio is following the preparations for the race from the stand, wrapped in an English overcoat he bought last year. This year, he hasn't replenished his wardrobe. He hasn't had time, but above all he doesn't want to add to the bills to be paid on top of those already on his desk. His mother, Franca, and even Igiea—a girl of six, for heaven's sake!—seem to do nothing but buy hats, dresses, gloves, shoes, and bags all over Europe. He's asked Franca several times not to overdo it, but she always listens with an air of indifference, barely deigning to look at him.

She replied only once, "I assume you don't ask the other women to skimp on jewels or hotels." A line delivered calmly, without anger, and accompanied by a glance so frigid as to make him feel uncomfortable.

He muttered a "What are you talking about?" of which he still feels ashamed.

The chill between him and Franca only makes the things tormenting him harder to bear. Starting with that damned shipyard on which he staked so many hopes: yes, it was completed, but the lack of commissions, the fall in prices, and the strikes undermined the project from its inception. In the end, he was forced to give up his shares in the shipyard company to Attilio Odero, the Genoese owner of the Sestri Ponente and La Foce shipyards. But even that wasn't enough to settle his debts—above all, the two million he owed the Banca Commerciale Italiana just for the shipyard—and he had to lay off workers, both in the yard and at the Oretea. He had to resort to asking for certain loans to be repaid to him—he who never bothered with such trifles.

On the political front, the situation was even worse: Giolitti was powerful, much too powerful. And he was defending interests that conflicted with those of the south, and of NGI in particular. Very soon they would have to start new discussions on the renewal of the maritime conventions: an uphill battle, filled with opponents, starting with Erasmo Piaggio, in whom he had placed faith and hope but who turned out to be a low-down profiteer like all the rest. After Ignazio forced him to resign, the man slammed the door on his way out, swearing to make him pay for his presumption. A scene that uncomfortably echoed Laganà.

And then there was the winery . . .

At this, his back stiffens and his mouth grows dry. Sitting next to him, Romualdo turns and looks at him. He knows him too well not to recognize his bad humor. "What's the matter?" he asks.

Ignazio shrugs. "*Camurrie*."

But Romualdo isn't content with this reply, not in that tone. He grabs Ignazio by one arm and leads him over to a discreet corner of the stand. They've known each other a long time; they don't need such ceremony. "What is it?"

A sigh. "The winery." He gives his friend a glance of remorse, regret, and shame. The thought of it has been eating away at him for days, since mid-April to be exact, when he had to sign over the lion emblem.

The winery was one of his family's first undertakings, created by that grandfather who passed away just when he himself was born. His father would never have permitted everything to go to rack and ruin. Although he's now been dead for fifteen years, Ignazio can clearly hear the words of blame and disappointment, the reproving gaze with which he would have nailed him. His father would never have lacked the money, or the esteem, or the respect.

Nobody would ever have asked his father for "more collateral."

"The winery? What do you mean?" Romualdo asks, puzzled.

"Some time ago I signed the contract to transfer the premises of the winery and the Marsala factory and with some partners set up SAVI, a new wine-making company to realize our assets, distribute the costs, and have a little breathing space. You knew that, didn't you? Well, last month I transferred the factories in Alcamo, Balestrate, and Castellammare, even the one for cognac, which we don't use anymore anyway." He pauses and moistens his lips. "Now we no longer own a single brick; we just have shares. And despite everything, the interest on the loans is eating me alive!"

Romualdo sees deep lines on his friend's face, lines he's never seen before. "I thought you still owned the winery, but . . ."

"Oh, no. I transferred everything to them, apart from the Marsala factory, and they paid me rent. Now I've given even that one away. I just hold the apartment building and the marsala that's ready to be sold." He sighs. "I need money. Money and time. You know what happened the other day? Fecarotta sent me a letter demanding payment. It's the second time that's happened. I couldn't believe it."

"Fecarotta? What did you get from him, a jewel for her?" Romualdo asks, indicating Franca.

Ignazio shakes his head. "No, for Bice," he murmurs, turning his head away. "She's driving me crazy, that woman."

Bice. Beatrice Tasca di Cutò.

Romualdo mutters an insult. "They're dangerous, the Tasca di Cutòs. I should know; I married one. *Curò*, there wasn't anything else you could have done, not with all the people who depend on you. Thanks to SAVI you've been able to take a breather, and of course you've had to make compromises . . . Is it your fault the wine market's on its knees?" He places a hand on Ignazio's arm. "First the phylloxera, then the crisis and the state taxes on alcohol."

"That was a blow. Rome tried for years to tax fortified wines, and finally they succeeded." Ignazio beats his hand down on the balustrade. "I looked for new avenues . . . years ago with cognac, then with table wines, but nothing clicked. And now it seems marsala isn't good anymore, because it's *too* alcoholic! And to think doctors recommend it as a tonic . . ." He lifts a hand to his temple, hardly able to breathe. He's angry now—it's an easy sentiment, that asks only to come out and receive relief. It doesn't feed on ideas or thoughts. And as always, Ignazio welcomes it, embraces it, makes it his own. "Even the Anglo-Sicilian Sulfur Company is no more. Not that I earned anything from it, but it's the principle, you know? The Americans have managed to exploit their sulfur deposits using a new process, so no more exports to the United States for us. And I wager that soon they'll be selling their products in Europe, so goodbye to our trade with France. There's nothing, nothing that's going right! Do you realize?"

"I know." Romualdo nods.

They remain side by side, without speaking. In the end, it's Ignazio who speaks first, and he does so softly, almost as if he struggles to put the words together. "Anyway, I never cared much for sulfur. The winery, on the other hand . . . Even Vincenzo signed, so I'm not sure how much he understood. He only ever thinks about enjoying himself . . . And, along with the factory, even the lion emblem has gone. Everything, everything is theirs now. All that's left is . . ." He makes an eloquent gesture.

Crumbs.

Romualdo looks at Ignazio with wide-open, incredulous eyes. He doesn't know what to say. Of course, the weight of everything has been on his friend's shoulders, since he was little more than twenty, and he's kept himself busy without sparing himself, even though sometimes he's launched himself into enterprises whose outcome was unclear. As for Vincenzo, he's just a *picciriddu* who plays with cars. What does he know about responsibilities, about choices to be made? But . . . Casa Florio without the winery? Without marsala? He finds that hard to fathom. "We've never talked about it . . . I mean, everyone knows there was this agreement, but not that you would have to . . ."

Ignazio lowers his eyes. "At least this way we've gotten something out of it," he replies. There is so much unsaid in that furtive look of his, in those words left unfinished.

Powerlessness, sorrow, humiliation.

"I tried, Romualdo. I tried with all my might, but there really were too many debts. For now, the banks are sapping everything . . . And the taxes! The taxes we have to pay!"

Romualdo stares at his friend. For a very long moment, everything around him stops. The crowd, the cars, the chatter, and the noises disappear, absorbed by a blinding whiteness. Only the two of them remain, immersed in a sensation that neither of them can explain to himself completely.

But one that approaches the realization that the first tremor of an earthquake has arrived.

Franca looks at Ignazio and Romualdo talking in private. She purses her lips. Two men who have refused to grow up, despite their few white hairs and heavy eyelids. Nothing good has ever come from their chatter. And this time will be no exception.

She adjusts her fur-lined coat, then turns to Giulia Trigona, seated next to her, grasps her wrist, and indicates the two men with a nod of her head.

Giulia gives them an irritated glance. "They're probably talking about some woman or other. My dear Franca, we married two men who are really . . . boring."

Franca gives a bitter smile and is about to reply when Annina Alliata di Montereale sits down beside her. She's red in the face, her eyes are shining, and she seems restless. She smooths her dress, leans forward to get a better view of the starting line, and adjusts her hat.

Her sister Maria Concetta takes a seat beside her with a sigh. "Annina, please show a little decorum. First you disappear for an hour, then you come here covered in mud and agitated. A lady should never be so . . . colorful. Franca, Giulia, you tell her, too, tell her to behave."

Annina raises her eyes to heaven. She ignores her sister and looks at Franca. "Don't you think it's a wonderful spectacle? What a pity the strike prevented the French teams from coming!"

Franca smiles. She likes Annina's enthusiasm, even if it also makes her a little sad. "Yes, it is a pity. Not to mention the terrible accident Jules Mottard had."

"An accident?" Annina exclaims. "Really?"

"During the tests, the car lifted at a bend, reared like a horse, then fell back down, twisting the wheels. He was hurt in his left shoulder and—"

"There, you see, Annina, how right I am when I tell you driving is very dangerous?" Maria Concetta interjects. "And you insist on getting a car!"

"If one knows how to drive and is careful, such things don't happen," Annina declares, piqued. "I'm convinced that driving a car is no more dangerous than riding a horse."

Giulia Trigona is equally skeptical. "For a man, perhaps. But a woman . . . would risk too much. It might compromise her ability to have children."

Annina raises an eyebrow. "It's only a matter of time before it's normal to see a woman behind the wheel of a fast car and—why not?—racing against men."

Franca laughs indulgently. "I seem to hear my brother-in-law." She looks at the road, finally clear of mechanics and on-lookers. The judges are about to give the go-ahead for the race to begin. Engines are started; the air is filled with cries and explosions. In the stands, everyone gets to their feet, while the brass band gives the signal, followed by a cannon shot.

This year, it is Alessandro Cagno's Itala that comes in first, also setting the best time, finishing the 450-kilometer course in nine and a half hours, almost 47 kilometers an hour. The second, another Itala, reaches the finishing line after ten hours. Paul Bablot comes in third, while Madame and Monsieur Le Blon, because of a series of flats, finish past the maximum allotted time, twelve hours. They do better, though, than other competitors—like Vincenzo Lancia or the American George Pope in an Itala—who don't even complete the race.

Annina's prophecy will come true in 1920, when Baroness Maria Antonietta Avanzo takes part in the eleventh Targa Florio, in a Buick. Unfortunately, her chassis will break on the second lap, but in 1928, Eliška Junková, known as "Miss Bugatti," will come in fifth in the race. Always gallant, Vincenzo Florio, with apologies to the winner, Albert Diva, will declare Eliška the symbolic winner of the competition. Between the 1950s and the 1970s Anna Maria Peduzzi and Ada Pace will participate five times, and other female drivers racing will be Giuseppina Gagliano and Anna Cambiaghi.

For seventy years, the race will be a stage that the greatest drivers will aspire to: from Felice Navarro to Juan Manuel Fangio, from Tazio Nuvolari to Arturo Merzario, from Achille Varzi to Nino Vaccarella. The very young Enzo Ferrari will race five times, from 1919 to 1923, coming in second in 1920, in an Alfa Romeo. And there will be dark years, overshadowed by low participation or serious accidents and tragedies. Like that of Count Giulio Masetti, the "Lion of the Madonie," who dies in 1926 in his Delage, numbered 1, which, from then on, will no longer be assigned to any car in the race. Finally, on May 15, 1977, Gabriele Ciutti loses control of his Osella and hits some spectators, killing two. The race is suspended on the fourth lap. "The Targa is dead," scream the newspapers, and for once they are not exaggerating. The "little circuit of the Madonie" will be abandoned forever.

But all this lies in the future on this damp morning of May 6, 1906. Nobody can know what a deep and indelible mark the Targa Florio will leave on the history of not only Italian but also world motorsports.

And yet a wager has already been won. Everybody—Italians and foreigners, drivers and spectators—has fallen in love. With the Madonie, the cars, the new world of speed, and a vibrant spectacle brimming with emotion.

Vincenzo Florio has brought the future to Sicily. And Sicily will never forget it.

⌒

"Oh, you have Poudre Azurea by Piver! It's my favorite face powder. May I use it?" Giulia asks, sitting down next to Franca.

"Of course. Go ahead."

In Franca's room at Villa Igiea, the sunlight is sweeping away the last hints of gloom from this late April morning. Igiea stands by the dressing table, watching the two women with an expression that is difficult to decipher, both curious and melancholic.

Giulia turns, tickles her nose with the powder puff, and manages to get a smile from her. Then she looks back at herself in the mirror. She is thirty-six and Franca is thirty-three; they're both beautiful and elegant, and yet over their faces is a veil, placed by the pain that both have felt and by the bitterness that has set down its roots in their hearts, like a plant impossible to extricate.

A tear appears in Franca's green eyes, and she quickly wipes it away with the back of her hand.

"Are you all right?" Giulia asks.

Franca shrugs. "Baby Boy would have enjoyed this race so much . . ." she murmurs. She shakes herself, wraps a lock of hair around a finger, and fixes it in the hairpin it has escaped, despite the care of Carmela, the maid who took the place of Diodata, who married a few months ago. Then she calls the governess and asks her to take Igiea away and prepare the little girl's luggage. She will watch the "motor dinghies" from the window of her room and then, as increasingly happens, she will go and spend some time with her grandmother at the Olivuzza.

When the girl has gone, Franca picks up where she left off: "You know, Vincenzo did well to organize this new event a week after the Targa Florio. So many people decided to extend their stay, and others have come from all over Europe. It's all very cheerful, and even Ignazio is a little less gloomy."

Giulia nods. "I've tried so many times to talk to him, to ask him: What about the winery? Or the sulfur? Or the shipyard? But he won't say a word. Or else he tells me I should concern myself with Casa Trabia and not interfere in his business. As if we were strangers." Franca remains silent and Giulia gives her a sidelong glance. "He doesn't say anything to you or Mother, I suppose."

"Oh, you know, running Villa Igiea keeps me very busy, and I have no desire to harp on about his business worries. As for your mother, right now she doesn't want to see anybody. It was all I could do to get her to take Igiea for a few weeks."

"Because of Donna Ciccia?"

Franca nods.

"Poor Donna Ciccia. Of course, she was old and bedridden, but to go like that, suddenly, because of pneumonia . . . I remember once, while she was trying in vain to teach me how to embroider, she said, 'You have to know how to do this if you want to be a good married woman.' How the times have changed!"

"For us, yes," Franca says. "For your mother, on the other hand, they haven't changed at all. And she's reacting much too . . . emotionally to the death of Donna Ciccia, almost as if it were a family death. As if we Florios haven't had enough death already."

Giulia sighs. She removes a flask of perfume from the dressing table, dabs a few drops onto her wrists, passes it to her sister-in-law, then abruptly gets to her feet and goes to the window. "It's becoming overcast, but a few clouds are certainly not going to stop Vincenzo and his races!" she exclaims, trying to lighten the mood. "You know, last night Pietro and I talked for a long time with Ludovico Potenziani, while his wife, Madda, chatted with Ignazio about the Targa Florio. I got the impression they were both very enthusiastic about these sporting challenges."

"Yes, in fact they both thought the second Targa was even better than the first. And yes, Madda made sure to tell me she loved it and will certainly be back. Did you know they've invited us to their Villa di San Mauro in Rieti?" Franca gets to her feet and puts on a ring with a large emerald that perfectly matches her green dress.

"Of the two Papadopoli twins, I confess I prefer Vera. I find her more . . . composed. They're intelligent women who've married not very bright men, and that was their fortune." A dry comment that cuts through flesh and bone. "I know they're friends of yours, that they were very close to you . . . in Venice, but I don't like them much. I find them a little too uninhibited."

Franca dismisses the memory of Venice and of Giacobina, that little girl born only in time to die, taking with her all Franca's hopes. She doesn't want the grief of it to drag her down again, preventing her from enjoying the pleasures life still has to offer. She has realized that if she wants to be serene, she must forget, ignore, not see. That an awareness of one's own unhappiness is often the worst of sentences.

"I can almost hear my mother," she murmurs to her sister-in-law as they descend the stairs.

Giulia raises her eyes to the ceiling. "Donna Costanza is very observant," she says sarcastically, lifting the hem of her skirt. "To me, they're like two saints hanging on a wall."

Franca smiles. "They both have angelic faces, it's true . . . But I think they know how to get what they want from a man."

Giulia laughs. "Well, even you have your band of admirers, I think. D'Annunzio dotes on you, and there was also that *marchese* who sent you bunches of flowers every day you were in Rome . . ."

"I let them dream," Franca comments.

On the ground floor they are greeted by a commotion that rises in intensity as they cross the drawing rooms. Dozens of guests have come to watch the race of the "motor dinghies," which Vincenzo Florio organized, modeled after those of Monte Carlo and Nice. But the Pearl of the Mediterranean—that's the name of this competition—is a much more serious and better organized race than its French counterparts, even if the latter have become must-see events for those fascinated by speedboat racing.

Ignazio is sitting in the garden. With him are the Potenzianis and Giulia's eldest child, Giuseppe, who's about to turn eighteen: a handsome boy, with a brash air that somewhat recalls his uncle Vincenzo.

Prince Ludovico Potenziani, who has a long, thin face, is wearing a hat to shelter him from the sun. "It's only April 28th, but it really is very hot," he is saying.

Madda's lips curl in a laugh. She has a soft face and bright, luminous hair, very different from Franca's and Giulia's dark hair. "Oh, come on, stop complaining. We're in Sicily, the land of sun, and it's almost two in the afternoon! And besides, smell the sea! It's also wonderfully alive here." She leans forward to take a canapé a butler is offering her. As she does so, the neckline of her dress opens to reveal her breasts, which are perfect despite her two pregnancies. Giuseppe's eyes, as well as Ignazio's, linger for a moment longer than necessary on that patch of skin.

Giulia turns her back on the little group and whispers to Franca, "What did I tell you?"

They all rise and walk to the little Greek temple that juts out over the sea, where a large number of armchairs have been arranged, with big canvas sheets above to shield them from the sun. Franca, Giulia, and Madda sit in the front row. Ignazio calls a waiter to serve lemonade to the ladies and white wine to the men. Ludovico Potenziani sits down on a deck chair in the shade. Giuseppe takes a seat at the back of the group.

"Where's Vera?" Franca asks Madda. "I haven't heard from her in weeks."

"She's in Venice with Giberto, I think. He's one of those husbands who cares a lot about the unity of the family." Madda looks around and places a hand on Franca's arm. "Villa Igiea really is a beautiful place." She smiles, offering her face to the sun. "One can't help being happy here. You and Ignazio are very fortunate. And you had Edward VII as a guest not long ago!"

"With his wife, Alexandra, and his daughter Victoria, yes. They were delighted by Villa Igiea and by the Olivuzza and in particular by Vincenzo's little villa. Ignazio offered them our Mercedes and the Isotta Fraschini he bought not long ago, so they took the opportunity to visit Palermo in comfort. It's a real pity they weren't able to stay for the race . . ."

"Ludovico is so boring," Madda comments in a low voice, glancing at her husband. "He never wants anything. He complains about everything, hates novelty. Not like your Ignazio, who's an enthusiast and loves company. Now, there's an amusing man!"

"Fairly typical of Sicilian men, and of the Florios in particular," Giulia cuts in. "They're always doing things, for good or bad, and they know how to charm, while also knowing when it's time to return to the fold." She glares at Madda.

At that moment, from the wharf, they hear Vincenzo's voice, amplified by a brass megaphone, greeting the guests and, amid applause, announcing the names of the competitors: first those in the class of racers—the *Flying Fish*, owned by Lionel de Rothschild, the *Gallinari II*, with its Delahaye engine, and Emile Thubron's *New Trefle III*—then those in the class of cruisers: the *CP II*, built in Naples, Zanelli's *Adele*, and the *All'Erta*, with its Gallinari body and FIAT engine.

A cannon shot gives the starting signal for the race, which immediately becomes a fascinating duel between the *All'Erta* and the *Flying Fish*, the *Adele* trailing. It's the *Flying Fish* that wins in the end, cutting through the finishing tape after two laps—one hundred kilometers in all—in two hours and eighteen minutes.

Franca and Giulia have followed every moment of the race with attention and enthusiasm, constantly asking Ignazio and Ludovico questions about the helmsmen, about the boats, and about the speeds. Madda, on the other hand, sighed after the first laps that all the noise was giving her a headache and that she was going for a walk.

But when Giulia turns to look for Giuseppe, she sees that the boy's chair is empty.

And she's unable to hold back a grimace of dismay.

Winter in the Olivuzza is like a ghost. It treads with soundless steps, wearing a veil of golden dust, like the tulle with which the dead are usually covered. It hides in the shadows that spread between the rooms, makes the velvet curtains sway, glides over the floors with their black-and-white chessboard pattern, and carries with it the echo of days when the house was full of children's voices and laughter. It is a sad ghost, but by now Giovanna knows it well. And it keeps her company in these rooms that are so familiar to her.

Until February 8, 1908, when destiny scatters the cards.

It's the dead of night when Giovanna is woken by the screams of the servants, by hurried footsteps, by the loud slamming of doors. She's confused, and for a moment wonders what the acrid smell is that's invading her nostrils and making her cough. Then she understands. She smells, more than she sees, the fire.

*It's close*, she tells herself. She gets out of bed, goes to the door, and flings it wide open. The first-floor corridor is wrapped in a cloud of black smoke, which seems to be climbing the tapestries and the gilded wooden doors. She grabs a shawl and rushes out of her room, straight toward the upper floor, where Igiea sleeps. But on the stairs, she runs into the nurse, who has the little girl in her arms and is hurrying to get her to safety, followed by two barefoot maids in their nightdresses.

The women hurry out of the house and a few servants run to greet them and wrap Igiea in a blanket. They are yelling, asking questions, praying. As they give Giovanna a pitcher of water to ease her coughing, they tell her that several of the men are still inside, trying to stop the flames from spreading to the rest of the Olivuzza.

But it's only when the fire engine arrives that Giovanna turns. The heat of the fire seems to caress her skin, displacing the cold of that February night—and the cold of fear. Indifferent to the servants' screams and Igiea's sobs, she watches the flames wrapping her house, listens to the crackle of the beams breaking and the screech of the windowpanes shattering. And the only thing she can think is that, when that red light has been put out, when that infernal heat has extinguished, she will finally be able to go back to her room, to her bed, and sleep. She will be able to return to her life, surrounded by her memories, protected by what's dearest to her, watched over by her ghosts. *Everything will be as it was before*, she repeats to herself.

She stays like that, motionless, her hands pressed to her belly, until Franca and Ignazio arrive: Franca was attending a reception at the Trabias'—she had fainted when she received the news—while Ignazio had been watching a wrestling match with Vincenzo, where he was informed by the carabinieri. Franca wraps Igiea in her fox-fur cloak, then goes to her mother-in-law and takes her hand in a tender gesture. But Giovanna does not react and remains still even after Ignazio puts his coat over her shoulders.

He's the one who decides. He calls the driver and gives orders for all the women to be taken to Villa Igiea. They need to rest—there's nothing they can do here anyway. Nothing, at least until the flames have been extinguished.

Sitting between Franca and the nurse, Giovanna pulls her son's coat around her. Then, after the car sets off, she closes her eyes and covers her face with her hands.

The next day, it's Ignazio who's the first to survey the devastated rooms. He's been told by the firefighters that it was an accidental fire: perhaps a hearth that had not been put out, perhaps a spark that fell on a curtain or a rug . . . But what does that matter now?

With a heavy heart, Ignazio wanders between the blackened walls, passes his fingers over the fragments of tapestry cracked by the heat, clambers over furniture reduced to ashes, shards of valuable porcelain, blackened and disfigured paintings. Finally, he comes to his mother's bedroom.

All that remains of it, and of various drawing rooms and, above all, of the wonderful ballroom, are the walls. The other rooms on the ground floor—including the study—are miraculously intact. And fortunately, the fire did not spread to the newest part of the Olivuzza; his room and Franca's, the dining room, the winter garden, and the green salon have all been saved.

Sitting in an armchair in the garden of Villa Igiea, wrapped in a large shawl, Giovanna listens to her son's account; painful as it is, Ignazio knows that it would be pointless to hide the truth from her. He speaks slowly, trying not to let any bitterness seep through, but Giovanna senses it on her skin, almost like an echo of last night's heat.

Ignazio removes something from his jacket pocket. "Here, I found this on the floor of your room," he says, handing her a diamond necklace all dirty with soot. "I'm sorry. I fear the pearls and cameos are ruined. We'll look for them anyway."

Giovanna takes the necklace. The gold has been warped by the heat and the stones are opaque. She turns it in her hands and hardly recognizes it. No, it can't be one of her husband's gifts. Then she remembers the large inlaid ivory box on the dressing table, the one that contained her delights.

And suddenly she understands.

She will never again hold Giovannuzza's sewn-canvas shoes. Her Vincenzino's baptism shirt, finished in *petit point* by Donna

Ciccia. Ignazio's last bottle of perfume. Her glasses. Her coral and silver rosary. The photographs of her husband, of her son in a sailor suit, and her dead grandchildren, arranged on the chest of drawers so that they were the first things she saw in the morning and the last things she saw at night. All the clothes in her wardrobe. The blouse she wore on her wedding night. The medallion with a lock of Ignazio's hair. The prayer book in which she kept a portrait of little Blasco. The books with Vincenzino's German exercises. His violin. The damask curtains. Donna Ciccia's rosary. The large portrait of Ignazio, painted when he was still young and healthy.

Her life, in ashes.

*But also . . .*

She's never had the heart to get rid of the rosewood-and-ebony box in which Ignazio kept the letters of the woman he loved. Giovanna found it after his death and, more than once, was driven by jealousy to take it out of the chest and burn it, but she never did. Nostalgia won out over resentment. Even what she had hated most had become dear to her. Inside that box was a trace of Ignazio, of his love; however painful it was, and even though that love had not been reserved for her, those letters made her feel close to him.

And now they have gone up in smoke.

Now they are just ashes, carbon, and soot.

And Giovanna doesn't know how she will keep going, now that even the last of her ghosts has disappeared.

Annina Alliata di Montereale likes cars and speed. She is courageous and resolute. She looks to the future without fear.

Vincenzo immediately sensed that. And he had confirmation of it when, two months ago, in July, she asked him to marry her. Yes, she asked him. In that, too, Annina was extraordinary.

They were on their way to the sea when he invited her to drive instead of him. In the other car, Franca smiled indulgently, Maria Concetta crossed herself, and the chauffeur decided to go much more slowly than usual. Then Annina floored the pedal and overtook the other car, throwing her hat into the back seat and lifting her face to the sun. Then she sounded the horn and in doing so brushed Vincenzo's arm. He blushed like a schoolboy.

They stopped near the seaside resort of Romagnolo. In front of them, the coast of Aspra and Porticello and a sea of a turquoise so brilliant it hurt your eyes. She quickly hopped out of the car, adjusting the sleeves of her peach dress, her mouth fixed in a half smile. Vincenzo grabbed his jacket and joined her, and they began walking side by side.

"Don't tell me off for being reckless, all right? You knew I would drive like that."

"I'd never tell you off. I like speed—you know that."

She nodded, then grabbed his hand and squeezed it. "I know. We're perfect together." Her face turned serious. "Marry me."

He stared at her in astonishment. A woman making a marriage proposal?

And besides . . . Get married? Him? Give up everything, his lady friends, his life, his amusements, his travels, his car races . . .

"Yes."

His reply came from the soul. Because with her he wouldn't have to give anything up, because they shared the same passions, because they were both hungry for life. Ever since Annina had entered his life, he hadn't looked at anyone else. Of course, he occasionally spent an evening at the Casa delle Rose, but that was expected of a man, wasn't it?

Vincenzo was silent for a few moments, his eyes wide open. "I should have been the one to ask, you know."

She shrugged. "You can make a public declaration, with a ring and everything, for the sake of our family members and acquaintances. They expect it anyway and are dying to have something they can chatter about, or even malign. I want to know if you want me as much as I want you."

He didn't reply, but kissed her, lifting her from the path that led to the sea.

"Oh, my God! What's this?" cried Maria Concetta, who had caught up with them in the meantime. But not Franca. She didn't smile; she sighed and looked away.

Annina isn't a girl like the others. Jewelry and clothes interest her only to a point. She's pragmatic, cheerful, full of life, and above all determined to live without compromise. She claims respect. She's not like Franca, who, after years of quarrels, has chosen to ignore her brother-in-law's relationships.

Vincenzo knows that. With her he will have to change his ways, he thinks, as he opens the door of the little villa in the middle of the grounds. He is greeted by the smell of wood and the gentle smell of the citrus potpourri on the large center table. He looks around: by the entrance, which also doubles as a sitting room, wooden vaults rise from the walls to interweave in sinuous lines on the ceiling. On the left, a fireplace of majolica and wood; facing him, a large window that looks out onto a terrace covered with white canvas and furnished with wrought-iron divans. Ducrot furniture—couches upholstered in green, a large console with flowery lines—completes these spaces in which light and wood seem to merge into one another.

He heads for the basement, where the automobile workshops are, but also a billiard room, which doubles as a *fumoir* and gaming room. While he waits for his cousin Ciccio d'Ondes to join him for a game of billiards, he checks the cues in the racks and rubs chalk on the tips. The huge room, also upholstered in green, is cool and silent: the ideal place to spend this summer afternoon without any disturbance. He has often brought women here and spent whole afternoons with them, playing cards and using his clothes and those of the day's beauty as stakes.

This thought both pleases and embarrasses him. When the fire broke out at the Olivuzza in February, he feared for a moment that the fire would also engulf his little villa. He can remember how desperate this made him feel: this place is a part of him, reflecting his desire for freedom and independence, his constant search for surprising things.

*This is a bachelor's house*, he tells himself with a sigh. He'll have to change something or else find another place to live with Annina. Something they can build together.

He's always thought only of himself and now he can only think of her by his side. And for the first time in his life, he feels confused. He's too young to remember his mother's devotion to her husband, and he doesn't know how much love his grandmother Giulia gave to the grandfather whose name he bears. All he has before his eyes are countless marriages of convenience, either social or economic. The mere idea of the cage of lies and suffering that some couples have built around themselves makes him shudder.

Of one thing he is certain: he wants Annina in his life. On the one hand, he'll try not to hurt her; on the other, he'll try to give her everything she deserves.

Love and respect. These are new words for him, just the beginning of a journey to a fascinating and unknown land.

But with Annina by his side, he feels he can go to the ends of the earth.

≈

That afternoon in late October 1908, in the study of the Olivuzza, Ignazio rubs his eyes and picks up a sheet of paper. Yet another bill: WORTH—ROBES, MANTEAUX, LINGERIES, FOURRURES.

The list below these words almost makes him feel dizzy:

*1 Robe de soie en velours gris taupe, panneaux de tulle même*
  *ton, brodée de paillettes grises mates et scintillantes, ourlet de*
  *skunks*
*1 Corsage en tulle garni d'épis de blé mur*
*1 Costume de piqué, gilet de lingerie*
*1 Manteau du soir en velours cerise garni de chinchilla;*
  *manches rebrodées or de motif "étincelle"*
*1 Robe de dentelle d'argent et satin bleu ciel . . .*

"Sending Franca, Igiea, and my mother to Paris to replenish their wardrobe after the fire was a really bad idea . . ." he says to himself, staring in dismay at the figure at the bottom of the list. At other times the sum would have been of little consequence to him; now it is a branding iron. As are the bills from Lanvin and Cartier, where his wife took her mother-in-law to replace some of the luxuries that were lost in the fire.

On the other hand, his mother's mood had darkened even more, Igiea had caught fright, and Franca . . . Well, sending her away did help to avoid any scenes and the acid comments she'd been making since she found out about his relationship with Vera Arrivabene.

Franca's mother, first of all, and then Giulia were right: you cannot trust the Papadopoli twins. Madda is no longer hiding her interest in the nineteen-year-old Giuseppe Lanza di Trabia. As for Vera, her husband is more than ten years her senior, a stiff naval officer. True, he's a friend of Ignazio's . . . but that hasn't been enough to stop him.

Vera is beautiful, bright, full of life: she makes him feel good and lightens his heart, and that's what Ignazio desperately needs. Within these walls, he feels oppressed.

He pushes away the bills from Worth, Lanvin, and Cartier and skims through those for the restoration of the Olivuzza. He's had to redo as many as eight rooms—including the ballroom—not to mention all the cleaning and painting needed to remove the carbon black from the walls of other rooms. Franca and he have considered taking the opportunity to build a circular anteroom next to the ballroom, the kind of space that's become fashionable for chatting and relaxing.

"Relaxing, of course," Ignazio murmurs.

A light knock at the door. "Avvocato Marchesano, Don Ignazio," the butler announces.

With heavy steps, Giuseppe Marchesano comes in and approaches the desk. For some time now he has been the family's lawyer, after having served as a deputy as well as the civil lawyer in the Notarbartolo murder trial. But his brief interrogation of Ignazio goes back seven years. Since then, the wind has changed course many times, and Marchesano has adapted. In addition, he's certainly not the only one, in Sicily, to have a past that contradicts his present.

Ignazio doesn't even stand. He looks warily at the huge portfolio that Marchesano has set on the desk, then fixes the lawyer with an expression halfway between impatience and anxiety. "Give me some good news," he says as soon as the door closes behind the butler. "I need it."

The lawyer's mustache—as black and compact as his hair—quivers. "I fear I can't help you there." He sits down and points at the portfolio. "They've written to me from the Banca Commerciale." He pauses. "From the head office in Milan."

Eyes closed, Ignazio rubs the base of his nose. "Go on."

"At the meeting on November 10, they will ask you to officially transfer the NGI shares you gave as collateral to two companies, La Veloce and Italia. They've chosen these two companies because they're affiliated with NGI, which means the shares will remain within the group." He speaks calmly, measuring his words. Ignazio Florio knows what it means, he isn't stupid, but he needs to accept the fact that the Banca Commerciale Italiana, Casa Florio's biggest creditor, no longer trusts him.

And they're trying to force him out of NGI.

Ignazio covers his face with one hand. "They're scared," he says. "They're afraid we'll sell the NGI shares cheaply to some foreign company to get ready cash, thus allowing dangerous competitors to enter the market."

"That's obvious. They've been keeping an eye on you ever since you sold shares to Attilio Odero. Practically speaking, you handed him the shipyard. What is it they say? You let the fox in the henhouse—that's it."

It's true; almost three years have gone by since he transferred the shares of his shipyard company to scrape together a little money, a move that basically excluded him from the activities of the company. It's a sacrifice that still hurts—and that didn't even solve the problem.

"That bastard Piaggio is behind all this. Ever since I dismissed him, he's been determined to have NGI chewed up by his Lloyd's Italiano. And I'm ready to bet that Giolitti is in agreement and can't wait to get rid of me! He and all his friends!"

Marchesano raises an eyebrow but makes no comment. He unties the strings of the portfolio, takes out a sheet, and squints at it.

Then he takes a pince-nez from his pocket and puts it on. "Over time, you've ceded more and more NGI shares to the Commerciale, and now there's practically nothing left in the coffers. You even gave them the last SAVI shares, as collateral for a loan, and God knows if you'll be able to get them back. In addition, the state navigation conventions are up for renewal soon, and your competitors will be able to make better offers."

"So when it comes down to it, what does the Banca Commerciale want?" Ignazio's voice has grown thin. "Because they have to give me something in return. They surely don't expect me to divest myself of everything!"

"The Banca Commerciale holds the shares temporarily and is offering you the chance to buy them back in May or November of next year, obviously at a higher price." Marchesano removes his pince-nez and crosses his hands over his belly. "To be quite honest, Don Ignazio, you're right: these are brutal circumstances. If those shares are not redeemed, you will be ousted from NGI and everything associated with it, especially the Oretea Foundry, but also the slipway. Nevertheless, given the situation of the company, I don't see what . . ."

He takes out another sheet of paper and hands it to Ignazio.

Ignazio looks at these figures. In their purity, the numbers are pitiless.

And the situation they summarize is tragic.

He feels his hands shaking and his stomach tightening. He reaches out his arm and grabs the bell. He wants Vincenzo to be present, too.

Up to now he has sheltered him from everything, he's never explained in detail what's been happening. He wanted Vincenzo to enjoy his youth without being burdened with responsibilities, as he himself was. He has permitted Vincenzo everything, spoiling him like a son, the son he no longer has.

A thought crosses his mind, striking the earth like an electric current.

*Will there still be a reason to fight?*

His brother doesn't take long to arrive, but the wait seems endless. Ignazio and Marchesano remain silent while the shadows lengthen in the room, taking possession of the shelves, twisting around the feet of the desk, and rising to the surface, among the papers. It seems almost as if the wood is breathing, emitting a creak.

One final very long moan.

Vincenzo arrives out of breath, in his shirtsleeves and sporting attire. He has grease stains on his hands and light-colored trousers, and he looks cheerful. "What's going on, Igna'? I've been repairing my car with the mechanics and . . . Oh, Avvocato Marchesano, you're here too?"

"Come in."

His brother's grim tone extinguishes the smile on Vincenzo's face. He closes the door and sits down next to Marchesano. Ignazio passes him the sheet of paper with the figures and orders him to read.

Vincenzo obeys. As he reads, his brow furrows and he shakes his head, again and again. "I don't understand . . ." he murmurs. "All that money . . . How is it possible?" Vincenzo turns pale and scans the columns again with his fingers, as if, by so doing, the figures might change. "When did this happen? Why didn't you tell me before?"

"Because it all started nearly fifteen years ago and you were too young then. Do you remember the failure of Credito Mobiliare?

They were connected to our bank, and because of that people were confident enough to deposit money with them, and then . . . I settled their debts, repaying savers with money from Casa Florio. That's where it all started. I used up all that money and now . . ."

He falls silent and points to the papers on the table.

A series of attempts, a mountain of failures: from the agrarian consortium to the Marsala winery. From the shipyard to the Anglo-Sicilian Sulfur Company. And even Villa Igiea, whose shares are now almost all pledged to a French bank, La Société Française de Banque et de Dépôts—yes, he's had to go all the way to France to get a bit of money.

"I had so few assets, I've had to beg for loans from other banks. And now the interest is due . . ."

"Only the *tonnaras* are still active," Marchesano says, confirming what Vincenzo, whose finger has lingered over the entry for the Aegadian Islands, has been thinking.

Ignazio slumps back in his chair and looks at the lawyer. It seems as if a part of himself is convinced that some solution, some way out, can come from that overweight man. But the other part, the rational, lucid part, is screaming at him that Casa Florio is a prisoner of its debts.

And now everyone knows, not only in Palermo but all over Europe. It's no longer only a question of the bills from the tailors, the jewelers, the furniture makers. Or of the fact that the hotels on the Côte d'Azur or in the Swiss Alps now ask that the bill be paid the moment he checks out, when before all it took was a handshake and the understanding that the money would be paid soon. Then there are the promissory notes, an increasing number of them, waiting to be paid. And the mortgages that have been taken out on the houses and factories over time.

"Yes, the Aegadian Islands are the only thing that still brings in any money," Marchesano says. He gets to his feet and looks at them. Beside him, a young man who until now has thought only of enjoying life but is now crushed by these figures, even if he doesn't yet fully understand their real meaning: for him, money has never been something to worry about. In front of him, Ignazio. All at once, this elegant forty-year-old strikes Marchesano as old and tired. As if the weight of a curse has landed on him. A man without an aim in life.

Without a son to whom he can leave everything.

Marchesano feels sorry for him.

*Not that the Florios can claim it's impossible, or accuse anyone else,* he reflects. The writing has been on the walls, and this communication from the Banca Commerciale is only confirmation of years of risky activities, of advice given but not taken, of thoughtlessness.

Ignazio blinks as if waking from a long sleep. "With the cards in our hands, we won't even be able to get those shares back," he comments bitterly.

Marchesano can only open his arms wide. "I told you: these are very harsh conditions. But they're also the only ones they're prepared to offer you." He puts his hands in his pockets and takes a few steps away from the desk. "The situation is serious, but not unsolvable, Don Ignazio. We have to think up a recovery plan. A way of finding a new direction. Because right now Casa Florio has no credibility." His tone is calm, his words like knives.

Ignazio puts his hand over his mouth to stop himself cursing. He shudders, brings his hand down onto the desk, and cries, "Damn!"

Vincenzo gives a start and shifts back in his chair. He's never seen Ignazio so angry or so desperate.

"The Banca Commerciale already has our bank . . . the shares, the customers . . . And it's had them for six years! As collateral for the money I asked for! And now they want the rest?"

"But at that time they opened a line of credit for five million—"

"How much?" Vincenzo cuts in.

The lawyer turns to look at the young man and this time is unable to hide the pity he feels, a pity tinged with annoyance. "Six years ago, your brother was given credit by the Banca Commerciale, but he's continued to sink further in debt year after year, guaranteeing it with the temporary shares, starting with those of NGI. You, Signore, have been kept out of this for too long. It's good that you should see the storm clouds gathering over your future."

Vincenzo opens his mouth to speak but is unable.

He's starting to understand. He remembers. The *Aegusa*, the yacht on which he spent so many carefree summers as a child. Sold. And the same thing happened to the *Fieramosca*, the *Aretusa*, and the *Valkyrie*. Then there was the sale of Villa ai Colli . . . "I always thought you transferred Villa ai Colli to the nuns because Franca no longer wanted to set foot in the place where Giovannuzza died. Instead of which . . ."

A pained line appears on Ignazio's brow. He shrugs, as if to say: *Yes, that, too, for the same reason,* then reaches out his hand across the table, grabs another file, and pushes it toward him. The label says: SALE OF THE LANDS OF THE TERRE ROSSE. The properties of Giovanna d'Ondes, her dowry.

Vincenzo shakes his head, incredulous. He reaches out his hand to open the file, then pulls it back, as if scorched. "What does *Maman* know?"

"Of the situation we're in? Very little. She's aware we're having difficulties, but . . ."

"And Franca?"

Ignazio's glance is more eloquent than any words.

"Before anything else," Marchesano says, "you have to decide if you want to get back the SAVI shares you offered as collateral to the Commerciale and thereby keep participating in the activities of the Marsala winery. You have private accounts that should be settled as soon as possible."

"But there are still resources . . ." Vincenzo murmurs. He gets to his feet, waves his hands, then indicates the list of assets. "There's the property, the shares . . . I'm sure even the SAVI shares have some value."

Ignazio coughs. "But didn't you hear that those shares were given as collateral for the debts? So, basically, we can't count on them, given that it's almost impossible to buy them back. Yes, there is some credit to be recovered, but very little. Most of our wealth now comes from Favignana and the houses." He opens his arms wide, as if to embrace what surrounds him.

For a moment, Vincenzo thinks again about his little villa in the grounds of the Olivuzza and about the preparations for his marriage with his beloved Annina. He promised her a fairy-tale wedding. And now . . .

Marchesano's voice interrupts his thoughts as the man places an index finger on the papers. "You both understand what needs to be done." For the first time, he raises his voice. "You have to *reduce your expenses*. I understand that for you it's difficult to accept, but you have to start somewhere."

"Where? With the Teatro Massimo? The civic hospital? Do you know how things were there? The state the pavilions were in? I intervened to put it back on an even keel . . . And now I'm supposed to abandon everything?"

"Don Ignazio, you're involved in too many things that don't bring in any revenue. You have to put a stop to them."

Ignazio pushes himself back from the desk, leaps to his feet, and goes to the window. His hair is disheveled, his tie loose. "Cutting the funds from the charity would mean revealing to the whole world that we're no longer the Florios, that our name, the name of my father and my grandfather, no longer means anything. Do you understand?"

Marchesano doesn't reply immediately. He puts his hands over his lips, as if wanting to hold back what he's thinking. But in the end, he speaks. And Ignazio and Vincenzo will remember them forever, those words of stone, even when they are old, even when they no longer have their own house and are forced to live as someone else's guests.

"You no longer have a name people can rely on, Don Ignazio."

Vincenzo collapses into his chair. Ignazio stares into empty space, then closes his eyes. For the first time, he is thankful that his father is dead, because he would never have been able to bear such shame. And it matters little that he would never have found himself in this situation.

"Have we reached that point?" Ignazio murmurs.

Marchesano stiffens, takes out his pocket watch, and pauses. There's so much he would like to say, but the words are like burning embers in his mouth: he has no desire to offend. In the end, he makes up his mind. "We don't have many options, except to turn to those in high positions."

"The Banca d'Italia and its director, that shark Bonaldo Stringher?" Ignazio shakes his head vigorously. "No! He'd put a chain around our necks. He has too many allies among the industrialists. They're all waiting to get rid of me and divide Casa Florio among themselves like mangy dogs."

"They might, yes, but I doubt it. Right now, the main objective is to protect the economy of Palermo and Sicily, and it suits everyone to move in that direction." Marchesano clears his throat. "We'll have to ask for an emergency meeting with Stringher before the partners' meeting." He takes a deep breath, then continues, looking him in the eyes. "You've started businesses that turned out to be failures. You've supported companies that closed down after a few years. You burdened yourself with the construction of a shipyard that never went into full operation and so had to sell it. You've made mistakes through pride and inexperience. Lots of people have given you good advice, but you pushed them away. On top of that, you've made too many enemies, starting with Erasmo Piaggio, whom you dismissed disrespectfully. That's why, yes, we have reached this point, and yes, the name of the Florios is now worth only as much as the paper it's written on. Your estate is gravely compromised, and all that's left is for you to find a way to at least keep your dignity: a way to get out of this with your head held high."

When Marchesano leaves, Vincenzo takes his head between his hands and stares down at the Persian rug without seeing it. Ignazio walks up and down the study.

"Stop it." Vincenzo's voice is hoarse with anger. "Keep still, damn it."

Ignazio goes up to him. "What do you want?" he says aggressively. "Can't I even walk?"

"You're getting on my nerves," Vincenzo replies, pushing him away. Does he want to quarrel? Yes. To scream, to understand, to rebel, because what he's just heard can't possibly be true. It's impossible; he can't believe it.

Ignazio grabs him and shakes him. "Keep calm."

"Why did you never tell me?"

"Would you have understood? All you think about is cars and women . . . And besides, what was the point in distressing both of us?"

Vincenzo leaps to his feet. "Oh, you're a saint, are you? How much have you spent on your women, eh? The jewels you gifted all of them, not to mention the houses, like the one you gave Lina Cavalieri! And now, with Vera, you're endlessly going back and forth to Rome . . . Nothing to do with business, I'm sure!"

"I won't allow you to judge me. I'm the one who pays for your pastimes, or have you forgotten? Do you know how much it costs to organize the Targa?"

They confront each other. Vincenzo pushes him away, muttering an insult. They are almost the same height; they resemble each other. But the fifteen years' difference is noticeable, today more than ever.

"You had a duty to tell me what was going on. I didn't realize we were so . . ." He looks for the word but can't find it.

Ignazio finds it for him. "Desperate? Yes, damn it, that's what we are. And don't rule out the fact that we'll have to sell some properties to settle our debts." He swallows air, fully conscious that they'll actually need to do a lot more than that to give Casa Florio breathing room.

Vincenzo tries to calm down, but he's scared. It's not that exciting fear he feels when he's racing. No, this fear freezes his blood and thoughts and wipes out the future. He looks around, as if not recognizing the place he finds himself in, as if the furniture and the objects that have always formed part of his daily life suddenly belong to someone else. He paces around the study, lightly touching the marble panel that depicts an episode in the life of Saint John the Baptist. It's a work by the great fifteenth-century sculptor Antonello Gagini, and Vincenzo remembers that his father bought it when he was very small; it always struck him as huge and very heavy. Next to it is a painting by the school of Raphael. Then there is the desk, the leather armchairs, the Persian rug . . .

And, beyond the door, in that house and in his life, there are the majolica vases, the bohemian crystals, the German porcelain, the English shoes, the exquisitely tailored suits . . . How can he accept that none of this belongs to him anymore? What kind of existence awaits him?

"I'm sorry." He hears Ignazio's voice behind him.

Vincenzo turns and embraces him. "We'll get out of this with our heads held high, Igna'. You'll see . . ."

But Ignazio shakes his head and breaks free of Vincenzo's embrace. "And you . . . you're supposed to be getting married . . ." he says, his voice faltering.

At this thought, the line on Vincenzo's forehead relaxes. "We'll postpone it till next year. Annina's an intelligent girl. She'll understand."

"Just think what they'll say about us. Starting with Tina Whitaker and her forked tongue!"

Vincenzo makes a gesture as if to say: *What does that matter?* "We'll try to pull through in some way," he replies. Part of him stubbornly thinks that there's a solution, some kind of way out, because there has to be a way of pulling through. His family has done so much for Palermo and for Sicily. How can all that be forgotten?

Ignazio nods and sighs, despondently. But his mind is running away, looking for something to comfort him, and he finds it: Vera, her calm smile, her serenity. And yet next to that idea another one forms: a thought both bright and cruel. He tries to dismiss it immediately, but in vain. It was that very lightheartedness Vera has given him that allowed him to still have faith in the future. That gave him hope.

A hope that is inside Franca. Yes, his wife is pregnant again. Five years after the death of Giacobina, Franca is expecting a child, and God only knows how much he hopes it will be a boy.

◈

"Shall we go to the Royal Cinématographe? Oh, if only you knew how moved I was last night by *Francesca da Rimini*! And how I then cried with laughter at *The Monkey Dentist*!"

"As you wish, dear," Franca replies. She turns to the chauffeur. "Via dei Candelai, at the intersection with Via Maqueda, please." The Isotta Fraschini turns carefully, dodging the holes in the flagstones.

Her new pregnancy, only just announced, has filled Franca with a strange uncertainty. It isn't fear for the child, nor is it a consequence of Ignazio's constant bad humor—he's in Rome right now on business, anyway. *And not only business*, she thinks. The image of Vera Arrivabene has come into her mind, but she quickly dismisses it. No, it's a sensation that's both lethargy and impatience. She would like to go away, perhaps to Paris or the Alps, but the doctor has forbidden it: so she divides her time between the Olivuzza and Villa Igiea, invites her female friends to play cards, reads a lot—she's just finished the new tragedy by her beloved D'Annunzio, *The Ship*, though this time it bored her a little—and goes often to the *cinématographe*, in the company of Stefanina Pajno, whose chatter always amuses her, and Maruzza, who loves to watch those "scenes from reality," perhaps because they remind her of when she was young and affluent and could go traveling with her father and brother.

"The Regio Teatro Bellini is a nicer *cinématographe*, though. More elegant," Maruzza says, with an unusual hint of joy in her voice.

Stefanina opens her hands wide. "But the common people don't care about elegance. All they care about is stories, even if it's just a puppet show." She gives a muted laugh. "I'll confess something to you, my dear Franca. When I was a girl, I watched a puppet show from the window of my room, with my nurse next to me, because my parents didn't want me to mix with the crowd. And when the storyteller started his narration and put on funny voices, I was excited. I was afraid, I laughed and cried, even though the nurse covered my ears so I wouldn't hear the cursing. Well, with the *cinématographe* I feel the same . . . liberation!"

"And besides, it gives everyone the chance to see the world and learn about stories that aren't even in books," Maruzza says enthusiastically.

"Precisely." Stefanina adjusts her blue afternoon dress, leans back in her seat, and looks out the window. "Everything's changing, accelerating, even in a lazy city like Palermo. I'm not talking only about the new streets that are finally sweeping away the alleys in the harbor with their slums, or about the automobiles, or even those flying cars your brother-in-law Vincenzo likes so much! I'm talking about the women. Very soon even the women here will be like Parisiennes and abandon corsets. Perhaps they'll have rallies at the Politeama like the suffragettes in London. You read about that, didn't you? There were fifteen thousand of them, in the Albert Hall! It really seems that all of a sudden women are in a hurry to do new things, to run headlong into the future. All the same . . ."

"Yes?" Franca says, turning to look at her.

"Sometimes I think these changes are just superficial. And that in fact we women are still behind, clinging to the past."

"Independence is always frightening," Maruzza comments. "But we can't hide from progress."

"But neither can we erase the past. And it wouldn't even be right to do so. For example, at the *cinématographe*, I find it unbecoming to be sitting next to my laundrywoman or a coachman. It strikes me as a thing that goes against . . . well, the social order."

Maruzza raises her eyes to heaven.

Franca listens but remains silent, then passes a hand over her belly. Perhaps that's another reason for her anxiety. What kind of world will her child inhabit? What will its place be in this city that's all atremble, ready to follow the future, but with its face turned to the past?

The wainscoting has been polished with wax and gives off a delicate scent. Along the walls, bookcases full of leather-bound volumes alternate with dark-hued paintings. The shiny marble floor glistens in the sunlight. It's a brazen sun, anomalous for November, even here in Rome. And it even seems mocking.

Giuseppe Marchesano and Ignazio Florio are sitting in front of an imposing desk. Everything in this room seems to fulfill the specific aim of inspiring awe, even the large double door covered in Moroccan leather, now closed behind them.

In front of them, Bonaldo Stringher, general director of the Banca d'Italia, leafs through the portfolio that Marchesano has presented him with.

Ignazio is finding it hard to breathe. He's aware of the beads of sweat forming on his temples and wipes them away with a furtive gesture.

"I see you've softened your stance," Stringher says. He has a face that seems carved in marble, a broad receding hairline, narrow, penetrating eyes, and a manner that's both energetic and detached.

Ignazio's back stiffens. "We all have a right to change our minds," he replies condescendingly.

Marchesano is unable to hold back a grimace of irritation. *Ig-*

*nazio Florio manages to be arrogant even on the edge of the abyss*, he thinks.

Stringher runs his hand over his dark vest and lingers on the gold chain of his watch. He looks at it, as if needing to calculate how much time he can still grant the two men.

"I've exchanged thoughts with our prime minister about your case. Giolitti is of the opinion that Casa Florio must be safeguarded, not so much because it's yours but because it's necessary for guaranteeing employment and public order in Sicily, which are already difficult to manage."

Marchesano would like to reply, but Stringher raises a hand to stop him. He looks around, then takes an extinguished cigar from an ashtray. He relights it, looking straight at Ignazio as he does so.

"So you would be ready to entrust the management of your estate to an external administrator? And what about your brother? What does he think? After all, he owns a third of your property."

"My brother trusts me absolutely."

Stringher's glance is skeptical. "So there won't be any problem getting his signature on these documents?"

"You'll have it," Marchesano intervenes. "Both Florio brothers commit themselves to entrust all their activities to an external administrator for a period of ten years, in return for an allowance that guarantees their way of life."

Bonaldo Stringher raises an eyebrow. "Is this allowance also meant to maintain the parasites with whom the Florio brothers surround themselves? Just to get a sense of the figure we're talking about."

"Parasites? No, good friends who need our assistance and support." Ignazio is unable to restrain himself. "My family has its dignity to maintain, Signor Stringher. Of course, we've made . . . I've made various mistakes in the administration of the family estate. I admit that. But I bear an important, respected name. I won't allow anyone to humiliate me and . . ."

Marchesano places a hand on his arm and squeezes it. *Be quiet, for heaven's sake*, his look seems to be telling him. "As I've told Signor Florio, he will have to make sacrifices, but nothing he cannot deal with. He and his family will have to be more prudent . . . Not, of course, to live like common people."

Stringher sits back in his armchair and regards both of them, rolling his cigar between his fingers. "The NGI shares you will transfer to the designated companies are not sufficient to cover your debts. You need about twenty-one million lire."

Ignazio gives a start. The amount takes his breath away.

"I've managed to obtain a deferment of payment until December for the SAVI shares you gave as collateral," Stringher goes on, running his finger down the account. "But you also have other deadlines to honor."

"But the conventions . . ."

"I wouldn't place too much trust in them, Signor Florio. Lloyd's Italiano is already moving in that direction. You should think about transferring part of the NGI fleet to them. That could certainly improve your position."

*So I was right*, Ignazio thinks, staring at the edge of the Persian rug, his vision clouding over. *That damned Piaggio! It seems that the aim of his life is to take from us Florios everything we've ever achieved.*

What Stringher is thinking, meanwhile, is connected to the conversation he had with Giolitti. The minister for transportation is trying to steer through the renewal of the maritime conventions. According to Giolitti, their nature has to change, because for now, they restrict other companies, Ligurian or Tuscan companies for example, from offering services at more advantageous prices. It's not a question of north or south, as far as Giolitti is concerned: it's just that the state can no longer afford to support companies that run a monopoly. And Stringher knows perfectly well that there has already been an auction for the renewal of the transportation services, even though, for various reasons, no company has taken part in it. Stringher knows this but says nothing, because, unlike Ignazio Florio, he knows when it's the right time to speak.

Stringher knows his own power; he knows to whom he owes loyalty.

And if, on the one hand, going to the aid of Casa Florio means helping the economy of an entire island, on the other, the government has made it extremely clear to him where its own interests lie. And the two things do not necessarily coincide.

Ignazio feels a chill. In that silence, the only one who manages to speak is Marchesano. He gets to his feet, looks at Stringher, and says, "Thank you, Director. We'll let you know our decision."

"Donna Franca, here you are! I was looking for you everywhere until Nino told me you were in the garden. In this cold!"

Maruzza, usually so calm, is unable to conceal her anxiety. She covers Franca with her shawl and warms her hands. Ever since she got back from Messina, Franca has refrained from talking, has been sleeping little and badly, and has hardly eaten. Now she's here, sitting motionless on the stone bench in front of the aviary, only a woolen jacket covering her dark gray velvet dress.

"Come back inside the house, I beg you. I've asked the *monsù* to make you some tea and lemon tart, the kind you like so much. Let's go inside—it's going to rain soon."

In response, Franca raises her head and looks at Maruzza with a strange smile. "They were there. I saw them . . ." she murmurs. "Only I could see them, but they were there."

"Who, Donna Franca? What are you talking about?" Maruzza's voice becomes shrill with worry. "Come, let's go and warm up in front of the fire. You need rest and warmth. Mastro Nino has lit the big one in the crimson salon."

But Franca doesn't move. Once again, she looks straight ahead, and her fingers claw at the dark shawl that Maruzza has draped over her.

In her eyes, there's an image she doesn't want to wipe out.

The beach at Messina.

At dawn on December 28, 1908, the earth between Sicily and Calabria shook. It had happened before and would happen again. It has always been a zone for earthquakes, for eddying seas and strong currents, and the Florios have always known that, even though more than a century has passed since an earthquake prompted the brothers Paolo and Ignazio Florio to leave Bagnara Calabra in search of their fortune in Palermo.

But this was no ordinary earthquake. It was the hand of God, raining down from the sky onto men and things to destroy them. The earth split in two, broken like a crust of bread. And left only crumbs.

Reggio Calabria was devastated, many villages—including Bagnara—were reduced to a heap of rubble, and Messina became dust and stone in just under two minutes. Then the spirit of the earthquake took possession of the sea, raising it, and exceptionally high waves crashed down on what remained of the city and those who were on its streets. Fires broke out; there were gas leaks and explosions. Finally, the rain arrived to clear the dust, dirtying it instead of washing it away, blinding the survivors who wandered dazed amid the ruins. The newspapers filled pages and pages with details, each more frightening than the last: the chasms from which hands and legs protruded; the moans, at first strong and heartrending, then ever weaker; the people fleeing to the countryside or else remaining motionless, petrified, screaming without pause. And there were also stories of men digging frantically through stones, beams, and corpses in search of something to steal: the eternal story of jackals rummaging through other people's pain.

In the days that followed, there was a profusion of news: anguish and dismay turned to an initiative to provide emergency help, which could arrive only by sea, given that the roads were impassable thanks to landslides.

The king, who arrived in Messina together with Queen Elena on December 30, on board the *Vittorio Emanuele*, said this himself in a telegram to Giolitti. *Here there is carnage, fire and blood. Send ships, ships, ships.* Then news came that Nicoletta Tasca di Cutò, Giulia Trigona's sister, had been buried under the rubble with her husband, Francesco Cianciafara. Fortunately, their sixteen-year-old son, Filippo, was saved.

At that point, Franca could no longer be content with the newspapers and bombarded Ignazio with questions. She wanted to know what the cruiser *Piemonte* of the Regia Marina had done—it was in the harbor at Messina when the tragedy occurred and was the first to intervene—what help had arrived from the English merchant ships, but above all what NGI was doing. And he explained that they were carrying food and aid, that four of NGI's steamers were ready to take survivors on board, that the *Lombardia* and the *Duca di Genova* were arriving from Genoa with provisions for about two thousand people for a month, and that the *Singapore* and the *Campania* would dock in Naples with three thousand displaced people on board.

But that wasn't enough for her.

When Ignazio announced that he was planning to go to Messina, Franca asked if she could go with him. When he refused, she implored him. Giovanna and Maruzza told her there were too many dangers for a pregnant woman, that there was a risk of disease and infection, that she was needed in Palermo in the charity committees for the evacuees, that she shouldn't tire herself, that the fright could harm the child . . . all to no avail. On the morning he left, Franca made sure she was outside the door, with her traveling coat and a suitcase. In a tone that brooked no reply, she said, "I have to be there, too."

They boarded a steamer and then, after transferring to a motorboat, found themselves on the beach at Messina. While Ignazio supervised the unloading of food and medicines and participated in the emergency teams, Franca walked amid the tents and the makeshift camps, ready to help in every way possible.

And it was then that she saw them.

Children, lots of children. Filthy with mud and blood, asking for a piece of bread or digging among the broken plaster, looking for a sign of life where now there was nothing but dust and death; gray, motionless babies with their mothers obstinately pressing them to their breasts; naked children making their way with difficulty through the heaps of rubble, asking desperately for their mothers; children staring at her, alive but with no life in their eyes.

The memory of her own children overwhelmed her. In every pair of eyes she saw those of Giovannuzza; in every uncertain step she encountered Baby Boy; all the babies reminded her of Giacobina . . . She even followed a little girl with a white nightdress and long black hair who resembled her firstborn; she called out her name, but the girl turned and looked for her mother, a woman sitting close by with a little boy asleep on her knees.

For a moment, she envied that poor unfortunate who despite losing everything still had her children.

And from that moment on she couldn't think of anything else.

"Only I could see them, but they were there," she repeats, reaching out her hand as if she could stroke Giovannuzza's face and ruffle Baby Boy's curls.

Maruzza goes to her, puts an arm around her, and lays her forehead on her shoulder. "You have to let them go, Donna Franca," she murmurs. "They're with you always, but they're no longer on this earth. And as painful as it is, you must mind those who are still on this earth. Igiea and . . . this little creature here," she concludes, placing her hand on Franca's belly.

Franca bursts into tears. She cries for those orphans she was unable to help. Yes, they welcomed about fifty evacuees—above all, children—in their ceramics factory, converted to a makeshift hospital; she and Giovanna took care of three of them personally, but one died of his wounds, another was reclaimed by his grandfather, and the third grew fond of her mother-in-law, refusing to leave her alone.

But she doesn't want other people's children; she wants her own, her own.

And yet she no longer has them. For her they are shadows wandering around the Olivuzza, little angels destined never to grow. Sometimes she hears their little steps on the stairs; at other times, half asleep, half awake, she seems to feel the caress of a little hand or the kiss of two little lips. Then she wakes with a start, her heart in her throat, and in the darkness looks for a sign of their presence, their smell, a laugh . . . But she's alone.

And yet Maruzza is right, just as the wife of that fisherman was right five years ago on Favignana when she was thinking of . . . There is Igiea, and there is a child who will be here in a few months.

A boy? She hopes so but finds it hard to believe. In her life, hope has so often changed to poison.

Franca wipes her tears, then, supported by Maruzza, she gets to her feet and looks at the aviary. In this house, in these grounds, there are too many signs of the past, too many memories.

"Shall we go back to Villa Igiea, Maruzza?" she says, her voice a mere breath.

"Yes," Maruzza replies, wrapping her arm around her. "Let's go home."

⌒

It's March 1909 when a meeting of lawyers and bank directors convenes in Bonaldo Stringher's office to discuss the situation of Casa Florio.

The two brothers are not present. In their place are Ottavio Ziino and Vittorio Rolandi Ricci, the lawyers who, together with Giuseppe Marchesano, represent the interests of the Florios. It's Rolandi Ricci who's taken on the unpleasant task of defining the situation. There's no more time, he says. Yes, more than money, it's time that's lacking: there's a real risk that soon there'll be nothing left to save. Prefect De Seta has added to the pressure, asking Stringher for a quick solution to the matter.

The fact is that there is unrest again in Palermo.

Not only because four shots were fired on Piazza Marina on March 12th, killing Giuseppe "Joe" Petrosino, who had arrived in Palermo from New York, to strengthen ties between the Sicilian Mafia and the American Black Hand. Nor because the eternal Damocles sword of the conventions not being renewed—which would mean the disappearance of Palermo's maritime industry—still hangs over the city. On March 21st it is brought to a complete standstill—

involving the factories, the schools, the shops, the streetcars—which only by a miracle does not explode into an uprising.

Too many rumors have been circulating for far too long and people want to know. They pass in front of the Olivuzza and stroll in the garden of Villa Igiea, craning their necks, peering, straining to hear something. They try to catch a movement at the windows, examine the cars parked in front of the entrance or the coaches that are still used for afternoon excursions, listen to the music coming from the drawing rooms, scrutinize the guests at the parties and teas, and wonder if the crisis really is as serious as they say.

Pushy and hungry for information, Palermo is waiting to understand what will happen, and does so with a wicked smile, because there are many who think the reckoning has finally arrived for that arrogant fellow Ignazio Florio. But the smile conceals fear. If the Florios go under, it will be hard for the city to remain afloat. From work to charity to the theaters, too many things are at risk.

News arrives from Rome that makes Ignazio tremble. After meeting Casa Florio's lawyers, Stringher writes that Ziino, Rolandi Ricci, and Marchesano—with the blessing of the Banca d'Italia— are trying to create a consortium of banks to take charge of the debts and administer the Casa. Stringher's tone is curt, even though his words are cautious. As far as he's concerned, Ignazio is a troublesome beggar, an incompetent who's whining because the banks have stopped listening to him.

On the other hand, Ignazio no longer knows who to turn to. One afternoon near the beginning of May, he goes to the office of the Banca Commerciale to discuss yet another extension but isn't even allowed to see the director, who, according to the secretary, is "very busy." "If that's the case, I certainly shan't be the one to disturb him," he replies curtly, and turns and leaves, while the other employees watch him go.

He has never felt so humiliated.

Once he would have been able to buy the branch, he could have become the master of their lives. Now he's been shown the door like some bothersome supplicant.

Back home, he can't find any outlet for his anxiety. He wishes he could talk to someone. Not a friend, not even Romualdo, because he's too ashamed, but someone who understands him. His brother? No, Vincenzo has gone out in the car with Annina and Maria Concetta. They've fixed the wedding for the summer and have decided to live partly in the little villa at the Olivuzza—Vincenzo is having it refurbished so that Annina "will have her space"—and partly on Via Catania, a cross street off the elegant Via della Libertà, in a modern building in the middle of one of the most rapidly expanding areas in the city. *A building they still have to finish paying for, for heaven's sake!* Ignazio thinks with a touch of annoyance.

Franca isn't here either: she's at Villa Igiea, organizing an evening that will alternate card games and musical entertainment. She's always liked playing cards, and is good at it, but lately it seems to be the only thing she thinks about. At first, Ignazio was pleased: on returning from Messina, Franca didn't want to see anyone for weeks and spent whole days cooped up in her room at the Olivuzza. More recently, though, he has come to realize that this hobby is becoming ever more expensive and has asked her to limit her bets. But she seems deaf to all his appeals.

In truth, things between them have worsened yet again.

Franca's pregnancy, which brought them together and gave them back a little hope, ended on April 20, 1909.

A girl.

They've called her Giulia, like Ignazio's beloved sister. She has strong lungs and temperament to spare, this baby who now fills by her presence alone the children's rooms that have remained empty for too long. Immediately after her birth, Igiea—who's now nine—stared at her for a long time, then asked the nurse if she, too, would die like the others.

The nurse smiled at her, embarrassed, and with a caress assured her that no, she would live. Franca, luckily, didn't hear. But Ignazio did, and felt a pang in his heart, because that simple question reignited the fire of his grief.

Of his five children, only two are left. And what's more, two girls.

Immediately after the birth, Ignazio gave Franca a platinum bracelet. Not a sapphire one—he had given her that when Baby Boy was born. It didn't really matter if the expense added to his debts. He took her hands and kissed them. She looked at him for a long time before speaking, reclining on the pillows, her face swollen and tired.

"I'm sorry," she said at last, in a low voice, her green eyes huge and resigned.

*I'm sorry it isn't a boy. I'm sorry I'm too old to give you another. Because despite everything, I have loved you and have placed my faith in you and our marriage. But now there's nothing left, not even the ghost of the love that united us. I know you have another woman. And she's not one of your passing conquests.*

All this passed from Franca's soul to her eyes, and the bitterness that she felt poured out onto Ignazio, forcing him to lower his eyes and nod.

Because that's how it was and that's how it is. He thinks about Vera. *She* understands his frustration, *she* knows how to support and encourage him. To calm him, at least a little.

He imagines her coming to him and embracing him without speaking. She helps him take off his jacket, sits him down on the divan in the suite of the Roman hotel where they meet, and places her head next to his. She doesn't nag him, she listens. She doesn't judge him, she welcomes him.

Because although Franca was his first great love, it's equally true that she wasn't the only one. *Because the way of loving changes, because people change and the way in which they need to feel loved changes,* he reflects. *Because fairy tales come to an end and all that remains in their place is the desire for an embrace that comforts, that takes away the fear of passing time and gives you the illusion that you're not alone.*

But Vera is in Rome, and far away.

Ignazio roams the house, and as he passes, the servants stand aside and bow their heads. He asks where his mother is, and someone points him to the green salon. Giovanna is sitting in an armchair, with her embroidery next to her, but her arthritic hands lie in her lap. She is dozing.

He goes to her and kisses her on the forehead. She wakes up. "So, my son . . . what did the people at the bank say?"

He hesitates for a moment, then says, "It's all right, *Maman.* Nothing to worry about." The lie brings an ache to his heart.

She smiles and, with a sigh, closes her eyes again.

Ignazio sits down next to her and takes her hand. What could he say to this poor woman, who already had to give up the lands of her dowry, the Terre Rosse where she spent her youth?

He looks at the photograph of his father on the little table next to the armchair. And yet for once, strangely, he doesn't read an accusation of incompetence in that stern look. Rather, it seems to him that his father is saying: *Be strong, have courage, because that's what the moment requires.*

*There's still hope*, Ignazio thinks as he heads for the study. And he repeats it to himself when he peers into Igiea's room and sees her playing quietly, while the nurse cradles Giulia, who is fast asleep.

The Florios are still solid, they have means, they have a name, no matter what Marchesano thinks, damn it! The Banca d'Italia's experts have investigated and said that there is money, that the family still has assets, and that his personal debts, which caused so many eyebrows to be raised, are not the main cause of his problems.

He enters his study and slams the door behind him.

"I'm not giving up," he says out loud. "You'll all see who you're dealing with."

Such is his irritation with the men of the Banca d'Italia and the Banca Commerciale, who not only treat him like an idiot but also stick their noses everywhere and keep investigating him, that Ignazio doesn't realize he has a viper in his midst. Vittorio Rolandi Ricci, one of his lawyers, writes to Stringher that, despite the gravity of the situation, the Florios are still feasting with champagne, throwing money on the gambling tables, and indulging expensive whims.

Stringher blows his top. But in his own way. He writes to Ignazio a letter that is both harsh and icy, filled with blame, scorn, accusation, condemnation, and mistrust. Above all, he makes an explicit threat to abandon him to his fate.

Reading this letter causes something to burst in Ignazio. It's not the first time he's felt humiliated, it's not the first time he's been ashamed, but Stringher's formal, detached tone shakes him to the depths and makes him unusually clearheaded. He must respond.

So he locks himself in his study and writes. He makes a rough draft, choosing his words with care: he doesn't want the director of the Banca d'Italia to realize how mortified he feels, but neither can he risk irritating him further. He writes, rereads, changes, meditates. He declares that he will dismiss the excess staff, reduce the expenses of running the house, and limit everything else as much as possible. He even tries to justify himself, to explain, but then feels that his excuses are inconsistent and strikes them with a decisive stroke of the pen. Finally, biting his lower lip, he copies the letter on the typewriter and burns the rough draft.

*I can't do more than that*, he tells himself as he seals the envelope and slumps in his armchair, rubbing his eyes. How he would love a glass of cognac, his cognac . . .

At that moment he hears the engine of the Isotta Fraschini and the barely murmured words of the chauffeur.

Franca has come home.

Ignazio takes his watch from his pocket. The letter has made him lose all sense of time.

It's two thirty.

"So late . . ." he murmurs. Then a thought strikes him.

*How much has she lost tonight?*

He leaves the study, strides through the drawing rooms, and intercepts Franca just as she's entering her room. She's holding a gold handbag with a diamond clasp—one of the last purchases from Cartier—and a bundle of IOUs.

Seeing this, Ignazio starts to shake. "How much have you lost?" he hisses.

She lifts her hand and looks at the papers as if they don't belong to her. "Oh, I don't know. I signed and that's it; I told them I'll pay by tomorrow."

Wearily, Ignazio raises his hands to his temples. "Who are *they*? And how much are you supposed to pay?"

Franca walks into the room, startling Carmela, who's been asleep on a chair. She throws off her shoes and hands the IOUs to Ignazio with a curt "Here you are." Carmela, her eyes lowered in embarrassment, starts to unbutton Franca's faille dress with its black and silver paillettes.

Ignazio skims through the figures and turns pale.

Having reached the last button, Carmela looks up and sees that Ignazio has a hand over his mouth, as if to stop himself from screaming. Franca notices her discomfort. "You may go, dear. You can put things away tomorrow."

Carmela slips out.

Franca, in her petticoat now, looks at Ignazio for a few moments, her eyebrows arched, then sits down on the bed.

"Do you realize how much you've spent?" Ignazio's voice is unrecognizable. Shrill and at the same time tinged with tears. "Do you realize that while you've been enjoying yourself, I was alone here, like a poor devil, writing a letter justifying myself to that dog Stringher? I humiliated myself on behalf of this family, and you . . ."

Franca slips off her stockings. Her last pregnancy has made her heavier, and her face is starting to show signs of all the misfortunes, the excesses, the sleepless nights. "I don't need to know what you do with your time. Besides, I think Vera enjoys these confidences more than I do."

"You've never wanted to know anything about me or how I was feeling!" he screams, throwing the IOUs at her. "Have you ever asked me how I was, how my business was doing? Or else what I went through after the deaths of our children, what it meant to me?

I've never made you want for anything: clothes, jewelry, travel . . . And you've been so ungrateful! It's always you, you, you . . . There was only ever you and your grief. Have you ever thought that I had to take care of everything, to keep everything together, while you concentrated on having the rest of the world feel sorry for you? I also lost three children—you know that? I no longer have an heir, someone to entrust Casa Florio to once I'm . . . I've lost my future, but that's never mattered to you." He goes to her and looks her straight in the eyes. "And now they're going to force me to let them have control, as if I were some kind of idiot, incapable of administering my own assets. You knew things were going badly, but you continued to turn away, to lead your own life, to spend without thinking. And to humiliate me, yes, because I can't honor these IOUs, either tomorrow or God knows when. But you don't care about that. You're selfish. You're damned selfish, and you came into this house only because of your pretty little face!"

Franca looks at him in a detached manner. Perhaps she's been drinking, or perhaps she's simply tired, but she doesn't react immediately. She gets to her feet, puts on her nightdress and her robe, then sits down again on the bed and strokes the blanket. "How can you accuse me of being selfish with all you've made me go through over the years?" she replies at last. "You say I've never supported you in your business, but Villa Igiea is famous all over Europe and that's due entirely to me, to what I've done, and do, every day for the guests. No, Ignazio . . ." She bends down to pick up an IOU and crumples it. "You're the one who's always done whatever his pleasure dictated. The one who's spent a fortune on his lovers, more than I've ever spent. You've enjoyed yourself without caring about me, about how I felt. And knowing that at the end of every affair, when you got bored or tired, I was there waiting for you, not asking any questions. But now all that's over, Ignazio. We each have our own way of escaping grief, and neither of us can blame the other for having tried to survive, despite everything." A hint of melancholy tempers the rancor she no longer bothers to hide. "You know what the truth is? It would have been a thousand times better if we'd never married."

Ignazio feels the blood drain from his face. He swallows.

They look at each other for a long moment.

Then he leaves the room and, in the darkness, heads for his own room.

"That Florio's an ingrate! Did you read my letter in which I described my encounter with him a few days ago? He says the deal we've come to with the banks would exclude him from the administration of Casa Florio. He's threatening to withdraw from the deal and ask for a legal settlement in Palermo under which he'll pay off his debts over seven years, thanks to an administrator officially appointed by the court but chosen by him. What does he think he's doing? Who does he think he is?" Vittorio Rolandi Ricci stops and sighs. He knows he has no need to moderate his tone with Bonaldo Stringher. They've known each other for years, and although they have an absolute respect for form, they've developed a strong, candid complicity: they don't need to use too many words because they share a common knowledge of how finance and power work.

Stringher doesn't reply immediately. He rises from his desk, goes to the window, and draws back the curtains, letting in the light of a bronze sun that seems to reclaim all its power before the darkness takes possession of the room. He's observing the late-afternoon traffic on Via Nazionale as he says, "Yes, I read your letter. You were very precise and honest, and for that I am grateful." *The exact opposite of Florio, with his letter full of good intentions that melt like snow in the sun after a few days,* he thinks. *The man has been spoiled by the privileges he's had and thinks he still has.* For a moment, he wonders if it's appropriate to show the letter to Rolandi Ricci. *No, there'd be no point,* he decides in the end. *Some weapons one should use only when they are needed. If they are needed.*

Rolandi Ricci's bright eyes are filled with anger. "The man is blind! Despite the efforts we've made, and the draft deal we submitted to him, he comes up with the idea of mortgaging the Aegadian Islands, his most important source of income! What would he have left?"

Stringher goes back to the desk, sits down, nods. "Yes, only a fool, or a badly advised person, could think up something like that. In truth, I suspect he's both those things. We're doing what we can, but we can't save someone who doesn't want to be saved."

"The fact is, he hasn't really grasped what will happen if he rejects our deal. He doesn't know that legal settlements would result in the very thing they're trying to avoid . . ."

"In other words, bankruptcy," Stringher completes the sentence, passing a finger over his lips, following the line of his mustache. "So much for reputation and respect!"

"In fact, it's as if he's opening the door to speculators," Rolandi Ricci says, crossing his hands over his round stomach.

"Or maybe that door's already open . . ." Stringher murmurs.

Rolandi Ricci looks at him questioningly. He knows very well that Stringher never makes hasty statements.

"I think the Florios are moving in that very direction. You noticed Marchesano wasn't at the last meetings, didn't you? Ignazio Florio's attitude, as you've described, his having second thoughts, the solutions he's proposing, merely confirm the . . . rumors that have reached me. He's looking for alliances elsewhere." Stringher leans forward. "We're working conscientiously, and the government has asked us to help Casa Florio, mainly to safeguard public order in Sicily. But if the Florios don't join our consortium, or if they're badly advised, we have no reason to stop the creditors from going after their assets. Casa Florio will be ruined and other entrepreneurs will occupy the space left by their activities. Do you understand me?"

A pause. A long silence, punctuated by the noises of the street and by the heavy breathing of Rolandi Ricci, who eventually sighs and says, "Yes. I understand you perfectly."

At the end of May 1909, the lawyer Ottavio Ziino, his face ashen and stony, communicates to an impassive Stringher that the Florios are withdrawing from the consortium. "They've taken different measures," he concludes tonelessly. "They were unable to accept the proposed conditions."

Bonaldo Stringher listens to him and shakes his head, then looks at Ziino with limpid detachment. "I would ask you to report back to your client that this is a stupid decision and that he will suffer the consequences. He has betrayed my trust and the trust of the creditors, he has acted in an obtuse and underhand manner, and his behavior will precipitate his ruin."

Ziino is unable to conceal the shaking of his hands but doesn't lower his eyes.

Stringher gets to his feet and adjusts his tie. "From this moment on, Ignazio Florio no longer concerns me. The creditors will be free to divide the assets of Casa Florio among themselves in whichever way they prefer. I shan't lift a finger."

In Palermo, the news is like a gust of the tramontana. It blows from the offices of the Banco di Sicilia to those of the Banca d'Italia, bearing its load of anxiety. In the drawing rooms, the rejection of the consortium is mixed with the gossip about Vera Arrivabene: it was she—say those in the know—who advised him in that direction. She, and not his wife, because Ignazio—again according to those in the know—has taught Donna Franca never to involve herself in his business. Others maintain they have learned "from *very reliable* sources" that some advisors of Ignazio have already made agreements with certain industrialists who . . . Yet others pontificate that Casa Florio is a sinking ship. And we know where the wreckage will wash up.

The news spreads through the streets, to the factories, and gets as far as the harbor. Immediately voices are raised, generating uncertainty and confusion. Commercial agreements and transfers of property matter little to the workers, the sailors, or the poor who survive on charity. They've sensed what's awaiting them, and the threat is more tangible than ever: if the Florios' money is coming to an end, their misery is about to start.

When Ignazio communicated his decision to the family, Vincenzo merely shrugged and said, "Go ahead," before running off to Annina's house to organize the wedding, which will take place in a few months' time. Giovanna, pale and in pain, made the sign of the cross, murmured a prayer, then took Igiea by the hand and walked away.

Sunk in an armchair, her hand in her lap, Franca listened to him without batting an eyelid. "Do you really think we'll manage to get out of this mess?" she eventually asked, having first lit a cigarette.

He shrugged and murmured an "I hope so" that Franca barely registered.

But then she did something she hadn't done for a long time: she went to him and embraced him. That affectionate impulse was exactly what Ignazio needed. And something inside him crumbled, revealing that a trace still remained of their love, despite all the quarrels and recriminations.

He pulled away from Franca and took her hand. "Why?" he asked, looking into her green eyes.

"Because that's how it is," she replied, maintaining his gaze. And after so long, a glimmer of tenderness shone through.

There are many things Ignazio would like to ask her. Was it really his fault, the fault of his infidelities, or does she feel at least a little responsible for the shipwreck of their marriage? Has she really always been faithful to him, or has she yielded to someone's advances, as is rumored? Why did the death of their children, instead of uniting them, separate them even more?

But he remains motionless and silent as she goes off to prepare herself for one of her parties at Villa Igiea. Another reason for bitterness: lately, the gaming rooms of the villa have been frequented, among others, by some not so respectable people: professional cheats and card sharks, moneylenders and prostitutes, who mainly take advantage of innocent or bored bourgeois. But they do help bring in money for the till, and the Florios need that desperately.

When Ignazio hears the front door close behind Franca, he covers his face with his hands.

Yet another opportunity to speak, to explain himself, has been lost.

The agreement intended to save Casa Florio is signed on June 18, 1909. Overseeing the operation is a certain Vincenzo Puglisi, who has put the Florios in contact with the owners of a Piedmontese company, the Pedemonte and Luigi Lavagetto brothers, as well as the owners of a canning factory in Genoa, the Porodis. The output from the *tonnara* at Favignana and Formica is ceded to them for five years, and a very large mortgage is taken out on the whole Aegadian archipelago.

*What an idiot*, thinks Bonaldo Stringher in his office in Rome, as he reads the confidential reports that the regional offices pass on to him. *It won't just end badly. It will end in ruin.*

Rolandi Ricci enters the office just as Stringher is closing the portfolio and lighting a cigar. He sits down without waiting to be invited. "So the Banca Commerciale has won."

Stringher remains motionless for a moment, then gets to his feet and puts the papers in a cupboard. "Yes, Florio hasn't realized that Lavagetto and Parodi have signed a subrogation in favor of the Commerciale, so that if one day they find themselves in difficulty, they will hand over their credit to the bank and he'll be forced to deal directly with the Commerciale."

"Which would then acquire the Aegadian property without batting an eyelid, leaving them out on the street," Rolandi Ricci concludes.

Stringher's laughter is contemptuous. "The Commerciale gives the money to Lavagetto and Parodi, who give it to the Florios, who will pay the debts contracted toward the Commerciale with that very money . . . A classic clearance account, in other words. But from it, we've gained two debtors who are infinitely more reliable than Ignazio Florio. When I think of what the man has thrown away . . . I can't imagine a more potent example of idiocy applied to finance. He hasn't bought back the SAVI shares, so he's out of the winery. He's practically out of NGI—he no longer owns either the shipyard or the slipway . . . It'll be a disaster. It's just a matter of time."

⌒

"Incredible! There are so few of us . . ."

"Oh, yes, my dear. A reception on the cheap, not at all the way things were just a few years ago. Remember when everyone was given a gold or silver trinket at the end of every ball?"

"Well, anyway, I learned that they've had to dismiss a number of servants and that Ignazio has given up his English tailor . . ."

"Whereas *she* hasn't given up a thing. Did you see that dress?"

"French or English? The dress, I mean . . . Anyway, since the birth of her last child, she's grown a lot heavier . . ."

"Of course, with that *corsage* of platinum and diamonds and those pearls around her neck she can still wear anything . . ."

Franca ignores these wagging tongues, which follow her like a swarm of wasps. *These parasites can say what they like*, she thinks. She has long since stopped caring about anything. In a dress of green lace and silk that matches the color of her eyes, she moves between the tables, which are decorated with centerpieces of white flowers and satin ribbons, checking that everything is as it should be and that no guest is neglected. Her smile is her shield.

The little band launches into a waltz, and Vincenzo and Annina dance, for the first time as husband and wife. It is July 10, 1909, and a little happiness has returned to the Olivuzza.

Annina is beautiful in a dress that shows off her slim waist and a veil held in place at the sides of her head by lilies of the valley. Vincenzo is handsome, too, but above all, he has the look of a man in love; he presses his wife to him, twirls her around, then stops, laughing. They kiss without shame, as if they're alone in the world.

Franca can recognize true happiness. Even though there is none in her own life, she can still sense love; she knows its smell: an intense perfume, as sweet as the lilies of the valley that adorn Annina's veil.

She feels nostalgic for happiness.

She watches them dance and prays that their feelings do not wither, as happened to her and Ignazio. She prays above all that Vincenzo does not make Annina suffer. In him the spirit of the Florios moves: he's enterprising, resolute, far-seeing; all the same, his brother has always protected him, financing all of his undertakings. Annina is only twenty-four, beautiful, self-confident. But she too has lived a gilded existence. Together, will they find the strength to weather the storms that will inevitably arrive?

Franca sighs and looks around for her husband. He's in a corner, scowling, not far from the armchair where Giovanna is sitting, next to Maruzza.

As usual, Ignazio has told her nothing about what's happening. He keeps asking her not to bet too much at baccarat or roulette, to save, to limit her spending on clothes, even though he knows that, in the eyes of the world, she can't give up on renewing her wardrobe every year or having long stays on the Côte d'Azur or in the Austrian Alps. But now even Franca is aware of the serious crisis threatening Casa Florio. She spoke openly about it with Giulia Trigona only a few weeks ago, admitting that yes, the rumors about their difficulties were not entirely unfounded.

Her friend embraced her, in tears, but couldn't help telling her that the whole city had known this for some time. Early in June, her husband, Romualdo, had become mayor of Palermo and she had heard him describe in anguished tones the strikes among NGI's dockworkers and clerks, but also at the ceramics factory, the bloody clashes between workers and carabinieri, the shops on Via Maqueda smashed up, the café on Piazza Regalmici completely destroyed, the passersby manhandled, the barricades in front of the church of the Crociferi . . . All because people couldn't and wouldn't reconcile themselves to the fact that the naval conventions would not be renewed, since they were now—or so it seemed—in the hands of Erasmo Piaggio's Lloyd's Italiano, and Piaggio had no interest in involving Palermo and its people.

After Giulia's words came the fiery articles in *L'Ora*, which Maruzza has been reading aloud to her, and which merely increased Franca's anxiety. She is upset at the idea that such hell broke loose at such a short distance from the Olivuzza and from Villa Igiea. This unrest was one of the reasons the wedding of Vincenzo and Annina was postponed for some days and the reception reserved for close family and friends. A grand-style party would have exacerbated the mood of the workers . . . not to mention that it would have placed too great a burden on the family finances.

Annina's sister, Maria Concetta, joins her and loops an arm through hers. "They're really lovely together, don't you think?"

"Yes. Lovely and happy. I hope they stay that way."

A man with a triangular face and a thin mustache passes them. He's wearing a suit covered in dust and carries, slung over one shoulder, a tripod on which is mounted a large box that looks both delicate and heavy. He smiles at Franca and bows his head by way of greeting.

Maria Concetta can't help but give her friend a questioning glance.

"It's Signor Raffaele Lucarelli, a friend of Vincenzo," Franca explains with a smile. "He's made . . . what did he call it? Oh, yes, 'a wonderful film from real life'—in other words, a cinematographic record of the wedding. He says he wants to show it in his theater, the Edison."

"So the whole of Palermo will be able to see the wedding? *Mais c'est époustouflant!*"

"First Palermo and then probably the whole of Italy . . . You know, that's how Vincenzo is. He can't resist novelty; he wants to demonstrate to the world that he's always one step ahead of everyone else. He doesn't care what other people think."

Maria Concetta moves closer to Franca and grips her arm through the long ice-colored glove. "Like Ignazio . . ." she murmurs.

It's a discreet and well-meant allusion. Franca nods and tries to hide the bitterness that has crept into her eyes at the thought of Vera Arrivabene. A few days ago, she went into Ignazio's study to talk to him. She didn't find him but immediately spotted the letters from her. There they were, on the desk, in a silver tray. One of them was close at hand, next to Ignazio's answer, which was already in an envelope and ready to be sent. She read it. They were the words of a woman in love, revealing trust, complicity, joy. Everything that she and Ignazio had lost.

Feeling like a thief, she put everything back in its place and tiptoed out of the room.

*Is it possible that Ignazio reciprocates this woman's love?* she asked herself as she closed the door.

"That's how he is. But he always comes back to me." This is what she says now to Maria Concetta, making an effort to smile.

How many times has she said those words, including to herself, in sixteen years of marriage? *He always has to come back to you,* Giovanna told her many years ago. *If you want to hold on to him, he must know that you will always forgive him. Close your eyes and ears, and when he comes back, keep quiet.* And that's how she behaved. She suffered, waited, and forgave in silence. And then she learned to stop suffering, to live without waiting for him, to forgive him without effort. To accept him and herself.

Now, though, she can't help wondering if it's different with Vera. And if, in the future, there won't be a new solitude. A solitude in which even the ties of grief that link her and Ignazio are broken. A solitude in which one survives only if one agrees to live in the company of ghosts.

"What will you do after the newlyweds leave for their honeymoon?" Maria Concetta asks. "Maruzza told me you'd like to go away for a few days."

Franca nods, then rummages in her bag for her cigarette holder. She gestures to her friend to follow her into the garden. "Yes, Ignazio wants to go to the Côte d'Azur: he needs a little peace and quiet." She lights a cigarette. "These have been terrible days for everyone, and there will be others, I fear. Igiea and Giulia will come, too, as well as my sister-in-law."

Maria Concetta moves her hair off her forehead and looks behind her. From the buffet, around which the guests are crowding, comes a burst of laughter, followed by applause. Vincenzo must have said something funny. "My mother's worried," she says. "Apart from the unrest in the city . . . Well, you know the rumors that are floating around about the situation of Casa Florio, and she'd like Annina not to be involved. She's lived an easy life, always free to do what she wanted, and she doesn't want her to be in any difficulty."

"I don't blame her," Franca replies. "All it takes is for one person to let the odd word drop here and there and what's just a difficult patch is immediately conflated with total ruin."

Maria Concetta stands in front of her and looks her in the eyes. They've been friends for years; they can be honest with each other. "Do you want to know what my sister said about those rumors?" she asks gently.

"Tell me."

"She said that, as far as she's concerned, the Florios could go back to living on Via dei Materassai, as poor perfume sellers, and it wouldn't matter a jot to her, because she loves Vincenzo and wants to be with him."

Franca feels a great tenderness. She's almost forgotten that such strong, pure sentiments exist. And this thought is reflected in the gesture Maria Concetta makes, taking both her hands and saying in a quavering voice, "Take care of her, Franca, I beg you. She's so young, so ready to throw herself headfirst into life . . . She doesn't know, she can't know, how difficult it is to be a wife and mother. She needs a friend to support and protect her."

Franca embraces Maria Concetta, her throat tight with emotion. "She'll be like a sister to me. I'll take care of her. She's a Florio now. And for us Florios, nothing is more important than family."

"Don Ignazio, where should we put these?"

Ignazio turns, looks at the workmen who are unloading the crates and the furniture that have been taken from the NGI office. That building on Piazza Marina is no longer his. He will no longer stroll along the Cassaro, nor see the gray slates of the square or the shiny streetcars. And perhaps he will no longer hear creaking, no longer see cracks opening up.

It didn't take long for Luigi Luzzatti—the new prime minister, but an old fox of politics and finance—to arrange things: in June 1910 he entrusted the running of the maritime services to a company just established in Rome. And this company has taken over the majority of the Florios' ships. For some time, Ignazio will continue to be the vice-chairman of the board of NGI, and Vincenzo will actually be present at the fateful meeting on April 25, 1911, in Rome, when NGI's head office is transferred once and for all to Genoa.

But that doesn't change the reality of it: the Florios are out of NGI.

Together with Vincenzo, Ignazio has started a company managing maritime rights. A small undertaking, although it's an opportunity to remain in a field in which—he can admit it openly now—he no longer counts for much of anything. They have taken an office on Via Roma. Brighter, certainly, and modern, with a fine view over the buildings that have swept away a section of the historic center, part of that obsession with renewal that still seems to run through the city like an electric current.

Ignazio gestures to the workmen to follow him up the stairs. He indicates two large rooms, one next to the other. "The low furniture, the paintings, and my father's desk in here; in the other room, the bookcases and the security cabinets."

"So you brought it in the end."

Vincenzo's voice makes him jump. Wearing a straw hat and a linen suit, he peers in and indicates with the tip of his stick the heavy mahogany desk the workmen are moving into position.

"I couldn't leave it there," Ignazio says.

"I don't have much love for all this old junk, for the family traditions, but it's only right it should be here, when it comes down to it." He gives his brother a sidelong glance. "Don't be sad. Just think, we'll have less trouble and will soon be back on our feet, thanks to the agreement about the *tonnaras*."

"I hope so," Ignazio replies.

Vincenzo wouldn't understand, he knows. He always looks forward, has never felt tied to the past. Perhaps he doesn't think that leaving his father's and grandfather's desk to some unknown person would have been an insult to the very name of the Florios. And he probably barely grasps the consequences of the end of their connection with NGI. It's only a matter of time: Ignazio will have to abandon the Oretea Foundry, which his grandfather Vincenzo started against everyone's advice and which made some of the most beautiful cast iron adorning Palermo. And he will have to sell the slipway: some Palermo parliamentarians are already moving to seal an agreement with Attilio Odero, the owner of the shipyard. Apparently, the agreement stipulates that the workers will be relocated so there won't be too many dismissals, but nobody believes that: Odero has quite different interests, and the new company has offices in Rome, Genoa, and Trieste. Everywhere, except Palermo. Everything has ended up in the hands of northerners, especially Ligurians. Yes, Ignazio knows how things will end up, and so do the people in Palermo, those who look askance at him and no longer step aside to let him pass.

Ignazio turns to his brother. They're alone in the room, which by now is cluttered with boxes and furniture. "You . . . you also think this is all my fault," he says.

"Yes and no," Vincenzo replies. Without anger, without recrimination. "You had too many things against you, and you didn't realize. You tried to keep everything going, but you weren't always capable of handling the situation."

He doesn't have the courage to add anything else. Besides, what point would there be in throwing it all—the mad spending, the princely gifts, the constant travel, the lavish receptions—in his brother's face? After all, he, too, has always taken everything he wanted, whether a car or a woman. *Perhaps with Annina everything will change*, he tells himself. *I'll learn to appreciate simple, unpretentious things* . . . He smiles at the notion, then sees his brother putting a silver-framed photograph of Baby Boy on the desk and feels a twinge in his heart. *I always thought I was brave because I'm not afraid to race cars or fly in planes*, he thinks. *But living with indelible grief, doing so every day, and forging ahead—that's real courage. An-*

*nina and I will help you to bear your grief, my brother. Because there are ties that are even stronger than blood. We'll never say it, because we are men and there are some things men don't say to each other. But that's how it is.*

He goes to Ignazio and puts a hand on his shoulder. "We'll do whatever it takes to survive," he says. "And we'll do it together."

ᕲ

Ignazio is hurrying along the corridors of the Quirinale, barely aware of the guards trying to slow him down. It's a liveried employee who stops in front of them and gestures to them not to intervene, because this is a rather delicate matter.

Distressing, in fact. A tragedy has struck Romualdo Trigona, Ignazio's lifelong friend, almost a brother to him. His wife, Giulia, has been stabbed to death in the Albergo Rebecchino, a third-class Roman *pensione*, by Baron Vincenzo Paternò del Cugno, a cavalry lieutenant from Palermo.

*How is it possible?* Ignazio asks himself, panting. *How?*

He's unable to find an answer.

But he does know where it all started.

Almost two years ago, in August 1909, during a party at Villa Igiea. That's where Giulia and Vincenzo met. An unsatisfied, neglected wife who drew the attention of the scion of a noble and not particularly rich family. An affair like so many others, to be kept hidden from the eyes of the world, to be conducted in secret.

Instead, it soon became public knowledge. Giulia even left home and sold some of her properties to be able to maintain her lover. Documents were drawn up for a legal separation.

In the scandal that overwhelmed the Tasca di Cutòs and the Trigonas, Franca did her best to make Giulia see reason, reminding her that she was condemning her daughters, Clementina and Giovanna, to a life marked by shame and an indelible social stigma. But Giulia wouldn't listen to reason; even if she left Vincenzo, she said, she would never go back to Romualdo. He was a womanizer, a spendthrift, and a coward, a man incapable of assuming responsibility for anything.

Ignazio, for his part, tried to confront Vincenzo Paternò. Thanks to Ignazio's network of relatives and acquaintances in Palermo high society, it didn't take him long to find the fellow and talk to him. Paternò del Cugno turned out to be a charismatic but arrogant young man, who even accused him of having designs on Giulia. He made no secret of his own interest in her wealth, given that he had heavy gambling debts. The encounter became heated, and angry words were exchanged. They almost came to blows.

Ignazio breathes heavily, more from the grief that is oppressing his chest than from his exertions. He could have done more, he tells himself. Everybody could have done more, and yet nobody intervened.

And now Giulia is dead.

He stops on the second floor and gives the employee a questioning glance. The man points to a double door at the far end of the corridor, the last of the apartments reserved for ladies-in-waiting and gentlemen of the king.

He goes to it and knocks.

On the other side, sobbing.

Ignazio goes in.

Romualdo is slumped in an armchair. Next to him, his valet.

"He killed her . . . the bastard killed her . . ."

Ignazio throws aside his hat and coat, kneels at Romualdo's feet, and embraces him. Romualdo clings to him like a shipwrecked man to a piece of flotsam. He's sick, and not only because of what has happened. For some days now, he's had a fever, and it's obvious he's only just gotten out of bed.

"He killed her . . . the bastard! Even after all that happened, I—" A burst of sobbing cuts off this flow of angry words. "Giulia . . . I never would have wanted her to end up like this." He clutches the lapel of Ignazio's jacket. "What about him? Is it true he killed himself?"

Ignazio takes Romualdo's head in his hands. "He shot himself in the temple, but he's only wounded, apparently. It seems she agreed to meet him to tell him that she wanted to leave him and he . . . already had it in his mind to stop her. He had a weapon with him and . . ." He can't go on. He, too, must make an effort to hold back his tears.

Romualdo beats his own forehead with his closed fists. "We don't even kill animals like that . . ." He grabs Ignazio abruptly by the shoulders. "I should have realized it! You know, only a few days ago that wretch came here, to our apartments, all excited. I was told that Giulia tried to calm him down, but he started shouting: 'You coward, you slut, you want to leave me now? I'll kill you!' I should have realized!"

"I don't know." Ignazio has heard all about that terrible scene. "Now calm down." He raises his head and looks around for the valet. "Two cognacs," he orders. He takes the glass and tells his friend to drink it all down.

Romualdo obeys and seems to regain control of himself, even though his hands continue to shake. "Did you see her?"

"No. I came straight here to you. Franca . . . is there, at the hotel, along with Alessandro. All I know is that the Prince of Belmonte has gone to give the news to Giulia's father, who was about to leave for Frascati. The poor man already lost a daughter in the Messina earthquake . . ."

But Romualdo isn't listening to him. "She wanted her own way, and I couldn't bear it. You know what I went through, you even know that the queen asked us to try and reconcile, but she wouldn't hear of it . . ."

Ignazio nods again. He was with Romualdo just two days ago, when he and Giulia signed the legal separation, and knows how much he's suffered. He forces him to drink the other cognac. "I know."

Romualdo covers his face. "Murdered like a common whore," he stammers. "What a terrible thing!"

Ignazio grips his shoulder. "Think of it this way. From now on, you'll no longer have anything to be ashamed about. Now you're a victim just as much as she was—more than she was. And you'll have to be careful about how you respond. You'll have to go to the king and queen and talk to them."

Harsh words, Ignazio knows. But he's the only person who can be so direct with Romualdo.

His friend needs to react in the right way. He belongs to one of the most important families on the island; he's a high-ranking politician; he's been mayor of Palermo.

Romualdo looks at him. He's still in a daze, but he's grasped the meaning of Ignazio's words. "Go to the king and queen," he repeats mechanically. "But I also have to talk to my in-laws."

Ignazio nods vigorously. "Of course, of course . . . Especially to Alessandro. After all, he's your brother-in-law, and don't forget, he's also a political opponent." He pauses and forces Romualdo to look at him. "We've known each other since we were in short pants, *curò*, so listen to me. You have to be strong. Even knowing how she ended up, even though it may seem to you the worst possible shame, you have to bury her in your family chapel. Make sure it's you who organizes the funeral. Your wife was the mother of your two children, and you should never forget that."

Nodding, Romualdo runs his hand through his hair. No, he can't forget that Giulia was a Trigona. But he'd rather forget the scenes that made their life more a war than a marriage, because he, too, is responsible for that failure. Out of the grief, the memories of his own constant betrayals resurface, especially the last one, with an actress from Eduardo Scarpetta's company, with which Giulia often confronted him.

He knows Ignazio is right: the murder of Giulia is a blow to his social credibility and therefore to his political career. It's up to him to regain his dignity and demonstrate that in his family there are still values and that he's there to defend them.

Romualdo gets laboriously to his feet. He sways as he proceeds to dress himself. Every now and again he stops and looks at the emptiness around him, and his body convulses with sobs. Because we can hate each other, wound each other, separate from each other, but death is a seal that crystallizes everything and leaves the living to bear the burden of existence. Death is pitiful for those who go, but a sentence without appeal for those who stay behind.

And Giulia's death has sealed their bond forever.

For his part, Ignazio knows what he must do. He will commission two articles from Tullio Giordana, the editor of *L'Ora*: the first in defense of Giulia's memory—a good, kind woman, but the victim of dubious passions—and the second in support of Romualdo, honest and noble, but the victim of tragic circumstances. Only one person is the guilty party: Vincenzo Paternò del Cugno.

That's how it will be. That's how it *must* be.

⌒

The return to Palermo is strange and grim. Franca continues organizing parties at the Villa Igiea but also dedicates much time to her mother, who has remained alone after the death of her son Franz, at the age of thirty, a few months ago. Ignazio divides his time between Sicily and Rome, officially for business, in reality to be close to Vera, who has become the main focus of his thoughts. Whenever he comes home, he's brusque and bad-tempered, partly because his creditors won't leave him alone.

There's a tinge of melancholy hovering over everything. Giulia's death has revealed to both of them what a tragic outcome an unhappy marriage may have. Luckily, the children and Vincenzo and Annina make the days happier.

On a bright May morning, Franca joins her sister-in-law in the stables, which have been converted to a car-repair workshop. Annina has been waiting on Igiea to finish her music lesson and now she's brought her here to look at the cars. She's demonstrating how the steering wheel works. "You see? It's connected to the wheels and makes them turn. The first time the mechanics, your uncle's friends, come here, I'll ask them to show you everything properly."

Igiea nods, but without much interest: the time has passed when she wanted to be a driver. Now she prefers to draw, to look at photographs, or go to the *cinématographe* with her mother or with her uncle and Annina, but above all she loves the sea. On a little table in the Olivuzza, there's a photograph that shows her, together with her mother, on the steps of one of the big mobile cabins they use for changing. She's on her feet and looking at the camera, gravely, while Franca is behind her. Giulia—everyone calls her Giugiù— isn't there, because she was still too little to go bathing. That image is very dear to both of them: they were living through a moment of serenity that's rare and, as such, precious.

Annina rubs her hands together to clean them, then she and Franca head for the house, Igiea skipping ahead of them, followed by one of her beloved Persian cats. "You know, Vincenzo wants to go to Switzerland for a few weeks. We may leave in July, because first he has to resolve the latest complications connected to the Targa." The complications, they both know very well, are the sums of money that are still owed to the organizers and transporters. "Vincenzo's idea of moving the stands from Buonfornello to Cerda was really a clever one. Did you see how many people came? And what a view!"

Franca nods. "Yes, I confess that after the last two years I was a little worried. Remember two years ago, when there were so few participants that Vincenzo himself decided to take part? Well, at least that was his excuse."

Annina laughs and raises her face to the sun. She's not afraid of her skin getting red. "Vincenzo was born to organize events and devise new things. He knows how to involve everyone, and he pushes them to give the best of themselves." Then she turns serious. "And I have no intention of letting him out of my sight even for a moment. I didn't like how some of the female guests looked at him."

Franca looks away. She'll never say what she thinks, which is that she's afraid her brother-in-law has not only inherited the charm of the Florio males but also assumed his brother's worst habits. But she likes Annina too much. "Always be careful," she says. "You must always keep your eyes open."

Annina's lips curl in a smile. "Men always go where they're led. And I'm making sure I control him well."

The perfume of the roses in the garden is so strong as to be intoxicating. Igiea runs to her nurse, who is sitting on a bench. Giugiù is taking her first steps and her elder sister encourages her, clapping her hands.

Annina lightly brushes the petals of a Noisette rose and sniffs the spicy aroma. "Every now and again I think about Giulia Trigona, the poor thing. I've never had the courage to ask you, but . . . is it true you saw her?"

Franca shudders. "No. I went first to the hotel and then with Ignazio and Alessandro to the Verano cemetery for the autopsy, but they wouldn't let me go in."

"Do you have any news of that man?"

Franca sighs. "I can't get a word out of Ignazio. According to the newspapers, he's in Regina Coeli and can hardly speak because the pistol shot took away the right side of his face. In any case he'll have to stand trial for premeditated homicide. I think it's likely that Ignazio will be called as a witness." She lowers her head, swallowing a lump of tears. "I feel really bad that I wasn't more insistent with her. I should have been closer to her. I knew that he was constantly asking her for money, that he even threatened her. And Giulia really wanted to leave him because he'd become violent. If I'd been there more, perhaps . . ."

"Perhaps it would have happened later, but it would have happened anyway. She was the one who chose to go to that last appointment, and that was her biggest mistake."

But Franca can't resign herself. It feels cruelly jarring to speak of such a terrible end in the middle of this flowery garden. "She was as dear to me as a sister—more than a sister. I can no longer bear to be surrounded by all this death. I've lost too many people who were dear to me."

Annina squeezes her arm. "Then Vincenzo and I will bring life back to this house. Maybe with a child, a child who has a big smile like his father!" She laughs. "Yes, a new little Florio! What this family needs is a little joy."

Cholera is an ancient scourge with which the city is familiar, and against which Vincenzo Florio, Ignazio's grandfather, fought all those years ago.

The designated victims have always been the same, for centuries: people who live in poverty, who can't wash themselves properly, who live cheek by jowl. First one, then ten, then twenty. The commune of Palermo sends functionaries from house to house, but many people keep their doors closed out of fear: they know that if they're ill, they'll be taken to a hospital and left to die alone like dogs . . .

It happens very, very quickly.

From the lower floors, cholera rises to the upper floors, spreads from the historic center to the outskirts, reaches the villas, attaches itself to the flesh of the inhabitants.

Nothing and no one can stop it.

On the morning of June 17, 1911, Annina wakes feeling lethargic, with strong pains in her stomach. Vincenzo kisses her and touches her forehead. "You have a slight fever," he whispers. "I'll call the doctor."

By the time Casa Florio's doctor arrives, the fever has increased significantly. Annina can barely breathe. The doctor touches her, then retreats.

Cholera.

How is it possible that cholera has arrived at the Olivuzza? Everything here is clean, there's running water, there are baths, and . . .

And yet . . .

At the news, Franca is seized with panic. She's already lost a daughter to an infectious disease and doesn't want to run the chance of Igiea or Giugiù getting ill. She gives orders for the children to leave Palermo with Maruzza and the nurse. The doctor says that Annina should remain isolated; Ignazio begs Vincenzo to obey, to stay away from her, but Vincenzo shakes his head.

"She's my wife. I have to be with her." His usually sharp voice becomes a rivulet. "I won't leave her alone. She must get better."

It's he who lifts her in his arms and carries her to a room on the third floor of the Olivuzza, far from everyone. He clasps her to his chest, but Annina, in the grip of the fever, hardly recognizes him. Her face is covered in red blotches; her sweaty hair sticks to her skull; she's very weak. He tidies her hair and wets her forehead with fresh cloths. He sits by the bed, holds her hand, kisses it, sends away the alarmed maids, and changes the sheets and linens himself.

"Don't die," he begs her, holding her hand. "Don't leave me."

For the first time in his life, he has felt loved and welcomed, he has experienced the joy of sharing mutual passions, of laughing and becoming excited about the same things. It can't all end like this. It *mustn't* end like this.

"It's too soon," he says to her, his mouth against the back of her hand. "You can't leave me. We want a child—remember how much we talked about it? You promised me a child."

*Wake up*, he implores silently, looking at her motionless, waxen face. "Wake up," he says to her, and tries to make her drink. In the evening, Annina loses consciousness. On the ground floor, her sister, Maria Concetta, is weeping desperately, and so is her mother, but the doctor prevents them from going up. "It's bad enough that Signor Vincenzo is there. Let's hope he doesn't get ill, too," he comments grimly, looking at Ignazio, who is ashen-faced.

The two women decide to stay there for the night, so as to be close to Annina.

The following morning, the gilded mirrors in the drawing rooms of the Olivuzza and the panes of the windows reflect pale, marked faces. The servants look for soap and vinegar to disinfect themselves.

There's Giovanna, in her room, weeping and praying on her knees in front of the crucifix. There's Franca, terrified, holed up in her room, hoping that her children have not been infected. There's Ignazio, in a daze, seizing the telephone to call Vera and tell her what's happening, just to hear her voice.

There's Vincenzo, who feels his soul breaking into pieces.

And then there's Annina, in a bed soaked with sweat, who's stopped waking up, who can't drink, can't speak, her breath ever more labored and her body seemingly on the verge of falling apart.

On the afternoon of June 19, she has an attack of convulsions.

Vincenzo screams and calls for help. It's the fever; it's too strong. From the stairs, the voices of Maria Concetta and her mother, the cries of Ignazio and the doctor.

Annina writhes, struggles, pants.

He tries to keep her still but can't. She won't stop moving.

Then she stops, her eyes roll back, her back arches. She collapses in Vincenzo's arms, without breath, without a heartbeat.

And all at once, it's over.

# PART FOUR

# Lead

October 1912 to Spring 1935

*Cu avi dinari campa felici e cu unn'avi perdi l'amici.*
Those who have money live happily and
those who don't lose their friends.
—SICILIAN PROVERB

L EAD IS A METALLIC BODY, pale, earthly, grave, soundless, with little white and much pallor," writes Ferrante Imperato in his *Dell'Historia Naturale* (1599). Available in abundance in nature, easy to melt and work, it is used as far back as ancient Egypt. Phoenicians, Greeks, and Romans use it for making weapons like arrowheads or sling bullets for catapults, since lead bullets do not exist until the Middle Ages. They also use lead to make fishing tools (ballasts, sounders, and anchors), various kinds of welding, pipes (because it is resistant to oxidization), and pans for cooking and concentrating must in order to obtain "salt of Saturn" (lead acetate) to sweeten wine, so called because the god Saturn was associated with lead.

From Theophrastus of Eresos (third century BCE), we discover the origin of another essential use of lead: ceruse, a kind of "mold" made from corroding lead with vinegar vapors. Until the nineteenth century, ceruse, or white lead, illuminates the history of art: everyone uses it, from Leonardo to Titian, from Van Dyck to Velázquez, because the only other white pigment—whitewash—is unsuitable for oil painting. Moreover, it illuminates women's faces: as far back as the eleventh century, Trotula de Ruggiero, active in the Schola Medica Salernitana, explains in her *De Ornatu Mulierum* how to create a cream that "can be applied daily to the face to make it fairer": chicken fat, violet or rose oil, wax, egg white, and white lead powder. Queen Elizabeth I's ashen complexion is due to her application of a thick blend of ceruse and vinegar to conceal her smallpox scars.

It is a long time before people realize just how dangerous this illumination is. In the mid-seventeenth century, the German physician Samuel Stockhausen finds that litharge (lead oxide) is the cause of the asthma afflicting miners in the city of Goslar in Lower Saxony. A few years later, in his *De Morbis Artificum Diatriba*, Bernardino Ramazzini focuses on the work of potters and says, "[ . . . ] all that is toxic in lead, when thus melted and liquefied with water, is absorbed by them through their mouths, nose, and entire body, and consequently they soon start suffering serious damage [ . . . ] at first trembling hands, then paralysis, with a sick spleen, then comes stupidity, cachexia, and toothlessness, to the extent that it is rare to see a potter without a pasty, lead-colored face." This condition will be called *saturnism*, and will give rise to theories about its famous victims: many Roman emperors (including Caligula, Nero, Domitian, Trajan), heavy wine drinkers and therefore consumers of *Saturn salt*; painters like Piero della Francesca, Caravaggio, Rembrandt, and Goya, because of their intense use of ceruse. Apparently, Beethoven also paid with deafness for his love of Rhine wines, drunk in lead crystal cups and sweetened with lead acetate. Some claim that Lenin also died from lead poisoning because of the two bullets he received in a failed assassination in 1918, which were not removed until four years later. But the millions of men and women with humble jobs who also died of lead poisoning, from factory workers to miners, from linotype operators to milliners, are and will always remain anonymous. Primo Levi was right when, in *The Periodic Table*, he defined lead as "murky, poisonous, and heavy," and yet it is also thanks to this metal that we have Antonello da Messina's *L'Annunciata*, Da Vinci's *The Last Supper*, and Caravaggio's *Medusa*.

Art and destruction, beauty and death, locked in a single soul.

The FIAT brakes to an abrupt standstill outside the hotel's double doors and Franca gets out. She's wearing a fur-trimmed beige coat and a hat with a large veil over her face, her forehead furrowed by a worry line. She clutches the handle of her handbag as she walks gracefully up the steps to the lobby.

Maruzza rushes after her and catches up with her just as Franca is about to ask for Signor Florio's room number.

The concierge is polite but firm. "The signore is indisposed and cannot receive callers."

Franca glares at him scornfully, lifts her veil over the brim of her hat, and leans forward. "He may be indisposed for all women, but not me. I'm his wife. I'm Donna Franca Florio," she says, her voice brimming with anger. "Tell me my husband's room number or I'll have you fired."

Embarrassed, the man mutters, "I apologize. I didn't recognize you . . ."—which only adds to Franca's exasperation.

She sighs and turns to Maruzza. "Take the car and arrange all our things in the hotel. Then send the car back to me."

"Are you sure you don't want me to wait for you here?"

"No, thank you. You may go."

Maruzza squeezes her arm. "Be strong," she whispers in her ear. Franca sighs again.

She has been trying to be strong all her life. *To force herself* to be strong, she thinks, correcting herself as she climbs the stairs, her hand on the velvet banister.

An entire lifetime of bearing, accepting, closing her eyes. Because that's the way she had to behave. Because that was the only role available to Donna Franca Florio on the stage of this gossiping, prying city called Palermo.

And all that for the sake of love. Even after love stopped being love—because that's how it ended up—and she found herself without a purpose. Without a man who, for better or worse, had filled her life.

Until Vera arrived.

She approaches the room on the third floor and hears muffled footsteps before a man with a thick graying mustache opens the door. Behind him, on the bed, sits Ignazio in a red velvet smoking jacket, a bandage covering part of his face.

She looks at him with a mixture of anxiety and anger.

"Signora . . . we weren't expecting you so soon," the man says, inviting her to come in.

Franca knows Professor Bastianelli: he is their family doctor in Rome. Trying to ignore the vague embarrassment that has drifted across the room, he picks up his hat and bag and leaves discreetly. Franca and Ignazio are left alone.

Franca removes her hat and coat and slips off her gloves. She is wearing a smart brown dress with a plain string of pearls around her neck. She goes and sits down in the armchair at the foot of the bed, crossing her hands over her legs, and stares at him for a long time.

Ignazio doesn't shy away from her gaze. "Forgive me," he says at last, lowering his head. "Once again, I've upset you."

"No worse than any other time," Franca replies with a tense smile. "If anything, I was rather scared for you."

Faced with this reaction, and those eyes filled with resigned sadness, Ignazio feels something he has recently had to contend with more and more: a sense of guilt. He has tried to deny it, to push it away his whole life. He has succeeded and is still succeeding, when it comes to tackling his increasingly precarious business situation. But it's quite another story with Franca. Now guilt is constricting his throat, pressing down on his chest, making it hard for him to breathe.

"I'm sorry," he murmurs. He rubs his hands on the edge of the bedsheet, his finger tracing an imaginary pattern. "When Vera's husband, Giberto, found out about me and his wife . . . I know how painful it must be to hear these things from me . . ."

Franca remains impassive.

"He attacked me here, in the lobby of this hotel, a few days ago," Ignazio continues, "and challenged me, demanding satisfaction. The duel was . . . unavoidable." He gets slowly to his feet. The wound to his temple is not serious, but it is unpleasant and causes dizziness. "We agreed to meet at Villa Anziani the day before yesterday, as I told you on the phone. We fought with sabers. He was furious—he lunged at me with the violence of an uncontrolled demon. He wanted to kill me, or at least disfigure me."

Franca suddenly bursts out into a long, hearty laugh, covering her mouth with her hands. "Oh God, you men are so ridiculous!"

Ignazio looks at her in shock. Has his wife gone crazy?

Franca shakes her head, her laughter waning into a smile of perfectly balanced pain and incredulity. "A duel with sabers, like a third-rate novel for servant girls. And Giberto demanding to defend his honor after . . . How long have you and she been seeing each other? Four years?" She looks down at her hands and touches her wedding band. "If I'd challenged to a duel all the women with whom you've had affairs, half our female acquaintances would be dead or disfigured . . . Or *I* would be. Only a man would behave with such stupidity."

Ignazio keeps staring at her. "What . . . what do you mean?"

"I mean that you may not remember how many women you've had, but I do. At least those I've heard of. I've had to learn to smile and shrug, as if it's only natural that my husband should have one affair after another. Dozens of them. And you know what?" She looks up, her green eyes now clear and almost calm. "After telling myself so often that I didn't care, I've truly ended up not giving a hoot."

He goes to a small table, picks up a bottle of cognac, and pours himself a glass. "But I've always come back to you."

"Because you wouldn't have known where else to go."

"Don't be silly. You've always been my point of reference."

Franca walks over and stands facing him. "Still telling yourself that lie, Ignazio? Be my guest, only don't tell it to me. I'm too tired. When I married you, I was a naive girl, and perhaps you, too, were filled with hopes . . . You know, I sometimes miss that young woman who was so sure her one duty was to be at her husband's side and love him in spite of everything. How I fought and suffered to feel worthy of you, of your name . . . of being a Florio."

Her voice has a hardness he has never heard before. "Franca—"

"You've never shared anything about your business with me. You've never told me what you talked about with your politician friends in Rome and Palermo. For so many years I thought that was right and proper. After all, I didn't know any other women involved in their husbands' dealings. I was your wife and I had social duties; someone like me shouldn't be interested in those things. But now . . ." She hesitates, these words clearly wounding her. "Now I know that you share these things with Vera. Don't bother denying it: I know she's advised you on more than one occasion. Even Vincenzo confirmed it."

Ignazio swallows air, not knowing how to respond. How can he explain to her how he feels when he doesn't know himself? How can he tell her that, yes, he loves her because she represents the most beautiful and important part of his life, because together they have been masters of the world, but that in the end that life has shriveled like paper burnt to ash? How can he confess to her that when he looks back, all he sees are wild parties, travels that were actually escapes, nameless female bodies, money squandered on seeking a pleasure as intense as it was ephemeral? And how can he admit that when he looks ahead, all he sees is the unavoidable decline of old age, accompanied by financial ruin?

He can't. Because to tell her everything would mean to give body and voice to the most painful reality for both of them: the absence of an heir for Casa Florio. His name, the name of his uncle—an "honest and brave man," as his father said—will end with him. There is no one he can give the ring he wears under his wedding band. He hoped at least to have a nephew, but since Annina's death over a year ago, Vincenzo has become even more restless and rebellious. No, there is no one, and never will be . . .

Franca notices Ignazio toying with the family ring. She knows that gesture. It means embarrassment, suffering, anxiety.

"I know you blame me," she mutters.

"For what?" Ignazio doesn't look at her but stares at the wall opposite, beyond the barrier of the half-open window.

"For giving you only one son. Only one."

He sighs, more irritated than despondent. "I don't blame you for anything. We had one and the Lord took him away. Maybe he wanted to punish us for something."

"Even your mother wouldn't say something like that."

Ignazio's sense of guilt clamps his chest again. He *has* thought, in his darkest moments, that the Lord wanted to punish him for the series of follies and betrayals that his life has been. But what does it matter now? Even if he did have an heir, what would he bequeath him? Only debts and dust.

"You know I've never held back. I've always been there. I've always been a faithful wife."

Ignazio can't bear it anymore. He needs an outlet, a way of unburdening himself. "Stop it once and for all!" he bursts out. "Why don't you talk about the men who chase you across Italy, who yearn for you, starting with D'Annunzio and that *marchese* who showers you with flowers, and finally Enrico Caruso, whom I was foolish enough to sign up for the Massimo when he didn't know anybody! I know he still writes to you . . . How long has it been? Ten, fifteen years?"

Franca waves her hands in annoyance. "It's pointless accusing me, and you know it. They all flirt with me, but nobody has ever taken any liberties beyond words. Because I've never given them reason or occasion to. I've always been equal to your wishes. And all that for what? There's always been a woman who's better than me, more desirable, more charming. Do you deny it?"

Ignazio stares at her in silence, with anger and shame.

*I've always been equal to your wishes.*

The ideal wife. Stunning. At ease in every circumstance. Relaxed but measured. More elegant than anyone else. With brilliant, sharp, intelligent conversation. A lover of music and the arts. The perfect hostess. Wasn't it he who prompted that shy nineteen-year-old to become this sophisticated, demanding woman standing now before him? He wanted a wife to show off, a trophy other men would envy. He never really sought in her a life companion.

He was so blind. So immature.

He realizes this now that he has found what he really needs elsewhere.

"I . . ."

She looks down at her hands and weeps silently, then asks in a weak voice, "What does Vera have that I don't?"

Ignazio wipes her tears with the back of his hand. "Franca . . . You're different. She's . . ."

"What more can she give you than I've given you all these years?"

He can't bear Franca acting as both judge and jury. He walks away and stands with his back to her. "She's everything you can no longer be," he says. *Full of enthusiasm, passionate, alive.* "She welcomed me into her life, while you've excluded me from everything. Any excuse to keep away from me: evenings gambling, taking trips with your female friends . . ."

Franca turns pale, eyes open wide. "*You're* blaming *me* for not being by your side?"

"Ever since the problems began, you've . . . disappeared. You haven't been there for me. Vera has been. And that's made a difference."

"But you never asked me to!"

"You're my wife. I shouldn't need to ask."

Franca sways.

She has given him her whole life and it wasn't enough for him. Now he's practically accusing her of not giving him more. Wasn't it enough that she turned a blind eye to all his betrayals? That she faced the whole world with dignity after the deaths of their children? That she was always at his side? No, it wasn't enough for him. Franca suddenly realizes that Ignazio wishes she had destroyed herself totally and remained invisible until he called her, dependent on his needs, his urges. But then he met Vera and understood that the power of love wasn't submission but equality and walking side by side.

Ignazio had grown up at last. But to do that, he had cast her aside, along with all that existed between them.

*So he, too, can truly love*, she tells herself, more surprised than embittered. *And he loves a woman who's not me.*

"I understand. There's nothing more to add." She throws back her shoulders and raises her head. Dignity and pride are the only two things no one will ever be able to take away from her. "I'm going to the Grand Hotel," she says. "You can find me there." She picks up her coat. He doesn't stop her. He drops his arms, watches her, searches that face that's able to hide pain.

This is delayed, denied pain, kept quiet for too long. And now it burns inside him, too, corroding him like acid.

They will be together in the eyes of the world, but they will live separate lives. They will share a dining table, but not a bed. And they will never again look back.

"I'll be in touch," he says, but she's already out the door.

Franca goes downstairs, holding on to the banister, although her fingers are trembling.

The ice that's been inside her for years—since her children died, but perhaps even earlier—suddenly turns into a flow of lava. She feels its intolerable heat, feels it bubbling and swelling. It seems to be stifling her. She collapses on a step, her forehead resting on her arm, breathing with her mouth open, her head spinning violently.

*What do I have left?*

*Igiea and Giulia, of course, but what else?*

This thought falls away and folds in on itself. The tears that were pushing to get out a moment ago have dried up.

There's nothing else to add. She gets back up and walks out, taking small steps, she who has always had a relaxed, elegant stride. Outside the hotel stands the vehicle Maruzza has sent back. As the driver opens the door and she's about to get in, another car stops outside the entrance.

A woman gets out.

Her delicate face is tense, her disheveled hair escaping her cream-colored hat. A small suitcase peers out from under a woolen cloak the same color as the hat.

The woman pays the driver, then turns.

At that moment, their eyes meet.

Vera Arrivabene stares, astonished. She lifts a hand, as if to greet Franca. After all, they have known each other for years and have been good friends. It would be a natural gesture.

But it only lasts an instant.

She clenches her hand and lowers her arm. She sustains Franca's gaze, shameless, remorseless. Her face is white and delicate, like that of a Madonna, with just a hint of pink.

Franca stands motionless, simultaneously looking at her and ignoring her.

Vera turns her back on her and practically runs up the steps into the hotel.

Only then does Franca take a seat in the car and say, "To the Grand Hotel."

Vincenzo Florio is sitting on a chair, looking out, resting his chin on his fist. He hears a sound behind him and barely turns toward it. One of the two women with whom he spent the night is waking up.

She looks at him through heavy eyelids, brushes her reddish hair off her face, and taps her hand on the mattress, inviting him to join her. The other woman, a brunette with an ample bosom, is snoring softly, mouth half open, tousled hair down her naked back. There is a smell of sex, sweat, and champagne in the room, in addition to a fragrance with powerful flowery notes.

He shakes his head and resumes looking outside.

It's raining over Paris, on the sycamores of the boulevard, on the slate roofs. It has been raining for three days. He's weary of this chilly, unpleasant June. He should go to the Côte d'Azur. Alternatively, he could join Franca, who's in Switzerland with his nieces. As for Ignazio, he might be in Venice or Rome with Vera—who knows?

His breath condenses on the windowpane. He draws an *A* with his fingers and erases it abruptly.

*Annina.*

It has been three years since his wife's death. Three years during which he has done nothing but travel and hop from one bed to another, trying to shake off the unease that oppresses him and constricts his throat.

He's having a relationship with a woman of Russian origin. He sometimes thinks he's grown attached to her, but nights like the last prove the opposite. The truth is that he no longer cares about anything or anyone; for the sake of a little distraction, he has actually involved himself in the family business, even though Ignazio has never taken him very seriously.

"Annina will always be a part of you and your life," Franca told him a few days after the funeral. Vincenzo was on a bench in the garden, motionless, his head in his hands. She sat down behind him without touching him. "You'll keep wondering about the things you would have done together, the words she would have said to you, when she would have smiled. You'll imagine talking to her, just like I do . . ." She paused, looked up at the horizon, and dropped her voice. "You'll think about what it would have been like to have a child and watch it grow. A part of you will continue to live with her, in your mind or your heart . . . in a time and place that don't exist." Only then did she squeeze his hand, and he burst into sobs. "Only, that won't be your real life. Reality will be here, with the emptiness, the absence, and the words you'll never again be able to hear. And in the end, imagining the impossible will become so painful that you'll choose to give it up. You'll start looking at the present and feeling a little better. I know this sounds absurd, but trust me. No one knows better than I . . ." She put her arm around him and together they wept, each with his and her own grief.

Vincenzo shakes his head. In the past three years he has recalled Franca's words and waited for his suffering to relent. But Annina is still here next to him, a constant presence. Maybe—he has wondered—women see things in the darkness of grief, things men can't begin to guess. It's their curse and their salvation.

Even now, at this very moment, she's before him, in a dark skirt and a white blouse with a lace collar. She's about to get behind the wheel of one of their automobiles, but then stops and looks at him with a reproachful expression, as though asking: *Why have you gotten yourself in such a state?*

"*Vincent, chéri, viens ici . . .*"

The redhead is calling him, heedless of the fact that the other woman is still asleep. He wishes he could send them both away, make them disappear.

Instead, he gets up, walks away from the window, removes his shirt, and lies down next to her. He lets her touch him, closes his eyes, and thrusts into her body almost violently. He doesn't care what her name is, who she is, or how she lives outside of this room: it's a body that gives him pleasure and warmth.

And he clings to that little bit of life he manages to snatch.

⌒

The lobby of the Hotel di Champfèr in the Engadin, where the Florios, the Lanza di Trabias, and the Whitakers are staying, is in turmoil. Tense faces, telegrams changing hands, telephones ringing, valets dashing between rooms like ants. For about a month now—ever since a very young Serbian nationalist assassinated Archduke Franz Ferdinand and his wife, Sophie, in Sarajevo—there have been endless, contradictory rumors of a possible declaration of war on Serbia by Austria. The ultimatum presented to the Serbian government in Belgrade by the Austrian ambassador on July 23 leaves little hope for a peaceful resolution.

Sitting in an armchair, Franca peruses the Italian and German newspapers, confused and unable to remove herself from this back-and-forth volley between exaltation about war and the "feverish intensity required by the gravity of the circumstance" that Italy is apparently adopting in order to maintain the peace, according to the *Corriere della Sera*.

"Here I am, Franca. *Désolée d'être en retard.*" Giulia Lanza di Trabia kisses her on the cheek and looks around. "Aren't Norina and Delia here?"

"No, they came by with Tina a couple of minutes ago and said they'd promised to spend the afternoon with her. They'll join us at five for tea. They're thirty years old, but that woman sometimes treats her daughters as if they were children."

"So much the better," Giulia says, smiling and putting on her gloves. "Shall we go?"

They nod to Giovanna, who's on the terrace, getting some sunshine with Maruzza, then leave by the back door of the hotel.

Giulia takes a deep breath of the crisp air. "What a shame Igiea and Giugiù aren't here, too!"

"I actually had a letter from Zurich this very afternoon: the governess says Igiea's back treatment seems to be effective. As for Giugiù, she's like her father: she always says the mountains are 'boooring' and spends her time running around the house. What's the poor dear supposed to do, after all? She's only five . . ."

With a firm step, Giulia takes the path to a pine wood that extends over the side of the mountain.

"And you? Have you heard anything from Giuseppe?"

"No." Giulia's tone is sharp. Her eldest son has always had a restless, rebellious nature. "With all that's happening, it would be more prudent for him to be here or in Palermo . . . If he would at least let us know where he is." She pauses, lips pursed. "I think he's in Venice with that woman."

"Madda . . ." Franca looks around at the pointed treetops soaring to the sky. A panoramic route opens before them amid the trees. They slow down and almost come to a halt. The air is balmy, fragrant with greenery, steeped in the smell of musk. Every so often, birdsong breaks the silence. "The Papadopoli twins don't know what fidelity and respect for the marriage bond are."

"Don't!" Giulia responds with a grimace. Unlike Franca, she has never taken particular care of her looks, and time has done her no favors. Her face has grown sharp and lined. "When I think of how she ensnared him! He was a boy when they met, and she already had a daughter. Giuseppe wants me to meet her . . . but that would be madness! She's married and she's left everything for him. No, I refuse to see her: it's indecent even to mention her name."

Franca squeezes her arm. "You're right. You're so right."

"I suppose my brother is still with her sister, Vera."

Franca responds with an exasperated sigh.

Giulia makes a gesture of contempt. "To leave four children and a husband to be with a man—a married man at that . . . The world's gone mad!"

Franca stops abruptly and looks at Giulia. "Do you remember what you told me all those years ago in the winter garden at your house?"

Giulia stares into the distance and smiles. "You were so scared . . . Everything and everyone frightened you, including my mother."

"But you told me that I had to claim whatever was mine by right, that I should be proud to be a Florio, to bear this name."

"Yes, and so you did. Always, even when times were particularly tough."

Franca smiles bitterly. "Yes, I learned to. It cost me a great deal, but I managed it in the end. In the eyes of the world, I've been a Florio, and always will be. But inside . . ."

Giulia takes her by the hands. "Inside, you died so many times. Because of what you went through, because of Ignazio's behavior . . . I know that, too."

"Yes, but there's something else. Until two years ago, I was convinced I knew my husband. I'd long stopped defending him and quietly accepting his defects. But I was sure we were still united by love."

Giulia raises an eyebrow.

"Yes, I still call it love. In any case, there was a bond between us. Then Vera came along and Ignazio fell in love with her. And I was left truly alone."

"Franca, darling, you're not alone . . . I'm here, and so's Igiea, and Giugiù . . ."

Franca throws her shoulders back and looks into the distance. "Yes, thank heavens you're here. But when I look in the mirror, I can only see myself, as though the world didn't exist. I see a broken woman who nevertheless lives on." She takes a deep breath. "That's what I wanted to tell you: that thanks to what you said, I've learned not to depend on anybody and to keep on going in spite of everything."

"And no longer feel anything?" Giulia murmurs.

"You know that's not possible. How long ago did Blasco die?"

"Twenty-one years," Giulia replies in a breath.

"And has there been a single day when you haven't thought of him?"

She shakes her head.

"Our dead never leave us, and their presence is both pain and consolation."

Suddenly, Giulia bursts into tears, holding her head between her hands. "You speak of the dead and I . . ."

"What's wrong?" Franca asks, anxious. She has never seen her sister-in-law cry like this. "Are you unwell?"

Giulia shakes her head, still sobbing. "No, no . . . I didn't want to say anything so as not to worry you, but I'm very afraid, Franca. I spoke to Pietro last night. He's in Rome and he says terrible things are afoot. He thinks the Austrians are going to attack Serbia and that will prompt France, Russia, and maybe Britain to go to war. And I'm scared because I have sons, and God only knows what might happen."

"But the papers say the Italian government is mediating . . ."

"Pietro is very skeptical about that," Giulia replies, drying her tears. "War is at the gates and the Lord only knows how it'll all end up. I can't bear the thought of my sons going to fight. Giuseppe is twenty-five years old, Ignazio twenty-four, and Manfredi twenty. They're grown men, they're Lanza di Trabias, and their place is on the front line. It's their duty."

Franca doesn't know what to say. First the Olivuzza and then Villa Igiea have always been open to all. She can't even remember how many Englishmen, Frenchmen, Germans, and Russians she has met.

Politicians and artists, bankers and entrepreneurs, with their families in tow. They have talked and dined together, danced till dawn, played cards or lawn tennis, laughed at jokes or gossip. They have dived into the sea or scaled Monte Pellegrino, spent happy hours on Favignana, made long excursions on Ignazio's yachts or in Vincenzo's cars. She thinks about the kaiser, the English monarchs, Empress Eugénie . . .

And now these same people are deciding whether or not to ravage Europe.

Giulia's sons are so young . . . Actually, Giovannuzza would be twenty-one now and maybe she would have to watch her husband leave. Ignazino is only sixteen, though, so he's too young to—

*Wait. Stop. They're not here anymore. But Giulia is here.*

She puts a hand on her sister-in-law's shoulder. "Pietro's probably exaggerating. He always makes things out to be worse than they are. No harm will come to your sons."

"I hope not." Giulia takes deep breaths to calm down. "Yes, I'd better think about the future of my daughters, Sofia and Giovanna. They're already seventeen and eighteen."

"Or about that hooligan Ignazio," Franca adds with a tense smile. She cannot bear to see Giulia in so much distress. "We must look ahead, to life carrying on, and not to these dreadful things we're unsure of."

When they return to the hotel, though, they quickly realize that the earlier turmoil has turned to fear. Anxiety has become physical; there is an unpleasant stink of cigarette smoke and sweat in the air. Groups of people surrounded by trunks and suitcases are besieging the concierge, asking for their bills at the tops of their voices, swearing, begging for attention, letting rage get the better of them. In a corner, a woman is sobbing and two children are sitting on the floor, crying, ignored by everybody.

For a second, Franca's mind slips away to the night her son died.

Then she looks around in panic, searching for a familiar face, and finds it: Maruzza stands up from the couch where she's been sitting next to Giovanna, who is praying with her rosary, eyes closed, and comes to her.

"Austria has declared war on Serbia. And they say other countries will soon be involved."

"What? When? And what about Italy?" Franca and Giulia speak in unison, and Maruzza raises her hands to stop them. "I telegraphed Ignazio to warn him," she says to Franca. "The Whitakers are already packing their bags. Everybody's leaving the hotel to go back home."

Giulia lifts a hand to her chest, as if to steady her heartbeat. "I'll have to speak to my husband and my sons. Yes, you're right: we must return to Italy. Franca, do you have with you the documents that state you're a lady-in-waiting to Queen Elena?"

Franca nods, confused. "Yes, but—"

"Good. I'm sure those documents are valid as a diplomatic pass for you and your family. Call Zurich and tell the governess to get the girls ready for immediate departure."

Franca nods. "I'll do it right away."

"And talk to Ignazio," Giulia adds, dropping her voice. "His place is with you now. And he'd better realize it."

⌒

"Of course I'm aware of the danger. All the same, my specific duty is—"

"But we've been the emperor's guests in Vienna! And you want to volunteer against him? It's absurd!"

"We're at war and everyone has to play his part."

For almost a year, Franca has hoped that Italy would stay out of the conflict. The fear of war has grown inside her gradually and she has hidden it for a long time in a dark corner of her soul, the way she does with anything she can't accept. But she can no longer avoid it now.

She gets to her feet and paces up and down the room, struggling to control her tension. A little earlier, she was at Palazzo Butera and found Giulia devastated because her sons are about to go to war. Franca adores those boys: Giuseppe, Ignazio, and Manfredi are a part of her life; she has watched them grow up and become men, while she was losing hers. The very thought of seeing them in uniform gives her a pang of anxiety, so she can't even imagine what her sister-in-law is going through. That's why she's decided she will avoid saying goodbye to them. That way she won't be forced to admit that this is all really happening. She's tired of defending herself against life and the world.

She leaves the room and walks to the little temple overlooking the sea, squinting in the light. It feels absurd to talk of war in the serenity of Villa Igiea's garden, amid blossoming plants, with the fragrance of summer in the air. Along the avenues that slope down toward the coast, amid the boxwood and pittosporum hedges, two gardeners are bedding out young plants while talking softly. Only the sounds from the harbor in the distance interrupt the whistling of the wind in the palm trees.

They're living now in Villa Igiea, with Giovanna, Maruzza, and Miss Daubenye, the girls' English governess. The Olivuzza has become too large, with too many expenses, and a garden that demands too much attention. Their hotel apartment is much better, still luxurious but easier to manage. Besides, Villa Igiea is half deserted at the moment, since the guests—almost all Italians—left a few days ago.

Ignazio approaches her, but Franca clenches her hands and asks, without turning, "And is it really necessary that you join up immediately?"

He hesitates and looks in the direction of the Arenella *tonnara* and Villa dei Quattro Pizzi, which his grandfather loved so much. The deep blue soothes his irritation. His forehead relaxes as he remembers cruises on board the *Aegusa*. But only for an instant. *A past life*, he thinks bitterly. "Necessary? Yes," he finally replies. "At the moment, I can arrange it so that I get an assignment far away from the front and suited to my skills. And I'll do the same for Vincenzo, who otherwise would run the risk of ending up on the front line, since he's younger than I. He's an excellent driver and a gifted mechanic, so he could be useful for transportation on the sidelines. He's also thinking of starting a small factory to manufacture airplanes or seaplanes in partnership with Vittorio Ducrot, and apart from that he mentioned a project involving a truck that could be useful to the army in the more rugged terrain . . . You know what Vincenzo's like: always on the go."

Franca shakes her head. "He'll do something foolish. He's a daredevil."

"Of course he won't!" He strokes her arm. "We won't be in any danger. You'll see."

She turns to look at him. Ignazio now has a few locks of hair with a dusting of gray, and his lips, once thin and elegant, are marked with bitterness. "Do you think it'll be over soon?" she asks, hands joined over her black skirt.

Ignazio shrugs his shoulders. "I couldn't say. It was supposed to last just a few weeks, and there's been fighting for a year already." He drops his voice and touches the white lace sleeve of Franca's blouse. "In any case, the war can only make things worse."

His voice is filled with a resignation Franca struggles to interpret. She wants to ask, and nearly does, but then a noise makes her turn.

"Forgive the intrusion. If I'd known you were engaged, Signor Florio, I would have waited before talking to you."

"Do come here, Signor Linch. Good morning."

Carlo Augusto Linch takes long, soft strides toward them. Ignazio goes to meet him, while Franca simply gives a nod. She is wary of this Argentinian, partly because she knows so little about him: only that he studied in Milan and at the Zurich Polytechnic, that he managed a factory in Germany, and that he returned to Italy once the war broke out. He immediately gained the trust of her husband and brother-in-law, winning them over with his good nature, his reassuring character, and his easy way with words. They both decided to involve him in the administration of their property, or what was left of it. Three months ago, in February 1915, Linch became the Florios' administrator and legal representative.

Franca stands aside and watches the two men. She hears the words, "Because the Casa Florio estate is . . ." and raises an eyebrow. What estate, when even Cartier and Worth—where she's been a client for over twenty years—now ask her to sign "documents" guaranteeing the payment of bills? Not to mention what happened just yesterday: a maid quit because she hadn't received her wages regularly. A true lack of respect toward people who had given bread and work to half of Palermo.

"And you, Signora? What are you going to do?"

She gives an embarrassed little laugh. "Pardon me, I wasn't listening to you. What were you discussing?"

"No, I was saying . . . What are you going to do to support our country at this time? Will you give your services as a Red Cross nurse?"

"Oh . . . Yes, certainly. At the hospital here in Palermo, I suppose."

Linch smiles at her, then looks away, as though her reply didn't convince him in the least. "I'm sure you'll be able to adapt to this difficult situation. There are times of great sacrifice ahead."

Franca squints. She senses reproach for her conduct behind his words, for her expenditures, and especially for what has now become her only pastime: cards. Chemin de fer, baccarat, poker. When she plays, her sadness becomes less oppressive, her thoughts lighter, and time passes. Of course, money also slips away in these hours, because she places high bets. And she is "luckier than is fair," as her gaming table companion, Marie-Thérèse Tasca di Cutò, known as Ama, Alessandro's wife and poor Giulia Trigona's sister-in-law, always says. *But not lucky enough*, Franca wants to reply.

"I think I have the necessary papers in my office," Ignazio is saying to Linch. "I'll get the car ready so we can go together."

"No need. I can tell you everything here and now."

Franca looks at Linch, then at her husband. Once upon a time, she would have walked away quietly, because this is men's business. But now she wants to listen and understand. *If my husband's mistress knows all our business, why should I remain in the dark?* she thinks with irritation. So she follows them to the small willow drawing room in a corner of the Villa Igiea terrace, tells a servant to bring a carafe of lemonade, and sits down gracefully in an armchair.

Linch gives her a furtive, vaguely puzzled glance. Franca responds to it with a long look of defiance, then turns her attention expectantly to Ignazio.

Linch is embarrassed. He has never before discussed business in the presence of a woman. Franca's expression is so sharp that he almost stammers. "So then—if you will allow me . . ."

Ignazio sits down without looking at his wife and takes a sip of lemonade. "Do please go on."

Linch cautiously opens the portfolio he has brought with him and puts it on a table. He touches the papers—letters, notes, and accounts—as if to gather his thoughts, then steeples his fingers before his face. "As you know, a few days ago I completed a thorough examination of your financial situation. As I mentioned to you, I was planning to go to Rome to try and form a group to come to the aid of Casa Florio. The Banca d'Italia could be essential to fixing your debts, above all the contract with Lavagetto and Parodi for the *tonnaras* on the Aegadian Islands. It's now clear that that was an unfortunate decision, and it has made everything infinitely more complicated. Of course, in the beginning, you had a healthy injection of cash that allowed you to pay some of Casa Florio's arrears, but the revenue from the *tonnaras* has been entirely insufficient to cover even the interest. Moreover, the mortgage you . . . imprudently obtained from the Société Française de Banque et de Dépôts to cover other losses is proving to be very damaging."

Ignazio listens, impassive. Franca tries to keep up, but too many things in this speech are unclear to her.

"And then there are the blocks of shares that guarantee other loans and make the debts of Casa Florio heavier. I intend to ask for the blocks of shares still in your possession to be sold in order to obtain more liquidity, as well as subsidies on the part of other banking institutions, subsidies guaranteed by collaterals on your real estate, which would be sold at a later stage." He stops and sighs. "In a nutshell: you need a lot of money, and that obliges you to ask the banks for loans and offer them as collateral real estate like the Olivuzza, but also your plants in the Castellammare district. Assets that will have to be sold in the future."

Ignazio gives a start. "Our villa . . . and the *aromateria*?"

"Yes—as well as the other warehouses and apartments."

"Even the house on Via dei Materassai . . . my father's house?"

His voice is thin, like a thread blown by the wind through the pine trees.

"I'm afraid so."

Ignazio runs his fingers through his hair. "My God . . ." He laughs, but it's a broken, perverted laugh. "To be honest, I haven't been there for ages . . . As a matter of fact, my wife doesn't even want to go to Quattro Pizzi either, even though we had it refurbished because I was already expecting to have to give up the Olivuzza . . . But to sell the house on Via dei Materassai . . ." He clenches his hand into a fist and rests his chin on it.

Franca suddenly feels out of place. She has never seen Ignazio's father's house, and her mother-in-law has rarely mentioned it. It's true, she has never much cared for Villa dei Quattro Pizzi: it's not that it's ugly, but it's too small for their needs, and in a working-class district like the Arenella. It really wouldn't be suitable for receiving guests, who would have to travel down streets crowded with wagons and poor people in order to get there.

But to hear it stated like that, like a reproach, is a humiliation she didn't expect.

Linch picks up a sheet of paper. "I'm afraid we won't have much room for negotiation with the Banca d'Italia. I've tried requesting a meeting with Stringher, but they told me he's very busy and, above all, not interested."

"I'll bet!" Ignazio leaps to his feet, knocking against the table and making the carafe wobble. "That son of a bitch wants to punish us for what happened in 1909, when I withdrew from the consortium—that's the truth. And he's never cared anything about Casa Florio!" Ignazio is almost yelling. "He's always wanted to strip us of everything, even our dignity!" He takes a few steps, mutters an insult in dialect, and puts his hand over his eyes. "I'll have to write all this to Vincenzo . . . I think he's on his way back from Paris," he adds, almost to himself. "I don't know anything about his lifestyle now . . . He spends more time in France than anywhere else, and only comes back here to organize the Targa Florio or some other competition . . ."

"Just calm yourself and sit down," Linch says firmly. "We can talk about that, too."

Ignazio walks back to the wicker armchair with the air of a condemned man on his way to the gallows. All at once, Franca feels sorry for him. Instinctively, she reaches out her hand to console him, to let him know that she is with him. But Ignazio sits down without looking at her and she moves her hand back to her chest.

"You need to put limits on a whole series of activities and, in tandem, reduce your expenses," Linch explains, articulating the words clearly, as if calming a wounded animal. "The charity donations, for example . . ." Here, he gives Franca a brief, almost furtive glance. "But also the spending on clothes and jewelry. Or expenses like all those pocket watches with your trademark that you give your suppliers . . . In other words, unnecessary expenses in general. Your sponsorship of the Teatro Massimo and the Targa needs to be significantly scaled back."

"That old story again?" Biting the knuckles of his fist, Ignazio rocks back and forth slowly in the armchair. "Cutting off the charities, the subsidies to the Massimo . . . Avvocato Marchesano came up with that at least seven years ago! Does nobody realize what name I bear? It would be like parading through the streets of Palermo with a banner saying: 'Ignazio Florio is bankrupt!'"

"Perhaps if you had made that choice then, you would be in a less critical situation now. And yes, I admit, the decision is a painful one, but it's more necessary now than ever, if you want to save yourselves." Linch leafs through the papers, takes out another one and shows it to Ignazio. It's a promissory note bearing Giovanna's shaky signature. "Do you see this? I asked the Banca d'Italia for an extension and they granted it to me only because it has your mother's assets as collateral."

For the first time in his life, Ignazio Florio blushes.

Linch is unable to hide how sorry he feels. The lines on the sides of his mouth seem to deepen, and he lowers his eyes. "Many sacrifices will be necessary from everyone," he says, turning to look at Franca, who instinctively crosses her arms over her chest. "It would be useful, for example, to offer pledges to the banks as collateral for the debts." A long pause. "Pledges in jewels."

She turns pale and shakes her head vigorously. "No, you can't ask that of me." Her voice is sharp, like glass on glass. "Not my jewels. There are diamonds in the safe, he knows that," she goes on, pointing to Ignazio, who appears to ignore her. "There's no need to . . . use mine."

"As I was saying, everyone has to be prepared to make sacrifices, including you, Signora." Linch doesn't raise his voice, but his tone brooks no argument.

Franca is dismayed: nobody has ever talked to her like this, let alone a foreigner.

Ignazio shrugs and sighs. When he speaks again, he does so in a sad tone. The tone of a defeated man. "So be it. The houses, the jewels . . . What difference does it make now? The king is naked!" He stands up again and resumes walking slowly. He stops next to one of the pillars and strokes it. Through his memory pass images that make his lips curl in a gentle smile. "There was a time when I would have done anything to protect what belonged to me. I would have fought; I would have accepted mortification and humiliation. But now there's nothing and nobody left to fight for. I'm a tree without shoots, and very soon our country will be the same way. This war will bring only disaster, while it lasts and when it's over. So for what, for whom, should I struggle?" He turns to look at them. "I have nothing left of what made me a Florio." He counts on his fingers. "I sold the winery, my grandfather Vincenzo's first business. I tried to build a shipyard, but it failed, and with it NGI, which my father built up. I allowed the Oretea Foundry to go to rack and ruin. I fed the *tonnaras* on the Aegadian Islands to the sharks, convinced I would be able to get back on my feet, but to no avail. When I asked for help, I was given ropes to hang myself. What do I have left? The Banco Florio transformed into an office for pen pushers, and this hotel, which is going to be empty with a war on . . . I'm about to lose everything, even my home. That's the story of my family." He looks at Franca. "So why should I care about your jewels? All we have left is our dignity and a little pride. Make sure you don't waste them."

Franca gets abruptly to her feet, grabs his wrist, and yanks it. "You can't do it!" She takes both his hands. "Think about me and your two daughters!"

At that very moment, Igiea appears at the French doors. She's fifteen years old, with a graceful figure, short hair, and a delicate face that resembles her mother's. She takes a step onto the terrace, raises her hand to shield herself from the sun, and looks at her parents. The fact that they're quarreling is no novelty to her.

"*Maman*, Maruzza and I were wondering if we can go and see Princess Ama later . . . Can Maruzza come or should she stay with Granny? You know she hasn't been very well."

Franca's white, stiff hand lets go of Ignazio's wrist. "We'll go to the Tasca di Cutòs later. Yes, it's best if Maruzza stays with your grandmother."

Ignazio waits for his daughter to leave, then walks past Franca to Linch. "Do everything that's necessary to save what can be saved," he says in a low, calm voice. "You'll have what you need as collateral for the still unpaid promissory notes."

Linch gets to his feet. He's a few years older than Ignazio and is almost as tall as him, but slimmer. "I need a list of all your expenses, Signor Florio. Every outlay, every purchase, every unpaid bill. I need to see the invoices, too, and from now on, please, don't buy anything without consulting me first. Can I rely on you to tell your brother the same thing?"

Ignazio nods. He has understood that Linch will be merciless with him and Vincenzo. "I'll try. In a few days I'll be leaving as a volunteer, as you know . . ."

"A laudable gesture. I'll make sure I keep you up to date and I'll do everything I can to make Stringher and the Banca d'Italia soften their stance." Linch clears his throat and walks over to Franca. "Signora, I fear this goes for you, too. Can you make me an up-to-date list of your expenses?"

Franca nods. She stares at Monte Pellegrino, as if admiring it, but in reality she's consumed with a fierce anger, mixed with humiliation. Her expenses? Of course. But then what about everything that Ignazio spends on Vera in Rome, given that he's now living with her? Not to mention the fact that—she's almost certain of it—her husband's decision to go to war is also connected with that woman, who, she's found out, has enlisted as a volunteer nurse.

Yet again, she has been pushed aside and is having to bear the brunt of other people's mistakes, as well as her own. *Not my jewels*, she thinks. *They'll never have them.*

⌒

The room is warm, too warm. The red damask curtains let in the red light of sunset through a blanket of clouds that conceals the horizon. Sitting in an armchair, Maruzza is leaning her head on the palm of one hand and with the other hand holding open the pages of D'Annunzio's *Maybe Yes, Maybe No*, left by Franca at Villa Igiea years ago. The writer himself had given it to her with a dedication that read: *To Donna Franca Florio in great devotion*, and she'd had it bound in Morocco leather finished in gold.

*Yes, all those years ago, when war was far in the future and nobody knew what was going to happen*, Maruzza thinks with a sigh.

Franca comes less and less often to Palermo. When she isn't traveling, she spends long periods in Rome, usually at the Grand Hotel, with her daughters and with Ama Tasca di Cutò, who has left her husband, Alessandro, and their children and is seen about with a young *cavalier servente*.

At this thought, Maruzza closes the book abruptly. *One should never judge*, she reflects, *but really, those Tasca di Cutòs don't know how to restrain themselves*. And to think that, in all these years roaming about Europe in the company of the Florios, she's seen it all . . . She thinks again nostalgically of those long stays in Montecatini, in Switzerland, or on the Côte d'Azur, and the money that Franca spent on her, too.

Not anymore.

She raises her eyes to the ceiling, her face expressing a sorrow that's impossible to hide. The war has insinuated itself into everyone's lives like a damp patch slowly peeling the plaster off a wall, leaving it chipped. Men are allowed to act, to fight, in the hope—or is it the illusion?—of being able to change things, of returning to normalcy. Women, on the other hand, can only wait for the storm to pass and, in the meantime, contemplate the devastation, wondering if life will ever be able to resume its course.

And God knows what life will be like afterward.

"Maruzza . . . Maruzza . . ."

The voice comes from the heap of blankets in which Giovanna is wrapped. Frail, tired, pale, stiff with arthritis, she's resting in an armchair: she divides her days between that and bed. "Haven't my children come yet?" she asks in a plaintive whisper. "Don't they know I'm sick?"

Maruzza goes to her and strokes her face, wiping away a tear. "Donna Giovanna, they're at the war, you know that . . ."

"Yes, I know . . . but I'm their mother and I'm sick. They could have let them come for a couple of days . . . And what about Franca? Where's Franca?"

"In Rome with the girls, Igiea and Giugiù."

"Ah . . . Rome . . . Maybe she could come for a while?"

Maruzza leans over, kisses her forehead, and talks to her, trying to calm her. Her breathing is labored again, she notes, perhaps because she's getting agitated at the thought of her children being far away. After so many years, she feels closer to this woman than to her own relatives. She has seen her grow older, becoming ever thinner, suffering because of the deaths of her grandchildren, the financial difficulties of Casa Florio, and the lost dignity of a name that was once powerful and respected.

She has seen pain and disappointment on her face when her sons asked her to guarantee their promissory notes or asked her to pay the interest on debts they were unable to settle themselves.

And now she's alone and sick. Angina pectoris, say the doctors: that's how they've classified the pains that shoot from her arms up to her chest and make every breath painful. The sufferings and anxieties—past, present, and future—have finally taken their toll.

Maruzza moves through the room, fills a glass, and pours into it a few drops of a medication that should calm the beating of that sick heart. Giovanna drinks, resigned, then asks her to open the curtains because she wants to see the sky and the last rays of the sun. Maruzza obeys. The sunset is a bronze light that pours into the room, illuminating the Ducrot furniture and the photographs on the chest of drawers. Above them, the portrait of her husband, Ignazio. A new painting, done after the fire.

It's on this that Maruzza lingers. *Is it really possible to love just one man your whole life?* she wonders. Because it's obvious that Giovanna has always kept in her heart that husband she herself has known only through the accounts of the other family members. A self-controlled man, sparing with his emotions: calm, kind, capable of great acts of tenderness, but also cold and ruthless. Giovanna seems to catch these thoughts, because she calls her over, motioning her to approach.

"Let me look at him," she says, her features softening. A vague smile appears on those lips made hollow by age. She raises her hand and points at the chest of drawers. "Bring me the photograph of my son Vincenzo."

Maruzza is about to take the photograph of the Vincenzo she knows, but then she realizes. Her hand stops in midair and moves toward another of the photographs, this one of a child with a gentle, serious face. She hands it to Giovanna, who kisses it and places it over her heart.

"My flesh and blood," she murmurs, and tries to lift herself. "They told me I was lucky . . . I, who had nothing left to cry for." She kisses and strokes the photograph. "If he were still here, things might not have ended up like this. You know what scares me, Maruzza? That when I'm gone, my sons will fight each other for money. They're never at peace, those two, never patient . . . Where are they, why don't they come back here to me? Ignazio, Vice'. . . *unni siti*—where are you?" she cries. She becomes agitated and makes an attempt to rise. Maruzza tucks in her blankets and tries to calm her.

"I told you, they're at the front. Maybe they'll come back in the New Year. For now, don't think about it, Donna Giovanna, and above all don't get upset, because when you do your chest hurts."

"They'll find nothing but my bones," Giovanna says sullenly, still clutching the photograph. "Turn my chair to the window—I want to look outside," she adds in a voice that briefly gains strength again. "At least I still have that. I don't have anything else left, not even my house, not even my health. Nothing. *Sulu l'occhi pi' chianciri*—only eyes to weep with."

With some difficulty, Maruzza turns the chair in such a way that Giovanna can see the city, from which the color is draining; very soon, when the curfew starts, it will lose every trace of light. Shrouded in darkness, Palermo will fall asleep, as frightened as a little girl looking into the emptiness of night and finding only pain and anguish. And then it will withdraw into itself, falling into a merciful, dreamless sleep.

Maruzza strokes Giovanna's hair, then says, "I'll go get your dinner. I asked them to make you chicken broth. I'll be right back."

Villa Igiea has been partially requisitioned and turned into a hospital for officers. Along the corridors, nurses and men in uniform or in pajamas move about, dragging crutches and sticks. Everything echoes with those faltering steps, rhythmic thuds like a drum. Even the air in the villa has changed: where once there hung a fragrant mixture of cologne, cigars, flowers, and face powder, there is now the heavy odor of sickness, mingling with that of the food prepared in the basement kitchens. The carpet runners have been removed, the games room is occupied by rows of beds, and the clicking of the chips has been replaced by moans. Even the sinuous moldings on the stairs are splintered and covered in a layer of dust.

Outside the kitchens, Maruzza waits for the dinner to be ready.

Propped against the wall is a mirror in a solid gold frame, and she can't help looking at herself in it. The tired face, the deep lines, the gray hair gathered in an untidy bun . . . In Donna Giovanna's room, time seems to stand still, and yet here they are, the marks of its passing. They are all there, together with those caused by anxiety about the war and the family's financial hardships. No, fate has not been kind to her.

She raises her eyes to the ceiling.

*Yes, she's very sick. I can't wait any longer,* she tells herself. *I have to find a way to bring at least her daughter Giulia here, so that she can comfort her. Though how can the poor woman comfort her mother when she has two sons on the front line?*

The door to the kitchens is flung open, interrupting these reflections of Maruzza's. She takes the tray the cook passes her and heads back to the family apartments. On the stairs, she guesses she will have to force Donna Giovanna to eat—it's what she's had to do most of the time these last few weeks. She enters the room. "Here it is: as promised, a light chicken broth," she says gaily. "And there's also some orange juice. You will eat, won't you, Donna Giovanna? At lunch you didn't eat a thing . . ."

No answer comes from Giovanna. The blankets have fallen to the floor, and her body seems to have tilted to the side, now slumped over the arm of the chair. Her hand is still clutching the photograph of her son. The lips are turned down with the weight of an infinite solitude.

Her gaze is distant, beyond Palermo, beyond the horizon. She has left just like that, in silence, without her children by her side. Alone. And perhaps, Maruzza tells herself as she closes her eyes and a curtain of sorrow falls over her heart, perhaps, in spite of everything, she is the luckiest of the Florios.

She has seen the sun rise, but she won't see it set.

The first days of January 1918 leave a metallic taste in one's mouth, the taste of mourning. Franca walks across rooms and down corridors, her kid gloves in one hand, the other on the fur collar of her cape. Behind her, Maruzza, dressed all in black, and a maid bundled up in a blue overcoat, worn at the elbows. She is one of the few who have remained at the Olivuzza: most of the servants have been dismissed because of the restrictions imposed by Linch. The three women advance slowly, in silence, leaving tracks in the dust on the floor. Around them, furniture covered in white sheets, rolled up carpets, a few objects—a pen, a pair of glasses—left behind by someone or other.

They reach the green salon. Franca has always liked this cozy, light-filled room looking out on the garden. Now, though, it is dark and cold, imbued with a moldy smell. Franca opens the French window, and a gust of wind brings in the topsoil and dry leaves that have accumulated against the shutter. Then she turns and spots, among the furniture, a sewing loom covered in dust and spiderwebs, like threads interlaced one last time by nature. It's her mother-in-law Giovanna's loom.

She was buried in the family chapel a few days into the New Year; they'd had to wait for Vincenzo and Ignazio to return from the front and Franca to arrive from Rome. After so many years, Giovanna d'Ondes was finally reunited with her beloved husband and with her son Vincenzo.

And today, Franca has come back to the Olivuzza to preside over another kind of memorial service.

Very soon the big house will be put up for sale; before then, it will have to be cleared of furniture. They will have to decide what to keep and what to sell. That's what Carlo Linch has requested.

Ignazio and Vincenzo have had to leave again for the front, so the responsibility falls to her. Some of the furniture will go to the house on Via Catania, where Vincenzo will live when the war is over; other items will be moved to storehouses at the Arenella in expectation of better times or moved to their apartment in Villa Igiea. The rest will be sold to make a little money.

This is what Franca has come to do: to choose what to preserve of the life that is being torn away from her. As if she hasn't already had to give up so many things! As if they haven't already taken away everything of value! She will have to say farewell to the French furniture, the candelabras bought by Giovanna in Paris, the ebony-inlaid coin cabinet, the Aubussons, the great collection of antique vases and majolica, the marble panel by Antonello Gagini in Ignazio's study . . . but also the paintings by Antonino Leto, Francesco de Mura, Luca Giordano, Francesco Solimena, and Francesco Lojacono. Yes, even the Velázquez. Only a few will go to Villa Igiea. Of the others, all that will remain at the Olivuzza will be empty space left on the bare walls.

Every now and again Maruzza comes up to Franca and points at something.

"That one," Franca replies with a nod, and Maruzza tells the maid what to write in the little notebook she holds in her hands.

Franca leaves the green salon, reaches the red marble staircase, crosses the gallery, and lingers for a few moments to look out at what remains of the winter garden: only dry plants, bare trunks, and rottenness. Then she lowers her gaze and heads for her room. She stops only for a moment in front of a little display case that houses a group of statuettes purchased over the years in Saxony, France, and Capodimonte: groups of children playing alone or with puppies, varying in their styles, identical in their smiles and in the playfulness captured by the whiteness of the porcelain.

Pure memories of a time when innocence seemed something of value.

"These," she says, her voice suddenly hard. "I don't want to see them again."

She opens the door to her bedroom. In truth, there is almost nothing left in it, but she was happy in this room, Giovanna, Ignazio, Igiea, and Giulia were born in this bed, and perhaps the memories are still here, enclosed in the rose petals on the floor, in the tiles in front of the French windows, in the stiff handle that closes the shutters, in the lopsided smiles of the cherubs in the corners of the ceiling . . .

*But what memories?* she thinks angrily. This room has witnessed more moments of pain and jealousy than happy ones. It houses an emptiness of the soul that Franca has long been unable to shake. *There is only stuff here, pointless stuff. Dead stuff.*

Maruzza, who is still in the doorway, says, "I'll have the servants take away part of the trousseau and send it to Rome."

Franca turns. "The used linen can be given to charity, or else they can keep it for themselves . . . if they haven't already." Her tone is contemptuous. "Well, it's what happens. Do you think I don't know?"

Maruzza merely nods, a grimace curling her dry lips.

"Let's hurry up. I want to get back to my daughters."

She looks into Ignazio's room, with a curt gesture points to just one item of furniture, the sophisticated burr-mahogany shirt case, closes the door, and walks back, passing the winter garden and entering the dining room. "Away with all of it," she says, meaning even the coral and copper peacocks and the great fireguard. Passing the children's rooms, which still contain games and books although the children are long gone, she merely nods, as if to say: *Away with it.*

She heads toward the oldest part of the Olivuzza, where the fire broke out ten years ago and which was subsequently rebuilt. There are still bills to pay for that work, and she can't help thinking: *If everything had burned, at least I would have been spared this torture.*

She takes a few steps, then, all at once, stops in front of a door. She seizes the handle, but her hand doesn't move.

At last she opens the door and goes in.

In the semi-darkness, she makes out the armchairs and divans heaped up against the walls, the empty consoles, devoid of crystal vases, the silver centerpieces and gilded bronze clocks, the rolled-up carpets, the tables covered with dusty cloths. She raises her eyes to the Murano lampshades, opaque with dirt, and the gilded moldings on the ceiling, imprisoned behind a veil of spiderwebs.

But the thing that draws a heartfelt sigh out of her is the silence. There was never silence in this room.

It was the realm of music and laughter and chatter, of rustling dresses, the tinkling of glasses, the tapping of shoes.

It was the ballroom of the Olivuzza.

Franca advances and stops in the middle of the room.

She looks around.

And all at once she sees figures that have escaped the laws of time. Men and women who are no longer here but who have smiled, danced, loved here. She can hear their voices and it's almost as if they brush against her. She herself is one of them, a shadow among shadows: young, beautiful, with Ignazio's hand at her side, laughing and looking at her with desire. Not far away are Giulia Trigona and Stefanina Pajno, and Maria Concetta and Giulia Lanza di Trabia. There's the smell of her perfume, La Marescialla. There are satin and mother-of-pearl fans, champagne glasses, white gloves, diamond bracelets, dance cards lined in silk, lace corsets. And there's the sound of mazurkas, polkas, waltzes . . .

But it lasts only a moment; it's only a mirage of the dust raised when the maid opened the shutters to let in a little light. That same maid now stands looking at her, waiting expectantly.

Another step. The shadows fade, the dust settles.

Franca retreats and leaves the room without answering Maruzza's questioning glance. Maruzza remains motionless for a moment too long and then is forced to follow her.

"We also need to take the Saxony porcelain service and the silver kitchenware," Franca is saying.

Maruzza nods and turns to the maid. "Make a note. And we should add the silverware from the big cabinet and the crystals—isn't that so, Donna Franca?"

But Franca has stopped listening. She's tired of this list, tired of fighting the memories that every object, even the most insignificant, evokes in her. The chair on which D'Annunzio sat at dinner after the performance of *La Gioconda* at the Teatro Massimo. The piano on which Puccini sketched out *Che gelida manina*, and which her own children used for a brief period. The table on which she and Ignazio laid out large sheets of paper to design the furniture for Villa Igiea. The camera that Vincenzo gave his eldest brother, and that which he used in the garden of the Hôtel Métropole before . . .

She looks at the objects, as if they're calling her, then quickens her pace and almost runs toward the exit, as if pursued by them. *It's the fate of men to be happy and not to realize it. It is their curse to waste times of joy without realizing they're as rare as they're unrepeatable. That memory can't give you back what you have felt but will instead give you back the measure of what you have lost,* Franca thinks, while the other two women continue to chatter about linen tablecloths and silver forks. She looks at them, and an infinite sorrow sweeps over her. She would like to weep, to cry out: *You're thinking about things, and I'm thinking that soon these things will no longer belong to me, whereas once they spoke of me, of Ignazio, of our children, of this family. Now love has slipped away, leaving me with nothing but lines of bitterness. Do you know what it means to really feel loved? To hope to be loved? To feel infinitely alone?*

Instead, she remains motionless and silent. Because, despite everything, she is still Donna Franca Florio and she can show the world only one face, the face of pride.

At last, the three women get back in the car to return to Villa Igiea. Franca feels her heart grow lighter as they leave the house behind, even though she was once happy there. In a few days, she and her daughters will go back to Rome. Palermo, with its cold, opaque light will be far away, and she'll be able to stop remembering.

She doesn't yet know that in a few years' time even the memory of that house and those grounds will have faded. That everything will end up in the hands of a real estate agency that will divide the garden into allotments, knocking down almost everything and building apartment buildings where the aviary and the little neoclassical temple once were, where the avenues lined with rose-bushes and tropical plants once stretched into the distance and her children played and Vincenzo drove his cars.

She won't hear the noise of the saws cutting into the centuries-old trees, or the blows of the axe splitting the trunks of the yuccas and the dracaenas. She won't see the hedges being pulled up or the creepers torn off the burning gazebo.

Of that luxuriant garden, very little will survive. Two palms, confined to a small patch of earth, on which the windows of a clinic will look out. A flower bed, where the salon facing the garden once stood. The olive tree next to the entrance, the one particularly dear to Senator Ignazio, repotted in a concrete tub inside a parking lot.

Around the little villa designed by Basile—where Vincenzo and Annina loved each other—a small green patch will remain. There will even be moves to tear down that fairy-tale house and replace it with yet another apartment block, yet another concrete monster. Fate will decide otherwise.

But that's another story.

◦つ—

The sky is a blinding blue this February of 1918, an unhoped-for gift after days of rain. The front is a few kilometers away, on the Piave: bands of smoke form columns and clouds, reducing visibility and obscuring the horizon. The Italian and Austrian cannons are silent, a sign that the armies are preparing an offensive. Very soon shells will start to rain down again and soldiers will emerge from their trenches to conquer a handful of ground at the price of dozens, of hundreds, of dead. The fear of dying in a bayonet attack is such that some deliberately contract infections or mutilate themselves, so as not to fight. At least that's what Ignazio has been told. And he can well believe it.

Ignazio, at the wheel of an ambulance car, stops not far from a building surrounded by tents marked with red crosses. It's a country house transformed into a field hospital, with rows of men lying on stretchers, some bandaged, others waiting for treatment, yet others dying or dead.

Ignazio moves cautiously along a muddy path punctuated by dark patches that he has by now learned to recognize. He was told that the blood of war has only one color, but it isn't true. It's dark red when it gushes from a wound. But it's black when it drips from corpses.

From the tents, the smell of iodine reaches him, combined with curses, screams, and moans. He pushes on until he reaches a tent behind what must have been stables. He goes in. It seems to be populated only by women dressed in white, nuns and nurses. If nothing else, the wounded here seem calmer, but it doesn't take him long to see the horror of it: they're all mutilated, and some have even had parts of their faces blown away by grenades.

A woman rises from the bed over which she was bending, sees him, and raises her hand in greeting. Then, having wiped her hands on her apron, she comes up to him.

"I wasn't expecting you so soon."

The war has been cruel to Vera Arrivabene, too: although her tiredness and the rings round her eyes can be remedied, nothing will ever straighten her stooped back or erase the deep lines around her mouth.

Ignazio brushes the back of her dirty hand. "I wanted to be sure of seeing you. It seems the number of attacks is increasing."

Vera strokes his arm. "That's right. Dozens of poor boys are coming in now. How are you?"

"Alive."

He motions her to follow him outside. They sit down on a bench behind a ruined wall and Ignazio lights a cigarette. His hands shake slightly. "The news from Palermo isn't good. What's left of Casa Florio seems like the pastime of some malign deity. At least I managed to pay for the work the Albaneses did on the Olivuzza and Villa Igiea, which is something that's been going on for years, and we confirmed Linch as administrator until April 1926. For an appropriate salary, obviously." He pauses, looks at Vera, and strokes her cheek. "I'm sorry. I'm burdening you with all my troubles as usual, and I haven't even asked you how you are."

She bows her head. "Yesterday I attended a poor man who'd lost his legs, a peasant from Frosinone . . . He died in my arms. He was afraid because they'd called up his son and there was no one left to take care of his farm, given that of course his wife and daughters couldn't start pushing a plow. It hurt me to see with what desperation he clung to me. I couldn't even give him a little morphine . . ."

"I know. I see them." He takes a deep breath. "What's happening is absurd. They're calling up those who were drafted in '99, practically children." He stares into the distance. "I'm worried about Giulia's son Manfredi. Right now, he's in Versailles, an officer attached to the permanent interallied committee, but I know he's longing to get back and fight. As for her other son, Ignazio . . ."

"Have you heard anything?"

"It's been three months since his plane disappeared. First they told us he was in Switzerland, then that he was a prisoner in Germany . . . I have a bad feeling about it."

"What about your brother, Vincenzo?"

Ignazio takes a deep drag on his cigarette. "He's not far from here—at least I think so. He wrote to me that he's still making modifications to his truck, even though it's been in production for two years. I've seen a few prototypes. It actually climbs mule tracks so steep you wouldn't be able to tackle them otherwise. Lucky him! All he needs is a wrench and a few nuts and bolts and he can forget the rest of the world!"

Vera takes his face between her hands and kisses him. "Am I a horrible person if I say that I'm happy to be here with you right now?"

"No, you're an adorable person." He tucks back a lock of hair that's escaped her cap. Even though she's tired and worn out, as far as he's concerned Vera is still beautiful. Even though there's a new desperation in her eyes. Even though those lines will never fade. "You're a brave woman, who's unafraid to do something even in a world that's gone mad."

Vera embraces him and they stay like that for a long time, not speaking.

But Ignazio's thoughts turn to Franca. He hasn't seen his daughters for months, but he's pleased to know they're safe with her. As for Franca herself, Ignazio soon realized that she had decided to stay well away from this wave of death. Of course, she's on various humanitarian committees and involved in collecting funds for soldiers at the front, but she has no idea what it means to transport men covered in blood, to see houses and villages destroyed, to tremble at every explosion.

He's tried to talk about these things in some of his letters, to seek her understanding, but by now Franca is like a piano without a pedal, incapable of producing sounds that vibrate deeply. It's as if nothing can touch her anymore, as if emotions are out of focus to her, indistinct. The deaths of her children and the loss of their house are not merely a wound that won't heal: they are a sore on which she constantly spreads salt to convince herself that her grief is stronger than anything else in the world. It's become an idea she's almost unable to do without.

Great sufferings are selfish; they don't admit comparison. They know only the devastation inflicted on the soul that houses them.

And it's this that's keeping them apart.

"Florio!"

"Here!"

Vincenzo emerges from under the truck he's repairing, leaps to his feet, and elbows his way to the man distributing the mail. He hasn't received many letters since his mother died, so he's surprised to see three envelopes addressed to him.

He weighs them in his hand, then looks for a quiet spot to read them, and finds it in a corner of the repair shop. One is from his brother, another from a French model he met in Paris two years ago, Lucie Henry. A relationship that began by chance but may be turning into something serious . . . *Now's not the time to think about that*, he tells himself, putting the envelope to one side. The third one is from his sister Giulia.

Ignazio brings him up to date on what Linch is doing for their business. The factory to produce seaplanes, which Ducrot established in Mondello and in which Ignazio has shares, is finally doing well. Vincenzo smiles, pleased that his idea has borne fruit. Then he skims through the lines in which Ignazio tells him that the Olivuzza has been stripped bare and that the furniture he may want to take for himself is now in the storehouses of the Arenella. With a touch of remorse, he thinks how much it must have cost Franca to choose what to keep and what to sell: he himself would never have had the courage. When the war ends—it must end eventually, he's been telling himself since time immemorial—he will move once and for all to Via Catania. A new home, a new relationship: without memories, without pain.

Because sometimes the past is a curse, a stone weighing on the soul that can't be lifted even by force of will. And this is what he's thinking about as he opens his sister's letter. Giulia's handwriting is tiny and angular, and the paper bulges oddly in a few places. He starts to read, distractedly at first, then hurriedly, and finally he rereads everything, once, twice. It's true what they say: a heart breaking doesn't make any noise.

It doesn't matter what the cause is, a bereavement, a loss, a love never forgotten or never lived. The fragments are there, and they hurt. They may be able to heal in time, but the scars are ready to reopen as soon as the next blade strikes.

And this blade has the name of his nephew, Manfredi.

After his long stay in France, he returned to Italy, eager to fight. And he was killed a few days ago, on August 21, 1918, at the age of only twenty-three, after part of a grenade entered his right ear.

Vincenzo knows now what those bulges are.

Tears.

Giulia, too, like Ignazio, is seeing her own sons die. Twenty-five years ago, Blasco, now Manfredi . . . and nobody has heard from Ignazio for eight months. The only male remaining is Giuseppe, who is also under arms.

He leans against the wall for support, then has to sit down on the ground because his legs have given way; he feels his eyes fill with tears and he rubs them so that nobody should see him weep. He remembers his nephews, and his soul overflows with all kinds of images, with pain, and regret, and sorrow.

There they are together, in Favignana, or on the *Sultana*, or traveling, or riding velocipedes at the Olivuzza. He relives the moment when he showed them the first motorcycle he was given by Ignazio. Whereas Ignazio insisted they call him uncle, he himself was never able to: the age difference was too small. They were playmates first and then companions in adventure.

His heart feels like lead. First one sob, then another, shakes him. The grief is a hot, heavy bullet in his guts. Now Ignazio and Manfredi, too, are gone. Just like Annina, who didn't even have time to give him a son. Just like his mother, to whom he was unable to bid farewell. Just like the Olivuzza.

Like all that was his and that he hasn't managed to hold on to.

⌒

The end of the war hasn't put an end to the pain. Perhaps it's really too early for such things, Franca thinks, looking at the stack of cards piled on the little pink wooden table at the entrance to the apartment in Villa Igiea. She picks them up and shuffles through them, but she already knows what they contain: Palermo is declining her invitation to the party she was planning to throw in a month's time, in mid-February 1919. Her hope was to revive the splendor of the hotel, but for now her efforts seem in vain. Too many bereavements, too much destruction: the city needs a period of silence and peace in which to wipe away its tears. And Villa Igiea's recent past as a military hospital certainly doesn't help.

She puts aside the cards with a weary gesture and walks to the balcony that looks out on the grounds. Wrapped in a blue overcoat, Giugiù, who's almost ten, is trying to persuade the governess to take her to the sea, which is unusually choppy today. Meanwhile, Igiea, who's eighteen, is almost certainly shut up in her room reading, perhaps one of those English novels she often buys in Rome. Franca once leafed through a few pages of a volume she found on her night table, *The Voyage Out* by Virginia Woolf, and immediately closed it in annoyance. That story of couples forming, then separating, seemed to her unpleasantly familiar.

She should be grateful her daughters haven't suffered too much because of the war, even though the family certainly hasn't emerged from it unscathed. Vincenzo has returned to Palermo and apparently resumed his role as the organizer of sporting competitions and various other events in the city. Every now and again, he has left his house on Via Catania and come to Villa Igiea to see his nieces, but even though when he's with them he makes an effort to always be cheerful, it's clear that the war has left its mark on his soul, together with the still unhealed scar left by Annina's death. As for Ignazio, he's still in Rome with Vera, heavily involved in business affairs of which she knows little or nothing but which are certainly not helping solve their financial woes. They saw each other when he returned from the front, and Franca almost found it difficult to recognize her husband in that stooped fifty-year-old with his marked face and lifeless expression. Apart from anything else, he had been greatly affected by Giulia's tragedy: after the death of Manfredi, the hopes of seeing her other son, Ignazio, alive vanished when, a year after his disappearance, his body was found . . . or rather, what was left of it. Since then, just like her mother, Giulia has insisted on remaining in mourning and now lives shut up inside Palazzo Butera, never receiving visitors, not even her brothers. Fortunately, her son Giuseppe not only survived but was even appointed private secretary to the prime minister, Vittorio Emanuele Orlando, at the Paris peace conference. Her daughter Giovanna became engaged to Ugo Moncada di Paternò; and her other daughter, Sofia, is sure to find a husband soon. For them, at least, life goes on . . .

*True, but definitely not the same life as before. What life, then?* Franca asks herself now.

The world born from the ashes of war is alien to her, almost repulsive. It's a world that has erased men like Kaiser Wilhelm II, a world that turned out the lights of a whole era and now gropes in the dark. And that makes her feel old, even though she is only forty-five.

She makes up her mind to sit down at the desk and answer her correspondence. The Congregazione delle Dame del Giardinello is asking her to help some young war widows; Stefanina Pajno is inviting her to a musical evening; she must write a thank-you note to . . .

Someone is knocking at the door. An unusually insistent knocking. One of the hotel's maids opens the door and converses with someone. Then Franca hears a familiar voice.

"Donna Franca! Donna Franca, please, I need to talk to you . . ."

With a sigh, she gets to her feet and goes into the next room.

And there she finds herself face-to-face with Diodata, her personal maid from the Olivuzza. For a moment, a ribbon of memories unrolls between them and Franca allows herself a smile. How many times did that woman help her brush her hair? How many dresses did she lay out for her? She was always attentive and discreet . . . including, and above all, during her rows with Ignazio.

She smiles at her, goes up to her, and lets her come in, dismissing the maid.

"You look well," she says to her, knowing she's lying. The woman in front of her is merely the shadow of the sturdy, rosy-cheeked girl who spent so many years in her service. She's grown thinner, marked by lines, and is wearing a misshapen hat and a coat that has more than one patch.

"Thank you. You, too, Signora, are looking very well." Diodata bows her head. She's embarrassed. "Donna Franca, please forgive me for coming here like this, without even writing you a note. I know it's not done . . . But, you see, I heard you'd come back from Rome and you're the only person I know who can help." All at once, her eyes grow damp and her face seems almost to crumble. "I beg you, Donna Franca. I'm desperate!" She raises her fists to her forehead. "You remember why I left, don't you? Tanino Russello, the farmer who brought the vegetables from the countryside and had a piece of land near the town of San Lorenzo, asked to marry me." She almost blushes. "We were both alone in the world and we thought we could make a go of it together. We didn't have any children, but if you remember, he was quite old and had a limp. That's why he didn't go to the war, which we thought was a blessing . . . But three months ago, he came back home with a cough . . . and the next morning he had a fever so strong that I was afraid and called the doctor. But the doctor didn't come right away; he sent someone to say there were a lot of cases like this all over Palermo, all because of this influenza they call Spanish: people who had a fever that wouldn't go down, who had pains in their necks and couldn't breathe, who ended up with blood coming from their mouths and were dying by the dozen . . . and that's how it was. After four days of very strong fever, Tanino started coughing up blood, and the next morning he was gone." She raises her head. Her eyes are filled with grief and despair. "I also had this Spanish thing after him, but the Lord didn't want me. I'm still here. I had to sell the piece of land he'd been cultivating that we got by with, but the money's almost gone, because the land isn't worth much at all, not these days . . . I'm alone and desperate; there'll be nothing left of me when I die. If I don't find someone to take me into service . . ." She seizes Franca's hands. "I beg you, Donna Franca, take me back, even if just for a while . . . Or maybe one of your friends might need . . ."

Overwhelmed by this flood of words, Franca instinctively takes a step back.

Of course, this violent, often fatal influenza isn't news to her: they were already talking about it during the war, but the newspapers only devoted a few small items to it, urging caution and pointing out that this or that public place had been disinfected. Among her acquaintances, nobody has fallen ill, and so Franca has convinced herself that there is no danger here in Palermo. "My dear Diodata, what are you saying?" she exclaims. "Is it possible the Spanish flu has affected so many people even here?"

Diodata nods vigorously. "You have no idea how many people have died, Donna Franca. Anyone living far from the city, near the sea or in the country, was saved, but the poor people . . . In Castellammare, La Kalsa, La Noce, La Zisa . . . there isn't a household that hasn't had at least one person sick or one dead." She wrings her hands. "Some locked themselves into their houses, others washed their linen every day with sulfur soap . . . and there were even those who went around with cloths over their faces. But it didn't really help."

Franca has fallen silent. Her terror of illness has become a powerful wave that clouds her vision and recalls in all its crudity the memory of Giovannuzza's death. "My daughters . . ." she moans, staring at Diodata with a blend of horror and incredulity.

"You're the only person I know; I served you for twenty years. I beg you, don't leave me out on the street. I'm strong, I can work. If I could, I'd go to America, as some who worked in the kitchen have done . . . But I don't have enough money to eat, let alone leave . . ."

Franca has hardly listened to her. A thought has formed in her mind and now occupies it completely: *What if Diodata is still infected?*

She can't stay next to this woman a minute longer. Without saying anything, she goes to her room and takes out a few banknotes. Then she has an idea. She stops, considers it, and nods. She takes pen and paper and writes a few lines. She puts the money and the note in an envelope, then goes hurriedly back to the door.

"I can't take you back, Diodata, I really can't. But take this," she says, holding out the envelope. "There's a little money, together with a message for my brother-in-law Vincenzo. You said you'd like to go to America, didn't you? Well, go to him, on Via Roma, and tell him I sent you. I've written to him to find you a ticket for the next ship if he can."

Diodata takes the envelope, incredulous. Then she bursts into tears. "Oh, Donna Franca, thank you! I always knew you were a saint!" She comes closer and tries to kiss her hand, but Franca backs away.

"No, there's no need to thank me for so little," she protests.

Diodata looks at her and dries her eyes, which are filled with a gratitude that only makes Franca more uncomfortable. "I'll never forget you," she murmurs. "You and your children will always be in my prayers, both those who are alive and those who are angels. You were always good to me, and you still are."

Franca seizes the handle of the door. "Go quickly to Via Roma," she says, almost making a shield of the door. "Goodbye and good luck, Diodata."

She closes the door while the woman still thanks and blesses her, then runs to the bathroom to find the sulfur soap. Frantically, she scours her hands and arms.

But it's not only the Spanish flu she's afraid of. It's the poverty she has seen in Diodata she wants to cleanse herself of, that sense of dirt and impermanence and misery. And the sense of guilt, the awareness of what the decline of Casa Florio has heralded. Because it's not only her life that's changed. Many others have changed, and for the worse. And that's a responsibility she's unable to bear.

*Rome is very beautiful, but it's also tiring. In Paris, on the other hand, it's as if one's inside a painting by Pissarro. It does the heart good to come here every now and again . . .* The April sun lightly grazes the windows of the buildings on Rue de la Paix, and memories as light as veils dance before Franca's eyes: her honeymoon, walks by the Seine with friends, horse races at the Grand Palais, nights at the Opéra . . . *It's as if nothing unpleasant can ever happen here*, she thinks, and smiles, listening to Igiea and Giugiù as they discuss the hats they saw at the Café de Paris, where they had lunch: Igiea really doesn't like the new fashion, in which flowers have been banished, to be replaced by ribbons and feathers, while Giugiù is an enthusiast for the new style.

For two years now Franca has been living in Rome, in an apartment in the Grand Hotel. Not only because it's a city where she can fulfill her role as a lady-in-waiting but above all because everything is simpler there: fewer servants, fewer expenses. And yet, the first few times she went back to Villa Igiea for a few days and sat down in the little temple facing the sea, she seemed to hear Palermo calling her. The city wanted its queen back, with her carefree parties, applause at the theater, waltzes danced until dawn, her *monsù*'s melon ices. But then that voice, too, grew weak until it faded completely. *Perhaps Palermo has understood that when the happy times are over, one can only hope that a few people remember them*, she told herself.

The only thing Franca can't get used to in Rome is the omnipresence of politics, the fact that every event in Italy has an immediate, tangible echo there. Everything that once upon a time came to her filtered through items in the newspapers or from someone's account now seems closer to her, and often more threatening. Like that horrible attack at the Teatro Diana in Milan a few weeks ago in which at least fifteen people died, including a little girl. The following day, Rome was strewn with flags bordered in mourning black and the whole city seemed to be sunk in a well of grief. Not to mention the strikes, the constant clashes between Socialists and Fascists . . . Perhaps that fellow Benito Mussolini, who went to see Gabriele d'Annunzio at Gardone Riviera just a few days ago, is the right man to bring a little order back to Italy . . .

"Did you hear me, *Mutti*?" Igiea has come to her side and gives her a little pat on the hand. "My future mother-in-law is expecting me to show her my wedding dress when it's almost ready. She's planning to give me a few family jewels and wants to be sure they match."

"Yes, she mentioned that to me, too, just as she told me that she would have preferred an Italian fashion house." She shrugs. "Worth is the house we Florios have always used. It's the best, and I want you to have the best for your wedding." She can already imagine Carlo Linch's objections—"Donna Franca, you promised me you would reduce your expenses!"—and Ignazio's reproaches, but she doesn't care. She wants Igiea to have the wedding she herself wasn't able to.

Giulia opens wide her clear eyes. "What about me?" she asks, unable to hide a touch of childish jealousy.

"For you, Giugiù, we'll go to Liberty's on Boulevard des Capucines." She leans forward and strokes her.

"The last time I went there, I was with Maruzza. I miss her, you know?"

"I miss her, too," Franca sighs.

It's been a year since Maruzza married Count Galanti, the manager of Villa Igiea. A late marriage for both of them, and one that in her case was an escape from the storms that keep breaking over Casa Florio. When Maruzza gave her the news, Franca merely nodded and murmured a few words of understanding. Her daughters, on the other hand, were overjoyed and gave Maruzza lots of hugs.

*What wonderful girls*, Franca thinks. *They really are a delight.*

Giugiù is only twelve, but she's already blossoming. And Igiea, who's twenty-one, is a young woman with very clear skin and long, elegant hands. On the ring finger of her left hand, she's wearing the ring that Duke Averardo Salviati gave her when they became engaged. They will marry in a few months, on October 28, 1921.

They met during a vacation in the Abetone, a place filled with memories for Franca: it was where she met Giovanna and Ignazio asked for her hand.

Affection and melancholy mingle for a moment. She's happy

that Igiea has found a man who loves her tenderly and has such a prestigious title. She couldn't have hoped for a better marriage for her daughter, especially as the Florios' financial situation hasn't improved—on the contrary. But she really hopes that this union will not be like hers with Ignazio. That it will be peaceful. That they will love and respect each other. *Why shouldn't it be so?* she wonders, almost to reassure herself. *I have no reason to think otherwise.*

They come to the main entrance of Worth, but just as they are about to go in, a little boy in a sailor suit pops up as if from nowhere and embraces Franca's legs.

"*Le carrousel! Je veux monter sur le carrousel!*" he whines, shaking his blond curls.

His nurse soon arrives, panting and apologizing profusely. She eventually drags the boy away, now weeping desperately.

Giugiù bursts out laughing, but Igiea has noticed the sad look that comes into her mother's eyes. She was very small when Giovannuzza and Baby Boy died but carries their images inside her. She goes to her and puts an arm round her shoulders. "*Mamma . . .*" she whispers.

Franca does her best to hold back the tears. "I'm sorry I wasn't able to give you and Giugiù a quiet life. Perhaps I haven't even been a good mother."

"Don't say that," Igiea replies. "You've always been here for us. And *Papà* . . . has made many mistakes, but we've never missed his affection," she adds in a calm voice. "That . . . woman who's with him will never be able to replace you. Now that I have Averardo, I understand many things. For example, that it's possible to love two people at the same time, but with different kinds of love. Perhaps *Papà* needs both."

"No," Franca retorts sharply, raising her head. A crack opens, letting out a flood of pain. "If you divide it, love between a man and a woman falls to pieces. I gave him all of myself, while he . . . he doesn't know what love means. Because he was never able to really take care of me. He didn't know how to do it, nor did he understand that sometimes you have to give something up to allow the other person to be happy. I'll continue to love him because he's my husband and your father, but . . ."

Igiea straightens up, looks her mother in the eyes, and clasps her hand. "But you will always be close. And that's the one thing that really matters."

～

Vincenzo takes a deep breath of the warm air of Paris. He smiles, then looks at the woman walking by his side and plants a kiss on her forehead. She laughs: a lively, spontaneous, silvery laugh.

Black hair, dark eyes, perfect nose: a face that reveals a free, cheerful character.

He finds it hard to believe that he's found a woman who wants to be with him, despite his constant mood swings. Lucie Henry entered his life by chance, but it's not at all chance that she has stayed with him. They survived the war and now they live together, dividing their time between Paris and Palermo.

Lucie returns his glance and huddles against him. "Do you think your sister-in-law will be pleased to see me? Last time, she didn't seem particularly happy with my presence."

He shrugs and twirls his silver-tipped ebony stick. "Well, that's her problem. I'm here to see my nieces and you're my *petite amie*. Do you mind if I call you that?"

"I had a daughter out of wedlock. I've known many men. Now I'm living with you without being your wife. In Sicily they would call me something else, but I don't care."

Vincenzo covers her hand with his own. They have stopped in the middle of the street. He strokes her cheeks and says in a low voice, "Do you remember? The war had only just started, and you were still posing for that penniless painter . . . The night we met, I was drunk and you'd quarreled with him."

She laughs softly. "Do you think I can forget? You were supposed to be going back to Italy soon, so we started seeing each other in secret, like two youngsters . . . And then I introduced you to Renée." She pauses. "I wanted you to meet her because—"

"You have a wonderful daughter," he cuts in. Images replace words, and the memory grows warm, as golden as honey. With her narrow eyes, as bright as Lucie's, Renée examined him closely before going to him, then asked her mother if he was a friend of hers.

Lucie's abrupt embarrassment disappeared as soon as Vincenzo leaned down and ruffled the girl's hair, saying, "*Non, ma petite*. I'm someone who loves your mother."

Then he looked up and his eyes met Lucie's.

They were blurry with tears.

His memory leaps forward. The two of them standing in Lucie's room, near the balcony with the white curtains drawn across it. They don't touch each other; they're still fully dressed. They're looking at each other. Nothing else: they are motionless in that wonderful, undefined moment in which two people begin to make love with their minds even before their bodies.

Lucie is the only woman who's been able to alleviate his grief over Annina.

"Let's go," he says. He runs his hand along her arm until it reaches her hand, and their fingers intertwine.

They find Franca, Igiea, and Giulia in the tearoom of the Hôtel le Meurice. The suffused light pouring down from the crystal chandeliers is reflected in the wood paneling, touches the white tablecloths, and shimmers in the milky glow of the porcelain.

Franca is sitting stiffly in an armchair. Igiea, who's beside her, is pouring the tea for herself and her mother. Giulia is engrossed in a novel.

"Oh, there you are." Vincenzo goes to them, kisses his nieces, and lightly brushes his sister-in-law's cheek.

"Forgive us if we kept you waiting." Lucie, behind him, bows her head in an informal greeting.

Franca points to the armchair in front of her. "Not at all. We've had so much to do today. Igiea chose her dress at Worth and then we dropped into Cartier's . . ." She ignores Vincenzo's raised eyebrow, turns to the waitress who has approached, and asks her to bring more *petits fours*.

Lucie clears her throat, her eyes moving from the girls to Franca. *She's very beautiful, and has innate class,* she thinks. *But she seems so cold, so distant . . .* Her hands are together on her lap, her back is stiff, and the smiles that hover over her lips as she talks to Vincenzo about the wedding preparations never reach her eyes. All at once, though, Lucie senses that she in turn is being observed. Or rather, judged. By that beautiful woman, of course, but also by her daughters. Igiea is giving her vaguely haughty glances, while Giugiù stares at her with boredom and puzzlement. *Are they comparing me with their mother?* she can't help wondering.

Vincenzo seems unaware of this play of glances. "Your parents aren't sparing any expense for this wedding, are they?" he says to Igiea with a hint of irony.

Franca's beautiful mouth widens in a complacent smile. "For a daughter, it's the least we can do. And besides, the conventions should be respected, especially as the families involved—the Salviatis and the Aldobrandinis—are among the most important in Italy."

"*Mamma* knows what's best for me," Igiea declares. "The Roman nobility cares a lot about—"

"The Roman nobility?" Lucie's eyes open wide. "Are you saying the wedding will be in Rome?"

"Of course. Igiea will live in Rome, or at Migliarino Pisano, where the Salviatis have their family estate," Franca replies. "But I'm also organizing a large party at Villa Igiea for our Palermo friends who won't be able to come to the receptions in Rome, so that they get a chance to meet the groom."

"The receptions?" Vincenzo asks. "Isn't one enough?"

"The real reception will be after the civil ceremony. After the religious service, we'll have a breakfast for intimates, about a hundred people. Your brother wanted it that way and I agreed to his requests."

"Uncle, you do remember that, as a witness, you will have to go to confession, don't you?" Igiea cuts in. "As you know, my future mother-in-law, Duchess Aldobrandini, is very religious, and Cardinal Vannutelli, who will celebrate the wedding, is a very close family friend."

Vincenzo raises his eyes to heaven and laughs. "I haven't confessed in I don't know how many years. I fear that my dissolute life will upset that poor priest!"

Lucie stares at Igiea. It strikes her as impossible for such a young girl to be so loyal to traditions and appearances. In the end, she's unable to contain herself and she exclaims, "But . . . we're in the twentieth century!"

"If there's one thing that never goes out of fashion, it's knowing how to behave correctly," Igiea retorts with biting elegance. "And we Florios must behave impeccably that day." Glancing at her mother, she continues: "My father knows how important it is to live up to the name he bears. That's why he will be with *Mamma* for as long as is necessary." She breaks off because the waitress has arrived with the tray of *petits fours*. In the abrupt silence, Franca gives Igiea an appreciative smile. She's proud of her daughter, of her determination. Of her delicate but clear way of setting boundaries.

Vincenzo, on the other hand, bows his head, grasps his spoon, and runs it across the tablecloth, back and forth. He has understood what his niece is telling him. At last he summons his courage, looks up at Lucie, and sees a deep sadness in her eyes. Yes, even she has understood: her presence at the wedding will not be welcome.

"Aren't they bound to secrecy . . . priests, I mean?" she asks, not very confidently.

Igiea reaches out her hand to the *petits fours*, hesitates, then chooses one. "It is not a question of what one says but of what one chooses to reveal. If something is not seen, it simply does not exist." She has spoken in a low breath, her lips lightly coated in sugar. She looks up and for a moment her eyes meet Lucie's.

And in those eyes, there is a judgment that brooks no appeal.

Franca puts down the receiver, gets up from the armchair, and allows herself a tender little laugh. Maria Arabella, the daughter of Igiea and Averardo, was born just over a month ago, on September 6, 1922, and both mother and child are doing well, perhaps partly due to the fact that they are living in the country, on the Salviatis' beautiful estate. What has most cheered her, though, is Igiea's voice: calm, self-confident, serene. The voice of a woman who has found her place in the world and feels appreciated and respected by her new family.

The telephone rings again and Giulia runs to answer it.

"Hello? Oh, Uncle Vincenzo! . . . Yes, we're fine. What about you? How's Aunt Lucie? And Renée? What about Grandma Costanza—have you seen her? . . . Oh, good! . . . What? You're organizing a motorboat race between the Arenella and Villa Igiea and want to know if we . . ."

Franca has understood and immediately shakes her head.

"I'll ask *Mamma*, but I don't think we'll come . . . Palermo is too sad in November . . . Oh, you know, yesterday we saw a film actually set in Sicily? It's called *Il viaggio* and Maria Jacobini is in it, she's very beautiful, and . . ."

Franca's smile fades, as does the image of Palermo that Vincenzo's invitation has evoked. It hardly matters now that the last stretch of Via Roma has been completed or that there are new streets and big stores. Those are all things for the lower middle classes, people with no style. Most of those nobles who illuminated Palermo for so many seasons have been unable to emerge from the darkness of war and the economic difficulties that followed and are leading an isolated existence. Or else they have moved, perhaps to Tuscany or Rome, as she has. And they try to travel as often as possible: the hotel rooms of Paris, of the Austrian Alps or the Trentino are comfortable, elegant places without a soul, without memories.

Only Giulia has found a way to remain linked to the past. Constantine, the ex-king of Greece, has chosen Palermo for his exile and Giulia spends her days with him, Queen Sophia, and their small entourage, who are often at Villa Igiea.

A ghost who has chosen the company of other ghosts.

Franca's eyes come to rest on the drawer of the little desk against the wall, one of the items of Ducrot furniture she managed to bring to Rome. She knows there's a bundle of papers in it, left there by Ignazio a few months ago, on the occasion of his last visit. Perhaps it was carelessness, or perhaps he did it deliberately—who could say? She saw them and, in that jumble of numbers and bureaucratic formulas, one thing was clear to her: the mortgage on the Olivuzza, arranged with the Société Française de Banque et de Dépôts, had been cancelled—God knows how—and much of the building, with a substantial section of the grounds, had been sold to Girolamo Settimo Turrisi, Prince of Fitalia.

She closed the portfolio abruptly and immediately put it in that drawer, trying to forget it. It was painful to think of the end of her own world, but unbearable to have concrete proof.

No, at least for a while she won't be going back to Palermo.

But nor does she want to stay in Rome. What may happen after that gigantic gathering of Fascists in Naples, at which Benito Mussolini said, "Either they give us the government or we will fall on Rome and take it," as if the city were his prey?

"Listen, Giugiù, what would you say to going on a little trip?" she asks Giulia as soon as the telephone call is over. "We could go to Stresa, and then to Viareggio, to the Hotel Select as usual. And we could ask Dory to come with us."

Giulia gives a little cry and starts dancing happily. Mother's new American friend, Miss Dory Chapman, is a woman who has traveled all over the world and who knows lots and lots of incredible stories, but above all she's always in a good mood. Even Giulia has noticed that when she talks to her, her mother is less sad than usual. "That'll be wonderful," she says, giving her a kiss on the cheek. "Yes, we need a little cheering up."

Franca doesn't know why Ignazio has joined her at the Hotel Select in Viareggio on this cloudy November evening. She has noticed that he has a troubled air and has brought a couple of suitcases with him, as if he left in a hurry. As usual, though, she doesn't ask any questions. In silence, she takes a string of pearls and a bracelet from her gold mesh bag, puts them on, and puts the bag back in the little trunk. Then she drapes her sable-edged cape over her shoulders and says simply, "Are you coming?"

"Where are you going?"

"To the casino, just for a few bets and a little chat. Not that there's much else to do here."

He shrugs. "Do you mind if I don't go with you? It's cold, it's about to rain, I'm exhausted, and I'd happily go to bed."

"Your room is opposite Giugiù's. Here's the key," she replies curtly. "And besides, I'm going with Dory and the Marchese Di Clavesana. I'm not alone."

In the corridor, Ignazio walks away without even saying goodbye.

*He's seen more dawns than the sun and now he's become an old man who complains about a few drops of rain,* Franca reflects with a smile as she descends the stairs to the lobby, where Dory, who has been waiting for her, immediately comes up to her. "Here you are, my dear!" she cries, pulling her fur stole around her. "Are you wrapped up warm enough? You Sicilians have such need of heat! The Marchese Di Clavesana is waiting for us in the car. Shall we go?"

Franca smiles. *Yes, Giugiù is right: this woman really does cheer you up.* "Of course," she replies.

A distant peal of thunder is heard as one of the hotel's valets closes the door behind them.

⌒

It's just after midnight. Two black-clad men are walking rapidly along the service corridors of the Hotel Select. They climb a flight of stairs, then noiselessly open the door of a storage closet. There, amid the brooms and the baskets of dirty linen, they find an apron. One of the two men grabs it, shakes it, and smiles.

Jingling. Keys.

The two men leave the storage closet and climb to the *piano nobile*, where the most luxurious rooms are. By the light of a little wall lamp, they insert the skeleton key in the lock, which clicks open without a squeak.

They are inside.

The room is spacious, illuminated only by the light of the street-lamps outside. They make out the bed, a robe lying between the pillows, the dressing table, and a chair on which there is a slip.

One of the two men slides a handkerchief into the lock of the door, then points to the dressing table. There in front of it, on the stool, is a little trunk.

*The* little trunk.

With a knowing nod, they put it on the mattress, and force it open with a picklock.

There it is, the gold mesh bag with Franca Florio's jewels. They open it, rummage inside, find the little velvet pouches, remove them, and before emptying their contents go to the window. The pearls and precious stones flash in the dark.

Then one of them replaces the pouches in the bag, while the other man goes to the opposite side of the room and places his ear against the door that partitions Franca's room from the American's.

No sound. They can continue.

They put the little trunk back on the stool. Then they fling open the wardrobes, open the suitcases and hatboxes, and carelessly rifle through the clothes. Finally, they grab the bottles of cream, uncap them, open wide the window, and toss them down among the hedges. Everyone will be convinced that they escaped that way, jumping down into the garden.

Next, they go into Dory's room. The booty here is less impressive: a gold pen, a little notepad, also bound in gold, an envelope with five thousand lire.

Then they close the door behind them, and as silently as they arrived, they leave.

Inspector Cadolino is holding the sheet of paper in hands that are almost trembling. Even his voice is hesitant. "I'm sorry to disturb you again, Signor Florio, but Commissioner Grazioli will be here soon from Rome and I'd like to make sure the list is complete. May I?"

Ignazio, holding a fist against his mouth, nods.

"Thank you. So: one string of one hundred eighty large pearls, with diamond and ruby clasp; one string of three hundred fifty-nine pearls with diamond clasp; one string of forty-five large pearls; one string of four hundred thirty-five small pearls; one platinum necklace with large drop pearls and large diamonds; one small platinum and gold purse with pearl monogram and pendant; one gold brooch with diamond monogram and royal crown with Turkish knot . . ."

"My wife is a lady-in-waiting to Queen Elena and that's her badge."

"Oh, yes, of course . . . One wristwatch with ribbon diamonds; one square gold wristwatch; five large pearl rings; one ruby and diamond ring; one long diamond chain segmented into three parts . . ."

Franca isn't listening. She sits, her hands in her lap, staring into the distance. Not only does she no longer have her jewels—her protection against the ugliness of the world—but ever since the theft was discovered, two days ago, it has felt to her that she's in prison, as if she were the thief. Constant interrogations. Policemen everywhere. Journalists waiting outside the hotel. Questions after questions, to her, to Dory, to Ignazio, even to Giulia. Unknown hands rummaging among her clothes and in the drawers, spreading a powder for fingerprints, searching and interrogating chambermaids and valets. For what? They're not even sure if the thief was alone or not, if he got in through the door or the window, or how he escaped. Yes, there was a smear of cold cream on the window, but . . .

". . . one large bracelet with platinum chain; one bracelet with two rubies and diamonds; one platinum bracelet with four large pearls; one bracelet entirely of diamonds; one platinum and turquoise bracelet . . ."

*I have nothing left.*

". . . one diamond and sapphire bracelet; one platinum ring with three diamonds; various ruby and diamond brooches; one diamond and ruby braid . . ."

*I am nothing anymore.*

"Have you finished?" Ignazio asks. He's weary, at the end of his rope, and makes no attempt to hide it.

Cadolino nods, bows to Franca, and leaves the room.

Ignazio goes to her and lightly touches her face. She looks at him as if she hasn't even noticed his presence.

"We'll find them—you'll see," he says, trying to console her. In reality, he, too, is shaken and incredulous. Those jewels are worth a fortune and could be collateral for the debts that are choking him. Linch knows that, too; he called him immediately to find out "the extent of the damage."

Franca twists a handkerchief. "What was most dear to me after my daughters . . ." she whispers. "It seems I can't keep that which I cherish most, that my fate is to lose in the most painful way possible the people and things of which I'm fondest. What sin am I meant to be atoning for? Why must I be punished like this?"

Ignazio embraces her. "Now, now, my dear Franca . . . We've been through much worse. Remember, these jewels are easy to identify. The thieves can't have them dismantled by the first jeweler they come across. And nobody will want to be accused of receiving stolen goods. For what you'd get out of it, it's far too risky."

Franca opens her eyes wide. "Taken apart?" she stammers. "My necklaces? The rings . . . my pearls?" She shakes her head frantically. "No, no . . ." she keeps repeating. Ignazio's words are futile. Franca starts to shake, hugging her chest as if trying to hold herself together. "Do I have to suffer that too?" She weeps softly, her face distorted by a pain that's the sum of all the suffering she's had over the years. As if the thief, besides robbing the jewels from her, has stolen the one thing that still protected her soul: the memory of happiness.

And yet, at least this once, fate is kind to her. Leading the investigation is a highly capable deputy inspector from Milan, Giovanni Rizzo. He's a bulldog, someone who really knows his job. He quickly identifies the two thieves, the Belgian Henry Poisson and the German ex–Air Force officer Richard Soyter. They had been following Franca for days, studying her habits and those of her friend, and committed the deed at a time when they were sure both Ignazio and Giulia would be asleep.

Rizzo lays a trap for them in Cologne, thanks to the naïvéte of Poisson's girlfriend, Marguerite. What with unlikely and contradictory testimony, bold declarations—"What was Signora Florio supposed to do with her jewels, she who has so many?" Poisson apparently said when he was arrested—suitcases stopped at the border with Italy, and legal blunders, it will take until 1926, in other words, four years, for the two thieves to be sentenced in absentia by the Italian courts. By the time the trial is held, people have lost interest, even Franca, who doesn't bother to attend.

It was enough for her that she got back all her jewels, in January of 1923. With a mixture of surprise and compassion, Giovanni Rizzo watched her open the pouches, one by one, lift the pearls to her face, stroke the diamonds, and slip on the rings. "They're back . . . they're here and they're mine," Franca murmured, weeping with happiness.

Her life, or at least a part of it, has been restored.

Even though more than ten years have passed since Ignazio had to abandon his office on Piazza Marina, for him the creaking has never stopped and the cracks have never been filled in. On the contrary. The Olivuzza torn to pieces, reduced to a new neighborhood of the city. Villa Igiea, which by now has lost its reason for being: the rooms are deserted; the casino brings in hardly any income. The ceramics factory practically transferred to Ducrot. The head office of the Banco Florio and the premises on Via dei Materassai sold to men of cunning and of dubious reputation, who got rich while Italy sank into war. Even *L'Ora* has for some time been in the hands of the rich miller Filippo Pecoraino. Then, in 1926, the regime will close down the paper and restart it the following year with the subtitle *Fascist Daily for the Mediterranean*.

In this endless storm, the one bulwark is Carlo Linch. Omnipresent, punctilious, tireless, he stubbornly continues to press for a reduction in expenses, especially Franca's—"They're still too high!"—and sometimes even brings up Igiea's wedding, even though that was four years ago. "It cost an arm and a leg! Clothes, jewels, even three receptions! Oh, if only you hadn't squandered so much . . ." he cries in exasperation when times are particularly hard. And yet he's not an insensitive man: saving what remains of Casa Florio is a task he carries out with a sacrifice deserving of a better cause. Wicked tongues insinuate that he has benefited financially and that certain choices made during his tenure were not entirely aboveboard. Be that as it may, he still has hope, and because of him, so does Ignazio.

For a brief moment, that hope had three names: *Ignazio Florio*, *Vincenzo Florio*, and *Giovanna Florio*.

It wasn't easy, but in the end the Banca Commerciale granted the Florios a line of credit for the purchase of three English ships, intended for freight. With one of them—the *Giovanna Florio*—Ignazio even entertained the idea of a route between the Mediterranean and Baltimore. But all these ambitions were scuttled by the crisis in the Italian merchant industry, which has been undermined by unsustainable costs and ever more meager profits. Over the course of a few years, the three ships will end up decommissioned in Palermo harbor, the sad reminder of yet another dream gone up in smoke, until a captain from Piano di Sorrento, Achille Lauro, rents them for a ridiculous sum and, thanks to them, starts to build his naval empire.

Another flame, another hope: after months of discussions with the ministry for the Merchant Navy, in December 1925 in Rome, a new company, the Florio–Società Italiana di Navigazione is set up, and some lines across the Tyrrhenian Sea will be assigned to it. This desire not to give up the sea is Ignazio's, aware as he is of how closely the name of the Florios is linked to the sea. But it's Linch who has seen to everything, overcoming the ministry's mistrust and taking charge of the operation, while Ignazio has launched himself into another enterprise entirely: he has gone to the Canaries with the intention of there opening a *tonnara* to intercept the banks of tuna before they enter the Mediterranean.

*Of all the crazy ideas he's had, this is the craziest of all*, thinks Franca, curling her lips as she reads the letter that has just arrived from her husband. She's in the bedroom of her house in Rome, a small villa on Via Sicilia, elegant in its sober architecture that vaguely recalls that of Villa Igiea, and filled partly with furniture designed by Ducrot, but also with many precious objects from the Olivuzza, like the Bohemian crystal service and the set of Saxon plates. Those parties with hundreds of guests are a distant memory, but a dinner in Franca Florio's house still has to be a major social occasion.

Ignazio's letter brings little cause for cheer: the tuna are actually becoming scarcer, but there are banks of sardines he's planning to exploit, provided he can find a little money for the plants and the workers. Vincenzo and Lucie are with him right now: they have rented a small villa where they live without luxury or any particular comfort, just like the locals. The photographs enclosed with the letter are less grim. One shows Ignazio and Vincenzo together on a bed; in another Ignazio is alone, sitting in an armchair; in yet another Lucie is cooking. There are also scenes of fishing, the interior of the *tonnara*, fishermen's huts, a beach at sunset . . .

Franca angrily throws aside the photographs. Ignazio hasn't

once asked her to join him, even if only for a few weeks. People have asked her why she hasn't gone there, and she has replied that the islands are too remote and primitive, unsuitable for Giugiù . . . "And besides," she always concludes with a smile, "I can't see myself organizing a dinner surrounded by savages."

*Lies.*

She isn't in the photographs, but Franca is sure that Vera is there with him. She can sense her presence, even though she can't see her. Ignazio may be thousands of kilometers away, but she can read him like a book; she discerns the truth behind his words as no one else can. It's a code she has learned at her own expense.

"Is that a letter from *Papà*? Can I read it?"

Giulia has entered the room like a gust of spring wind. Franca smiles and hands her the letter. How beautiful her Giugiù is. She's sixteen, with slim legs and fair hair. Igiea has a delicate, classical beauty, whereas Giulia is as vivacious and charming as her father, with whom she has a strong bond.

Giulia reads the letter out loud and lets out a cry of joy on discovering that her father intends to return to Rome soon on some business or other. At that moment, the maid appears in the doorway.

"Signor Linch is here, Signora."

Surprised, Franca gets up from the dressing table. "Linch? Whatever can he want?"

Giulia shrugs. "Maybe he's brought some papers to give to *Papà*, seeing that he's about to come back," she says and makes to follow her mother into the little drawing room where the butler has admitted Linch. But Franca stops her in the doorway. Linch is often the bearer of bad news, and she doesn't want her daughter to be upset. "Giulia, my dear, go check if the cook is preparing the *parfait de foie gras* for tonight's dinner." Slightly peeved, the girl sets off for the kitchen.

Carlo Linch is standing there, still in his coat. He seems to be in a hurry. "Good day to you, Donna Franca. Forgive me for coming without notice, but I must speak with you."

She motions him to a seat and takes one herself. "With me? Of course, go on," she says once the butler has closed the door behind him.

"I shall be brief and . . . I fear, unpleasant," Linch says with a frown. "I must remind you once again that you go out too often and—"

"Oh, how tired I am of that same old story!" Franca interrupts with obvious irritation. She looks down at the rug, which once adorned a room in the Olivuzza. "We've already made all the cuts we can and even asked for an extension on what we owe for the work done in this house, while waiting for the money that should arrive from our shares in the navigation company."

"But in this villa, you have nine people at your service. You need only half that number. Not to mention your gambling debts and your constant traveling. In your husband's absence, it therefore falls to me to ask you to show more . . . self-control."

Franca's cheeks grow flushed with indignation. "How dare you? My husband has never told me what to do and now you—"

"I haven't finished, Signora."

Franca adjusts the folds of her skirt and stares at Linch, waiting.

"I appeal to your common sense. Reducing your expenses here in Rome is no longer enough. You should go back to live in Palermo."

"What?" Franca's voice is like a thread on the verge of breaking.

"Go back home. There, you will be able to take care of what you still own and help your family."

Franca looks at him for a long time in silence. Then, all at once, she throws her head back and starts laughing maniacally.

She laughs for a long time, so loudly that tears come to her eyes. She continues to weep even after her laughter subsides. She leaps to her feet. "Home?" she says, her voice now grim but steady. "Tell me, Signor Linch, you who knows everything: What home am I supposed to go back to? The Olivuzza and its grounds no longer belong to us. A house where we welcomed the whole world: heads of state, musicians, poets, actors! Or else Villa Igiea, where I'm now just a guest?" She pauses and gives him a long, hard look, her green eyes brimming with anger. "Or perhaps you're telling me that the home I should return to is Palermo?" She swallows saliva, tears, and bitterness. No dam can hold back her rage now: she has been nursing it for too long. It's a tidal wave, a storm surge that rips through sand and rocks. She walks up and down the room, the hem of her dress swaying about her calves. "Palermo that had bread and work from the Florios for more than a century, that donned the airs of a great European city with that Teatro Massimo my husband financed. They all came to us, cap in hand, asking for help or a subsidy, certain that the Florios would never refuse them charity. It was a city that asked and promised but deceived us. In Palermo, gratitude lasts three days, like the sirocco." She stops and passes a hand over her forehead. A lock of hair falls across her face. "So tell me, tell me who I should go back to! There's no longer anyone waiting for me there. Those who called themselves our friends, who came to ask for a loan, who accepted our gifts and now turn the other way when they meet us? Or else those who bought the Olivuzza for a pittance, after dividing it up among themselves?" She straightens up and crosses her arms over her chest. Her eyelashes are beating faster, and her voice breaks. "You can tell me many things, Signor Linch. But you arrived in Palermo when the hyenas were already tearing to pieces what little remained of our life. It's impossible for you to understand what it means to lose respect, because you never saw my Palermo. The city of the Florios was vital, rich, full of hope. And now it no longer exists. It's only a spiderweb of unknown streets, lined with buildings inhabited by ghosts."

Silently, Linch puts his hand in his pocket, takes out a handkerchief, and holds it out to her. She takes it and thanks him. A line of face powder remains on the batiste fabric.

"I understand," Linch says, bowing his head. "What can I tell you? Try to live as best you can with what you have left. It's never too late to be prudent."

These words provoke another sob.

"But you, too, must understand that I cannot withdraw my . . . request," he goes on. "The business really isn't doing well. I'm making the case for the new maritime conventions with Minister Ciano in person, but there are many obstacles, starting with the fact that your husband has again hardened his position toward the Banca Commerciale, even though the bank owns most of the shares and titles of credit involving Casa Florio. He should be more accommodating, instead of which . . ."

"He doesn't inform me of those things. You know that perfectly well." Franca lowers her head and looks at the carpet.

"I supposed as much." Linch takes his hat and plays with the rim. "Our hopes are tied to the fact that your husband fought hard for the industrialists to support Mussolini's list in the administrative elections in Palermo. He still has influence down there, and he was listened to . . . Now we just have to hope that the government remembers and is grateful." He makes a slight bow. "Thank you for hearing me out, Donna Franca. If you change your mind, you know where to find me."

Franca is left alone.

A sudden need for fresh air makes her fling the French window wide open. She throws back her head and takes a deep breath, the air wiping away her tears. The wind lifts the curtain, and for a moment she is surprised to see her own reflection in the glass. But this time she can't tell herself she is still beautiful despite the years and the suffering. This time she sees the marks made by the absences, the vanished affections, all that she has lost. They are there in her eyes, which have lost all liveliness, in the ever-deeper lines, and in her now gray hair.

*I've become a shadow surrounded by shadows*, she tells herself. *Nothing but a reflection in a pane of glass.*

In the silence of the narrow corridor in Villa dei Quattro Pizzi, Ignazio walks with a bowed head. From an open window the light lapping of the waves reaches him, together with the smell of seaweed. A smell that takes him back to the summers of his childhood, to Favignana, when the whole family moved to the building his father built.

Christmas 1928 has just passed, and the New Year has tiptoed in, joylessly. Even though she's in Milan right now, Franca is living in Rome with Giulia: having been evicted from the little villa on Via Sicilia, she's now in a house on Via Piemonte.

Ignazio swallows air. Reaching the door of the square tower, he throws it open, but doesn't go in. He merely looks at the January light and the dust dancing above the majolica floor. Then he looks out at the gulf spread out in front of him. The sea is a cold, shiny sheet of metal, punctuated with a few small fishing vessels returning to the little harbor. Beyond the water, he glimpses the garden of Villa Igiea.

A blow to his heart. One more.

Even Villa Igiea no longer belongs to him. A few months ago, he and Vincenzo transferred it to a finance company that now, through Linch, manages almost all of what they own: from the Florio–Società Italiana di Navigazione, which is smothered in debt, to the *tonnaras* in the Canaries—another failure—and from their shares in Ducrot's company to Vincenzo's house on Via Catania . . . and even Villa dei Quattro Pizzi, in which he himself is now living. To remain in Villa Igiea, Ignazio would have had to pay rent; being unable to afford it, he was asked by the new manager—kindly—to leave. Then, after the kindness, came the eviction notice.

*Semu nuddu 'mmiscatu cu 'nenti*, he tells himself. He knows that's how people think, that's how he is considered by everyone. *We are nothing mixed with nothing.*

He studies his hands and asks himself who is to blame. He's asked himself the same question dozens, perhaps hundreds, of times: he's off-loaded the blame onto his partners—obtuse, incompetent, shortsighted—but then told himself that in reality it was his opponents who clipped his wings. He has fancied himself the predestined victim of bad luck, then convinced himself that his ideas were too bold, too far in advance of their time to be successful.

Today, though, he no longer has the strength to lie to himself.

He blinks to stop the tears and, as if in a dream, sees his father watching the *mattanza* in Favignana, stopping to talk to the workers at the Oretea, calculating how best to exploit the sulfur mines, tasting the marsala with eyes closed, watching the train come into the farm at Alcamo, arguing with Crispi in a hotel in Rome . . . Bad luck, the ineptitude of others, or the fact that the world was not ready for his enterprises: these are ideas that would never have even occurred to him. He always acted with a sense of responsibility, of duty, and that was enough for him. He had a single god, Casa Florio, and a single religion, work. Like that grandfather who died just as Ignazio was being born and who was alive for him in the stories his father told: a simple but implacable man, a Calabrian spice merchant who, starting from dire poverty, won the respect of an entire city. He was the one who had decided to build this villa in the Arenella, and to make it so extraordinary as to arouse the admiration of kings and queens.

Ignazio wonders if it isn't actually the blood of the Florios that has betrayed him, because he was always convinced that that alone was enough to make him good at business. That expertise and entrepreneurial skills were there in his blood, kneaded into his bones and muscles. Instead of which, there was something more, something he's never had. A desire for redemption? The will to succeed? A sense of duty? An ability to read other men's minds and sense what they want?

He doesn't know. He will never know.

All he knows is that now is no longer the time to lie to himself. At the age of sixty, it's pointless to look for justifications, to convince himself that in the smithy of fate someone—God or someone working for God—made him a suit of armor so heavy it ended up crushing him.

The fault is his and his alone.

"It's only a matter of days," the doctor said last night. "Keep the windows open, but make sure he's in the sun and talk to him about nice things. Let him have a few treats."

Ignazio nodded and walked him to the door. Then he burst out crying like a child.

He didn't cry like that even when Giuseppe Lanza di Trabia died as the result of a tropical fever two years ago, in 1927, leaving his beloved sister and brother-in-law in the same situation as him: with no male child to continue the name. This must really be the curse of the Florios, Ignazio had thought, touching the family ring.

And now Romualdo. Tuberculosis is carrying him away. When Ignazio found out he was gravely ill, he had him brought back from the sanatorium in the Alps, where he was wasting away his last days, so that he could die in his own city. And then he decided to house him here, in the Arenella. He owed it to him.

He enters the room. Romualdo's skin is tight over his cheekbones, and he has deep rings around his eyes.

Ignazio sits down by the bed, just as the uncle whose name he bears once did with his brother Paolo.

"How are you?"

"Blooming," Romualdo says, and laughs. He has always laughed, and continues to do so even in the face of death. "Get the cards out, go on, we'll have a game."

With a heavy heart, Ignazio obeys. But Romualdo has difficulty in following the game and often stops to chat. All at once, though, he breaks off, puts the cards on his chest, and looks toward the wall. "You know, every now and again I think about her."

"Who, *curò*?" Ignazio shuffles the cards, preparing the next hand.

"My wife, Giulia." He sighs. "I think how they gave Paternò a life sentence and I never believed it was enough. But now I can't even remember the animal's face. Giulia, on the other hand . . . *mischina*. Now that I'm dying, too, I feel sorry for her."

"Stop that," Ignazio cuts in. "You're not dying," he adds with a casualness that sounds forced.

Romualdo turns, looks at him, and raises his eyebrows. "Don't talk rubbish, Igna'."

Ignazio lowers his eyes to the cards. The images blur. "With all the women we've had, here we are, alone like two poor wretches."

"What are you talking about? You have Vera, don't you?"

"Vera doesn't want to see me anymore. She says it's not the right time . . . and I don't know what to do. I miss her."

"What about Franca?"

Ignazio puts the cards down and gives a bitter smile. "Ever since I offered her jewels as collateral for loans from the Banco di Sicilia, she's practically stopped speaking to me. It's been two years now . . . It had already hurt her when she found out that Boldini sold the painting to the Rothschilds. You know what she told me when she handed over the gold mesh bag with the jewels?"

"What?"

"'You promised you would give me everything. And instead, you've taken everything away from me.'"

Memory dilates the images, slowly, painfully. Franca wrapped the jewels, one by one, in a velvet cloth, almost as if it were a shroud, then put them back in the bag. She was crying. She left the pearls for last, running them through her fingers, one string after another. "I've been told that pearls are tears," she murmured, clutching them in her fist. She lifted them to her face, for a last caress, then shut them up in a case and handed them over.

That image still torments him. "Poor Franca. She was right," he says softly. "I made her suffer a lot."

Romualdo shrugs. "We've told each other enough nonsense, Igna'. Both of us." He takes the cards from his hands. "Now it's all over."

"And what do we have left?" Ignazio asks, perhaps more of himself than of Romualdo.

"Why is there always supposed to be something left? We've lived well, Igna'. We didn't stand watching; we took life by the horns, and we enjoyed it without thinking too much. I've reached death without regrets. I've been the mayor of Palermo. I've been rich and powerful, like you. We've had wonderful women in our beds. We've had money, travel, champagne . . . We've had a life, Igna'. We've dreamed big dreams, we've been free, and we've always defended what really mattered to us. Not money, not power, and not even our names. Dignity."

Ignazio remembers Romualdo's words the day they are forced to leave even the house on Via Piemonte. He came back to his wife after being abandoned once and for all by Vera, who had a deep spiritual crisis in 1930, following the death of her son Leonardo during an aerial drill over the Adriatic. Ignazio and she were now united only by the ferocity of the divine punishment for what they had done: first the deaths of Ignazio's children, then Leonardo's death, were the punishment they deserved for having been un-faithful. That's what Vera told him, and Ignazio couldn't find any-thing to say in reply. He merely embraced this woman who had given him such peace. Who had always carried a smile for him and who now, through her tears, implored him to redeem himself, to repent for the harm he had done his wife and family. Then, after giving her a last kiss on the forehead, he walked away.

But those words entered his soul, planted roots in that sense of guilt he had denied for so long. They drove him to return to Franca, to share with her what little now remained.

He didn't give up, not immediately: going from one city to an-other, he kept trying to do business deals, even small ones, even at the cost of humiliating himself. But his name now aroused pity, contempt, and sometimes even derision. Ignazio Florio had let an empire collapse. Ignazio Florio had been unable to administer his own heritage. Ignazio Florio was a fool, a failure.

He once again found himself envying Vincenzo, because he had a brave, pragmatic woman beside him, a woman who really loved him and had done everything she could to salvage something, starting with the jewels and furniture his brother had given her over the years. They didn't see each other often: together with Lucie and Renée, Vincenzo traveled between Palermo and France, between Via Catania and her family home, at Épernay in Champagne. The last time he met him, Ignazio had the sensation that the fifteen years' difference between them had been suddenly bridged: he found himself looking at a man who looked much older than his fifty years, tired and full of burdens. Basically, he told himself that his brother, like him, had always done what he had wanted, regardless of the consequences. And perhaps it was because of his excesses that he hadn't had children. *Has he resigned himself to the fact?* Ignazio asked himself at the time. But once again, he said nothing.

A slight cough. Behind him, the butler and a maid. Both of them are wearing their coats.

"Signore, we're going. If you'd like to pay us our last month's wages . . ." the man says, politely but firmly.

"As for the other months, we hope you can at least give us an advance . . ." the maid adds.

Suddenly, Ignazio feels acute embarrassment. Don't these two know that the bones have already been stripped bare by lots of other predators?

He puts his hands in his pockets and takes out a wad of banknotes. The last ones.

"Here. I'll let you divide it up," he says to the butler, then turns his back on them and goes to Giulia, who has witnessed the scene, standing motionless in the doorway.

He strokes her arm and smiles at her.

She smiles back at him, then goes to the bed, on which two small suitcases lie open.

"Do you need any help?"

"*Papà*, you already asked me," she replies, a flash of irony in her eyes. "You've never packed a suitcase in your life, and you would put in a mountain of things, higgledy-piggledy. Sit down. I won't be long."

Ignazio sighs and obeys. It's toward Giulia that he feels the greatest sense of guilt. Two years ago, she had a serious nervous breakdown. Luckily, Igiea and Averardo took care of her, putting her up at Migliarino Pisano. They helped her to recover, to eat normally, to sleep peacefully.

They made her feel loved.

He was still with Vera at the time. As for Franca, after paying her daughter a visit, she saw fit to leave for Paris, having lost God knows how much at the casinos on the Côte d'Azur. She couldn't bear any more suffering, let alone that of her daughters, she said on her return, by way of justification.

In the end, Giulia recovered, but since then, she's become more detached, as if the world to which she once belonged no longer interests her.

"I'm sorry," Ignazio murmurs, almost to himself.

Giulia seems not to have heard. But after a few moments she asks, "For what?"

"For . . . what I'm forcing you to do."

"Fortunately, I'm going to see Igiea," she replies in a curt tone, shutting the suitcases. She puts on first her gloves, then her fur-lined coat. The Roman winter is particularly damp this year. "And above all I'm going to see Arabella, Laura Floriana, Flavia Domitilla, and Forese. They'll certainly be pleased to spend some time with their aunt."

"Your mother and I will come and see you. We'll come and see you and Igiea, my darling."

She nods and kisses him on the cheek. "Take care of Mother," she says, smoothing the lapel of his jacket, which by now is showing its age. "She isn't as strong as you."

*You don't know how she used to be,* Ignazio thinks. *I was the one who made her weak. I was the one who broke her.*

After a last caress, Giulia walks away along the corridor, opens the door, and goes out. The Salviatis' car is waiting for her outside. All Ignazio can do now is stare at the dimly lit room, the empty walls, and the elegant furnishings that are about to be auctioned. A fate similar to that of the furniture that has remained in Palermo, confiscated by the municipal tax office because of a series of unpaid taxes. Not much, in truth: a lot of it was already sold in 1921, during an auction that lasted more than a month.

But in his eyes there is no longer either sadness or regret. There is only a gleam of dignity, that dignity that his friend Romualdo defended to his last breath and that, for Ignazio, now has the same color as resignation.

Franca is sitting on the bed, her hands folded on her lap, staring down at the floor. Ignazio comes in but doesn't look at her. She, too, looks much older than her sixty-one years. Ignazio knows why; he knows it's not only because of her bad habits and excesses. And because he knows that, he avoids as much as possible looking at that hardened face, those lifeless eyes, those hands covered in stains.

He goes to the armchair where his coat is, takes it, and drapes it over his shoulders. He smells an echo of her perfume, the same as always: La Marescialla. "Shall we go?" he says.

Franca nods.

Ignazio picks up the two small suitcases and they leave the house. The rest is already at the Hotel Eliseo, a modest but clean and quiet hotel near Porta Pinciana. Averardo and Igiea kept insisting, but Franca was adamant: moving to the Salviatis' house would be too big a blow to their dignity.

On the street, some stop to greet them, while others turn away. Everyone in the area knows who they are. They walk side by side in silence. With the years, the difference between them has grown. She has always been taller than him, but now Ignazio really seems shrunken, while Franca has retained her nimble, harmonious gait. It takes an effort, but she can't do otherwise.

Because the world is looking at her, and whatever happens, she is always Donna Franca Florio.

The Roman spring is cold, but the people in the head office of the Banca Commerciale don't seem to notice. Perhaps because the room has been filling up since early morning, perhaps because the wait has gotten them all excited, perhaps because it's in the nature of secrets to give off a heat that burns anyone who gets too close to it.

The auction catalog doesn't declare the provenance of the lots that are being put under the hammer, but the people taking their places in the room have no need for a name on the paper. Because the brooches and the diamond bracelets, the ruby rings, the emerald bracelets, the long strings of pearls, can only have belonged to one person.

*To her.*

The Roman nobility is in the know and has sent its representatives, with specific instructions. There are those who have preserved the memory of a particular brooch by Cartier—or Fecarotta or the Brothers Merli—ever since they saw her wearing it at a dinner, a first night, or during a chance encounter. Envy has turned into a yearning for possession. It's as if the splendor of a jewel can preserve a trace of the charm and grace of the person who wore it, and now these men want to take possession of it in order to shine by reflection.

The many jewelers present, on the other hand, seem more detached. They recognize one another, greet one another formally, their eyes filled with a touch of defiance. Then they skim the pages of the catalog and reflect on the starting price of this or that item, imagining how to take the jewels apart and mount the stones differently, in a more modern, less recognizable style.

Then a murmur runs through the room. Giulia Florio has appeared in the doorway: she is wearing a hat with a half veil and a black coat. The youngest of the Florios stops, her hands tight around the strap of her velvet handbag, her eyes haughtily studying the faces of those present, one by one, as if wanting to imprint them on her mind.

*I know who you are,* those eyes seem to say. *You are here because you would never have been able to afford what my family owned. You are just crows stripping bare the bones. You can remove the stones from their mounts, separate the strings of pearls, melt the metal, but I will know what you did and I will know which of you did it.*

*You will never have my mother's elegance, or my father's class, or my family's greatness. Never.*

*And I am here to remind you of that.*

She advances confidently, with her head held high, and takes a seat. The auctioneer has seen her and recognized her: he hesitates for a few moments, but then begins to call the lots. In front of her pass the jewels that have accompanied her mother's life. In some cases, Giulia even remembers the last time she saw them. Like that gold brooch with the diamond monogram, which five years ago, in 1930, Franca asked to have back just for a few days, so that she could wear it during the wedding of Umberto II and Marie-José of Belgium. She was still a lady-in-waiting and so was expected to participate in such an important ceremony wearing the royal brooch. Giulia hasn't forgotten the humiliation in her mother's eyes when the bank informed her that it couldn't entrust to the Florios either that brooch or the pearl necklace for fear they would not be handed back. In the end, the bank gave in, but it had taken many petitions and reassurances from high places.

The auctioneer describes the jewels, and the bids succeed one another without a stop. The strings of pearls unleash a genuine frenzy. After the string of three hundred fifty-nine pearls has been awarded, at a figure that is probably equivalent to half its value, and after the audible exclamation of triumph from the jeweler who has purchased it, Giulia clasps her bag to herself and leaves the room with her head held high.

She will never tell her mother that she witnessed the sale of her beloved jewels. It was her father who showed her the letter from the Banca Commerciale informing him of the day and hour of the auction, and he looked at her, in silence, as if to say: *Help me.* Giulia returned his gaze, then shook her head, just once, and walked away.

Her mother and her father had to write the last chapter of this story together, without anyone's help. Just as they had written the other chapters, both the bright ones and the terrible ones.

She was merely a witness to the fate of Casa Florio. And as such, she had wanted to watch as their hand wrote the words *The End*.

Franca is sitting at the dressing table. The small room in the Hotel Eliseo is bathed in a bright light, which speaks of new life and spring. It troubles her, almost offends her. Ignazio has gone out for a walk. At least that's what he told her. In reality—as she well knows—her husband couldn't stand the idea of having to talk about what was happening at that moment. He simply whispered to her, "Forgive me," in the doorway of the room before he left.

She closes her eyes. Today is *the* day.

In her mind, she hears the blows of the little hammer punctuating the sale of her jewels.

The sapphire bracelet that Ignazio gave her when Baby Boy was born. The platinum one, a gift on the birth of Giulia. The diamond and platinum brooch in the shape of an orchid, received on the occasion of their first wedding anniversary. And then her pearls. The string of forty-five large pearls. The one of one hundred eighty. The one of four hundred thirty-five small pearls . . . and above all the string of three hundred fifty-nine pearls, in all their charm, the one she wore when Boldini painted her portrait . . .

Every blow echoes in her bones, the echo of a pain that reaches her soul.

All her life, those jewels were her shield. They protected her; they demonstrated to the world her strength and her beauty. And now where are they? Who will take care of them?

Where are elegance, style, self-control? Did they ever really exist, did they really belong to her? Or were they false certainties destined to vanish with the years?

She has the answer right there in front of her. It's in that face marked with bitter lines, in those sad eyes, in that pleated dress that hides a body grown heavy. In that soul that has fallen to pieces so many times it is no longer able to recompose itself.

*Don't be afraid to be what you are*, Giulia told her one rainy day, a whole lifetime ago. And she tried, in the only way that seemed possible to her. With love, in all its forms. For Ignazio, for her children, for the family, for the name she bore. She loved a lot and was loved a lot, but in the end it was love that created inside her an abyss of darkness and silence. *They say that love gives of itself unreservedly; but if you give everything of yourself you have nothing left to live on.*

That's what happened to her.

At first, her love for Ignazio was filled with desire, devotion, loyalty. She gave herself entirely to him, to what he was and what he represented. She was swept away by wealth, the frenzy of living, luxury. With the arrival of her children, her joy was unconfined. For a very brief and infinitely distant time, she felt alive. Even the malign gossip, the glances of envy, the poison of an entire city that so tormented her, now seem to her the signs of that complete, resplendent perfection.

But then the circle was broken. The betrayals began, the pain, the bereavements. She deluded herself that she could protect that love by continuing to love Ignazio in spite of everything, continuing to be what he wanted. Continuing to be Donna Franca Florio.

That was the start of the decline, not only of Casa Florio. *Her own decline.*

Now the star that lit up the sky of Palermo, brighter than any other, has gone out, becoming darkness within darkness.

Even her jewels, even those that were signs of a deceptive, desperate, misplaced love, have vanished. The illusion of having been happy is evaporated by the sun; it is dust on this golden spring morning.

She has nothing left.

All that remains is a mild tenderness toward Ignazio, born out of the years they have spent together. And there remains her love for her daughters, for Igiea and for Giulia. For them she harbors the hope that they don't make her mistakes. That they remain faithful to themselves and that they understand that love cannot live only because one of the two wants it.

And above all, that they learn to love themselves.

*Would I have loved less if I had known all this?*

No.

*I would have loved differently.*

She stares at a point in the mirror—one of the mirrors saved from the sack of the Olivuzza—but her eyes are engrossed, distant.

Then a slight smile curls her lips and softens her face.

There in front of her is a little boy sitting on a carpet. He has thick blond curls and mischievous eyes and he's laughing as he pulls the short white skirt of a little girl with diaphanous skin and green eyes, who holds a baby girl in her arms.

And there in a corner are her mother and father, her brother Franz, her mother-in-law Giovanna. Giulia Tasca di Cutò is there, too, young and beautiful as she was at the time of their friendship.

She looks at the children again. They look back and smile.

Giovannuzza. Baby Boy. Giacobina.

"We're waiting for you, *Mamma*," Giovannuzza says, although her lips don't move.

She knows. She knows they're waiting for her. And she even knows that her love for them was different. With them she was never afraid to be Franca and nothing else. She wasn't afraid to be fragile, to show her soul. And she realizes only now that all the rest has vanished.

So, only for them, there in the mirror, Franca is young and beautiful again. She's in her room, the one with the floor covered in rose petals and cherubs on the ceiling. Her green eyes are clear; her mouth is open in a serene smile. She's wearing a light white dress and her pearls.

And at that moment, as perfect as it's impossible, she's really happy.

As she never really was.

# Epilogue

## November 1950

*Cu campa si fa vecchiu.*
Those who live grow old.
—SICILIAN PROVERB

THE NOVEMBER OF 1950 is a frosty one, swept by a wind that smells of wet soil.

Ignazio shuffles down the concrete path in the Santa Maria di Gesù Cemetery and stumbles. Beside him, Igiea keeps having to stop and hold him up. Behind them, beyond the gates, there are people, many people. They have come to say their final farewell to Donna Franca Florio.

"My darling Franca . . ." he murmurs. Franca died, at the age of seventy-six, just a few days ago in Migliarino Pisano, in Igiea's house, where she had been living. Ignazio refused to see her. In his increasingly frail, hazy mind, Franca will always be the young woman in the straw hat and white cotton dress he met in Villa Giulia.

He looks up. The imposing Florio chapel looms above him. The wrought-iron gate is wide open, and just behind the marble lion sculpted by Benedetto De Lisi stands a dark coffin covered with a large wreath of flowers. An explosion of life in the midst of all the grayness.

Igiea shakes him gently and he looks at her, as though surprised to see her next to him. Under the veil, his daughter's face looks exhausted, her eyes red from crying.

"Would you like to say goodbye to her, *Papà*?"

He shakes his head vigorously. Igiea sighs. *I thought you wouldn't*, she seems to say. She turns to the young woman behind her, her eldest child, Arabella. "Keep an eye on *Nonno*," she says, stepping aside to allow her to take his arm. Then she walks up the short path between the graves and up the small staircase to the chapel, where her husband, her sister Giulia, and her brother-in-law Achille Belloso Afan de Rivera are waiting for her.

Ignazio looks at his daughters with wistful detachment. Yes, he knows they think his mind is in a muddle, lost in a past that's more imagined than real, and that they blame him for having made their mother suffer. And they're right.

Igiea and Giulia are grown women. They have their own lives, their own families, their own places in the world. They don't belong to Sicily anymore, and no longer bear his name. The only one who could have borne it is here, in the very chapel about to receive Franca.

He has often wondered in the past if he was afraid of death. Now he has the answer. No, he isn't afraid of it. He's had a full life and for a long time didn't deprive himself of anything. But now he's tired—tired of outliving all the people he loved, of being a dam that stems the tide of destiny while others are swept away.

Ignazio walks over to the foot of the embankment where the chapel stands. This is where the crypt is. "Where are you trying to go, *Nonno*?" Arabella asks, almost holding him back.

He simply indicates the small, black iron railing, opened for the occasion. "There."

It's even colder in the crypt. The tuff walls are cracked, coated with a layer of mold, and the iron chandeliers are bent, corroded by damp and the passing years.

And yet the two white sarcophagi in the middle of the crypt seem immune to the damage of time. The one where his father lies is covered in dust. Ignazio approaches and wipes it with his hand. As he does so, he scrapes the family ring against the stone, producing a hissing sound that makes him yank his hand away. The other sarcophagus, a monumental one, is that of his grandfather

Vincenzo, whom he never knew. Next to it lie his mother, Giovanna, and grandmother Giulia, as well as his great-grandfather Paolo and great-uncle Ignazio, who came to Palermo from Bagnara Calabra and owned the wretched *putìa* where it all began. His great-grandmother Giuseppina, Paolo's wife, is with them.

All the Florios are here.

They all had a future, someone to whom they could leave not just money but businesses, buildings, a name, and a history. And one flagstone after another, just like a road, this name and this history have come to him.

There is no one left now to keep their memory. This thought makes him so unbearably dizzy that he closes his eyes, as if ignoring the abyss is enough to stop him from falling into it. That's why he didn't want to watch Franca's funeral. Because up there in the chapel, next to her, lie his young brother Vincenzo and three of his own children: Giovannuzza, Baby Boy, and Giacobina.

The dizziness doesn't go away even when he leaves the cemetery and gets into Igiea's Alfa Romeo. Palermo rushes past his eyes, indifferent. Ignazio gives a start only when they drive past Palazzo Butera, devastated by bombs in 1943. His sister, Giulia, witnessed that atrocity, the death of her oldest son, Giuseppe, and of her husband, Pietro. She died only three years ago, on Christmas Eve 1947.

Ignazio looks down at the family ring. The ruin of Casa Florio is something distant now. When he remembers it, he feels a vague unease, but not grief. Even his dependence on his daughters and brother leaves him indifferent. He doesn't have a penny left, even though Casa Florio never officially went bankrupt. What racks his soul is the knowledge that with him a name will be lost. A history. Their history, stored in that little gold circle that has grown thinner over the years.

Igiea parks the car outside Villa dei Quattro Pizzi. Ignazio hardly notices. He's staring into space, lost in thought.

"*Papà* . . . We've arrived at Uncle Vincenzo's," she says. "I'll go up and say hello to him and Aunt Lucie but won't stay for lunch." She walks around the car and opens the door for him.

Ignazio gets out and points to the beach. "Wait," he murmurs. "Let me go look at the sea." He smiles at her, as though apologizing for his request.

They walk with difficulty, their shoes sinking in the sand, between the tiny pebbles that lie at the water's edge. Ignazio suddenly gestures to the tower on his left. "You know, your mother didn't like it here . . ."

Igiea points to the right, at a large green patch overlooking the sea. A small temple is discernable through the foliage. "I know; she preferred Villa Igiea. She stayed there for as long as she could." There's a hint of sadness in her voice.

Ignazio's eyes focus on the horizon, on the buildings of the shipyard, and beyond, on the outline of Palermo. "Look, leave me here for ten minutes," he says, indicating a flat rock not far from the side entrance of the villa.

Igiea is puzzled. "It's cold, *Papà*." The sea is swelling, splashes of foam flying in the air, filling it with brine. "Don't you think you'd be better off in the warmth?"

"No, no. Leave me here." He squeezes her arm. "Go say hello to your uncle and aunt."

Igiea nods, gives him a glance that's a blend of pain and understanding, then walks away.

Left on his own, Ignazio stares for a long time at the waves—indifferent and fierce—that come crashing against the cliffs.

Villa dei Quattro Pizzi, built by his grandfather; Villa Igiea, his and Franca's creation. His entire life and that of his family is contained in those two buildings.

Palermo. The sea.

They had been the absolute masters of Palermo. And many years ago, in Favignana, his father told him that they had the sea running in their veins.

The dizziness returns, violent and aggressive.

*It'll all be forgotten*, he tells himself, unable to restrain a sob.

He closes his eyes, then opens them again when he hears someone calling him.

"Don Ignazio!" An old man with tousled hair is coming toward him, holding by the hand a little girl with long black braids. "*Assabbinirìca*, Don Ignazio. I'm Luciano Gandolfo—do you remember me?"

Ignazio looks at him, frowning. "You used to be one of the servants at the villa, weren't you?"

"Yes, that's right. I was here even as a *picciriddu*, when your father was still alive—bless his soul. I was fifteen when he died. Me and my family have always served the Florios." The man leans forward. "I heard about your wife. She was such a beautiful woman, *recamatierna*. And you're here now, at Don Vincenzo's, right?"

Ignazio nods. He's a guest at his brother's—he who once owned houses everywhere, who reigned over the Olivuzza.

Next to them, the little girl starts picking up shells. She suddenly plucks up and stares at Ignazio with dark, intense eyes. "So you're Don Ignazio Florio, are you?" she asks.

Ignazio looks at her and nods. She must be ten or perhaps slightly older.

"Then you're Don Vincenzo's brother, Don Vincenzo with

the cars! My father often goes to talk to him when they bring us American engines for the motorboats."

"This is my granddaughter," the old man says. "My son Ignazio's daughter." He takes her by the hand and draws her closer. "My son's a mechanic."

Ignazio struggles to his feet. "Your son . . ."

The old man nods. "I named him after your father, because he was always so generous to us. And her, too." He indicates his granddaughter. "Her name's Giovanna, like your mother, who was so kind to us all, always."

The child smiles: she's clearly proud to be referred to by name. "I know all about you, Don Ignazio. My grandfather tells me and my brothers so many things . . . And my schoolmates, too . . . Their grandparents tell us all about the *tonnara* and Casa Florio." She pauses, looks at the shells in the palm of her hand, picks one, and gives it to him. "Everybody here knows who you are."

Ignazio takes the shell. "Everybody knows . . . really?" he asks in a faint voice.

The little girl nods. The old man adds, "*Caciettu*. Everyone knows your history, Don Ignazio. Yours, your brother's, your family's . . . There have been so many rich and important folk in Palermo, but no one like you. You're the Florios."

Ignazio looks up at the horizon, a lump in his throat. In the distance, amid the waves, there's a small boat with a white lateen sail. It looks like a traditional Sicilian *schifazzo*.

"True." He turns and smiles at the child and the old man. "The others are the others. We are the Florios."

# HISTORICAL BACKGROUND

## Part One: Cognac
### March 1894 to March 1901

Toward the end of 1893, the situation in Sicily worsens: on December 10, in Giardinello (near Palermo), a protest against taxes ends in tragedy, with eleven casualties and many injured; seven people die on December 25 in a similar demonstration in Lercara Friddi (also near Palermo). Many other protests break out across the island, often suppressed violently. On January 4, with the number of casualties reaching over a thousand, Francesco Crispi declares Sicily to be in a state of siege and appoints General Roberto Morra di Lavriano, Palermo's former prefect, as extraordinary civil commissioner, granting him full military and civilian powers. The repression—carried out with the help of forty thousand soldiers—is brutal: hasty trials lead to harsh sentencing and, as the general himself writes in his report, "individual freedoms, the inviolability of the home, the freedom of the press and of assembly and association" are abolished. Naturally, the *Fasci* are dissolved, but the social and economic demands that have brought together factory workers and day laborers, craftsmen and sulfur miners, as well as civil servants and teachers, extend beyond the island (protests and unrest break out from Puglia to Emilia, from Ancona to Brescia, and particularly in Lunigiana, where 250 people are arrested) and merge, at least partly, in the Italian Workers' Socialist Party, formally created in

1893 (on January 13, 1895, it will become the Italian Socialist Party, with Filippo Turati as its secretary).

It is therefore in a deeply uneasy social atmosphere that, on February 21, 1894, finance minister Sidney Sonnino announces to Parliament the necessity of tax hikes in order to address the country's economic issues. He encounters staunch opposition and resigns, but Crispi does not give up: his third government falls on June 4, but a new executive is already formed by June 14. Helped by the huge stir caused by the failed attack on his life by the anarchist Paolo Lega on June 16, 1894, Crispi succeeds, on July 20, in getting a series of economic measures approved, including an increase in duty on cereals and in the price of salt, and, above all, a 20 percent rise in income tax.

Crispi's government falls on March 10, 1896, devastated by defeat at Adua (March 1, 1896), a battle in which 14,500 Italians tried in vain to withstand an assault by 100,000 soldiers of Ethiopian Negus Menelik II (at least 6,000 Italians were killed). This is how Liberal member of Parliament Bernardo Arnaboldi Gazzaniga summarizes the disastrous African experience: "In twelve years of colonial politics [ . . . ] we managed to spend about five hundred million lire without any result, [ . . . ] spreading poverty and discontent among the populations" (speech in the Chamber on May 19, 1897).

Crispi is succeeded by Antonio Starabba di Rudinì, who remains prime minister until June 29, 1898 (in four separate governments). Partly because of the high cost of the colonization, Italy is in a very difficult economic situation, aggravated by insufficient crops (September and October 1896 register severe floods, particularly in Piedmont and Calabria) as well as by the rising cost of imported cereal and consequently of bread, which goes from an average thirty-five centesimi per kilogram to sixty. The profound popular discontent, which has by now taken on the features of a genuine social consciousness (fifteen Socialist members, including Leonida Bissolati and Filippo Turati, entered Parliament in 1895), finds expression in a series of protests that set the whole of Italy ablaze starting from early 1898 (in Florence, Ancona, Rome, Foggia, and Naples) and strikes that culminate in Milan's Piazza del Duomo on May 8. Invested with full powers, with twenty thousand men at his command, General Fiorenzo Bava Beccaris gives the order to shoot at the demonstrators, causing at least a hundred deaths. In the days that immediately follow, Bava Beccaris orders two thousand arrests, the closing down of fourteen periodicals, and the dissolution of the Trade Union Center. The king bestows on him the Order of Merit of Savoy "for important services rendered to institutions and civilizations."

Riots continue, however. On May 9, a state of siege is declared in Tuscany and the province of Naples, then, on May 11, it is Como's turn. Following Rudinì's resignation, the king calls on General Luigi Pelloux to form a government (June 29, 1898), and in February 1899, the general seeks approval for a bill proposing the militarization of railroad and postal workers, severe limitations on the freedom of assembly and the right to strike, and the preventative censorship of newspapers. There is violent opposition on the part of the Left, and after a long series of parliamentary clashes, Pelloux also resigns from his second mandate (May 14, 1899, to June 24, 1900). The moderate Giuseppe Saracco is appointed in his place and remains in office until February 15, 1901.

On June 4, 1899, King Umberto I grants amnesty to all those sentenced for the so-called bread riots, but that does not stop the anarchist Gaetano Bresci from killing the king with three gunshots on July 29, 1900, in Monza and stating, "I did it to avenge the pale, bleeding victims in Milan . . . I didn't mean to kill a man but a principle." Bresci is sentenced to life imprisonment on August 29 and dies—possibly by suicide—on May 22, 1901.

The thirty-year-old Victor Emmanuel III ascends the throne on August 10, 1900.

# Part Two: Porcelain
## April 1901 to July 1904

The end of the second Pelloux government (June 24, 1900) also marks the conclusion of an era dominated by "reactionary" politicians such as Crispi (who dies on August 11, 1901) and Rudinì. The new king actually turns to a representative of the liberal Left, Giuseppe Zanardelli, to form a government. As minister of justice in the first Crispi government, Zanardelli developed the new penal code (1889), abolishing capital punishment and establishing the right to strike (up until then considered a criminal offense). Zanardelli appoints as minister of the interior Giovanni Giolitti, who decides not to use repression against the wave of strikes in 1901 (over fifteen hundred in industry and agriculture) and 1902 (about a thousand in total), or during the first Italian general strike (September 15–20, 1904), confident that "the rising movement of the working classes [ ... ] is an invincible movement, because it exists in all civilized countries, and because it is based on the principle of equality among men" (speech to the Chamber on February 4, 1901). On December 1, 1903, Giolitti becomes prime minister (Zanardelli resigns on November 3 and dies about a month later) and presents his government to Parliament, saying that "it is necessary to start a period of social, economic, and financial reforms," given that "the improvement of the circumstances of society's less well-off classes depends above all on the growth in the country's economic prosperity." And so "the

Giolitti era" begins, marked by the government's mediation on the social and political fronts, intended to strengthen the liberal state thanks to the contribution of Catholics as well as Socialists. Giolitti exercises patience and determination with the former in order to overcome—in practice if not yet officially—the *non expedit* bloc vote; with the latter, he seeks a dialogue and spends a long time negotiating with Filippo Turati. But a coalition government with the Socialists will never materialize.

Giolitti can also rely on a favorable economic phase following the international recovery that began in 1896, strengthened in Italy partly thanks to government commissions, the continuation of protectionist policy (in the steel and textile industries in particular), growth in manpower, and foreign investment in banking (the Banca Commerciale Italiana was created as far back as 1894 with German, Swiss, and Austrian capital) forming ever closer bonds with the business world. This development, however, focuses on the "industrial triangle" (Turin, Milan, and Genoa) and fails to make a dent in the dominance of agriculture: it actually excludes Southern Italy, whose problems are never tackled organically but only with "special laws" that prove to be inadequate. One of the consequences is the increase in migration (which began after the unification of Italy): the three hundred thousand migrants during the 1896 to 1900 period grow to half a million between 1901 and 1904 (60 percent of it bound for the American continent).

In foreign politics, while still under the Zanardelli government, on June 28, 1902, Italy, Germany, and Austria sign the fourth Triple Alliance treaty (already renewed in 1887 and 1891), with the addition of a declaration in which Austria states that it has no interest in hindering possible Italian actions in Tripolitania (present-day western Libya): Crispi's failed colonial enterprise forgotten, Italy seeks to occupy a country with which it has important commercial exchanges. Concurrently, there is an improvement in relations with France: following the 1898 agreement that put an end to the "customs war," foreign minister Giulio Prinetti and French ambassador Camille Barrère reach an understanding by which Italy guarantees diplomatic support to France in Morocco, and France declares that it does not oppose Italian intervention in Tripolitania.

On July 20, 1903, Pope Leo XIII dies at the age of ninety-three. On August 4, he is succeeded by the patriarch of Venice, Cardinal Giuseppe Sarto, who takes the name Pius X. On June 11, 1905, with the encyclical *The Firm Purpose*, Pius X allows Catholics—in case of "strict necessity for the good of the souls"—the possibility of being relieved of the *non expedit*, since they must "prepare prudently and seriously for political life if they should ever be called to."

## Part Three: Lily of the Valley
### May 1906 to June 1911

The third Giolitti government takes office on May 29, 1906. It will last until December 11, 1909. The main concern of the "long ministry," as it will be called, is to bring in more social reforms. The Carcano Law (forbidding the use of minors of twelve for work, limiting women's work to twelve hours a day, and bringing in maternity leave) is approved in 1902; in 1904 the obligation to insure workers against industrial accidents is introduced; in 1907 night work for women is banned, and it is established that workers have rights to "a period of rest of no less than twenty-four consecutive hours every week"; while in 1910 the "maternity fund" is brought in. In the meantime, on September 29, 1906, the General Confederation of Labor is born, with two hundred fifty thousand members, and on May 5, 1910, the General Confederation of Industry is established.

In the economic field, Giolitti nationalizes the railways (June 15, 1905) and, even though only partially, the telephone services (1907), but the most important result comes from the "great conversion" of income (1906), mainly at the instigation of finance minister Luigi Luzzatti, a consortium of foreign banks, and the Banca d'Italia (in the person of its director, Bonaldo Stringher): the net annuity of 4 percent on shares of public debt (which amounts to about eight billion lire—that is, more than thirty-two billion euros) is converted to 3.75 percent (July 1, 1907) and then to 3.5 percent (July 1, 1912). The saving on the payment of interest amounts to about twenty million lire in 1907. The state balance closes in credit, the international reputation of Italy is consolidated, and the lira is actually quoted above gold.

After the international economic crisis of 1907—caused by the reckless speculation of the previous years and, in Italy, overcome thanks to concerted action between the government and the Banca d'Italia—Giolitti has to confront one of the greatest tragedies in Italian history: at five twenty on the morning of December 28, 1908, an earthquake of the magnitude of 7.2 destroys Messina and Reggio Calabria and devastates an area of about six thousand square kilometers, claiming between eighty thousand and a hundred thousand victims. While the government is accused of excessive slowness in the rescue operation, the king and queen go to Reggio Calabria as early as December 30 and take concrete measures to help the population. On January 8, 1909, an allocation of thirty million lire for the reconstruction of the affected areas is approved.

Having won the elections of March 7, 1909—which see the

Catholics enter Parliament for the first time—Giolitti resigns on December 2, perhaps as a result of accusations made by the southern Socialist Gaetano Salvemini, first voiced in an article in *Avanti!* (March 14, 1909) and then in the essay "The Minister of the Underworld" (1910); according to Salvemini, the backwardness of Southern Italy is due to a deliberate strategy on the part of Giolitti, who depends on election rigging and violence to maintain power.

On March 30, 1911, though, Giolitti forms his fourth government, which will last until March 21, 1914. And on September 29, 1911, he will give vent to the expansionist aims of Italy by declaring war on the Ottoman Empire and setting out to conquer Tripolitania and Cyrenaica (eastern Libya). This time, the African enterprise—supported at home by liberals, Catholics, and nationalists alike, and presented as the conquest of some kind of El Dorado—is successful: on October 11, Tripoli falls into Italian hands, followed on October 18 by Benghazi. With the First Treaty of Ouchy (October 18, 1912), Italy obtains sovereignty over Libya—"a sandbox," as Gaetano Salvemini famously defines it.

## Part Four: Lead
### October 1912 to Spring 1935

On June 30, 1912, a new electoral law is passed: men over the age of twenty-one who can read and write have the right to vote; the illiterate may vote, too, but they must be over thirty and have done their military service. Consequently, from just over three million, the number of voters increases to eight and a half million. The Socialists propose extending this right to women by altering the first article of the law as follows: "All adult Italian citizens, without distinction of sex, are voters," but the Chamber rejects the amendment on May 15, 1912.

The Socialists are a cause for concern for Giolitti ahead of the elections on October 26, 1913. The Congress of Reggio Emilia (July 1912) has decreed the expulsion of the moderates by maximalists—among them, the future editor of *Avanti!*: Benito Mussolini. Giolitti opens negotiations with the Catholics, which leads to the Gentiloni Pact (after Vincenzo Ottorino Gentiloni, president of the Italian Catholic Electoral Union). In signing an eight-point document, liberal candidates commit to fighting any "anti-Catholic law" that may reach the Parliament. This maneuver appears successful, but the majority obtained is ripped apart by forces that are contradictory (opposing the signatories of the Gentiloni Pact to anti-clerical liberals) and, in the case of nationalists and revolutionary Socialists, at least partly new. "Leave, Mr. Giolitti," Arturo Labriola tells the Chamber on December 9, 1913. "The country has grown surreptitiously, escaped your control, and speaks a new language [ . . . ] It's a new situation, a new politics, new men. Let the dead bury their dead."

Giolitti steps down on March 4, 1914, after the radicals have withdrawn from the government, leaving him in a minority. He suggests to the king his successor be Antonio Salandra, whose government takes office on March 21, 1914.

On July 28, 1914, the Austro-Hungarian Empire declares war on the Kingdom of Serbia following the assassination a month earlier of Archduke Franz Ferdinand and his wife, Sophie, by a twenty-year-old Serbian nationalist, Gavrilo Princip. On August 1, the United Kingdom declares war on Germany. Italy, for her part, takes an entire year to decide whether or not to go to war. It is a year of violent clashes between the neutralist front—Socialists, Giolitti supporters, and, above all, Catholics, since the new pope,

Benedict XV (elected on September 5, 1914), immediately takes sides against the war—and a smaller group of interventionists, small even in Parliament but capable of drawing people in with their fervent speeches, like the one made by Gabriele d'Annunzio from the Quarto cliff on the fifty-fifth anniversary of the Expedition of the Thousand. Bound by the Treaty of London, a secret agreement signed between the Italian government and the so-called Triple Entente (Great Britain, France, and Russia) and concealed from Parliament, Salandra obtains plenary powers from the king on May 23, 1915, and Italy declares war on Austria, thus trampling the remaining vestiges of the Triple Alliance. Preparations are made for fighting in South Tyrol and along the River Isonzo, in other words in territories Italy intends to take from the Austro-Hungarian Empire because Salandra considers them Italian.

The conflict soon turns into a frustrating trench war. After the defeat at Caporetto (October 24–November 19, 1917), when Italian troops are decimated by Austro-German artillery (at least 10,000 dead and 265,000 taken prisoner), General Luigi Cadorna is dismissed and General Armando Diaz is called upon to reorganize the army. The Battle of Vittorio Veneto, fought between October 24 and November 3, 1918, is crucial: the Italians defeat the Austrians and, on November 3, march on Trento and Trieste. That same day, at Villa Giusti, outside Padua, the armistice is signed. On November 11, Germany also capitulates. At the cost of millions of lives (figures vary from fifteen to seventeen million, over one million dead among Italians alone), Europe's political geography is irreversibly altered. In addition to these dead, there are those killed by the devastating Spanish flu epidemic (1918–1920), which, by the most recent estimates, involves around fifty million worldwide (six hundred thousand in Italy).

One man who takes advantage of the difficult postwar social

and economic situation is Benito Mussolini, expelled from the Socialist Party (November 29, 1914) because of his interventionist position. Using the widespread discontent among veterans, he creates the Italian Fasces of Combat, marked by heavy anti-Socialist rancor: an attitude soon also adopted by the middle classes, frightened by the strikes and factory occupations that become frequent during the so-called Red Biennium (1919–1920) throughout Italy. Even Giolitti, back for the fifth time as prime minister (June 15, 1920–July 4, 1921), is unable to resolve the situation. The Fasces grow increasingly violent and organize *squadrista* attacks on the workers and their organizations. On October 22, 1922, over forty thousand Fascists gather in Naples, determined to march on Rome. Prime Minister Luigi Facta asks the king to declare a state of siege, but Victor Emmanuel III refuses. Facta resigns and, on October 29, gives Mussolini the role of prime minister. When Mussolini presents his executive to the Chamber on November 16, he asks for plenary powers "in order to reorganize the tax system and public administration" and obtains them for one year, by 275 votes to 90. The Fascist Party (within the so-called National List) gets 65 percent of the votes in the elections of April 6, 1924, but in a vehement speech to the Chamber, Socialist member of Parliament Giacomo Matteotti asks that they be declared null because they took place in an atmosphere of violence and repression. On June 10, Matteotti is abducted. There is such dismay that, on June 23, 123 opposition members of Parliament decide to cease working at the Chamber until a light is shed on the event (the Aventine Secession). Matteotti's body is discovered on August 16 in a wood in Riano, outside Rome; on January 3, 1925, Mussolini assumes "political, moral, and historical" responsibility for the murder. In practice, this spells the start of the Fascist dictatorship, as demonstrated by the *leggi fascistissime* (very Fascist laws) proclaimed between

1925 and 1926, which, among other things, decree "the disbanding of all parties, associations, and organizations that carry out actions contrary to the regime," hold the head of the government to be the only agent of executive power, permit the dismissal of public servants considered "incompatible" with the party's directives, ban strikes, and stifle freedom of the press. At the March 14, 1929, elections (which take the form of a referendum, by presenting a list of names for the voter to approve or reject), eight and a half million people vote yes, corresponding to over 98 percent of the voters: a result partly influenced by the signing of the Lateran Treaty (February 11, 1929), an agreement between church and state that finally heals the fracture of 1871.

"We are the only judges of our interests and guarantors of our future, only we, exclusively, and nobody else," Mussolini says in Cagliari on June 8, 1935. History will prove him wrong: in 1940, Italy enters World War II, a conflict that alters the political, social, and economic balance of the whole world. And that is only the beginning. As Winston Churchill writes in 1948: "We have at length emerged from a scene of material ruin and moral havoc, the like of which had never darkened the imagination of former centuries. After all that we suffered and achieved, we find ourselves still confronted with problems and perils not less but far more formidable than those through which we have so narrowly made our way."

# AUTHOR'S NOTE

*Fall of the Florios* is a novel. It may seem an unnecessary thing to underline, but it isn't, not when talking about the Florios, a family that left such a profound mark on the history of Palermo, Sicily, and Italy, a family whose dramatic social and economic trajectory has long fascinated historians, who still have the difficult task of analyzing it in all its complexity.

Like *The Florios of Sicily* and *The Triumph of the Lions*, this novel is also based on documented fact, combined with situations and characters I have imagined or reworked for the demands of the narrative. Demands that also led me to the decision—often not an easy one—to privilege some elements of the Florios' story over others. In other words, I have made choices. But this is the fate of anyone who writes historical novels that touch on the present, and it is both a blessing and a curse.

However, having reached the end of my journey with the Florios—a journey that has lasted almost six years—it seems only right to list those works, mostly nonfiction, that have genuinely guided me in the writing of the three novels. First and foremost, the monumental work by Orazio Cancila, *I Florio: Storia di una dinastia imprenditoriale*, which is essential to an indepth reading of the affairs of the family over four generations. Secondly, *L'età dei Florio*, edited by, and with contributions from, Romualdo Giuffrida and Rosario Lentini, and *I Florio* by Simone Candela, which contains a wealth of information and interesting interpretations. Finally, *L'economia dei Florio:*

*Una famiglia di imprenditori borghesi dell'800*, which gathers contributions from various authors and also includes the catalog of the exhibition held in 1991 in Palermo, at Sicilcassa's Fondazione Culturale Lauro Chiazzese, an exhibition curated by Rosario Lentini, a man of great intellectual generosity and immense culture, who has written a lot about the Florios, especially about their business activities and their links with Italian culture and politics.

Next come works focused on more specific topics, and for that reason extremely revealing: *Le navi dei Florio* by Piero Piccione; *Villa Igiea*, edited by Francesco Amendolagine; *Giuseppe Damiani Almeyda: Tre architetture tra cronaca e storia* by Anna Maria Fundarò; *I Florio e il regno dell'Olivuzza* by Francesca Mercadante; *La pesca del tonno in Sicilia*, edited by Vincenzo Consolo; *Breve storia della Ceramica Florio* by Augusto Marinelli; *Boldini: Il ritratto di Donna Franca Florio*, by Matteo Smolizza; *Gioielli in Italia*, edited by Lia Lenti; *Le toilette della signora del Liberty* by Ketty Giannilivigni; *Il guardaroba di Donna Franca Florio*, edited by Cristina Piacenti Aschengreen; *Regine: Ritratti di nobildonne Siciliane (1905–1914)*, edited by Daniele Anselmo and Giovanni Purpura; *La musica nell'età dei Florio* by Consuelo Giglio; and the websites Targapedia.com (where, among other things, we can find the issues of *Rapiditas*, the "universal motoring magazine" created by Vincenzo Florio), Targaflorio.info, and Amicidellatargaflorio.com, genuine mines of information on the story of Targa Florio.

But nor can I forget the leads and suggestions I derived from texts such as *La Sicile illustrée* (issued from 1904 to 1911), *Palermo fin de siècle* by Pietro Nicolosi, and *Sulle orme dei Florio* by Gaetano Corselli D'Ondes and Paola D'Amore Lo Bue, as well as classics like *Princes Under the Volcano* by Raleigh Trevelyan, *Estati felici* by Fulco Santostefano della Cerda, Duke of Verdura, and the short stories of Giuseppe Tomasi di Lampedusa: thanks to them, I was able to investigate in depth a now vanished and yet incredibly fascinating way of life. I have also been able to count on my historical and artistic advisor, Francesco Melia, who revealed to me the complexity and richness of Palermo society at the turn of the twentieth century and who consulted countless texts and compared documents, including *Il blasone in Sicilia: Dizionario storico-araldico della Sicilia* by Vincenzo Palizzolo Gravina; *Vivere e abitare da nobili a Palermo tra Seicento e Ottocento*, edited by Luisa Chifari and Ciro D'Arpa; and *La pittura dell'Ottocento in Sicilia: Tra committenza, critica d'arte e collezionismo*, edited by Maria Concetta Di Natale.

Another valuable source was the documents digitized and accessible on Internet Archive and the online archives of *Corriere della Sera* and *La Stampa*. In articles dating from the period of the novel, I discovered detailed items on matters that otherwise would have fallen into oblivion. I am grateful to those—often anonymous— journalists who vividly recorded stories, characters, and events, but also to those who make their articles available. As is obvious, I also found of great value *Giornale di Sicilia* and *L'Ora*, true media leaders in those years.

In addition, there were many essays, testimonies, and articles on Italian political, economic, and cultural life from 1868 to 1935. If there are errors or inaccuracies in the novel, they should be ascribed exclusively to me and not to the people who helped me in my research.

Of the texts that trace the "private" affairs of the family, I found two of them essential. First of all, *Franca Florio* by Anna Pomar, her only real biography, published in 1985 and based on the testimony of Giulia Florio, last child of Franca and Ignazio—a book that reconstructs both an era and the personal story of this woman and her difficult life. I spoke at length with Marco Pomar, son of the author, partly about the fact that sometimes the information contained in the text did not coincide with what emerged from my research. I heartily thank Marco for how helpful he was, and I feel honored to have been able to walk the road charted by his mother.

*L'ultima leonessa*, published in 2020, not long before the death of its author, Costanza Afan de Rivera, is the other book, equally unique in that it retraces the life of Giulia Florio through the memories of her daughter. I still recall very fondly the occasions on which I had the privilege of speaking with Donna Costanza, and her passion in evoking the affairs of the family. Through her, I was able not only to grasp the most authentic aspects of a contradictory woman like Franca but also to truly understand the burden, and at the same time the pride, of bearing a name like Florio.

# ACKNOWLEDGMENTS

In these six long years, from the moment the scene of the earthquake with which *The Florios of Sicily* begins came into my head until these words of acknowledgment at the end of *Fall of the Florios*, I have learned the value of discipline, solitude, patience, and courage. Because writing is an act that is never an end in itself: it demands responsibility and inner strength. You are alone with words and with your own doubts, with the fear of not having given enough, with the feeling of being in hand-to-hand combat with a story that doesn't want to be tamed and having to choose which dry branches to cut off and which new foundations to build.

Instead, you eventually realize that every novel is a road full of bends and bumps, and that you can choose whether to dance down that road or proceed cautiously, lit only by the light of intuition. You know only that ahead of you have a lodestar: the story you want to tell. You do the best you can, you try to maintain the right detachment, and you let time help the words you are safeguarding to find their place. And in the end, you put your hand in the lion's mouth, and that wild beast you feared would maul you instead lets itself be stroked meekly.

Telling the story of the Florios was all this and much more.

And I wouldn't have succeeded if I hadn't had beside me people who helped me, with affection and patience. First of all, my husband and children, who never failed to support me, even at the most complicated moments, and who often actually followed me around Italy. It wasn't easy: truly, thanking you is the least I can do. And, together with them, my original family: my mother, Giovanna, and my sisters, Vita and Anna, *in primis*, nephews, nieces, in-laws, uncles, aunts, and cousins (especially the Basiricòs and the Rossellis). I have the privilege of being surrounded by people who love me, and that's not so common. I'm very lucky to have you all beside me and to enjoy your respect.

Then there are all my friends: Chiara, who's always there, one way or another; Nadia Terranova, who is an example and a valuable point of reference; Loredana Lipperini, who is my witch godmother (she knows what that means); Evelina Santangelo, who gave me helpful advice. But thank you also to Piero Melati, who has always shown me great respect; to Alessandro D'Avenia, who listened to me so attentively; to Pietrangelo Buttafuoco, an old-school gentleman with a great heart; and finally the group from Villa Diodati Reloaded: Filippo Tapparelli, Eleonora Caruso, and Domitilla Pirro, who at least on a few occasions picked up my pieces and made me laugh. And also thank you to Felice Cavallaro and Gaetano Savatteri, two of the finest and most authentic voices of Sicilian and Italian culture.

Thank you to Elena, Gabriella, Antonella, Valeria, Rita, Valentina, and the ever dear Elisabetta Bricca, extraordinary women and readers with whom I have shared a friendship that goes back decades; to Franco Cascio and Elvira Terranova, because they are there, and that's enough; to Alessia Gazzola, Valentina D'Urbano, and Laura Imai Messina, to whom I owe respect and great gratitude. Your stories are aways sources of inspiration for me.

Then there is a long list of booksellers I carry in my heart: some of them have not only been—not only are—people I work with but also true friends, and as such, I shall mention them by name: Fabrizio, Loredana and Marcella, Teresa, Alessandro and Ina, Ornella, Maria Pia, Bianca, Caterina and Paolo, Manuela,

# Acknowledgments

Guido, Sara, Daniela, Giovanni, Maria Carmela and Angelica, Arturo, Nicola, Carlotta and Nicolò, Valentina, Fabio, Cetti and her sisters, Barbara and Francesca, Serena, Alberto, Marco and Susan, Stefania and Giuseppe. To all of you and to all the other booksellers—whether independent or not—I want not only to say thank you but also to bow down to you, because yours is a noble and remarkable profession; if I weren't a teacher, I really think I would like to be a bookseller. That these books have become what it is, I owe to you, the passion you put into suggesting it to readers and the incredible way you have gone with it out into the world. Just as I must thank those who introduced you to my books, in other words, the agents of Prolibro (one can stand for all: Toti Di Stefano), led by their commercial director Emanuele Bertoni. You are my heroes.

Thank you to Giuseppe Basiricò, a gifted antique dealer and a person of enormous worth, to whom I owe countless postcards, books, and objects concerning the story of the Florios, and who encouraged and helped me right from the beginning of my research; to the Tortorici brothers for their respect and for allowing me to browse among the wonders on display in their art gallery; to Francesco Sarno, who placed at my disposal the catalog of the 1921 auction of the Florio family's furniture and who supported me with great diligence and attention.

I thank Professor Mario Damiani Almeyda, grandson of the Florios' architect, who has created a wonderful online archive of his grandfather's designs and who, one rainy morning, welcomed me to his rooms and showed me some unpublished designs for the Florio building in Favignana. He should also be applauded for the magnificent work of conservation and popularization that he has been performing for years all by himself. A special thank-you to Professor Piazza, who allowed me to visit one of the most beautiful and best-preserved areas of the Villa dell'Olivuzza, currently in the care of the Circolo dell'Unione di Palermo. I am grateful to Giuseppe Carli, owner of the historic Carli jewelry shop in Lucca and an aficionado of timepieces, who revealed to me the existence of a pocket watch made for the Florios for advertising purposes early in the twentieth century. A sophisticated reader and a man of great culture who impressed me with his intellectual generosity.

Thank you to those who welcomed me (and waited for me) during these months: Enrico del Mercato, Mario di Caro, and Sara Scarafia; thank you to Claudio Cerasa and all the journalists who have met me and talked with me without preconceptions and without filters. It has been wonderful to work with you. Thank you to the colleagues and principal of the Paolo Borsellino Institute, who continue to welcome me with the same affection as ever.

Thank you to Costanza Afan de Rivera: I would have liked to give you this book and see that half smile with which you always expressed your curiosity. It is a great regret for me to know that you will not read these pages.

Thank you to Sara di Cara, Mara Scanavino, and Gloria Danese: three people who have guided me, each in her own way, through these years. Toward them I have a debt of gratitude that cannot be expressed in words.

Thank you to Isabella di Nolfo and Valentina Masilli, who no longer take any notice of the fact that I am permanently crazy, and who know how to manage my anxiety.

An immense thank-you to Silvia Donzelli and Stefania Fietta, my agents. If they hadn't believed in this story from the beginning, it would never have seen the light of day. Thank you for your patience and for always being there. You are precious and priceless.

Thank you to my publishers, Nord: firstly to Stefano Mauri, Cristina Foschini, and Marco Tarò, who have always shown me respect and affection. Thank you for your sensitivity and intelligence, for considering me before anything a person and then an author, for welcoming me despite my obvious madness. Thank you to Viviana Vuscovich, who has taken *The Florios of Sicily* and its sequels around the world: nobody else could have performed the miracles you have performed. Thank you to Giorgia di Tolle, patience personified, and to Paolo Caruso, who had a very clear idea of things. Thank you to the marketing team, from Elena Pavanetto to Dr. Giacomo Lanaro, always attentive, always creative, always friendly. Thank you to Barbara Trianni: as well as being the fantastic head of the press office, she is a partner in crime—as well as a partner in shopping—but above all she is a remarkable, courageous, and determined woman. Thank you to Alessandro Magno, who is in charge of the people dealing with audiobooks and e-books: Simona Musmeci, Davide Perra, and Désirée Favero. And to Ninni Bruschetta, "the voice of the Florios." Thank you to Elena Carloni and to Ester Borgese, who picked up on typos and errors, and also to Simona Musmeci, who standardized the dialect. If I could, I would take a dirigible, attach a thank-you banner, and fly for hours above Via Gherardini. And there's nothing to say I won't do that one of these days.

Then there are three people who have been by my side through these years of research and writing.

Francesca Maccani, who has always believed in me, always. Who has never turned away, who has listened to my complaints and confessions, who has really been my guardian angel. I hope you receive all the good you have done me, and that is really a lot.

Francesco Melia, whose historic and artistic culture is impressive and who showed a remarkable willingness to collaborate with me. A person of enormous kindness and patience, a companion in adventures who was able to alleviate my insecurities, sometimes just with a joke.

Cristina Prasso. To her, one of the shyest people in the world, I have one thing to say. Thank you. Because if you too hadn't believed in it in 2018, and hadn't read my novel in one night, none of this would ever have happened. Thank you because you never dropped me for a minute, not even in those moments when the exhaustion became overwhelming and I was afraid I would never succeed in telling this story the way I felt it should be told; thank you for being not only a publisher and an editor but also a friend and a point of reference. Thank you for everything you have taught me and still teach me every day. Thank you because you are there, and because that is the way you are.

Thank you to all three of you. Behind these words there is so much unsaid . . . which should remain unsaid.

Thank you to those who read this novel and then recommend it, give it as a present, mention it on Instagram and Facebook because you loved it; but thank you also to those who don't love it and who are indifferent to it: reading is always, in every case, a way to take care of oneself.

Finally: Paolo and Giuseppina, Ignazio, Vincenzo and Giulia, Giovanna and Ignazio, Franca and Ignazziddu and their children. Each of you has given me something. And taught me something. My final thank-you goes to you.

# A NOTE FROM THE TRANSLATORS

A translator of our acquaintance likes to tell the story of how a client once asked her to translate a short text with the words: "Can you just type this into English for me?" Most readers, we would hope, realize that translation involves more than just "typing" from one language to another. But what they may not be aware of is how much of a translator's work consists of more than finding the best way to express in one language what was originally written in another—how much, in fact, involves *research*. This is especially true when it comes to historical novels or novels set in particular regions with their own traditional customs and dialects (the issue of dialect was mentioned in the translator's note to the first volume, *The Florios of Sicily*). We need to fully understand what it is that's being described before we can render it in English, and this occasionally requires a certain amount of background reading.

When particular events or people or places are mentioned, we need to find out if there is a widely recognized English name for them. And where technical terms are included (some of which might not be found in standard dictionaries), we need to do a fair amount of research to discover the English equivalents. This saga of the Florios contains a good deal of information about activities as varied as shipping, winemaking, and sulfur mining—each with its own specialized vocabulary and all needing to be researched.

Take tuna fishing, another of the Florios' businesses that features frequently in the books. What is a *tonnara?* What is the *mattanza?* These are just a few of the terms related to this topic that appear in the books. Not only do we have to make sure we grasp the specific processes to which they refer, we then have to decide, in the (frequent) cases where there is no exact English equivalent, whether to find a vague equivalent or use the original Italian and modify the text to make the meaning clear. If we have managed to make the author's work comprehensible, while at the same time conveying her tone and style, then we have done our job as translators—which is a lot more than just "typing"!

—KATHERINE GREGOR AND HOWARD CURTIS

Here ends Stefania Auci's
*Fall of the Florios.*

The first edition of this book was printed
and bound at Lakeside Book Company
in Harrisonburg, Virginia, July 2024.

A NOTE ON THE TYPE

The text of this novel was set in Adobe Garamond Pro, a
typeface designed in 1989 by Robert Slimbach. It's based
on two distinctive examples of the French Renaissance
style, a Roman type by Claude Garamond (1499–1561)
and an italic type by Robert Granjon (1513–1590), and
was developed after Slimbach studied the fifteenth-century
equipment at the Plantin-Moretus Museum in Antwerp,
Belgium. Adobe Garamond Pro is considered to faithfully
capture the original Garamond's grace and clarity, and is
used extensively in books for its elegance and readability.

HarperVia

An imprint dedicated to publishing international voices,
offering readers a chance to encounter other lives and other
points of view via the language of the imagination.